THE DESCENDANTS

THE DESCENDANTS

ROBERT CHURSINOFF

NIGHTWOOD EDITIONS

2022

1 2 3 4 5 — 26 25 24 23 22

Nightwood Editions
P.O. Box 1779
Gibsons, BC VON 1VO
Canada
www.nightwoodeditions.com

COVER DESIGN: TopShelf Creative
TYPOGRAPHY: Carleton Wilson
The historical photo at the top left of the front cover is from the Kooma J. Tarasoff Photo Collection.

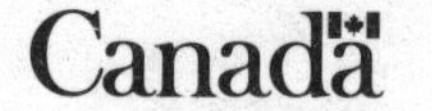

Canada Council for the Arts Conseil des Arts du Canada

Nightwood Editions acknowledges the support of the Canada Council for the Arts, the Government of Canada, and the Province of British Columbia through the BC Arts Council.

This book has been produced on paper certified by the FSC.

Printed and bound in Canada.

LIBRARY AND ARCHIVES CANADA CATALOGUING IN PUBLICATION

Title: The descendants / Robert Chursinoff.
Names: Chursinoff, Robert, author.
Identifiers: Canadiana (print) 20220261970 | Canadiana (ebook) 20220261989 | ISBN 9780889714403 (softcover) | ISBN 9780889714410 (EPUB)
Classification: LCC PS8605.H88 D47 2022 | DDC C813/.6—dc23

For all Doukhobors:
those practising and those newly discovering their roots.

I

Phantoms and Fury

In 1692 a Russian Army deserter and wandering hermit named Danilo Filippov establishes himself in a cave along the shores of the Volga River. There he attracts followers to whom he declares that the truth is not to be found in the Bible but rather in the Holy Spirit which dwells within every human being. In an act of heresy, he places a bible into a sack and hurls it into the river. In the decades that follow, a succession of nomadic preachers who are inspired by Filippov and other wanderers like him emerges to organize and develop the basic tenets of a new philosophy.

By 1785, followers of this philosophy officially become known as the Doukhobors.

The sect believes in the sanctity of pacifism and material simplicity. They reject icon worship, arguing that external symbols and elaborate rituals are not necessary for one's communion with God—beliefs for which both the Russian State and Orthodox Church despise the Doukhobors.

By the late 1800s the Doukhobors have embraced communal living, vegetarianism and abstinence from alcohol. In 1895 under the guidance of beloved hereditary leader Peter V. Verigin the Doukhobors reaffirm their resolute pacifism with mass anti-war protests staged across the Caucasus region in open defiance of Tsar Nicholas II. Considered treasonous by the authorities and heretical by the Orthodox church, Verigin is exiled to Siberia, and a policy of Doukhobor cultural cleansing is vigorously pursued by Russian authorities.

Slocan Valley, British Columbia, July 1998

When you love someone with the force of an atomic bomb, showing off to them on a half-pipe while attempting your first Frontside 180 Heelflip is no biggie. Neither is making them vegetable barley soup from scratch because they've got the flu; even if you suck at cooking, you try anyway. Or making an ass of yourself trying to serenade them at karaoke because you're tone-deaf. Or sacrificing a weekend of video games with your buddies to go to Doukhobor Festival with your girl even though you can't speak a lick of Russian and you find the event as boring as watching golf on TV. These all come easily when love is a never-ending heart explosion like it is for a mother and her child, or for the devoutly religious and their beliefs, or for two people who simply can't live without each other. Violence comes easily too. Even if you come from a super, natural province of a super peaceful country where you were surrounded by super chill hippies and super pacifist Douks. When protecting the one you love, violence as primal as the fang and claw, as instinctual as breathing will possess you, infect you like herpes, so freaking easily that you'll wonder if there will ever be peace at the end of the falling row of dominoes that this brutality has kicked off.

Or so Jonah Seeger thought as the Honda Civic screeched through the tight S-curves of the mountain road, its headlights sweeping the smoky wildfire night like a lighthouse on a foggy, hazardous coast. He imagined it was the biker's neck in his clutches instead of the steering wheel he now clenched with puffy, bloodless knuckles. Jonah glanced at Ruby with wild eyes, pupils big as saucers as though he were tripping on shrooms. What had he done? Was more shame on its way to his mother, already shamed because of her Sons of Freedom family? For how long could he and Ruby Samarodin just drive a loop through the West Kootenay towns?

With distant eyes Ruby returned Jonah's glance. The icy-blue glow from the dashboard made his long, brown hair appear streaked with grey, and his usually fresh, teenage face, ghostly pale. "None of us would even be here…" Ruby mumbled her mother's sermon from a breakfast that felt like a lifetime ago. She tugged on one of her platinum-blonde pigtails that strove to twist free. "None of us would even be here if it were not for Tolstoy," she continued, the *S* in *Tolstoy* whistling through the little gap in her front teeth like it always did when she was exhausted.

"If not for ole Tolstoy," Jonah said in an attempt to lighten the foreboding mood, "only half of me wouldn't be here."

"Mhmm." Ruby continued to stare at the sweeping headlight beams as she finished off her beer and tossed the can at her feet. Maybe her mother was right about Jonah after all; a half American, half Freedomite could never be a proper Doukhobor. And why was he driving? *She* was usually the one behind the wheel of her Civic, feeling cramped as though she were stuffed into an Apollo space capsule. In the passenger seat it was usually Jonah sitting in a normal way with his legs of normal length, shoulders of normal width, and bones of normal size. Ruby tucked her knees into her chest, on this night feeling abnormally small and hollow as an ant. The mountains that towered around her suddenly suffocated her like they always had when she was lonely, bored… or hopeless. She pulled out strands of hair as she rocked gently in her seat.

Jonah grabbed a bottle of water from the cupholder, twisted off the cap with his teeth and held it out to her. "Drink this," he said. "Please, baby."

Instead, Ruby groped around the footwell and found another rolling can of warm beer—*pfzt*—popped the tab. She could remember her mother standing rigid that morning, cracking eggs into a terracotta mixing bowl on the marble countertop of the kitchen island, hounding Ruby to practise her Sunday school lesson. "Resurrection…" Ruby muttered. "Tolstoy sold his final novel, Resurrection, to help pay for the Doukhobor exile to Canada." She should finish writing her song about outcasts and exiles, she thought. She tilted her head back and gulped the beer—her sixth in the two hours they'd been driving—then allowed a mouthful to soothingly pour out over her cracked lips and trickle down her aching neck. Bitterness toward her mother surfaced like acid reflux crawling up her throat. That morning, Virginia had convinced Ruby's dad that they would *not* be watching their daughter dressed as she was, prancing around on stage, playing rock 'n' roll. "You're nineteen for goodness' sake," her mother had said, "practically a woman, and need to start *acting* that way."

Warm, smoky night air blew across Ruby's face through the cracked window. Memories flickered in and out: sweating on stage in her crop top and itty-bitty roller-derby shorts; the air smelling of charred forest; the late afternoon sun a murky orange spotlight shining on her performance. But she could not remember what happened after her band finished playing their cover of Blur's "woo-hoo" song. Or why so many of her black-polished fingernails were broken now. And why weren't they still at the party with their friends, celebrating Jet Poison's first proper show?

Sleep tugged at her like a boulder tied to her feet, dragging her across the road and over the rocky cliff down into the depths of Slocan Lake hundreds of feet below. Now she felt Jonah's warm, calloused hand on hers, squeezing reassuringly, keeping her securely in her seat, safely in the car. When she looked down and saw how bruised and mangled his knuckles were, she flinched and yanked her hand to her chest.

Jonah eyed his hand, downshifted into second gear, and leaned into a tight S-curve and swerved back across the yellow line as a semi sounded its horn and crawled past them in the opposite lane. Ruby allowed herself to weakly flop against the passenger door. Jonah glanced at his skateboard lying on the back seat, its trucks and wheels surely spattered with blood.

"Where are we going?" Ruby asked.

"Babe… do you… do you remember what happened?" Jonah asked timidly.

Ruby rummaged through the purse sitting between her legs, saying nothing.

"The parking lot... Swanny... his brother... laid out on the ground?"

Ruby shrugged, shook her head. She pulled a small metal flask from her purse, unscrewed the lid, tilted her head back, and poured the amber liquid into her mouth, coughing and swiping her lips afterward. What she wouldn't give for a fat line of blow right now. All she knew was that it was time to get the fuck out of there. To check the rear-view mirror and watch the Slocan Valley, the Kootenays, recede into boring, stifling, depressing smallness. She and Jonah could start over anywhere. Anywhere but there.

A shrug of her shoulders, her continuing shock and denial, that's all it took for Jonah to know with laser-sharp clarity. He'd already called his brother, Julian, hours ago from a pay phone and told him to go to their mother's trailer right away, pack a few bags and get them to Grandma Polly's place for a few weeks—pronto. Sharon was used to fleeing the Kootenays when things felt out of control; this wouldn't be much different for Jonah's poor mom. Julian had cursed his name, then after he'd calmed down, asked Jonah where they'd go. *We* wouldn't be going anywhere, Jonah now thought to himself. No better place to leave Ruby than in the hands of her best friend, Nadya. He looked at the Civic's dashboard clock: five a.m. In two more hours, Cedar would find Jonah hiding at the edge of the Slocan River at the swimming spot underneath the old Passmore Bridge. From there his best friend would drive him south to the Paterson Boarder Crossing, and then to his dad's place in Spokane. And in a few weeks, maybe a few months tops, Jonah would come back to the Kootenays and try, with all his heart and soul, to make things right again.

By January 1899, Russian author Leo Tolstoy and his followers have been ardent supporters of the Doukhobors for several years. From his estate, Yasna Polyana, Tolstoy corresponds with the sect's exiled leader, Peter V. Verigin, engages in letter-writing campaigns to prominent international newspapers on behalf of the sect and donates the proceeds of his final novel, Resurrection, *to Doukhobor emigration. The efforts of the novelist and his followers finally pay off when Tsar Nicholas II permits the Doukhobors to leave Russia. And never return.*

In negotiations with the Canadian government, representatives of both Tolstoy and the Doukhobors are told that the religious sect will receive blocks of land to facilitate their communal way of life, that they will have some control over the education of their children and, most importantly, they will be exempt from military service.

Longing for a better life and desperate to flee persecution, nearly two thousand Doukhobors board the SS Lake Superior, *a vessel meant for cattle, in the Black Sea port of Batum.*

That winter and in the months that follow, a total of seven boats will bring over 7,500 Doukhobors to Canada, making it the largest single mass migration in the country's history.

Los Angeles, California, November 2004

Ruby strummed her Stratocaster with all the wildness and determination in her heart, its quaking strings threatening to burst as overdriven distortion blasted from her amp and pulsed through her like a solar storm. Continuing to strum, she kicked at the small floor fan in front of her, repositioning it with the tip of her cowboy boot. Underneath her leather jacket her black maxi dress momentarily billowed, her blonde hair fluttered. This set off a barrage of camera flashes from the photographers at the front of the stage in a bid to capture Ruby towering above them in all her alluring disarray. She offered what the press loved most, her gap-toothed grin à la Brigitte Bardot, then spun away to face the band.

Ruby and the rest of Caravana were onstage at LA's historic Wiltern Theatre, rooted deep into the turbulent outro of "Break the Halo." She could feel her bandmates thrumming in sync with her, watched Ted high up on a riser in the middle of the stage grimace as he bashed the drums and smashed the cymbals like they'd done him a grave injustice. Beside Ruby, Tomás was seductively writhing on his back, lost in a guitar solo as the sweat-soaked crowd bobbed and moshed along in front. The band was off the hook. Pure electricity. A blazing bushfire licking at the raised arms and flushed grinning faces of the fans. The members of Caravana were giving it their all, knowing it was the best show they'd played all year. They strummed and pounded, plucked and banged, broke sticks, skins and strings for every single one of their drunken darlings out there.

The last triumphant chords of the song faded as cymbal crashes bled into a din of cheering. Ruby was breathless and filled with gratitude. Gratitude for a month of sobriety. Gratitude for the healing power of music and Caravana's loyal, loving fans. Their people were whooping and howling for them. Whistling and clapping. Wanting more. Wanting everything they had. Wanting *her*, Ruby Samarodin.

She knew this, felt it clear her head, ease her breathing, swell her heart.

You love it, Ruby thought. Just like we do. This is why we do it and this is why you come. To experience a band in perfect symbiosis, firing on all cylinders, in the flow, every note and every move with each other second nature, and the crowd feeling this, giving back with all their hoarse, hollering throats and sweat-drenched souls. Ruby understood that was what two albums and over four hundred shows together in four years got you. There was simply no better feeling. Music had the power to erase all the bullying and abuse and shame and self-loathing.

At least for a while it could fill the gaping hole in one's soul caused by all the flaming shame arrows and grief-laden cannonballs life had thrust at you. Better than the best powdered high any day. Ruby laughed. Possibly even better than the orgasmic cunnilingus she'd taught Jonah to give her when they were teenagers. She whispered a blessing in Russian to Jonah, "*Blagosloveniye vam.*" Stay safe, darling, she thought, wherever you are.

Ruby took a sip of water then slipped her Strat over her head and exchanged it for the Larrivée acoustic. She wiggled out of her sweaty leather jacket and passed it off to the guitar tech. She returned to the front of the stage, strapped on her acoustic, stuck her guitar pick in the corner of her mouth and winked at the cameras. Ruby scanned the mayhem in the Wiltern as Tomás addressed the crowd. Her forearm was up, shielding her eyes from the blinding stage lights. A crowd of 2,300 packed the elegant old theatre. Cords snaked around Ruby across the vast black stage. She zoned out on the ceiling of art-deco skyscrapers laid out in an orange-red sunburst pattern that beckoned band and crowd alike to celebrate with abandon.

For a moment Ruby was transported back to the last summer day her and Jonah were allowed to play together as children. They were six years old at her place in the Slocan Valley, running through her mother's garden, Ruby pulling Jonah along, his red Superman cape fluttering behind him. They howled through rows of corn and its scratchy sandpaper husks, they navigated through impossibly tall sunflowers waving in the breeze and then ran to the overflowing raspberry bushes buzzing with bees. And that night they told ghost stories in the tree house and slept wrapped around each other.

A loud cheer erupted from the crowd over something Tomás had said. Ruby wiped sweat from her brow and looked over at him gesticulating wildly. His wiry naked torso was glistening with sweat that had been pouring from all manner of pathway: streaming from the thick brown hair that clung to his shoulders, dripping from the Roman nose that his bony face was attached to, dribbling from the bushy handlebar moustache that framed his jabbering jaw. Tomás was a master at banter and at that very moment had the audience engaged in an origin story Ruby could relate to: a teenage dirtbag who'd had enough of small-minded Bratislava, a secular outcast who ran away to Los Angeles to follow his rock 'n' roll dreams. Ruby still marvelled at his ability to engage nightly with the audience with sincerity and humour and passion. Like she and Tomás used to do with each other. Back when neither of them was trying to kick their poisons, back when living the rock star life seemed easier than facing reality.

Subpar shows in Denver and Reno had the band on its best behaviour at the Wiltern that November evening. They'd all agreed: clean performances—except for one or two drinks on stage—for the remainder of the tour. Ruby was glad she'd insisted, and relieved when everyone, especially Tomás, agreed. Besides, there'd be influential press in the house tonight and they didn't need any more negative reviews about a great band that was too wasted to deliver.

Tomás's tale of exodus was always Ruby's cue to make sure her acoustic was in tune for the next song. Her song. She spun around to see if the band was ready. Ted sat on the throne at his white mother-of-pearl DW drums, shirtless as usual, furiously wiping his face with a towel. Then there was little fireball Alice on her own riser beside the drums, pressing buttons on her Nord synth, cueing up a warm Wurlitzer sound. In front of her, old Vlad was grinning at the audience, his worn Soviet-era violin at the ready, tucked under his wispy grey beard.

Behind Tomás and directly in front of the drums, Chilly tousled his bleached-blond mohawk, gave Ruby a wink as he bounced on the balls of his feet and continued tuning his Rickenbacker bass. Beside him, lanky Ben was taking a long pull from his tall glass of whisky, his Les Paul slung low, its sunburst pattern like the Eye of Sauron glaring at the audience. Ruby brought her gaze back to Tomás. He was clutching his hollow-body electric at the base of its neck, holding it up triumphantly as though he were a soldier fresh from battle. Spit glistening like tiny diamonds in the stage lights sprayed out over the mic as he delivered his impassioned sermon.

Ruby took a deep breath to ready herself for what came next. Always in the middle of the set, to control the energy, to rein in the gypsy-punk mayhem, to give the band a breather, they'd play Ruby's song. Some days she was still amazed that it had touched so many fans, was such a beacon, was so transformative like it had been for her when she first wrote it as a teenage freakazoid. It was a song about outcasts and exiles. It was an ode to the Doukhobors, her people that she'd left behind. It was a song she'd started writing as a fifteen-year-old, long before her first gig in 1998 at the Slocan Valley Give'r Fest. Ruby momentarily tensed. She pushed down the terrible memories from that day, willed them not to surface.

She took another deep breath and focused on the love she felt coming from the crowd instead, thought of her song and its ingredients. It was a ballad that contained her landscape and her people: refugee-packed ships exiled across the heaving Atlantic; the broad, looming mountains of her southern British Columbia home, ripe for logging; lush, sparsely populated valleys cleaved by mighty, glacier-fed rivers; kerchief-clad babushki in long, threadbare skirts, stooped and toiling in the plentiful vegetable gardens; dedushki in overalls harvesting the bounty of orchards planted almost a century earlier and still happily bearing fruit; thriving communal villages with two-storey brick homes, workshops, barns and bathhouses, now abandoned to assimilation and left to collapse; the bombed bridges and burnt schools of the terrorizing Sons of Freedom; their miles-long protest marches, everyone naked and holy as the day they were born; big, boisterous family meals full of deliciously rich and savoury ass-fattening vegetarian cuisine; hundreds of Doukhobors packed into the Brilliant Cultural Centre for the annual festival, clinging to the last vestiges of culture as they sang solemn hymns, heavenly psalms and rollicking Russian folk ballads.

Ruby's song was her past and her future. It was for her family, for her teenage lover Jonah and especially for Sasha, her sweet, sweet son that she'd left behind. Every time Ruby sang her song, she was in service to the music. In service to her grief. Unreachable.

The ballad was quickly becoming an indie-rock hit for Caravana. The band referred to it as "the soother," while *Pitchfork* had recently called it the group's "Hallelujah." The fans—they eagerly offered reverential love for it at every show.

Tomás would segue from his story into Ruby's song perfectly every night; candour and warmth in his voice, as though everything between them was right and always had been. "...but we're all outcasts in our own way, aren't we?" Tomás would conclude, as he did on that sold-out night at their hometown show. The crowd roared. "Please give it up for the talented lady to my right... Ruby Samarodin!"

Ruby waved and stepped to the mic as the stage lights dimmed, save for a spotlight on her. "Thank you so much, Los Angeles. It's good to be home." Ruby giggled at this. Most of them hadn't a clue about her British Columbia roots a thousand miles to the north. "This is a song about outcasts and exiles, about starting over," she said with confidence. "Maybe you can relate. It's called... 'Spirit Wrestlers.'"

The crowd erupted. Ruby's heart started running. Her skin tingled. As soon as she began strumming the D chord—Vlad's violin and Alice's organ accompanying her—she knew that nothing would derail her. The fans at the Wiltern fell into rapt silence... at first. It was something that happened often when she performed "Spirit Wrestlers"—her ballad of praise, redemption and reckoning, a hymn that went far deeper than words could ever express.

Tomás was harmonizing perfectly now with Ruby. The entire band was restrained and spare, then grew louder, threatening to explode but never stepping over the edge. Ruby sang with care and intention, allowed the song to wash over her, granting her temporary absolution. Its sounds in her ears were a warm, tender mosaic of vivid greens, yellows, reds and purples. The song was made resonant and electric through her pain, through generation upon generation of her people's lives. With it she could stand naked and unashamed, allow joy to course through her, sing herself into her future. Now came Ruby's favourite part... the audience joining in halfway, singing along to every word and then at last holding the high C with her through the song's entire soaring, wailing conclusion...

When she strummed the final chord, Ruby opened her eyes, her head tilted back. A breath of silence was followed by a deafening and overwhelming clamour. The stage lights dimmed. She levelled her head. Ruby had been sober a month. A small victory. She felt loved by the fans. Her soul had been lifted. There might never again be a perfect show like this one. With tears in her eyes, she eased down onto her knees, placed her guitar at her side. Tomás watched her with a look of bewilderment. In the Doukhobor tradition of giving thanks, Ruby bowed deeply once to the band, then, still on her knees, pivoted and bowed deeply to the rapturous fans.

Fallujah, Iraq, November 2004

Jonah Seeger looked away from his rifle's scope and brought the silver Cossack pendant hanging around his neck to his lips and kissed it. He took two deep breaths and fist-bumped Mason, pale and huddled on his left side, then blew a loud kiss at Lewis who was peering through a spotting scope to his right. Even after that modest ritual his hammering heart still wouldn't stop trying to crawl out the side of his chest. Like most Marines though, he found the adrenalin-spiking moments right before all hell broke loose an irresistible craving. Absolutely nothing compared to the rush of battle. Or to the inevitable comedowns and scratching, stinging wounds of it. But no time to fret about that now. Crouching nearby, checking GPS coordinates, Sergeant Will Cafferty had let the fire team know. Very soon it would be go time.

It was early morning but for hours now Jonah had been in a prone position on his sleeping pad, staring through the scope of his bolt-action M40A3, several metres back from the basketball-sized hole blown in the wall. It was Jonah's preferred concealment tactic, ensuring that the only way the enemy could shoot him or Lew in the face was if they fired at them from the exact same height and angle. If the enemy found out where they were firing from in the first place. And if their position was discovered, then the enemy could always blast them with an RPG or lob some mortars their way. To Jonah, the idea that random rocket and mortar fire could leave you powerless over your destiny was intoxicating… and sometimes maddening.

A steady stream of sweat trickled from his Kevlar helmet down his neck and back. The shadow of a mosque's minaret lengthened along the dusty floor to Jonah's left. He peered through his scope again, could see the rising sun, a murky orb hovering low over the industrial desert city. Already it cooked the stagnant air, hazy from dust storms, and putrid from piles of garbage, backed-up sewer and rotting corpses. There was not, and never would be, any getting used to the gut-punch stench. Muted sunbeams sliced through shattered windows of crippled factories, landed in black, oily puddles and on mounds of rubble lining the street. Rusting shells of vehicles were littered about. Entire blocks of Fallujah looked like they'd been crushed beneath the heel of a giant's boot. The flash-bang strategy had worked. Nothing stirred… yet. Save for the last scattered groups of anxious, desperate insurgents, the festering city now lay abandoned, as though a plague had scoured its streets.

With the sun in his eyes now it was no use. He rose onto his knees and started disassembling his kit as Lewis did the same beside him. He scratched his stubbled chin and glanced at Private First Class Mason Orleski as the kid again muttered his prayers. Jonah patted his shoulder, gave it a reassuring squeeze. Mase was a fresh-faced nineteen-year-old from Scottsdale, Arizona who dreamed of becoming a veterinarian and marrying his high school sweetheart, a kid who'd pray to Jesus every morning so that he wouldn't have to take a life in battle. Surrounded by resolute patriots, über-warriors, kill-craving lunatics, and apathetic dirtbags, Mase was a breath of fresh air to Jonah. Hands down the nicest Marine in the entire battalion. During every mission the kid felt safest tucked somewhere between Jonah's solid, five-foot-eleven frame and Corporal Lewis Robinson who stood four inches taller and was built like a linebacker. Jonah could relate. He felt safe around Lew as well. Lew was Jonah's best friend; a twenty-four-year-old Black man from the rough side of Buffalo; an NBA prospect until he blew out both knees in college.

Jonah zipped up his rifle bag, looked at the knuckles of his gloves where he'd scrawled *SKATE OR DIE*, a copy of what was tattooed on the flesh of his fingers. He scoffed quietly knowing his skateboarding ass could've turned pro too if he hadn't done what any teenager trying to protect the love of his life would've done. Ah, Ruby Samarodin, Jonah thought. If only they hadn't met as kids, then fallen in love as teenagers, he might not be risking his ass as a Marine. He thought of a time when he still made plans for the future. A future with Ruby.

They'd settle like the Douks and hippies did in one of the rural riverside villages dotting the remote, forested Slocan Valley. Home. God, how he missed Ruby. The way they fit together perfectly when they spooned naked. Her strumming her guitar and humming songs all day, or scribbling lyrics on whatever paper was at hand. Her beachy blonde hair and the succulent little gap between her front teeth. He even missed Ruby dragging him to the stuffy Doukhobor Festival to watch her sing in the choir as he felt like a fraud surrounded by real Douks who spoke a language he didn't understand a lick of. Did he miss the not-so-subtle put-downs dished out by her mother, Virginia, or the way her dad, Big Nick, largely avoided speaking to him? Nope. But laying with Ruby on her giant bed, listening to her *80s New Wave for Baby Makin'* mixtape definitely made up for her parents' disdain.

Surely Ruby worried about him. Did she still love him though? Maybe. Hopefully. But he hadn't seen her since the summer of '98, exactly six years and—he counted with his fingers—four months ago. So, he couldn't be sure.

Jonah's hammering heart suddenly sank as the saddest bits of that telephone call ricocheted through his skull. By the time Ruby finally returned one of his calls it'd already been weeks since he'd fled south across the border to his dad's place in Spokane. Through heaving sobs and gulps of breath she told Jonah she was three months pregnant. Then she went quiet for too long with just the sound of sniffling on the other end. Finally, she managed to stammer, "The baby's not… not…"

"What?" Jonah asked. "Healthy?"

"He's not yours."

Jonah wanted to die right there in his father's kitchen.

"It's Swanny's," she said timidly. "A boy due in March."

Jonah leaned over the sink and filled it with sick. His vomit was a fish, his soul flopping around, gills sucking at air, dying. Not only was the baby not Jonah's but his love had cheated on him with that dirtbag Swanny Pritchard.

"I'm sorry," Ruby's voice had crackled through the receiver as Jonah held it away from the cold sweat of his face.

Jonah had called her unforgiveable names, then in an about-face muttered a sob-filled mantra, repeating how he loved her more than anything in the world.

Her voice turned icy. "What you just called me, Jonah. That's not love." She told him that if he truly cared about her, cared about her safety, the safety of her soon-to-be-born son, he would stay away. He would stay far, far away.

"I'm joining the Marines to fight in Iraq." In the moment it felt like a bluff. "Is that far enough away for you?"

After a long stretch of uncomfortable silence she finally spoke. "Please, please don't die on the battlefield... and don't kill anyone, because that's a sin." She told him she would pray for him. She told him she loved him. Then the line went dead.

They were crushing words that caused him to make the most drastic decision he'd ever made; one that led him to right where he was at that exact moment; in Iraq—stoked, wanted, needed, and, he wasn't ashamed to admit, gloriously scared shitless. If only Ruby could see twenty-five-year-old Jonah Seeger now; raised by a pacifist, Sons of Freedom Doukhobor mother. Yet here he was performing his duties as a United States Marine Corps Scout Sniper, Bravo Company, Third Battalion, First Marine Regiment. Oorah.

Jonah squeezed bright-yellow jalapeno cheese spread from their allotted Meals Ready-to-Eat pack onto a bone-dry cracker. He shoved it into his mouth, chewed loudly and dry-swallowed. From the distance came the wild howl of a feral dog. A helicopter roared by overhead. Mase continued his muttering incantations. Lew slurped a packet of beef ravioli. Sergeant Cafferty shuffled in his crouch and glanced back at his team. He squinted at Jonah. Jonah and Lewis had only been assigned to Sergeant Cafferty two weeks prior and Jonah still didn't know what to think of him. He was a forty-five-year-old career Marine; a blunt, five-foot-eight pit bull of a man with a deeply sunburned neck. In a way he reminded Jonah of the worst of his archnemeses from back home; Swanny's older brother, Clinton, the ultimate biker douchebag. The type of tattooed gym rat and loose cannon who, if you even looked at him the wrong way, would readily, eagerly snap. Jonah suddenly felt sick at the thought of Ruby in Clinton's truck with him... and then Swanny. His stomach did a somersault at the thought of how he'd done far worse to the Pritchard brothers than just look at them the wrong way. When Jonah finally did go back home, there'd surely be a reckoning. Years ago, the thought of what that would look like made Jonah tremble. Often, he imagined he might just run forever. But now, after five years as a Marine, Jonah was a warrior, more than capable of handling himself. In a way he was even looking forward to the rematch.

Jonah felt a hard poke to his shoulder. Lewis had shot him his bug-eyed, sour-lipped, don't-be-a-dumbass look. Jonah mouthed, "What?"

Lewis raised two fingers to his eyes. "Focus," he mouthed back.

Sergeant Cafferty turned to them and in a whispered hiss told them all to shut the fuck up, even though they hadn't actually said anything. Classic Cafferty. Jonah smiled. Sergeant C., Lew and Mase were his brothers, just like his skate crew was back home. They were Ruby and his mom and dad and brother, Julian. They were people Jonah would easily give his life for. They were his tribe.

With his sniper rifle packed away, Jonah checked over his M16A4, the standard service rifle for the Marine Corps, as the last chords of ACDC's "Hells Bells" reverberated throughout Fallujah. The Marines had psy-opsed the crap out of the city for another night.

On the street below a pack of stray dogs halted their roaming and glared up toward Jonah and his boys. Just as the dogs sniffed the air toward them and began a low growl that could reveal their position, the first shot of the morning rang out like a starter pistol in an empty stadium.

Jonah's heart leapt into his throat. Mason swivelled his head toward him, his usual look of worry intensified, making the kid's fresh face look twenty years older.

Jonah took three deep breaths just like Vietnam vet Ben Whitewolf had taught him on his very first hunting trip with his dad. Jonah winked at Mase and nodded. "Run like a bat out of hell, Mase," he whispered, "and you'll be fine. Promise."

Lewis turned to Mason too and nudged him. "I got you bro. Don't I always got you?"

Mason forcefully exhaled, wiped sweat from his brow and nodded quickly.

Jonah quietly went over the plan again for Mason's sake. "We exit this building through the back, run like hell to the apartment building two hundred yards south and meet up with the rest of the squad. We all clear the building, then me and Lew set up on the roof. We need to cover our guys on the ground who'll be pushing to objective line green."

"By the end of the day," Lewis said, "we be having a hot meal and an even hotter shower back at base, baby."

Sergeant Cafferty lifted his hand, about to give the signal. Jonah lived for this feeling. He gripped his rifle. He was ten years old again, gripping the nose of his skateboard, positioning its tail, about to drop into a massive half-pipe for the first time, knowing full well he'd zoom, wobble and then splat into the far wall. Pure exhilaration.

"Let's get these terrorist motherfuckers." Sergeant C. sliced the air in front of his helmet. Go time. Instinctively, Lewis, Mason and Jonah rose in tandem with him. Then, come what may, they were off.

They exited the building they'd been holed up in and snaked across the debris-littered street, aiming for cover behind what was left of some sort of store. Giving it all they had, they ran, ducked, ran and ducked some more. Even though Jonah's heart was pumping hard, thrashing like a rodent trying to escape its cage, he could barely feel his sixty-five-pound rucksack. His vision was now laser focused. He was in the zone. The target building was in sight, about a hundred metres away as they continued their sprint. But an explosion rocked their position thirty metres ahead. At full speed they all slammed back first into the remnants of a storefront and hugged its wall. Breaching charges exploded half a klick away... followed by the distant clang of boots kicking in sheet-metal doors. Then huge, hundred-fifty-millimetre shells screamed overhead. They pulverized the upper floors of a building a hundred metres away. Instantly the guys all hit the ground amidst a shower of debris. If Jonah's mom could see him now, she'd be gobbling a Xanax, binging on junk food and cry-praying into her balled fists.

When Jonah looked up, movement through the dust cloud caught his eye. He jutted his rifle out toward the street, about to pull the trigger, when he saw it was nothing more than a scurrying mutt. He relaxed his grip, let his rifle hang for a second, cracked his knuckles and spat out bits of the city.

"Keep moving!" Sergeant Cafferty shouted. They crawled along a bullet-ridden wall for a few metres until Sergeant Cafferty sprang up. They all followed, sprinting full on amidst the barrage of mortar rounds and a storm of heavy artillery fire. Jonah hoofed it even as his heart begged him to stop. He thought it might burst right then and there as bullets hissed by his head and the thud of nearby explosions rattled his bones. He heard desperate, adrenalized yelling amidst gunfire. Run, just fucking run, Jonah told himself. In his periphery he saw a burst of flames to his left. Behind him an explosion thrust a pile of already-exploded debris into the air.

"This way!" Sergeant C. yelled.

Jonah zigzagged and ducked as more bullets hissed by. With burning, wheezing lungs he willed his legs to keep moving. The swoosh of a rocket overhead, blowing up structures behind him. Running, wheezing, head pounding, the need to puke from such do-or-die exertion.

Sergeant Cafferty seemed to be leading them in circles. They stopped, quickly checked coordinates and carried on. But somehow, they'd gotten themselves into a maze of narrow, shadowy alleys flanked by two-storey buildings with way too many open doors and windows. Totally not ideal. An eerie silence descended as the sounds of battle suddenly ceased. They slowed their movements, crouched a little, stepped as quiet as ninjas. Jonah glanced behind him. No enemies. He wiped stinging sweat from his eyes. When he faced forward again, he saw Sergeant Cafferty motion for them to follow around a dark corner of the alley to the right. Lewis was scanning doors and windows on the right side of the alley and was about to turn the corner when all of a sudden Mason stopped in his tracks. Jonah followed the kid's gaze. The hairs on the back of his neck flared. Unaware of them, an Iraqi insurgent had stepped out of a doorway up ahead on the left side of the alley. He wore shabby jeans and a baggy blue sweater. And even though his head and face were wrapped in a red and white–checked kaffiyeh, Jonah saw that the insurgent was a teenager. No more than seventeen, eighteen. He clutched an old AK-47. A mortar round exploding in the distance behind Jonah caused the Iraqi to turn toward them. He spotted Mason first, frozen in place, staring back at the young insurgent.

Castlegar, British Columbia, November 2004

"Are you sure you won't come in?" Sharon asked her brother, Yuri, in her singsong falsetto, trying to sound more chipper than usual. His bushy eyebrows rose to their extremity. She slipped off her electric-pink headband that kept her auburn hair in check and pulled her embroidered *platok* from her handbag. She draped the kerchief around her face, a big, nearly perfect circle, even though it'd been almost five years since she'd stopped digging an early grave with a spoon, a fork and mountains of crap food. In the rear-view mirror she adjusted her coke-bottle glasses and made sure to tuck her hair under the *platok*'s fold. At fifty-two years old, it was high time she got herself some contact lenses, she thought. She noticed Yuri glance at her scarred left hand as she fastened the *platok* under her chin with a silver brooch.

Yuri removed a comb from his back pocket, slicked back what was left of his hair and snickered. "I walk in there with you," he said in his pronounced Doukhobor Russian accent, "and folks will scatter like cats sniffing jar of pickles."

Sharon snort-laughed. What would they scatter from more, she wondered? Yuri's history of arson, or his sexual history—which for some in their community—especially their late father—would be considered "abnormal"? "Not sure they'd even recognize you, Yuri." His dubious wince and head tilt said it all. Touché. But she was one to talk. Last some people in the community saw her, back in her youth, Sharon's midsection wasn't as girthy, didn't protrude to her ample bosom like it did now. Yuri, however, was the same elfin man he'd always been, but like an old oak tree his bark had grown more gnarled. Unlike his Freedomite heyday when he preferred all black, these days Yuri wore an oversized brown suit jacket, jeans held up with purple suspenders and a light-blue dress shirt. His white sneakers matched the white feather that he had tucked into his breast pocket. A peace offering to the Kootenays? Sharon wondered. Or in memoriam to his Dimitri, the White Dove? She'd liked Dimitri, assured Yuri she was okay with it, despite how their mother typically reacted—denial in the form of silence and deflection.

She hadn't seen Yuri in a couple years, and just like his Tolstoyan beard, his head of wispy hair was now fully white, slicked back with Brylcreem. He sat in the passenger seat of her 1980 Volvo station wagon looking out at the Brilliant Cultural Centre. It was an austere, imposing building constructed entirely of brick; fortified against arson, against the Sons of Freedom, against a fanatical version of Yuri, who thirty years earlier had tried to burn it down.

Typical of Yuri not to accompany her. Even as a boy his zealous acceptance of their parents' Freedomite ways ensured he was often on the run. Still, Sharon could relate to his hesitance. It would be her first prayer service since her disturbing drunken lapse in decorum at that doomed Samarodin Christmas dinner seven years earlier. And it scared the bejesus out of her. Plus, her Russian was rusty. And to top it all off, she came from an infamous family.

Sharon's Doukhobor beliefs were still oozing out of the room she'd locked them in back when she'd first fled the Kootenays in 1969. She supposed having a soldier for a son would drive any mother estranged from their faith back to it in search of solace.

Sharon left Yuri the keys to her car so he could keep warm. He found a radio station playing oldies hits and stared out the window humming along to an Elvis tune. She checked her watch. Darn it, it was about to start. She thought for a moment and then the Russian word for "prayer service" came to her… *molenya*.

Even though the November morning air was brisk Sharon left her wool coat unbuttoned. With a swaying gait and short steps she made her way through the gravel parking lot as quickly as what she liked to call her "hourglass figure" allowed her to. At the end of the parking lot was a wide cement walkway sloping up to the great hall. On either side sat apple trees, their bare, gnarled limbs reaching up to the overcast sky. Acres of grass turning Autumn brown flanked the hall.

Farther beyond were the homes of the predominantly Doukhobor neighbourhood of Brilliant.

Unlike much of her life, these days Sharon was happy to be living in the Kootenays. With a hodgepodge history of miners and loggers, Doukhobors and draft dodgers, ski bums, mill workers and artists, the region attracted and birthed an alluring and occasionally odd cast of characters. Like Yuri. Like herself, Sharon supposed. The entire area had never felt more like home than it did these days. Even Castlegar, where her marriage to Jonah and Julian's father Roy had dissolved, didn't have the same sting to it, or Shoreacres at the south end of the Slocan Valley where Sharon and teenage Jonah lived in a trailer and where she'd tried hard (with varying degrees of success) to get herself right. But it was her home now in Nelson, half an hour east of Castlegar, where Sharon felt most comfortable. Especially since over the years she had slowly shed piles of shame and witnessed her story unfold with a clarity and perspective that could only come with abstinence plus time plus distance.

Still, it wasn't easy. Sharon hesitated at the grey entrance doors. Without needing the confirmation of a mirror, she knew that her face was drawing in on itself ever so slightly as it tended to do when she worried. She had felt stable these past years living in Nelson. And even though the eating disorder was under control (for the moment), the overwhelming desire to devour an entire Deep'n Delicious chocolate cake that very second sent her stomach into a somersault. Was a stage entrance back into the Doukhobor community a good idea? Sharon wondered. Only one way to find out. She swung open the doors, strode in...

And immediately regretted it. As she approached the congregation of around fifty already lined up and ready to commune with their God, who did Sharon behold? Why, Virginia Samarodin of course: pious pillar of the community, resolute promoter of all things Doukhobor, Ruby's straitlaced mother, and Sharon's ex–best friend. Sharon's heart sank and quickened at the same time. Ginny, as Virginia used to be called, was looking svelte, proudly standing at the head of the congregation, about to lead that morning's service. She was in the midst of welcoming everyone when, at the sight of Sharon, Virginia coughed, sputtered and swallowed her words mid-sentence. Sharon stopped as all heads swivelled toward her. Was the murmur that rippled through the crowd due to the fact she wasn't the five-foot-five lightweight version of herself from her twenties? Or because she had shed sixty pounds and now stood at a robust yet respectable 170? Or was the crowd's murmur because she was there at all?

Sharon muttered an apology for her lateness and was about to spin around and flee when she saw her old friend Olga Makayev standing in the back row of the women, waving for Sharon to join her. Sharon knew full well she was there to pray to the universe, to God, the gods, anything, in an appeal for Jonah's safe return, as much as she was there for her own soul's comfort. She forced a comical smile, straightened her blouse and practically jogged to Olga. Sharon's short, stout friend welcomed her with a warm, rosy-cheeked smile and reassuring squeeze of her hand. Sharon looked around the large, carpeted hall as Virginia continued her welcome to the gathered. Pale light spilled in from the tall, narrow windows that lined the brick walls. At the front of the hall was a vast stage cordoned off by brown velvet curtains. It was just as Sharon remembered from her youth. Opposite the women were the men and boys lined up in rows. Towering over them, and trying not to stare at Sharon, was Virginia's husband, Big Nick Samarodin, tall and hefty as Paul Bunyan and with Viking-blond hair. Nick rested his massive hands on the tender shoulders of an adorable little boy standing in the front row. His grandson, Sharon assumed. All the men were in their Sunday best. Like herself, the women were wearing colourful dresses and white, silken head scarves. In front of Virginia at the head of the congregation sat a shiny wood table covered by a crisp white cloth. On top was a round loaf of bread that looked like a giant mushroom cap, flanked by a hand-carved wood bowl full of salt, and a pitcher of water. Sharon remembered as an eight-year-old being at a similar *molenya* in their Sons of Freedom village of Krestova. She'd asked her mother why there wasn't a Jesus hanging on the cross, or statues and paintings like she knew were in normal Christian churches. Her mother told her it was because Doukhobors didn't need to pray to crosses and statues, that icon worship was beneath them. The only symbols required were bread, salt and water, the stuff that life was made of. As a child Sharon thought it was silly, since people were actually made of skin and bones.

When Sharon last saw Virginia it was at that horrendously awkward 1997 Christmas dinner that both their families had endured. Drunk, fed up with the Samarodin sanctimony, and clearly delusional, Sharon had wobbled up from her seat at the table and, like a child lashing out, began to unbutton her… Oh God, she couldn't bear to think of it. With clenched eyes and a quake of her head Sharon squeezed the memory away. Instead, through the rows of ladies she demurely peeked at Virginia, who still seemed to be enjoying the sound of her own voice. Unlike Sharon's own pasty skin, and her stormy blue-grey eyes, Virginia was blessed with sharp, almond-brown eyes, sweeping lashes and a natural copper complexion. And while her nose was a tad pointy, her eloquent lips made up for that. Sharon took a small amount of shameful pleasure in noting, however, that unlike her own locks poking from under her *platok*, Virginia's had all but gone grey.

In the traditional Doukhobor manner Virginia started the hymn solo and was then joined a few seconds later by the entire congregation in unison. The familiar hymn, like all the songs sung at Doukhobor *molenya,* was full of sadness and longing. Sharon couldn't remember the words but feeling the vibration of herself humming along to it, and of everyone around her singing as one, made Sharon's chest lighten and her heart momentarily swell with joy as it used to when she was a child. After a few minutes the hymn finished, and Sharon watched a young man step out of the front row and turn to the elder beside him. The young man clasped the elder's hand, like he was shaking it, bowed to him once, kissed him on both cheeks, then bowed to him one last time. Several more men performed the ritual, followed by the front row of women.

Afterwards Virginia reminded the gathered of the significance of the ritual. "When we kiss and bow to one another it's because we see the special spark in each other. Like an invisible flame that lives in everyone. We call this flame, or spark, God. God is in all of us and knowing this makes us happy."

Sharon watched as Nick and Virginia's grandson shot his arm high into the air.

In Russian Virginia asked the boy what his question was. "*Chto,* Sasha?"

The boy was silent for a moment. He stuck out his belly as far as he could and rubbed it in circles underneath his white dress shirt, then poked himself in the belly button. He looked up at his baba. "God is an invisible fire that lives inside people?" He asked with his sweet, earnest voice.

The crowd chuckled. Virginia replied, "*Da,* Sasha, that's a good way of putting it."

After *molenya* had concluded, Sharon chatted for a while with her friend Olga, then, like a spy would, attempted to slip away unnoticed. She stepped out from the back row and waded through the dispersing crowd but ... there was Big Nick, with his grandson in his arms, standing like a wall in front of her. She spun around before he could spot her, aiming to beeline for the side exits, when she stepped straight into someone. Sharon's glasses were nearly flung off her head. She began apologizing as she readjusted them. "Oh, I'm so sorry. I was—"

The woman turned around beaming, but when she saw it was Sharon her smile evaporated as though it had never been there in the first place. "*Och* ... Sharon," Virginia said, her voice strained and nearly cracking. She waved her husband over, scrunched her face and eyed Sharon up and down with a look of disbelief. "*Chto ty... zdes delayesh?*"

What am I doing here? Sharon repeated the Russian question in her head to make sure she understood. "Oh, same as anyone I suppose," she tittered. "Getting closer to God."

"Aha, *pon'yatno*." Again, in Russian Virginia affirmed that she understood, knowing full well Sharon's Russian was rusty. She assessed her former friend and switched to English. "You... you've lost..."

Sharon nodded. "Yes. Sixty pounds." She glanced out the windows lining the side of the hall. The overcast skies had let up; sunshine broke through the clouds, beckoning her to escape outside.

"*Nu, privet*," Big Nick said in his hearty baritone as he stepped to his wife's side.

Sharon slowly translated in her head, remembering that *nu* was a Doukhobor catch-all phrase that meant, "Well?" or "What's up?" And *privet* meant "hello." "*Privet*," Sharon said to Nick.

"Fancy seeing you here." He placed his grandson at his feet.

People were milling about around them. Sharon was suddenly overheating. She glanced at Virginia, at her gold brooch fastening her kerchief of fine silk, and down at the designer leather purse that she clutched with the polished, talon-like nails of her perfectly manicured hands. Instinctively Sharon covered her scarred hand with her unblemished one and silently berated herself for doing so. She forced a smile, stooped over and spoke to the boy. "And who's this handsome young man?" He blushed, then clutched his grandfather's pant leg.

"This is Sasha," Virginia said. "Ruby and..." The words seemed to fade from her mouth. Virginia looked around for answers; then, as though the child had no father, she just said, "Ruby's son."

"Nice to meet you, Sasha. I love your name," Sharon said. Sasha nodded in agreement, his head of wavy brown hair bobbing adorably as he did. "How old?"

"Six in March. You may have heard, we're, we're helping raise him while..." Virginia lifted her chin. "While Ruby's away working."

Working? Sharon thought. She supposed being a galivanting rock star *was* work. But who was she to judge? There were plenty of times she'd fantasized about what it would be like if it were her that had left the family instead of Roy. She could've completed her nursing degree, possibly travelled the world, made something of herself, instead of eating through her emotions most of her adult life.

Sharon looked Virginia in the eye. "How *is* Ruby?" She liked the girl, her wit and spunk, her natural beauty, her singing voice. The few times she chose to stay with Jonah in his tiny room in Sharon's mobile home, Ruby was a pleasure: polite, helping with dishes, often praising Sharon's sense of style, happy to play Durak, Sharon's favourite Russian card game. And she could always see that Ruby adored Jonah even if, in typical teenage fashion, she tried not to show it.

"Oh, she's fine, just fine," Virginia said far too cheerfully. "Working hard, making a good living." She twirled her finger in the air. "Seeing the world." Virginia fidgeted, seemed as eager to escape as Sharon was. "Well, we should—"

"Does she get back much?" Sharon persisted, enjoying the rare occurrence of Virginia squirming.

Still clutching his grandfather's pant leg, Sasha said timidly, "Momma Ruby is away lots."

"We'll call her tonight," Nick consoled, stroking Sasha's hair.

Virginia stiffened. "She gets back as… as often as she can. And Jonah, he's… is he still…?"

"Alive? Yes." So nice of her to ask after a boy who wasn't good enough for her daughter, Sharon thought.

"Oh, I didn't mean…" Virginia looked to her husband for help.

"*Slava Bohu*. We're glad he's okay," Nick offered.

"Yes, thank God," Virginia echoed.

"Who's Jonah?" Sasha asked.

"An old friend of your mom's," Nick replied quickly.

"By 'old friend,'" Sharon air-quoted, "I think your dyeda meant *boyfriend*. Jonah was your mom's boyfriend. He's my son."

Clearly wanting to change the subject, Virginia asked, "So, when did you move back?"

Sharon raised her eyebrows. "I haven't left since moving back in '96."

"Oh *really*?" Virginia's tone was condescending now. "I just, well, you know, after that... Christmas dinner..." Virginia wobbled her head. "We just assumed you'd moved *again*."

Knowing she'd stayed through the prayer service when she could've fled, remembering the soothing feeling of the Doukhobor hymns thrumming through her gave Sharon a small measure of strength now. She held Virginia's eye. "I stayed," Sharon said, wanting to own her actions. "And I've stayed clothed." She chuckled awkwardly and considered that instead of attempting humour, now might be a good time for a long-overdue apology to Ginny.

Sharon was about to speak when Virginia laughed anxiously like a politician facing scandal. "Ha ha ha... Well, we should be off then." She took Sasha's hand. "Nice... nice to see you, Sharon."

Sharon watched Virginia turn and walk away. It was understandable that Virginia thought Sharon had moved away from the Kootenays, as she had done time and time again. For a moment her mind rewound to 1967 and the things that had sparked her friendship with Ginny in the first place. Sharon remembered first meeting Virginia in old Ms. Sedgewick's home economics class on the first day of grade eleven. Virginia had walked right up to her as she arranged her cooking area and complimented Sharon on her Cher-inspired hairdo; long, straight and silky with bangs. They partnered up in class and became fast friends over their mutual love of the film *Doctor Zhivago*, and an equally mutual disdain for Ms. Sedgewick, whose rants about vegetarian cuisine everyone knew held a subtext of anti-Doukhobor sentiment. They sang in choir together, took weekend shopping trips to Spokane, playfully sparred over which musician was better—Ginny's choice of Elvis, or Sharon's pick of Bob Dylan—and both looked forward to going through the nursing program together at Selkirk College. Throughout their friendship they'd resolutely avoided talking about their respective families and the worst years of the fracturing of the Doukhobor community which they both believed were finally behind them. And maybe that avoidance was the problem? On the surface they both played at being regular Canadian girls, but underneath they knew there was nothing regular about what they and their community had been through.

Their friendship finally collapsed in 1968. Sharon could see the blasted front page of the newspaper, could see it as clear as if Virginia were holding it up in her face. *Beware Your Neighbours!* it read. And there was the photo of Sharon with her grade eleven classmates; Igor Arishenkoff, Wally Pepin ... and Sharon herself, circled in red. If Virginia's parents hadn't given that interview to the *Vancouver Sun*, outing Sharon's family, outing scores of other Svobodnik (Freedomite) families, she might still be friends with Virginia. Sharon scoffed. Whatever problems there'd been between Community Doukhobors and the Sons of Freedom—and God knows there had been plenty—they'd traditionally kept it between themselves. They didn't go running to the press. Or crying to the police. Virginia's family, the Kalesnikoffs, had broken an unspoken rule. But it was that day in the school parking lot that Virginia showed her true colours, and a wedge was firmly driven into their friendship. Sharon was already plenty ashamed of having grown up in a Sons of Freedom family. What had given Sharon some semblance of self-respect was at least hanging out with regular, non–Sons of Freedom kids, along with any and all English-speaking people, whom Doukhobors referred to as Angliki, the English. She'd been making friends with popular girls like Virginia; boys were paying attention to her; up until the newspaper article she'd been able to distance herself from her family's infamy. One Friday afternoon after school though, in front of Virginia and Nick—who were high school sweethearts—and a group of friends, Walt Finney had asked Sharon to come to his house party. She'd had a thing for tall, handsome, normal Canadian Walt all year. What better way to celebrate the end of school than by getting to know him? Sharon swooned.

"You sure about that?" Asked Walt's best friend, local hockey star Phil Bozak.

Shut up, Phil, please just shut up, Sharon remembered silently pleading.

Virginia covered her mouth with her hand, and Sharon thought at least her friend would come to her defence. "Yeah," Virginia said excitedly, "she might burn the house down!"

Everyone, including Walt, erupted in laughter. Sharon blushed and did her best to laugh along. But at that very moment she vowed to get the hell out of the Kootenays the second she graduated. And then, for the next eighteen years, didn't speak another word to Virginia Samarodin.

In 1899 the newly arrived Doukhobors travel by train from Atlantic Canada to the Prairies where the government offers them land wrested from the Indigenous Peoples in the form of three reserves totalling 773,400 acres. There they establish over sixty farming communes. Each one consists of one-storey log dwellings built in the style of their former Caucasus villages, with mud-plastered, whitewashed walls and prairie-sod roofs. As many as two dozen houses line both sides of a wide dirt road running through the settlement. Common throughout each village is a sawmill, a flour mill, a flax oil press, a blacksmith shop, bathhouses, a pen for sheep, chicken coops, grain bins, horse stables, cattle barns, and sheds housing farm implements, wagons and supplies

In December of 1902 Peter Vasilevich Verigin arrives in Otradnoe village in Saskatchewan to assume hereditary leadership of the Doukhobors following nearly sixteen years of imprisonment in Siberia. A tall, robust, impeccably dressed man with luxuriant black hair and moustache, and dark, thoughtful eyes, Verigin is known to be deeply well read, and to possess a powerful personality with a quick, subtle and capable mind.

Slocan Valley, British Columbia, November 2004

Virginia took her *platok* off and shoved it into her purse, muttering under her breath. She cranked the heat up in the Suburban and switched off the radio.

"You okay, honey?" Nick asked.

"Did you see the way she was looking at me when she asked about..." Virginia glanced at Sasha leafing through a picture book in the back seat. "... Ruby?" She mouthed.

Nick rolled his eyes as he drove their vehicle along Poplar Ridge Road. "*Och*," he uttered, using the Doukhobor expression that doubled as a shake of the head. "She genuinely likes her, cares for her."

Virginia crossed her arms, felt a pang of guilt in her chest. Sharon had lost so much weight. After her sad display at Christmas dinner had she sought help? And even if she had, Virginia could see that Jonah being a stupid soldier was still a burden to Sharon. Rightly so. Virginia pulled down the visor, flipped open the small mirror and ran her fingers through her prudently short hair. Was repair between her and Sharon possible? The troubles between the Freedomites and other Doukhobors had been over for almost twenty years, yet the emotional residue burrowed on. An apology one day would be nice. But then again, Virginia could stand to apologize, too. Her chest tightened as the pang of guilt thickened.

"Nick, we have to tell her—" Virginia pointed out the window. "Who on Earth is that?" A Toyota minivan was parked on the side of the road at the foot of their driveway, its windows partially fogged. Virginia peered closer. At the wheel was a long-haired man wearing a red bandana, looking down as they drove by. "Stop the truck," Virginia commanded.

"It's nothing," Nick said. "Probably just lost is all. What do we have to tell Sharon?"

"Stop. Right now." Nick knew that tone and stopped the Suburban halfway up their driveway. Virginia climbed out the passenger door, did up her designer winter coat, tightened her pashmina scarf and strode purposefully down to the minivan. As she approached, she could hear a clicking sound coming from the engine. She stood a few feet away. The long-haired man avoided eye contact as he tried to start his van. She stepped to the driver's-side window and stared, her breath rising out into the late-morning air. He finally looked at her, rolled down his window.

"Can I help you with something?" Virginia asked.

"Uh… battery's dead and…" He gestured beside him to where a wheelchair sat folded and strapped to the floor. Trying to reach up to the battery under the van's hood from his wheelchair positioned on the driveway would be impossible. He tried to peer around Virginia, squinted his eyes to focus.

She glanced behind her. Nick was standing outside his open driver's door, holding Sasha in his arms. The man's long hair. The wheelchair. Parked where he was. Virginia just knew it. "You're *him* aren't you?"

"Him who?" the man asked, trying to start his vehicle again.

"My daughter, Ruby's… whatchamacallit. With the funny name." He sat silently staring at his steering wheel. "Well?" Virginia said. "Are you or aren't you, young man? Speak up."

Finally, he nodded. "Yeah, my name is Swanny. But I—"

Virginia held up a silencing finger, spun around and called to Nick. "Put him in the truck and come down here right now." She turned back to Swanny. "What do you want?"

He looked around his van as though the dashboard held the answer. "I… I just wanted to, to see…" Swanny gestured with his chin toward Sasha. "Him."

"Why?" Virginia's voice was stone cold. "Spying on us for that monster of a brother of yours?"

Swanny's eyes nearly popped out of his head. "No! God no. I'm not spying for him or anything like that. Well, I *am* spying." He forced a laugh. "But, but for myself."

Virginia shook her head at the lame attempt at a joke.

Swanny forged on. "Honestly, I was in the neighbourhood and I, I was just curious is all." He raised his hands in surrender. "Really. I swear to God." He slapped his thighs then gestured again to his wheelchair. "Plus, I get a little... bored sitting at home all day."

"Ruby's not here," Virginia said.

"I know, I know. I follow her career a bit. She seems to be quite successful."

"Mhmm." Big Nick was now at Virginia's side. "Nick, help this young man with his battery." She pointed at Nick's face. "And don't let him leave until I come back." Nick and Swanny both wore looks of utter confusion as Virginia spun and strode up the driveway.

Ten minutes later she returned carrying a cloth sack. Swanny's minivan was idling and Nick was curling up his jumper cables. She passed the bag to Swanny through his window.

"What's this?" He asked, feeling the weight of it and peering inside.

"A jar of raspberry jam, one of apricot, one jar of borsch and a jar of pickles. All homemade."

Swanny was astonished. "Thank you. But... why?"

"Because that's what Doukhobors do. And you look like you could use some food made with love."

Swanny nodded and looked at his spoils again. "I really appreciate it. Thank you, Mrs. Samarodin."

Virginia nodded. "And young man?"

"Yes?"

Virginia conjured all the times she'd scolded and grounded Ruby, thought of her and Nick's vow to protect Sasha no matter what, then said, "Don't ever come back here again."

* * *

Virginia was sitting on the front porch of her timber-frame home, nursing the one glass per week she allowed herself of the Château Mouton Rothschild Bordeaux. She was cozy in her coat, her feet warm in her

Uggs as the autumn sun was setting. She was taking a breather from all the emailing and telephoning: organizing the Doukhobor presence at next spring's peace walk in Vancouver; negotiating with the City of Nelson to display the Vietnam draft dodger memorial statue at City Hall; coordinating with the Doukhobor Ladies' Choir to sing at Vancouver Folk Fest; teaching Russian language classes; cooking with the ladies' funeral committee; volunteering at the Doukhobor Museum. "Oy, oy, oy," Virginia said. The list went on. Being of service, keeping her people engaged in their culture, spreading the spirit of "toil and peaceful life"—as one of the Doukhobor sayings went—was Virginia's self-appointed, never-ending duty. If not her, then who? Her mother's old age had slowed her own crusade, Virginia thought as she savoured a tiny sip of wine.

If people in the community thought Virginia to be a bit... rigid, as she knew they did, then her mother was positively Victorian. Mary Kalesnikoff, who wore tactically discreet polyester blouses and skirts, and never once missed Sunday prayer in Grand Forks, considered herself a model of Doukhobor purity and piousness. If she were there now, Virginia would be getting a talking to about the *one* glass of wine. With lips pinched tight, her mother would ask her what was wrong with her, "*Chto s'toboy ne tak?*" followed by a reminder that she never used to drink: "*Ty nikogda ne pil'a.*" Her mother would conclude her admonishment by asking, What would Uncle Verigin think? "*Chto biy podumal dyadya Verigin?*" It was a common question posed by devout older folks, even by those who weren't related to Doukhobor leader Peter V. Verigin as Virginia was on her mother's side. Poor Uncle Verigin died in a train explosion in 1924. The community was still split on the unsolved mystery: one side believed he was assassinated by government agents; the other side, to which Virginia belonged, believed the assassin came from within the Freedomite ranks. And it was precisely the manner in which the beloved and revered leader died that caused people in the community to still hearken back to him. Virginia asked her uncle's ghost what he would think of the Doukhobors now: "*Chto ty dumayesh' o dukhoborakh seychas?*" Would he be disappointed? she wondered. Resigned? The flock was spread far and wide; they'd been marrying non-Doukhobors for decades now; some loved their booze a little too much, had gotten into all sorts of dope, were forgetting their language and customs, and were even joining the army like Jonah Seeger did. Such a fool, she thought, then said it to herself in Russian: "*Woht durak.*" Ruby and Jonah weren't alone though. It seemed to Virginia that young people nowadays, Doukhobor or not, wanted desperately to be any place but where they were. Don't worry, Uncle Verigin, Virginia thought. There's hope. Because even though the world was getting crazier by the day, in times of trouble the flock always returned home.

Despite what her mother would think, Virginia continued enjoying her wine. She savoured it coursing through her as she took in the hilltop view from her house, the largest one for miles around. In the front yard clumps of soggy leaves clung like hanging bats to the otherwise naked branches of the apple trees; down the hill mist drifted overtop the emerald Slocan River as it snaked south where it eventually joined the larger Kootenay River; chimney smoke drifted up from her neighbours' modest houses; and high above, the snow line was halfway down the ridge. In less than a month winter would be at their doorstep, blanketing the entire length of the remote, hundred-kilometre-long valley.

Virginia thought of the awkward encounter with Sharon earlier that day. How inconceivable that Ruby might ever stray as far as Sharon did from her community and its values. How hard Ruby always sought to be the reverse of Virginia: impulsive, secular, craving the world beyond the Kootenays, brazenly determined to make a name for herself even if that ambition left splinters in its wake. And that was all *before* the night of that stupid music festival in July of 1998. For three nights afterwards Ruby had stayed at her best friend Nadya's. When she did finally come home, Nick was at the neighbours' helping with some carpentry while Virginia was placing a sprinkler in the garden's cucumber patch. She'd heard a vehicle come and go in the driveway, then moments later watched Ruby slink into the house through the basement door. Virginia was livid that her daughter would stay away for so many nights in a row, no doubt getting drunk and smoking marijuana with Jonah and their friends. She was fully prepared to give Ruby a tongue-lashing but when she went to her room and saw Ruby sitting on the edge of her bed, pale, shivering and crying, she knew something terrible had transpired.

"Luba, what's wrong?" Virginia asked, sitting down beside Ruby. Ruby was silent, quickly swiped away her tears with the sleeves of her hoodie. "Where's Jonah?" Virginia asked.

But at the mention of her boyfriend, Ruby's tears started to flow again. Virginia's relationship with her daughter had by then been strained for some time. They hadn't hugged in as long as Virginia could remember, but in that moment any tension between them had quickly dissolved. She put her arm around her baby and gently pulled her close. "Did something happen between you and Jonah? Did you get in a fight?" Almost imperceptibly Ruby shook her head. "Did he hurt you?"

Ruby jolted away from her mother, looked at her aghast. "No! Jesus, Mom, no. He'd never do that."

"Then what, Luba?" Virginia asked. "What's wrong?"

Ruby proceeded to tell Virginia of Jonah's terrible fight with the bikers at Give'r Fest and how as a consequence, one of them, Clinton Pritchard, now wanted Jonah dead. That's why she didn't come home right away and why Jonah wasn't with her. In fact, he had to flee for his life, to Spokane, possibly never to return.

That stupid, stupid kid, Virginia thought of Jonah then as she did now sitting on the porch steps drinking wine. How her family's life would've been better off had Ruby and Jonah never met. She looked at her half-empty bottle of Bordeaux, her memories begging for her to finish it off.

Virginia remembered how the following day she'd discovered Ruby's stage outfit in the clothes hamper and thought of the skimpy, misshapen and torn clothes as shameless. "*Besstydnyy*," she'd said at them. When questioned, Ruby grew agitated, defensively described how she'd fallen in the forest as they fled from the bikers. Seemingly confused as to why she'd wanted to wash her stage outfit in the first place, Ruby snatched the tiny red shorts and filthy crop top from the hamper and immediately threw them in the garbage.

In the days that followed, Ruby was often nauseous. She'd get confused as to what day of the week it was. Oddly, she washed her hands obsessively. Knowing that Jonah was perhaps gone forever, Ruby was as sad and listless as Virginia had ever seen her. It broke Virginia's heart. It wasn't until weeks later, when Ruby discovered that she was pregnant, that she regained some spark of innocence. But certainly not all of it. Teenage pregnancy brought with it a whole new set of challenges. As for what exactly happened at that music festival that night, Virginia might never know. One thing was for certain; her daughter came home forever changed.

Virginia downed the last of her wine, then groaned from strain as she stood and went back inside her house. She hung up her jacket and scarf and stepped out of her boots. She walked down the long hallway, then peeked into the living room where a robust fire crackled in the stone fireplace. Her eagle eyes spotted a fine layer of dust covering the set of antique matryoshka and the silver samovar that were displayed on a teak table next to a large mahogany bookshelf. How did she miss dusting the nesting dolls and tea urn yesterday?

She wondered where Nick was, then remembered he was getting the *banya* ready. The bathhouse was a Sunday ritual she looked forward to, especially the traditional Doukhobor songs they'd all sing as they sweated and purified together. Just like their ancestors had done for centuries.

Swanny Pritchard's stomach was a hollow pit, as though he hadn't eaten in days. And now it was afternoon and he felt even worse. "Something wicked this way comes," he said aloud in a terrible British accent he hoped would cheer himself up. "Never should've left your humble abode this morning, good sir..." He dropped the accent. "To stare at her house like a loser creep." At least he got some delicious preserves out of it. Followed by a stern warning from Ruby's... intense mother.

It wasn't entirely the autumn chill, Swanny considered, or the looming peaks of the Valhalla Ranges constantly throwing shade over the Slocan Valley that caused his mood. Nor was it the ass, leg and toe spasms that woke him in the middle of the night, signalling his need to piss. He thought it was probably loneliness, but he couldn't be sure. It felt even weightier.

Swanny tucked the small coffee Thermos between his legs, slicked his long, greasy hair back with his fingers, then pushed the lever of his wheelchair forward. He steered the chair off the kitchen linoleum and onto the carpet of the living room, his chair moving more sluggishly than usual. "Ah shoot." He rolled past his worn leather couch. "Battery's almost out of juice."

He stopped at the stereo system which sat on an old, rosewood cabinet beside the hallway that led to the washroom and his bedroom farther beyond. The stereo's radio was tuned to the CBC, the host discussing the war in Iraq. He shut off the radio, grabbed a remote beside it and clicked on the TV. From his sweatpants pocket Swanny pulled out the red bandana he'd had since he was a teenager. He folded it precisely, then wrapped it around his head and tied it snuggly. He looked down at his sweats torn at the knees and the food stains on his grey t-shirt. Man, how much he used to care about his appearance. "Who's there to impress now anyway?" Swanny scoffed, both at how pathetic that sounded, and at the fact that he was only thirty-five years old but constantly talked out loud to himself as if he were an old man trying to keep himself company.

Swanny tuned in to the American televangelist gesticulating wildly on TV. "Well if it isn't the devil himself." Bobby Popoff's oily smile and glazed, hungry eyes were those of a man possessed by Christian fundamentalism. "Uncle Bobby." Swanny was happy to have never met his mother's crackpot sibling.

He clicked off the TV. At least Swanny could count on his morning coffee to lift his mood; he took it dark, strong and without sugar. He slurped a sip then placed the Thermos back between his legs. On his bookshelf his forefinger traced the spines of several options. "Some Chuck Palahniuk? Nah, too depressing for current mood. Houellebecq's *Elementary Particles*... too bleak and loveless. I don't need any reminders. Leonard Cohen's *Beautiful Losers* perhaps? Not today." Swanny was about to reach for his copy of Tolstoy's *Resurrection* when a beeping noise sounded. It was accompanied by a flashing red diode on the small black and white security monitors that sat on the kitchen counter. He rarely got unwanted visitors. Just the way he preferred it. Swanny wheeled over to the kitchen and checked the monitor. Security cameras positioned up in trees revealed a black SUV tracking through the snow-dusted road that snaked up to his place. His dark mood had been validated. "Always trust your gut, Swan."

He made his way back to the living room and peered out the frosted window. No movement in the forest on either side of his property. Through the clearing in the sloping front yard, the farmland flanking the languidly flowing Slocan River was as peaceful as ever.

Okay, at least I'm not getting ambushed, he considered. Unless... He quickly wheeled back to the monitors. "Unless the SUV's a decoy and they're hitting the barn in the back?" But the monitor for his barn showed no movement either. Swanny knew he had less than a minute to prepare for the uninvited visitor. Only one thing could effectively calm him. He pulled a pre-rolled joint from the breast pocket of his plaid mac jacket, lit it up and took a giant pull. He adjusted his bandana, made sure it was snug. He took another pull of the joint then butted it out on the windowsill, slipped it back into his pocket. He exhaled a cloud of weed smoke and went back to his monitors. The SUV was on the small log bridge crossing the stream. At the fork in the road it turned left toward his home. "*Merde*."

Swanny directed his wheelchair through the kitchen and into the mud room, piled with boots and shoes, boxes, a few full garbage bags and other assorted junk. He grabbed his coat from the rack. As he reached for his pump-action shotgun leaning in the corner, a terrible pain spread hot lava from his ass crack to his toes. He winced, took a big breath and waited out the neuropathic sensation.

Before he opened the front door, Swanny checked that the gun was loaded, then placed it across his lap and covered it with a hoodie. He unlocked the deadbolts, pressed a large button at the side of the door which caused it to swing open with a low hum, allowing Swanny to roll onto the landing. He took another big breath and let the autumn chill wash over him. Then he unlocked the safety on the gun and quoted one of his favourite simple lines from *Slaughterhouse Five*, "So it goes..."

He pushed on his wheelchair's control lever. "Goddamnit." The battery was nearly dead. And now here he was in a compromised situation that might require that he move fast. He gripped his shotgun and watched the Hummer come to a stop between two large cedar trees a hundred metres away. He didn't recognize the vehicle but knew the type of douchebag gangsters who drove them. The vehicle's windows were tinted. He knew that rippers wouldn't be stupid enough to steal his marijuana crop by driving up his road in broad daylight. He wondered if it was someone who'd come to settle a family score. If there were more than one of them, he might not fare so well. Only one, and he'd sure as shit blast them with buckshot.

The Hummer slowly rolled forward ten feet.

"Shit." At that distance he couldn't make out who it might be. He brought his shotgun out from under his hoodie, placed his finger on the trigger, and waited.

This time the truck lurched forward another five feet, then skidded to a halt.

"What the fuck is this bastard doing?" He squinted at the figure to try make them out. No use. Swanny wasn't taking any chances. He raised the nose of the shotgun just as the driver's door opened.

"Stop right there and state your goddamned business." Swanny pumped the gun and was about to fire when he heard the familiar sound of thick necklaces clinking together as the driver climbed out of the vehicle. The man closed the driver's door and stepped forward. His large head was bald and shiny, his eyes hidden behind the type of mirrored wraparound sunglasses that only cops, gangsters and dudes with terrible style wear. But there was no mistaking that shrewd grin, the cackle and the mashed nose of a hockey enforcer. "Jesus fuck, Clinton." Swanny lowered his gun.

"Ha! Gotcha, motherfucker," Clinton said in his perpetually party-worn voice.

"I could've killed you."

Clinton shrugged his husky shoulders. "Ah, I suppose there's worse things." In his right hand he clutched a leather vest, in the other a bottle of Jack Daniels. "Why you gotta live way the fuck up here anyway?"

"So I don't get any visitors." Especially not from his brother… half-brother. "Why you holding that cut?"

Clinton stopped at the foot of the stairs, slid his glasses up onto his scarred dome. He was forty-one, only six years older than Swanny, but his worn catcher's mitt of a face and grey stubble made Swanny's brother look as though he was on the wrong side of fifty. Clinton really knew his way around a bottle of booze, so it wasn't at all unusual that his eyes were already far away with drink. Or was it something else this time? Swanny looked at the half-gone bottle of whisky. Clinton dropped his cleft chin to his chest. When he looked back up, his eyes red and watery, Swanny understood.

He suddenly felt the crushing bear hug of their father. He could hear the deep, uproarious cackle the burly man was known for. Hulk Hogan, Swanny and his friends would call him when they were kids; his blond handlebar moustache and gruff voice reminding them of the pro wrestler. Wild Eddie is what everyone else called him; how he could lustily devour an entire rack of lamb, then effortlessly drink any takers under the table, eagerly snort a fistful of cocaine, readily start a fight just for the hell of it, and astonishingly keep on partying until he was the last man standing. All things he passed on to Clinton... including the use of fists as battering rams whenever confronted, confused or disrespected. He shuddered at the memories.

Swanny's sadness and pain caught in his tightening chest. He exhaled heavily. "How'd it happen?"

"If yer askin' was it a hit? The answer is no," Clinton said. "The ole man had a massive heart attack yesterday. Died quicker than a moose meeting a Mack truck."

"Ah shit." Swanny looked up at the overcast sky. "Why didn't you phone right away?"

"I needed to come see you anyway. Gotta lay low for a few days." Clinton was at the foot of the stairs now. He tossed Swanny's biker vest at him. "There's your cut," he said. "Found it in Dad's closet. Funeral's Sunday in Kelowna."

Swanny turned it over in his hands. He ran his finger over the smooth black leather and the Hells Angels patches. Unlike his brother's patches would be by now, Swanny's were still clean and intact. "My mom know?" he asked.

"Don't know, that's your deal."

Suppose it is, Swanny thought. He knew that Clinton appreciated that Swanny's mother was good to him when they were kids, especially seeing as Clinton's own mother died when he was far too young. But after Swanny's mother left their father, broke his heart, Clinton kept his distance.

"You staying the night here then?" Swanny asked, trying to hide his wariness.

"What, not offering?" Clinton sounded offended.

"Yeah yeah, sure, yeah of course."

Clinton stared at Swanny like he always did when he wanted to make him uncomfortable. And when Swanny started to be visibly uncomfortable, Clinton would crack a smile. "Just fuckin' with ya. Got a room in Nelson. Gonna get me some Kootenay pussy tonight. But I ain't goin' anywhere till you an' I polish off the rest of this baby." He raised the bottle of Jack triumphantly over his head. "Got another in the truck, too."

Shit. "Sure," Swanny said. A gust of wind made him shiver. "Come on in."

"Stay a couple days at the ranch after the funeral, bro." Clinton stepped up the ramp. "I could put your ass to work. I just got a good shipment from Juárez that I need cut and weighed. Plus, the guys will be stoked to see ya, Swan. It's been too long."

Swanny turned his chair around and rolled farther into the house. Clinton followed. Swanny hung his coat up and returned the shotgun to its corner.

"Before you almost shot my ass, I was sniffing the air," Clinton said. "Your filters seem to be working good, couldn't smell anything."

"Of course. I run a tight operation here." Swanny closed the door and locked it. "It's not like I got neighbours close by to worry about anyway. Shoes off." Swanny pointed down at Clinton's black leather riding boots.

Clinton ignored the rule. He unzipped his black hoodie, revealing his Hells Angels vest worn overtop a faded jean jacket. Swanny zeroed in on the feared and respected Filthy Few patch in the top right corner; the one with Nazi-style *SS* lightning bolts on it; the one that meant you were willing to or had already committed murder for the club.

"Lotsa guys like yer shit, Swan. You're a good grower." Clinton took in his brother's home: dirty dishes piled in the sink, a simple wooden table with two chairs, two photos stuck on the fridge—the only one of the entire family, and one of Clinton and Swanny as teenagers, their father actually smiling, his arm around Swanny. Clinton peered into the living room: crappy leather couch from the '70s, La-Z-Boy recliner, bookcase. "Livin' like a fuckin' poor-ass hermit," Clinton said.

"Yeah, pretty zenned out up here. Me, my books and my plants." The two looked at each other. It had been half a year since Swanny last saw his brother, back when shit had really hit the fan for Clinton. Back when he had hair. Swanny knew how to keep the peace. He slowly nodded his head. "Good to see you."

"Yeah... too bad it's under these circumstances," Clinton replied.

"Last time wasn't great circumstances either." Clinton sat at the kitchen table, plopped the bottle of whisky down. "I read the news..." Swanny rolled up to the table across from him. Six months earlier Clinton had been involved in a notorious gangland slaying. What the press were calling the Richmond Six murders—four United Nations gang members executed, plus an innocent plumber and his young apprentice caught in the wrong place at the wrong time. "Three guys have been taken out already," Swanny continued, "as payback for what you guys did."

"Don't ya think I know that? And if it's not the UN fucks or some other affiliate, it's the cops who're closing in."

Despite their congenial name, Swanny knew just how vicious the UN gang could be.

"Fucked either way you look at it," Clinton said.

"Think *I* have to worry?" Swanny asked.

Clinton shook his head. "It's me they want. You've been out so long now and living here in the sticks; you're... I mean, don't go advertising who you are and all."

"You scared at all?"

Clinton tapped his fingers on the kitchen table. "More just, I don't know... some nights I can't sleep. All I hear is that kid pleading for his life, and the old man, the plumber, sobbing. Both of 'em pissing their pants." Clinton scoffed silently. "Tough guys or not, they always piss their pants."

Swanny shook his head. "Fuck." Damn their father for leading the life he did. And thank god for his own mother. She took it from Wild Eddie every time she tried to shelter Swanny from the violence, whenever she fought hard to rein Swanny in even as his father dragged him further into club business. What could Clinton have become? Swanny wondered as he looked at him. What kind of man would he be now if he hadn't been a born-and-bred biker? Swanny peered at his gaunt thighs and knobby knees protruding from under his sweatpants. If there was any kind of silver lining to paralysis it was that it ensured he escaped the worst of biker life. And if there was such a thing as karma, he wondered if his debt had yet been fully paid. Swanny looked at Clinton. "And the UN guys?"

"That was the easy part. Had it coming after what they did to our boys in Nanaimo."

"But if you hadn't shot the civilians..." Swanny trailed off.

"I know, they might've squawked, and I might be sitting in jail already."

Swanny looked away. "I see the kid's mother all over the news."

Clinton took a big swig of whisky, after which he grunted. "We know what we sign up for. You remember back in the day. Old man made me take out one a year for the first three years. 'My button man,' he'd say. Remember that?"

Swanny remembered. Button man, bag man, the son that could tie up loose ends. Clinton was never the same after that. Swanny let it rest for now, then changed the subject from bad to sad. "So, shit... Dad's gone, eh? Really gone."

Clinton lit up a cigarette and took a long drag. "At least it was quick and—"

"—peaceful," Swanny finished. If Clinton hadn't looked like he needed the ciggy fix so bad, Swanny would've told him to butt it out. "Want a break from the whisky?" Swanny offered.

"Watcha got?"

"OJ, milk... water."

"Christ." Clinton scratched his head. "You don't gotta monitor me fer fuck's sake. So I had some drinks—"

"—while driving," Swanny interrupted.

"Ah Jesus, Swan. Screw off." He backhanded the air. "Dad's dead. I'll drink and rage and fuck a bunch of peelers all day long if I want.

Don't fuckin' lecture me, Mr. I-ain't-an-Angel-anymore-I'm-a-hippie-dippie-fuckin'-pot-grower-now. Fuck's sake."

"Alright, alright… take it easy." Swanny watched his brother unscrew the lid on the bottle of whisky and suck back enough to make most men wretch. Without so much as a wince he passed the bottle to Swanny. He took a sip and was about to pass it directly back to Clinton. Instead he placed it on the table. Swanny considered the ensuing silence between them. It was the new normal. They spoke less and less the further Swanny retreated from the family business and the more Clinton became inescapably entrenched in it.

Clinton's cigarette had gone out. He tried flipping open his Zippo lighter, all cool-like, but dropped it instead. He grumbled incoherently. Like an aging pro wrestler whose best years were far behind him, Clinton seemed frayed at the edges, his hulking frame bent in on itself. Bravado underpinned by simmering violence. It had always been there. But now the bravado was nearly erased, replaced, Swanny realized, by some twisted form of sadness. Swanny recalled the only other times he'd seen his brother like that. Now as then he'd dealt with the pain the only way he knew how, the way Wild Eddie had taught them: self-medicating with copious amounts of alcohol. The first occasion was the day Swanny was paralyzed, when he became a cripple, as Clinton and their father would say. It took their father all he had to stop Clinton from embarking on a violent rampage. Wouldn't be good for the club. Revenge was a dish best served cold, Wild Eddie reminded them. And then half a year ago, the last time Swanny talked to Clinton, the Richmond Six murders. That day it wasn't rage that consumed Clinton. It was confusion, numbness and something Swanny had never before heard in his brother's voice—fear.

Swanny took another swig of the booze just as his legs spasmed, his knees knocking together like clacking teeth. Once they settled down, he passed the whisky back to Clinton.

Clinton grabbed the bottle, looked Swanny up and down in his chair. "Know if that fuckface Jonah Seeger is still alive? Still playing soldier in Iraq?"

"Jeez, where did that come from? As far as I know, why?"

"You damn well know why, brother. Even last week the old man promised me that you and I would never let it rest, what happened to you. He loved ya, Swan. Even when you turned your back on the club, he still loved ya." Clinton shook his head. "Fuckin' golden boy. You always were Dad's favourite. And you in that fuckin' chair is a goddamned disgrace."

"Is it?" Swanny wheeled to the modified kitchen counter, with its lowered sink, and lowered cupboards. He reached for a glass and poured himself a water.

"Pritchards don't let debts go unpaid," Clinton said sourly.

Funny. Swanny glanced down at his legs. What *was* the debt Jonah owed to Clinton?

"One day that war's gonna be over," Clinton continued, gripping the bottle by the neck so hard his knuckles blanched, "and when it does, the little Douk cunt will need to come crawling back home."

Fallujah, Iraq, November 2004

The stench of death as he and Sergeant Cafferty climbed the stairs punched Jonah in the nose and forced him to swallow a gag. Shaking uncontrollably as though he had Parkinson's, Jonah stepped onto the second-floor landing of the shelled building behind Sergeant C. His head was full of fog, his palms were sweaty, chest in a vice grip. His adrenalin spiked as if he were flooring it on the gas pedal of a Mustang. In formation they scanned from behind their poised rifles, more than ready to fire at any movement. The second floor was sparse: a rusting metal table in the far corner with two walkie-talkies, an empty bottle of water, and a can of Coke on it; a tattered and stained Iraqi flag hung on a bullet-riddled wall; chunks of rubble, windowpane glass and twisted metal were strewn about.

Jonah looked behind him. Where were the others? What in the hell had just happened? Just then, flashes of them in the alley moments before spiralled through Jonah's mind: Mason frozen, his gun aimed at the insurgent's baggy blue sweater; a muzzle flash and the head-rattling burst of automatic weapons' fire; Mason flung back against the wall; the insurgent's AK-47 swinging left toward an unprepared Lewis as the insurgent's head swivels right to see Jonah stepping forward at the last second; the terror in the young man's eyes; Jonah, terror in his own eyes, pulling the trigger, feeling the recoil in the crook of his shoulder; Lewis lifting a shocked and moaning Mason over his shoulder, running toward safety.

Long before that morning Jonah had seen the dead and wounded, rotting in the streets of Kandahar and Kosovo. He considered his own kills; they were well calculated, mostly from a few hundred metres away, and viewed through a scope. He was good at it too. "One shot, one kill" was their Marine Infantry motto. On the surface he'd feel a sense of completion at having performed his task. He'd pull the trigger, and if all went according to plan, he'd strike his target, a pinkish-grey mist would burst into the air, and the target would collapse. Like Blue Ball Cap, his first. It was as if he were at home playing *Call of Duty*. At least that's what he'd tell himself during and after every mission. But he'd never shot a man at close range while looking into that man's eyes; a boy, really, who had just shot one of Jonah's team members and was a second away from spraying bullets into his best friend.

A gloved hand clenching Jonah's jaw brought him back to the moment. Sergeant Cafferty had his eyes locked on Jonah's, throwing daggers into them. He mouthed, "Focus," then released his grip. He plastered himself against one side of the door, then gestured for Jonah to enter. Jonah's heart spiked again as he stepped in, gun poised, finger on the trigger. Sunlight streamed into the large room, a dust-filled beam highlighting the body of a man lying on his back on the dirty floor. His eyes and mouth were open, arms out to his side, his fingers still curled around an AK-47. Jonah approached him with caution as Sergeant C. checked two more bodies spread on the floor. Dried blood had pooled underneath the man in front of Jonah. He stood overtop and nudged the man's groin with the tip of his rifle. Not even a hint of life. There was no playing dead with that tactic. Another body lay on its back a few feet from a window that looked out onto the street. Shrapnel from a grenade blast had removed the man's face. One leg, severed just below the hip, lay next to a pillar behind him, while the other leg clung ridiculously by strands of shredded tendon and skin just below the knee. Jonah looked back to the fully severed leg, the mangled stump like fresh ground hamburger. He looked away and then quickly back again, astonished by the gore.

"All clear," Sergeant Cafferty said as he approached Jonah. "Get your shit together, Marine."

Jonah squeezed his eyes shut and tried to shake the fog from his head. "Lew… Mase."

"Downstairs. Medevac is five minutes away." Sergeant Cafferty stepped to Jonah, put his hand on his shoulder, squeezed it. "I understand your shock. But, Seeger, you need to pull it together. Mase is in good hands."

More flashes of the last few minutes came: Lewis applying pressure to Mason's spurting neck wound; Jonah unclasping Mason's chest armour as the kid stared up at the ceiling, eyelids twitching; Jonah holding his weak hand as Mase whispered... something to him; Sergeant C. barking orders for Jonah to follow him upstairs.

"Help me drag the bodies to the corner," Sergeant Cafferty said.

Jonah considered the young insurgent he'd shot in the alley and the three dead men in front of him; these "terrorists," as Sergeant C. had called them. It wasn't a jolt of sympathy that he felt; after all, the men died defending a cause Jonah didn't agree with. But it was a cause wasn't it? And at least they'd had the cojones to fight for what they believed in. Ironic, Jonah thought, he'd never considered the insurgents, the jihadists, as *terrorists* before... the very label his mother's Sons of Freedom people were stamped with.

Jonah ran his thumb and forefinger along his gold chain necklace, on the end of which dangled the silver Cossack crescent earring. He lifted the heirloom to his dry lips and once again kissed it. Unlike his outwardly distraught mother the day he left for boot camp five years earlier, his Grandmother Polly was quietly disappointed. Stoic Baba Polly. She was seventy then, still wearing her grey-streaked black hair long. She'd looked him in the eye and spoke with her prominent Russian accent. "Shame you don' know much about our hee-story," she'd said. "But remember one of our sayings, 'Sons of Freedom cannot be slaves of corruption,' hm?" She'd kissed him on the forehead, fastened the Cossack heirloom around his neck, then told him to come back to them alive. Without inquiring about the slogan, Jonah promised he would.

Jonah grabbed a dead man by his boots while Sergeant Cafferty lifted by the arms. As they dragged the corpse along the floor, Jonah remembered his mother reciting a Doukhobor prayer before he shipped off to boot camp. He'd been with Ruby at her family's dinner table when they said the Lord's Prayer in Russian, too. He never listened, never cared. But in that moment, he wished he knew even one line of a Doukhobor prayer, anything, even one comforting word that he could say for Mase. For the kid he'd killed, too. Even for the dead men in that room.

In November of 1902, a small group of radicals emerge in Saskatchewan from within the Doukhobor community after misinterpreting exiled leader Peter V. Verigin's philosophical writings. These radicals embark on a lengthy nude march in accordance with what they believe Verigin has instructed, while protesting homestead laws and even the Prairie climate. In later years the protest will focus on what they believe to be the morally corrupt rise of materialism amongst their brethren. It is the first recorded act of defiance by the group who would become known as the Sons of Freedom. An incensed Peter V. Verigin arrives in Canada months later and condemns their actions. As does an angry public, and an embarrassed government.

It is Leo Tolstoy alone who offers sympathy for the Sons of Freedom's actions when he writes, "this movement has shown that there lives in them what is most precious and important—a religious feeling, not passive and contemplative, but active, drawing them to the renunciation of material advantages... and woe not to them in whom it shows itself in a perverted form (I refer to undressing when entering villages), but to him in whom it has dried up."

Slocan Valley, British Columbia, November 2004

The cedar wood door of the bathhouse creaked open, orange light spreading across the lawn. Virginia watched as Sasha poked his head out to see tiny snowflakes drifting down, immediately melting where they touched the ground. Steam rose from Sasha's naked body, curling up and vanishing into the cool night air. Above hung the barren yellow branchlets of the old weeping willow tree; home to the cedar wood tree fort built by Nick for their son, Alan, then gleefully taken over by Ruby. Virginia remembered scolding Jonah up there during his sleepover with Ruby when they were six. She scoffed. God, why had she been so harsh? No wonder Sharon had given her an awful earful on the phone that evening.

The lilting crescendo of *Kalinka* drifted out the open door of the *banya*. Virginia hummed along to the voices of Nick and their closest friends, Elmer and Edna Maloff, singing her favourite Russian folk song. Virginia stopped humming. "Once around the *banya* and then we'll go in for a little more." Sasha squealed, jumped out the door and ran circles on the cold, moist grass, hollering and waving his arms in the air.

Back inside, Virginia joined in the singing as she gave a ladle full of cold water to Sasha. He carefully poured it over the cage of rocks that surrounded the wood stove. A loud hiss and explosion of steam filled the bathhouse. Sasha was scooped up by his dyeda and set down on the top bench next to Virginia where he watched the happy, smiling adults until they finished their song. Sasha scrunched his nose from the intense heat.

"*Ochen zharko?*" Nick asked.

"*Nyet, ne zharko,*" Sasha said, clenching his little fists, trying not to show that it was too hot.

Elmer stroked his bushy white moustache, rubbed his large belly that folded onto his legs, and turned to Sasha. He reached over and patted him on his knee, told him he was a good man, "*Ochen maladyets,*" and that he should keep learning the Russian tongue, "*Prodolzhay uchit' Russkiy yazik.*" He switched to English. "And keep having *banyas*. They clean you of any bad stuff. *Ponemayish?*"

Sasha nodded that he understood.

Virginia smiled at Nick. They'd been doing a good job raising Sasha. Her grandson tucked his knees up to his belly, something he always did when he felt comfortable and safe.

Edna lightly touched Virginia's forearm and spoke in Russian. "His mother is still in the States?" she asked.

Virginia nodded. "Oh yes, you know, working hard at her craft."

Edna wore a placating smile as she continued in English. "How are you and Nick holding up?"

"Fine, fine," Virginia said. It was somewhat true. For the past couple of years whenever Ruby phoned she sounded *rrastrepannyy*. The last time she came for a visit, six months ago now, her dishevelled appearance matched how she'd sounded on the phone. Ruby was distant, fidgety. Ruby had even suggested she take Sasha with her to Los Angeles for a while, that it would be good for her, with little regard for whether it would be good for Sasha or not.

Sasha stood. "What are you and dyeda holding up? Something heavy?" He hopped off the bench and crouched down near the door where it was cooler.

Nick laughed. "We're holding *everything* up," he said, spreading his long orangutan arms above him. Sasha giggled.

Edna adjusted her towel, then once again turned to Virginia. "Could you believe Sharon Seeger was at *molenya*?"

"*Ya znayoo,*" Virginia said. "And heavens, the weight she's lost."

"She was so thin, even when she moved away to Kelowna," Edna said. "*Och,* the trouble that family has caused." She waved the notion away in front of her. "I still can't believe what she did at your Christmas dinner."

"*Obespokoyeniy,*" Nick said.

Virginia weighed her words. "Maybe not so troubled anymore. She actually looked healthy."

"She used to be a Kazakoff, no?" Elmer said. "Polly and Serge's daughter?"

Edna nodded solemnly. "Uh-huh. Svobodniki. Crazy Yuri, the... *bachelor,* is her brother."

Big Nick scoffed. "Is that what they call those types? Bachelors?"

"She was the lady who asked about Momma Ruby?" Sasha asked. He scooped another ladle full of cold water from a bucket on the floor as Virginia nodded. "I liked her," Sasha said, splashing water on the hot rocks. "Svobodniki are Sons of Freedom? The bad Doukhobors?" Hot steam filled the room.

"Mhmm," Nick and Elmer said in unison.

"And her son is that... that soldier?" Edna asked.

Virginia nodded. "Used to date—" She gestured at Sasha. "—you-know-who."

"It's a shame, that family." Elmer rubbed his sweat-drenched belly.

Virginia thought back to her and Sharon's high school friendship. Sharon believed that if she ran far enough away from the Kootenays, people wouldn't know she was a Doukhobor, wouldn't ask her about it, or make fun of her about it like the Angliki used to do back then. Like even Virginia herself did. Back when the crazy terrorist crap of the Sons of Freedom was tarnishing *all* Doukhobors. Virginia slumped a little. Her parents were right to go to the press, were they not? After all, Yuri had burnt their home down. She'd come back from school to see the white stucco on their smouldering house charred black, the windows shattered and the roof half gone. Whenever she thought of that day, she could always conjure the acrid, smoky smell of arson.

Sasha poured yet another scoop of water on the hot rocks. "Sons of Freedom are the people who light houses on fire, and blow stuff up, and like to be naked?"

The steam was thick in the bathhouse now; the stinging hot air in the nostrils was almost unbearable. "They used to," Virginia said as she and Edna both moved to the lower bench. "They didn't believe in owning anything fancy like your baba's BMW, or a fancy house like the one we live in. Or owning too many things."

"Or sending their children to regular Canadian school," Edna chimed in.

Nick's baritone voice came from above. "The Sons of Freedom thought all those things would take them away from being good people living close to God."

"So, the *dooraki,* they destroyed their own... stuff," Virginia continued, "burned their own homes, to try prove a point." And those of the Doukhobors they considered too materialistic, she thought. "*Ti ponimaesh?*" Virginia asked.

Scooping more water, Sasha shrugged his shoulders.

"Because of all the bad stuff the Svobodniki did," Elmer said, "everyone around here, together with the police, they made fun of Doukhobors, and sometimes bullied those of us that weren't even Sons of Freedom. So, lots moved away and forgot about being Doukhobor because they were ashamed."

Sasha brought his finger to his lips. "Like when Raphael gets angry and loses control and Leonardo and the rest of the brothers need a time-out from him or else then everyone will think all the Turtles are angry and out of control?"

"*Kto?*" Virginia asked.

Sasha made a show of rolling his eyes and throwing his hands in the air. "Babaaa, you knowww. The Teenage Mutant Ninja Turtles."

Virginia brought her head back. "Ahh, yes..." She nodded. "Yes, like that."

Sasha was about to pour more water onto the rocks.

"That's enough, Sasha." Virginia patted the bench next to her.

Sasha scrunched his brows. "I think Momma Ruby left because she was ashamed, too," he said.

Route 40, New Mexico, November 2004

Ruby is on her bed holding Sasha in her arms when she falls asleep. She doesn't know how much time passes but she wakes to the sound of Sasha cooing and babbling. She looks around her but he's nowhere on the bed. Frantically she sits up, spots him on the floor. He's gotten into her purse and is sitting there on the carpet, his stubby little fingers poking around in a ripped-open bag of cocaine as though he's sneaking treats from a cookie jar. White powder is spilled onto his diapers, and onto the carpet around him. He takes his hand out of the bag and is about to lick his fingers. Ruby flies off her bed, screaming at him to stop. But it's too late. He laughs and sticks his entire cocaine-covered hand into his mouth.

Ruby woke from the nightmare gasping for air. She sat up with a start and banged her head on the bunk above. She was in her darkened sleeping pod on the tour bus as it rumbled down the highway to... she'd already forgotten where. El Paso? Dallas? Amarillo? She rubbed her forehead and lay back down. She'd had that damned nightmare again; the one she dreaded most, the one that filled her with guilt and always triggered her need for escape. When the nightmare happened in real life, she'd managed to stop Sasha a split second before he ingested the cocaine. But still... It was on that day she realized with perfect clarity that she was unfit for motherhood. A week later she'd jetted to LA to record on Caravana's debut album. Her parents agreed to look after Sasha while she was gone, what she'd said would only be three weeks.

Ruby propped herself up on her elbow and flicked on the bunk light. She remembered she'd had an okay show in Flagstaff, much better than last night's show at the El Ray in Albuquerque where her voice had cracked attempting the high C in "Spirit Wrestlers." So thoroughly lame and embarrassing. With her confidence shaken Ruby had decided to join the after-party in the green room the night before even though she knew nothing good ever came of them, except a few hours of life-affirming, hedonistic fun... followed by a day or two of horrendous hangovers. One drink turned into five, which turned into the party moving to the bus, which turned into beer and whisky-stained carpets, lines of coke on the kitchen counter—which Ruby thankfully avoided—a threesome for bassist Chilly in his bunk, a visit from the cops due to noise complaints, and the bus bathroom filled with poo; the biggest no-no on tour. There was little of the rock star glitz and glamour that Ruby imagined there would've been back when she was a kid spontaneously scribbling lyrics on found pieces of paper, or later filling notebooks with song ideas, or as a teenager, eyes glued to the TV for hours watching her favourite musicians strutting, posing and performing in videos on MuchMusic and MTV, or rehearsing with her own band in a cramped basement jam room. At first, she naively thought her sheltered upbringing would've somehow allowed her to bypass all the clichés that came with the business. By now though Ruby was well aware that like herself, on some level most of her peers in the biz had become musicians and sought some level of rock stardom less as a way to showcase their talents and more as a way to mask one monumental insecurity after another. The drugs did work. They made all the bland motel-room artwork and all the American suburbs that blurred by and all the identical Walmarts that much more colorful. Drugs made the exhausting predictability of touring life, of life in general, less predictable, less heartachey, less lonely. Less of a letdown. Ruby cackled in her bunk at the notion. Because she knew damn well that drugs didn't *really* do any of that. In the long run they did just the opposite.

Even though she'd resisted the urge last night to do drugs, the mere thought of them now, the tingle of anticipation, distant as it was, felt good. Her heart rate bumped up a few beats. The feeling was strong enough that she knew she needed to get up, make herself some food in the bus's kitchen, then sit in the forward lounge and zone out to a movie. Anything to divert the urge. I'll call home, Ruby thought, talk to Dad, and Sash. As she slid out of her bunk she wondered if

Tomás might still be partying in the back where she left him. The thought sent a faint tingle through her groin. Ruby braced herself on the top bunks as the bus tilted while rounding a curve on the highway. She wobbled toward the forward lounge, her stomach churning. She reached to open the door but against her better judgment stopped, spun around instead. She'd check the back lounge, try get Tomás to cool it, clean up, get some rest. She hadn't done any cocaine in a month but the mere thought of Tomás possibly doing some made her feel as though she'd just done a tiny bump herself. She opened the back lounge door; Tomás was sitting on the floor in his underwear resting against the couch, staring up at the TV in the corner, fixated on playing a video game. The back lounge reeked of dry, sour sweat and spilled beer. Tomás slipped a plastic bag behind his back without acknowledging Ruby as she stepped into the room. He looked rough, probably hadn't slept the entire bus ride. Ruby checked herself in the mirror that spanned the entire back wall. She was one to talk. Tomás had commented just the other day how her blue eyes used to sparkle and dance. Lately they were dull and grey. Her long blonde hair, limp. Ruby lifted her t-shirt, exposing her breasts. Perplexed, Tomás finally took notice of her. She cupped her more than ample boobs and squeezed. At least they were still the best pair she'd ever seen or felt.

Ruby sat down next to Tomás, spotted the plastic sandwich bag stuffed with smaller bags tucked behind him. Why even try hide it at this point? She tried to ignore the small jolt of adrenalin that seeing this brought her. "Tom, you can't keep doing this." He kept thumbing the controller, staring at the flickering screen, mouth open. "Tomás, did you hear me?" Ruby noticed he had his earbuds in. She elbowed him in the ribs. He flinched and looked at her, eyes bloodshot. His lips were dry and cracked. One nostril had blood caked around its rim, the other was caked with white powder. Ruby peaked her eyebrows, stared at Tomás in the eye and shook her head.

Tomás pulled his earbuds out. "What?"

"What're you doing?" she said. He rolled his eyes, lifted the video game controller up off his lap to show her. "No shit, Sherlock, but..."

Ruby pointed at her own nostrils. Tomás brushed his thumb across one nostril and swiped his forefinger under the other. He glanced back at Ruby, lifted his nose to show her. She nodded.

A shaky grin appeared on Tomás's face. "Thought you insisted that we cool our jets," he said, "but last night was fun, no?"

Oh, right, they'd had sex. Fuck.

He scrunched his face, pulled his head back. "What, didn't enjoy the quickie in your bunk?"

The corners of Ruby's mouth pinched as she shook her head. "I didn't do drugs, did I?"

Tomás scoffed. "No." He returned to playing his video game.

"I still think we need to cool it," Ruby said.

"Drugs? Sex…?" He frowned. "What is it *this* time?"

"Yeah, we're broken up, so let's cut out the sex. And we both know you taking a break on the party treats wouldn't be such a bad idea."

Tomás laughed. "I'm not the one who nearly blacked out on stage in Paris, babe."

"That was a month ago, Tom," Ruby said wearily. "I've been… pretty damn clean since then. Unlike yourself, hoovering up any powder or pill that comes your way. Jesus."

He glanced at Ruby. "You never messed up any songs back when you still partied with us, so…" Tomás jammed his earbuds back into his ears.

Asshole. A slow ember of anxiety formed in Ruby's gut. Apart from the stellar performance in LA, he was right. Ruby raised herself up onto the leather bench and looked out the massive tinted window. Flat, beige scrubland rolled by. In the distance were sparsely forested hills.

She looked at Tomás's back, his protruding spine. When she'd first joined Caravana the two of them were so good together; the ease with which they'd collaborate on songs, the tenderness in his touch, the considerate way he'd speak to her, and his understanding if in the middle of making love she'd need to stop. Now though their relationship had deteriorated into a tumultuous one, built mostly on dependency and lust. And stupid games. When she'd warm to him, he'd cool. Sensing this, she'd take a step back, until he needed her and wanted her again, at which point they'd have sex. Even just a few months ago it was still imaginative and blissful. Inevitably though it became tedious and banal, became just a thing they did, until they didn't for a while. They wouldn't sleep together for weeks until they both desperately needed to because they just needed something, anything. Nearly five years and two albums on and there they were, a full-fledged rock 'n' roll cliché. At least they weren't a broke-ass version of that cliché. They could afford to live off the gigs, royalties and song placements. They could bank a little money, and tour on a bus now, but still... Ruby sighed the deep sigh of someone considering how much her sacrifices had cost her. Bored of this merry-go-round, she thought.

Tomás put down his controller, reached behind him and pulled out a small bag of coke from the larger plastic bag. Ruby's adrenalin spiked again. A tingle formed in her groin and slid up to her fluttering belly.

She'd been clean for a month, what harm would a little bump do?

After all she'd already broken her sobriety the previous night with a few beers. She could always stop again for another month. Plus, she needed to get her singing confidence back after the last couple shows. She slid off the bench down beside Tomás, reached behind him and grabbed the bag. He tried to snatch it back from her, shot her a look as though she were about to run off and dump the drugs into the toilet. He tried to snatch the bag again, but Ruby twisted to her side. "Relaaax. Jeesus." Ruby reached in and pulled out a baggie and tiny coke spoon. She peeled open the little bag then scooped out a small pile of white powder. Her breathing became light, the tingle ran from her stomach, up her spine and deep into her brain. She reasoned that it was better to do a bump than to be a bitch the rest of the day. She brought the coke spoon up to her left nostril, pressed her right nostril and inhaled. She released her other nostril, lifted her nose into the air and sniffed hard. The sting shot through her nose, into her head and down her throat.

Searing white light. Crystalline clarity.

Satisfied, she tossed the bag back to Tomás, let the cocaine course through her. After a few minutes she popped up and danced to her own beat under the TV. She lifted the lid off of the cooler that was built into a corner cupboard and pulled out two Coronas. She handed them to Tomás to open, then looked at herself in the mirror. She fixed her hair, noticed her eyes had gotten a bit of their sparkle back. Her breathing was light, her heart beating with strength.

Tomás handed the open beer to Ruby. "Sorry I said what I did about you messing up songs. I didn't mean it." He laughed. "Hell, I do it all the time!"

Ruby sat down across from Tomás. She looked him up and down; his protruding rib cage, his long, dishevelled brown hair. Skinny asshole. A skinny asshole that she thought was so hot and so cool when she first met him. She'd been twenty. Sasha had been fifteen months old and Ruby was supposed to be a good Doukhobor girl from a good Doukhobor family. She'd never really been anywhere other than Vancouver, once to Toronto, and the... weird, infamous school trip to Russia. She'd escaped her motherly duties to watch Tomás play a solo acoustic set at the Royal in Nelson. His sad Slavic eyes were easy to fall into when he'd stare at her from the stage as he performed, laying himself bare.

Tomás clinked his beer with Ruby's. "Feeling better?"

"I was just thinking about the first night we met. Remember?"

"How could I forget?"

"Ah your voice," Ruby swooned. "Raw like Dylan, electrifying like Buckley." She'd been completely floored and knew immediately she'd complement his style perfectly given the chance. Back then her guitar chops had a long way to go, but she had a strong ear for melody, perfect pitch, and was gifted with her own ability to hush a crowd when singing; had been doing it since she was a child.

"After my show you bought me a shot of whisky and a beer chaser," Tomás said, "and told me I wouldn't be leaving town in one piece." They both laughed.

"I was sooo much sassier back then," Ruby said.

Tomás dug into his drug bag and produced two pink pills. He popped one into his mouth, chased it with a swig of beer. He handed the other to Ruby. "MDMA. One of these should just do us right before we get to Amarillo. Get you some of that sass back, gorgeous."

Ruby hesitated for a moment, then took the pill, swallowed it with a sip of beer. "Boy did we get drunk that night." Ruby wiped her mouth.

"Oh yeah." Tomás laughed. "And you did most of the talking."

"You were a good listener." Tomás sat through all her stories about the Doukhobors, the Vietnam draft dodgers that lived in the Slocan Valley, the outdoor raves she went to full of weirdo hippies. Ruby purposely left out anything about Sasha, Jonah, Swanny, Clinton. Any of it.

"My only chance to inject flattery into the conversation was when you needed to catch your breath," Tomás said.

Ruby slid across the floor and sidled up to him. "'I love your little space there,' you said as you slammed your empty shot glass on the bar. Then you parted my lips slightly, ran your finger over what you called—"

"Your Brigitte Bardot smile," Tomás said, running his finger over the gap in her front teeth.

Ruby playfully swatted his hand away. "Oh, remember how much you wanted to eat my legs?"

"I do!"

"Your eyes howled," Ruby said.

"Mmm, your long, perfect legs. Still just as delicious." Tomás ran his hand up and down her bare thigh. "They'd be the first thing I'd eat if we were stranded on a desert island and you died first."

Ruby laughed and her and Tomás leaned over and brought their heads together. "We didn't leave your hotel room that entire weekend," Ruby said bashfully.

"Ahhh, those were the days, hey babe?" Tomás spooned another pile of blow.

They were, Ruby thought. It was a much-needed weekend that helped her forget everything that she needed to. "And then the night before you returned to LA, I picked up your acoustic guitar..."

Tomás snorted the coke off the little spoon. "And serenaded me with a dreamy, bewitching song about destiny versus free will. 'The Killing Moon.' Echo & the Bunnymen." Tomás's eyes were wild as he gesticulated. "Your version was angelic, fantastic, beautiful, all of it, your voice, the song... It was all..." His fingers burst and spread out above his head. "Perfection."

Ruby blushed as she laughed. "And six months later your phone call. How could I resist joining Caravana? A... How did you put it?"

"A seven-piece, gypsy-punk troupe made for ass-shaking and never-ending celebration."

"Sold," Ruby said. And agonizingly torn. She'd dreamt of leaving the Kootenays her whole life, not of having children which was so many of her friends' desire. A child was a spiral of anxieties. Sasha was full of demands, he cried non-stop, preferred his baba's touch to Ruby's. She couldn't find the time to pick up her guitar, or when she did, she played without joy. Ideas for lyrics dried up. Some days she felt as hollow as a mannequin. How had her mother done it?

The door opened and Jolie, the ever-jovial, take-no-shit tour manager, popped her head in. Ruby liked Jolie; she reminded her of her best friend Nadya from back home.

"Y'all good?" Jolie asked in her southern drawl.

Ruby nodded. Tomás slid the drugs behind him.

Jolie frowned. "Sound check is at six tonight. Sold-out show. Get some rest." She closed the door and left.

Ruby thought back to the early days, playing to a hundred people a night in small towns and cities scattered across the US and Canada. It excited her. She was living the dream after all. Being on the road had always felt like a second home. She whispered the word *home*, drew the word out as though by doing so the idea might resonate more clearly for her. That the home of where she grew up and the home of where she spent the better part of four years might jostle for position, one revealing itself to have more magnetic pull than the other.

"You okay?" Tomás asked.

Ruby nodded and forced a smile. Her high from the little bump of cocaine was waning and the MDMA hadn't yet kicked in. With all the talk of her inaugural romantic weekend with Tomás in Nelson, and last night's sad dream about Sasha … today the road didn't much seem like home, Ruby concluded. She could feel the spiral coming on. And only one thing could stop it. Her adrenalin spiked, her belly tingled and her heart bumped up a few beats. She reached behind Tomás and pulled out the bag full of cocaine and ecstasy.

In 1905 tensions rise in Saskatchewan between the sect and the Canadian government when a fundamental difference in philosophy regarding land ownership causes the Doukhobors to fail to complete legal homestead requirements. A breaking point for all involved comes in 1907. Having originally assured the Doukhobors that they could live communally, the Canadian government reverses its policy. It reclaims 258,880 acres of land worth eleven million dollars to the community. Initially nearly a thousand members abandon communal living, refute the hereditary Verigin leadership, and continue to farm the land under Canada's homestead system. Maintaining their religion but not averse to integrating into Canadian society, they become known as Independent Doukhobors. The majority, who continue to follow the leadership of the Verigin family, are known as Community Doukhobors.

That same year, exasperated with Peter V. Verigin and his followers, the government informs the Doukhobors that they must now swear an oath of allegiance to the Crown or lose their lands. Having refused this request of the Russian Tsar, the Community Doukhobors refuse it in Canada, too. The seeds of distrust for Canadian authorities are planted.

Beginning in 1908, Peter V. Verigin leads over five thousand Doukhobors from the Prairies to southeastern British Columbia in what becomes the largest internal migration in Canadian history. There, the community purchases large plots of private land around Grand Forks, Castlegar and the Slocan Valley. Since the properties are not Crown land, no oath of allegiance is required. The Doukhobors quickly set about clearing land, building communal villages and earning income in the logging and fruit-growing industries. At last, they believe they will be allowed to realize their dream of a peaceful, communal utopia.

Castlegar, British Columbia, November 2004

"Oh, guess who died last week?" Olga asked as nonchalantly as someone about to reveal who had just paid them a surprise visit.

Sharon was in the sizable kitchen in the basement of the Brilliant Cultural Centre, chopping onions on a wooden cutting board. Recently she'd volunteered to cook for Doukhobor funerals, and whenever the ladies were preparing traditional dishes, talk would inevitably turn to those in the community who'd recently passed away. The last few times Sharon had volunteered it had been her old friend Olga Makayev who always kicked off the obituary discussion. Its frank, woe-free nature wasn't unusual to Sharon, as she knew Doukhobors to be as reconciled with death's imminence as they were to the inevitability of losing one's baby teeth, or every summer having wild animals traipse through one's gardens to feast on organic veggies.

Olga wiped her hands on her apron and looked Sharon in the eye. Her usually glowing heart-shaped face drooped into blankness. "Doris Clarkson died," Olga said.

Sharon braced herself as her knees nearly buckled. Her stomach churned, and her scarred left hand began to tremble. The spatula slipped from her hand, falling to the floor with a clatter. For the first time in nearly five years, she wished she had a Xanax in her purse. Even a Mars bar.

"Remember her?" Olga asked.

How could Sharon forget the matron from the New Denver prison school? She and Olga and hundreds of other Sons of Freedom children were incarcerated at that godforsaken place. Sharon could clearly see the obese Ms. Clarkson's limp as though the matron were right there looming over her, the dyed-red hair pulled back tightly and tied in a bun at the top of her head. How the woman tried to cover her constant sweating with a lurching rose-scented perfume.

More terrible visions flashed through Sharon's mind: eight-foot-tall chain-link fencing surrounding the school, Ms. Clarkson calling Sharon by her number—seventeen—then giving her the strap across her palms for speaking Russian, berating Olga for being Doukhobor, telling her that her mother and father weren't fit for parenthood. And the worst vision of all; unbeknownst to Ms. Clarkson, Sharon hiding behind a cabinet watching as the vile matron dragged her protesting brother Yuri into the janitor's closet by the scruff of his neck. Sharon was only six years old, couldn't understand what was happening to Yuri or why exactly any of them were even at that prison school in the first place.

"Sharon, everything alright?" Olga asked, rubbing Sharon's back.

Sharon groaned as she picked the spatula up off the floor and nodded. "I'm surprised that devil of a woman lasted as long as she did."

"*Tarakans* don't die easy," Olga said, which produced a few snickers from the other ladies in the kitchen.

"*Tarakan*?" Sharon asked.

"Russian for… cockroach."

Sharon nodded. "That, she most certainly was." She looked Olga in the eye. "How did you do it? How did you manage to… move past those days, and all the Freedomite crap we went through?"

Olga's smile returned. She brandished the spoon she held in her hand. "With this…" she said, as though it were obvious.

Sharon raised her arms in exasperation as she surveyed herself. "Are you kidding me? With food?" She marvelled at how junk food particularly had always helped restore her desire for self-preservation. Especially in the months after Roy had finally had enough of her monthly spirals of self-pity, shame and sorrow, and decided to leave her. That was 1986. After that she'd fled the Kootenays once again and rented a tiny apartment in the rough Rutland neighbourhood of Kelowna. There she gobbled pills that enabled her to assume a plastic likeness of herself in which she wore a ridiculously fake smile and elicited a marvellously fraudulent happiness that she believed was sparing her boys the cancers of second-hand suffering. But pills were no match for food. God, how many evenings she'd sat naked at the foot of her bed on the beige carpet that was peppered with the previous tenant's cigarette burns, surrounded by piles of dirty laundry, months-old *People* and *Us* magazines, and the remnants of her hurricane binge: Big Mac wrappers, crinkled bags of Doritos, an empty carton of Timbits, a jar of pickles, an Oreo Blizzard, a cleaned-out bucket of KFC, Mars, Kit Kat and Coffee Crisp wrappers, two cans of Coke. Afterward she'd wheeze as she surveyed her crumb-covered rolls of flab while clutching a bottle of Crown Royal. No need for a glass. Always she'd have the sensation of having watched herself from above, as though divorced from her being, her body labouring to contain her soul. God, how she wallowed in the swamp of her family's undoing. Not anymore. Stay the course, Sharon, stay the course.

"You remember, Mom wouldn't let me eat candies?" Sharon said. "The food of the oppressor. So, what did I do whenever she wasn't looking? I ate the Freedomite shame away with as many chocolate bars I could stuff into my mouth. And do you know that the day Roy left me, Jonah and Julian watched with jaws on the floor as I sliced a Tim Hortons donut in half, stuck a Mars bar in between, warmed it in the oven for five minutes then ate it like a goopy sandwich as I cried on the couch?"

"*Da idi tih?*" Olga said as she dipped a spoon into the large pot of borsch simmering on the stove.

Yes, really, Sharon thought.

Olga continued. "Listen, dear, I'm not talking about destructive food." She passed the spoon to Sharon. "I'm talking about food made with love, which is good for your soul."

Sharon took the spoon and brought the vegetarian Doukhobor specialty up to her mouth. Her coke-bottle glasses fogged up as she allowed the aromatic steam to bathe her nostrils. Sharon's entire body pleaded for the savoury, dill-garnished, creamy beet and potato soup even as her mind and her current Wild Rose cleanse screamed no.

She sipped it anyway. But before she swallowed it, Sharon let it swirl in her mouth, allowed herself to savour a moment of warmth, tradition and goodness. She swallowed… "Mmm. So, borsch is the trick to dealing with the past?"

"By growing the vegetables that go into the borsch, and by making the borsch yourself." Olga gestured at the ladies toiling on other dishes around her. "And by being with us ladies, like you've started to do. Then food becomes identity. It fosters community. Your cells remember it, they feel joy." Olga patted her own round tummy and laughed. "Don't be afraid to eat our culture like you've been eating that hippie-dippie yoga food."

"Can you email me some recipes later?" Sharon asked. "I don't have Mom's anymore."

"Of course," Olga said. "I promise you, after cooking for hours in your kitchen you'll feel reconnected to *nashi*. That's the magic of soul food, my dear."

* * *

Half an hour later Sharon was back in Nelson. She climbed the stairs to her quaint hundred-year-old rental house, placed the groceries on the porch and sat down on the top step for a moment. She regarded her station wagon that she'd parked out front on the street, laughed at how Jonah and Julian always teased her for being a hippie. She had driven the same car for the last twenty years, did yoga twice a week, these days bought exclusively organic produce *and* lived in the most bohemian town in the entire country. She supposed her sons were right. She was a hippie of sorts. A reformed Son of Freedom. A Doukhobor hippie.

Sharon felt the warmth of Luke Skywalker sliding along her back. He was named by Jonah before he'd deployed nearly six years earlier. "Hello Luke," she said. The cat mewed in response and planted himself on Sharon's lap for her to stroke his orange-grey fur. She looked down over town: its immaculately restored nineteenth-century heritage buildings; the mist hanging low over the narrow western arm of Kootenay Lake; the orange bridge connecting to the North Shore; the steep, snow-covered Selkirk Mountains beyond. She never tired of the view. She was considering how it always provided a measure of comfort just as a black SUV with tinted windows slowed to a grumbling stop on the street in front of her house. It was one of those stupid, gas-guzzling monstrosities they called Hummers. Sharon could make out a bald man wearing sunglasses staring at her from behind the steering wheel. Was it that older Pritchard brother again, come around on his annual check-in to make sure Jonah wasn't back? She shuddered just as a West Kootenay Power truck behind the Hummer honked for it to move. Sharon got up and watched the SUV lurch forward and speed away.

Before she went in, she collected her mail from the black box fastened to the wall beside the front door. There amongst bills and flyers was a postcard from Jonah. She held it to her chest, hiding it as though the man in the Hummer would see. She thought of Jonah, what he might've written to her, and her mood lifted, her heart glowing with warmth.

In the kitchen Sharon put the kettle on for tea and noticed her answering machine blinking red. Whoever it was could darned well wait. She quickly unpacked the groceries, then returned to the mail from Jonah. She adjusted her glasses and studied the vintage postcard underneath the kitchen light. It was a cracked and faded portrait whose title read, "Basra. The Venice of Iraq." A boatman in a ghostly white robe guided his narrow vessel with a long pole down a clear, turquoise canal; its banks lined with green grass, pink flowers, palm trees and ornate buildings flying Iraqi and British flags. Sharon could scarcely imagine the country once looking so pristine. She smiled knowing Jonah always selected postcards that showed a beautiful, sanitized version of wherever he was. She flipped the card over and read:

Mom,

I'm sitting in a sunny room in a dusty town in Iraq (that definitely does not look like the postcard, ha ha!). Of course Lewis is here. Mason and Sergeant Cafferty and the rest of the squad, too. We're still looking out for each other, keeping each other safe, so you don't have to worry. Just today Sergeant Cafferty asked me how a skateboarding Canadian kid came to be a Marine. Didn't know exactly what to tell him so I just told him Ben Whitewolf taught me to shoot like a pro. You know, Dad's Native buddy? Ex-Marine?

I know you think me being a Marine has brought more shame to a family that's already been shamed enough. But I'm doing important work here, Mom. Really I am. Helping liberate Iraqis from a tyrant. Anyway, I have no regrets. I miss you and I love you lots. Are you staying… you know, healthy? Still reconnecting with your Douk roots? You sure that's a good idea?

Oh yeah, you'll be happy to know, at your urging, I'm looking into transferring to a non-combat role in the military. I'll keep you posted.

Love, Jonah

Sharon hadn't talked to Jonah on the phone since right before his important mission to liberate a town called Fallujah. Sharon reread, "helping liberate the Iraqis from a tyrant." Liberation. That's what the soldiers called it now? *Soldier…* Sharon rolled the word around in her mouth. It didn't sound right. Never had. How had she raised a soldier? Fighting a war for America no less. Handfuls of Doukhobor men had enlisted during both world wars. But they were mostly from the more assimilated villages of Alberta and Saskatchewan. And since those wars Sharon had not heard of any other Doukhobor soldiers. Until Jonah. He was right, though. If she hadn't been so ashamed of her Sons of Freedom upbringing, of the things that had happened to her and to Yuri, the things he and her family had done, she would've never run away from the community, from her Doukhobor roots. She would've raised Jonah to fully understand his people and value their pacifist beliefs, to be a proud and peaceful Doukhobor. But, *oy Bozhe moy*, certainly not a soldier.

The day Jonah went off to war was the day Sharon quit her vices. Every day since had been a battle to keep it that way. Nowadays healthy food, continued acceptance of her body, a yoga class and a dose of Doukhoborism did the trick.

She'd gone decades without practising any of the traditions. But it was true what people said: the older you got and the closer to death you were, the more you circled back to the faith you were raised with for comfort. And while she herself was still alive and kicking, it was when Jonah had shipped off on his first mission to the Balkans that she knew his death at any given moment was a heightened and terrible possibility. Sharon's re-entry into the Doukhobor community started simply, with a phone call to Olga for a translation of *Dom Nash Blahodatniy*, Our Blessed Home, the prayer that Sharon had long forgotten. The following day Olga emailed the Russian version and the poetic, contemporary adaptation of it in English. It was an all-purpose blessing for safety that Sharon would invoke for Jonah (and Julian) once in the morning and once before bed every night.

Still, some nights Sharon couldn't sleep a wink from worry. A defective gene no doubt passed down from humanity's first mother. Especially when he was on a mission, as he called it, and unable to communicate for days at a time, it was all Sharon could do to not retreat into old habits. Did she stash chocolate bars throughout her house, keep a tub of Vanilla Swiss Almond Häagen-Dazs in the freezer, and have a packet of Xanax in the medicine cabinet as safeguards? Or as warnings?

Sharon turned her attention now to her blinking answering machine. She pressed play on the device; the female robot announced that she had one new message. His voice was unmistakable; time-worn, thickly accented, and with just a tinge of playful mischief.

"Hello seester. Yuri here. Do you have enough firewood? Need your driveway cleaned? I'm trying to make up for lost years." He cough-laughed. "I phoned Mother yesterday. She's okay. Have you heard from that soldier son of yours, eh? Anyway, I'll try you again later..."

Sharon listened to her brother breathing as he paused and considered what to say next.

"We should break bread soon, ah? Like old times. Maybe KC's in Nelson? I'm craving Chinese and haven't been there since... Dimitri... long long time. Well, okay then. Yuri signing off."

It was four years since they last had any kind of take-out together, but that most certainly wasn't the most memorable occasion. Once, back in '62 when Sharon was ten, Yuri had called from a pay phone. He asked if Sharon and their mother could order Chinese and meet him at Gyro Park in Trail after sundown. In the back seat of the car he wolfed down his chow mein, eyes darting around at the other parked cars. Sharon's mother had purposely avoided parking underneath a streetlamp, but the industrial glow of the sprawling Cominco smelter across the river illuminated the interior of the car in dappled orange light anyway. Yuri looked thoroughly dishevelled and smelled of house fire. Sharon and her mother both knew why. The arsons the night before had made the news across Canada and the US. Sharon never imagined Yuri would resort to such violence. But then why not, given what he'd been through at the prison school? After all the bullying he faced for never having a girlfriend, always hanging out with Dimitri. Yuri was born in the wrong era, Sharon thought. Once they finished their food, Yuri gave Sharon and their mother a hug and a kiss and told them he'd be going deep underground for a while. A while turned into a decade. Sharon had sat limply in the passenger seat, a knot in her stomach, refusing to hold her mother's hand. She'd watched Yuri forlornly as he loped away and disappeared into the shadows.

The kettle started whistling and Sharon turned away from the answering machine just as her phone rang, startling her, causing her to flinch. Maybe it was Yuri calling back? Or Olga? She picked up the receiver and was surprised to hear Jonah's voice. She adjusted her hair and took a quick sip of tea. But something was wrong. Immediately she could tell that Jonah sounded haggard. Like he hadn't slept in days, like he was hungover but instead of from alcohol, from tragedy. She could relate.

Must lighten the mood, Sharon thought. "Guess what, honey?" She asked as cheerily as she could muster. "After I get off the phone, for the first time in about twenty years I'm going to make borsch. In your honour."

Jonah laughed. "In my honour? Mom, I'm still alive."

"Oh, I… I didn't mean it like that," she said. "I was just—"

"We have a saying here…" Jonah interrupted, the moment of warmth having quickly passed. He sounded as distant as though he were calling from the moon instead of Iraq. "If we… If something happens to us here in Iraq at least we're knocking on heaven's door, you know? One step closer to paradise."

"Jonah, honey," Sharon said with deep concern in her voice, "don't say that, dear. Nothing's going to happen to you."

Jonah ignored his mother's concern and continued. "This is because the marshlands which lie at the confluence of the Tigris and Euphrates rivers are believed to be the inspiration for, or quite possibly the actual site of, the Bible's Garden of Eden. See? One step closer to paradise. Funny eh?"

Sharon didn't see the humour in it at all. A wave of anxiety suddenly and urgently washed over her as though she'd been shoved under a cold shower. "Jonah what's going on?"

"Nothing. I'm… I'm sorry, Mom," he said somewhat robotically. "Don't worry. I'm not seeing much combat."

Sharon could always tell when Jonah was lying. For nine months he grew inside her, love and nutrients migrating back and forth. His cells were imbedded in her skin and organs, his DNA nested in her brain. Call it a mother's intuition. Call it sixth sense. Call it a blood bond. Either way, Sharon just knew. "Jonah River Seeger… what happened? Are you hurt?"

"No, no…" he said, then fell silent for a long time.

"Honey, it's okay. You can tell me."

After a few moments Jonah spoke. "I… My friend…" He trailed off.

"I'm right here. You don't have to spell it out." At the sound of her baby boy's heaving breaths, Sharon's heart sank and began to break apart. She desperately wanted Jonah there beside her, back home where she could hold and comfort him. "Jonah? My love, listen to me…"

Jonah sniffed forcefully. "I'm here, Mom," he said timidly.

Sharon spoke in Russian, "*Hospodee Blahaslovee,*" then translated to English, "Lord grant us your blessing."

"Mom, what're you doing?"

"Just listen…" She took a deep breath, then continued in English. "Our true home is our connection to the Divine. Our trust in the wisdom of our souls. And the love and grace that surrounds us. Now and always. Wherever we go, God goes with us. Thank you, Divine One."

"What… is that?" Jonah asked.

"It's an old Doukhobor prayer made modern. I learned it for you and Julian, and I say it every day for my boys. I'll email it to you."

"Sure."

"And… here's one more thing you should know… *Vechnaya pamyat.*"

"What does it mean?"

"Say it, *vech-naya pam-yat,*" Sharon enunciated slowly and Jonah haltingly repeated after her.

"It means, 'In eternal memory.' Doukhobors say it when someone has… passed on."

Jonah grunted, took a big, pained breath.

"Whoever you're suffering for, son, whatever friend you've lost, you say it for them, okay?"

Jonah was silent.

"*Vechnaya pamyat.* In eternal memory. Say it. Even if what you've lost in that terrible war... is a part of yourself."

In 1912 fears of militia and rifle training being introduced into public schools cause the Doukhobors in British Columbia to stop sending their children to school because of their pacifist beliefs. A compromise is reached later in the year, but it's a compromise that won't last.

At the outset of World War I, Doukhobors remain exempt from military service. Despite this, sixty-two Independent Doukhobors (most of whom had recently migrated from Russia and were not staunch pacifists) voluntarily enlist with the Canadian Expeditionary Forces. However, with most of the Community and Independent Doukhobors refusing to enlist, anti-Doukhobor sentiment reaches a fever pitch, especially in the BC cities of Nelson, Trail and Grand Forks. To quell this, Peter V. Verigin makes headlines throughout North America when he announces the donation of several rail cars full of fruit preserves from the community's jam factory to soldiers on the front and to the wounded returning from battle.

Upon John Nevacshonoff's return from fighting with the 232nd Battalion in France, the native of Thrums, BC expresses his regret, saying he "had given three years of his life to the devil." He begs his sons to never go to war.

On September 1, 1918, twenty-two-year-old Doukhobor soldier William Gloeboff of Kamsack, Saskatchewan of the Eighth Battalion dies of wounds suffered on the Drocourt-Queant Line. Gloeboff is buried at Ligny–St. Flochel British Cemetery near Arras, France.

Slocan Valley, British Columbia, November 2004

Nick's baritone bellowed from Sasha's upstairs bedroom. "Ginny," he called loudly. "Don't forget the candles."

"Yes... I'm on my way," she yelled from the kitchen as she placed the last dinner dishes into the dishwasher. How could she forget the candles? Sasha had a fit if they weren't lit for him during story time. If the "protectors" weren't invoked. Her and Nick had done it for their own son, Alan, when he was four years old. Back then they simply and effectively called upon God and baby Jesus, Doukhobor ancestors and beloved elders. Invoking them calmed the night terrors that seemed to be typical of boys at that age. Then one day when Ruby was soothing Sasha to sleep, before her first exodus to Los Angeles, and much to Virginia's disappointment, Ruby included Muslim and Jewish religious figures, and animal spirits, and silly fairies. Wasn't their Doukhobor faith enough? But Sasha latched on to what his mother dubbed his protectors and from that night on there was no looking back. For the past four years Sasha demanded the ritual be performed on a nightly basis.

Virginia stepped from the hallway into Sasha's room, dimly lit by a lamp from IKEA that stood near the bed. Posters of Teenage Mutant Ninja Turtles, Spider-Man, SpongeBob and Dora the Explorer adorned the walls. In one corner of the room next to a dresser, Lego spilled out of a wooden box into a debris pile on the carpet. Scattered nearby were Power Rangers, Transformers, Hot Wheels cars and trucks, and his favourite... Barbie dolls. Why not Ken? Virginia always wondered.

Sasha was sitting in his Batman pyjamas, leaning back on his pillows that were propped up against the headboard. Nick had remembered to make sure the curtains were wide open; Sasha liked to see stars and moonlight and be awakened by the morning sun. As usual Nick had planted his gigantic frame beside Sasha, his torso towering above their grandson, Nick's side of the bed straining under his bulk. He had his orangutan arm around Sasha, his legs reaching well over the end of the bed.

Virginia placed a phone on Sasha's dresser, and candles on a small stone slab beside it. "Ready for the protectors?" She sat down beside her grandson.

Sasha scrunched his knees to his chest under the blanket and clapped his hands.

"And then we call your mom?" Virginia asked.

Sasha dropped his knees, looked up to his dyeda and then to his baba, shrugged. "Some kids at kindergarten call me orphan boy."

Nick drew his head back and banged the wall. Virginia's mouth fell open. "What?!"

"Is it because the man who made me with Momma Ruby is in a wheelchair is why he doesn't want to be my dad?" Sasha asked.

Virginia's eyes darted fast around the room. "Who, who told you that?"

"Johnny, Mara and Celeste say he lives around here and is in a wheelchair."

"*Pizdets prishol,*" Virginia muttered. Sasha peered up at her. Did he understand the meaning, "Here's a screwed siutuation"? She loathed lying to the dear boy. "We've told you many times, *kotyik*, that we don't know where he lives..."

"And he's not healthy enough to be a father..." Nick added, stroking Sasha's head.

"And Momma Ruby and him were only friends for a little while," Virginia added. "And they don't speak anymore."

Sasha squinted and pursed his lips. He wasn't stupid, Virginia thought. She desperately didn't want to lose his trust.

"What if he found me one day and came and took me? We would have to let him?"

"*Gospodi,* no no," Virginia said. She scooched up closer to Sasha.

"That would never happen," Nick said, squeezing Sasha's shoulder.

"But what if he did? And he was a robber and had guns?" Sasha fidgeted. "And tried to steal me?" He sunk down under his covers.

"Well..." Virginia felt as though she were in a car spinning out of control on an icy highway. She took a deep breath. "Your dyeda would do everything he had to, to make sure no one ever stole you." She eyed her husband while trying to hide her anguish from her grandson.

"Including hurting the robbers?" Sasha poked his head from beneath the blanket.

"Maybe... *choot choot*, if I had to," Nick reassured him.

Sasha sat up. "Only a little?" Nick nodded and Sasha continued. "Then you wouldn't be a Doukhobor after that for hurting the bad guys?"

"*Nyet.*" Nick shook his head. "I'd still be a Doukhobor."

"Okay, listen Sasha," Virginia said, "no robbers or bad guys or, or a man in a wheelchair who isn't..." Virginia expelled an exasperated breath. "No one's going to come here and steal you. Okay? We promise." Virginia held out her curled pinky finger. "I'll even pinky swear." Sasha locked his pinky with his baba's and smiled. Virginia picked the phone up off the dresser. "Ready to phone mom?"

Sasha shrugged. "Mmm..." He tightened his lips. "No. She'll prolly just be all tired."

Virginia looked at Nick, who frowned and shrugged his own shoulders. "Well, how about the protectors then?" Virginia asked. Sasha yawned and nodded. Virginia lit each of the three candles she'd brought. Sasha looked at his dyeda to make sure his eyes were closed. Then to his baba. Virginia closed her eyes and began speaking softly. "We call on the protectors to watch over Sasha Samarodin throughout the night, so that no bad spirits fly around him and disturb his peaceful sleep. First, we call upon all our Doukhobor ancestors who have gone before us, to protect Sasha." Virginia recited a long list of dead elders, then continued. "We call upon the spirit animals—the wolf, the bear, the coyote, the cougar, the eagle. And we call—"

"Babaaa," Sasha whined. He squirmed underneath his covers. "You forgot one."

Virginia opened one eye, whispered the spirit animal list under her breath. She glanced at Nick who mouthed, "owl." "Oh yes, we call upon the spirit of the night owl, too."

Sasha frowned. "Thank you, Dyeda, for helping Baba. And Baba, please try not to forget."

Virginia gave Sasha her best stern look. "I shall not forget again." She closed her eyes and continued. "We call upon all the guardian angels, the same ones that protect Ruby and her brother, Alan. We call upon Jesus, and Buddha, and Moses, and Mohammed, and Quan Yin. We call upon the ancient magical fairies, the pixies, elves and... and sprites from the invisible realms. And finally, we call upon the guardians of land, water, sky, fire and *all* the galaxies, to protect Sasha Samarodin as he drifts off into sleep."

With eyes closed, Sasha yawned again. Nick leaned over and kissed him on the forehead, then slowly, gently slid off the bed and quietly left the room. Virginia glanced back at her grandson from the doorway. It had been many years since Sasha had asked about his father. Lying to a grandchild in order to protect them from the harsh realities of the situation was a fact of life. Still, each time Virginia did she couldn't stand herself. What betrayal. Lying for her daughter. Lying about her daughter. Virginia's eyes welled with tears. She couldn't stand lying to anyone, let alone to Sasha, the innocent angel.

Over the years, Sasha talked less and less about his mother, hadn't said he missed her in months. Unlike Sharon, who time and time again kept finding her way back to the Kootenays, Ruby seemed content to be as far away as possible. Maybe for the best, Virginia thought as she closed Sasha's bedroom door. Maybe for the best.

In 1923, following the arson of several schools in Castlegar, British Columbia by the Sons of Freedom, government authorities begin seizing Doukhobor community property to pay for the losses and for rebuilding. In the following months, nine more schools are set alight in the Castlegar area in retaliation for the property seizure and as continued resistance toward forced public education of Doukhobor children.

In the decades that follow these instances of arson, a renewed renunciation of materialism expresses itself with ritual burnings of the Sons of Freedom's own homes, as well as those of non-Freedomite Doukhobors, often done while stripping nude and singing. For the Freedomites, these forms of protest are purposely public and provocative in order to court arrest and encourage martyrdom.

Slocan Valley, British Columbia, November 2004

Blazing halogen lights spread summer-like sunshine and warmth to a sea of marijuana plants. Sugar-coated pistils curled outwards past green leafy crowns and stretched toward their life-giving stars. Swanny was in his barn which had been converted to an ultra-modern grow room. He'd positioned his wheelchair on the platform of a small articulating boom lift he'd manoeuvred between rows of flowering plants. He bent the bud from a seven-foot-tall plant toward his nostrils, breathed in and savoured the skunky scent.

"Smell that," he said to Clinton, who looked even more haggard after two nights of partying in Nelson.

Clinton snuffed out his cigarette butt with his boot, then sniffed the bud. "What strain?"

Swanny swept his hand behind him. "This half, Green Velvet Crush." He pointed across the aisle. "That's Purple Dragon." He pulled the platform's lever and lowered to ground level.

"Your girls look good," Clinton said. "Speaking of girls ... I hired you one," he added matter-of-factly.

"You hired me a girl? For what?" Swanny wheeled down a short ramp off the platform onto the smooth cement floor.

"Cute girl from Castlegar." Clinton launched into a coughing fit ... "Fucking hell. Gotta cut back on the darts," he said, then coughed some more. "Brandi's her name. Twenty-five, big tits. Her uncle works for us running product between the Coast and Toronto. She's worked as a trimmer for plenty of growers. Told 'er to come up once a week, grocery shop, cook, clean, do some laundry. Told her I'd pay her extra to give you a massage ... with a happy ending now and then. Maybe blow ya."

Swanny squinted at his brother.

"You're giving me that what-the-hell look," Clinton said.

"Yeah. What the hell?"

"Whaddaya mean?" Clinton cackled. "Little worm still works doesn't he?"

Swanny shook his head and groaned in bafflement. "Yes. But I don't need any girl cleaning for me and paid to have sex with me, for Christ's sake." He wheeled to the far end of the barn. Clinton followed.

"It's not like I'm forcing her, bro."

"Well, that'd be a first," Swanny said as the neuropathic leg pain started its burning slither.

"Screw off with yer fuckin' lectures, Jesus."

From a metal shelf Swanny grabbed a plastic spray bottle and began spraying his plants. Clinton went off about how women loved how he treated them. Same old terrible story. While Clinton had learned all about women from their father, Swanny at least had his mother to keep steering him away from the violence. His father knew nothing of love. To him love was sex and sex was all about aggression, conquest and submission. Clinton was a carbon copy.

"You even listening to me?" Clinton asked, agitated.

"Nope."

"Bastard," Clinton said.

"Me?" Swanny pointed at himself. "Sure, one with a heart." He gestured his chin at Clinton. "You? You're *just* a bastard."

Clinton sniggered. "Still sore about that Ruby chick huh? I was pissed drunk and coked up. Never told me you were bangin' her."

Swanny stopped spraying his plants. His face turned sour. "Why would that even matter?" His heart was in fight mode now. An anger he rarely felt anymore flushed through him, shadowed by the lava that crawled through his stagnant legs. He looked down at them as they vibrated, knees knocking together. Blood was pumping loud in his ears, but all he could hear was the heavy metal music that blasted from Clinton's truck that day, muffling sounds of distress and the insane look of Clinton's coked-out rage, and Swanny reaching, grabbing, trying to make it right. Then, wham, crack and Swanny's red bandana lying in the dirt next to him.

In that moment as his legs quaked, Swanny glared at Clinton's crimson face with its flared snout and wanted nothing more than to clobber his brother senseless. "Look how *you* being pissed drunk and coked up turned out for me." Swanny fought to contain his pain. "And always your talk of revenge."

Clinton's eyes threatened to burst from their sockets. He sneered and made the garbled, throaty sounds that always preceded him losing his shit. Today for the first time in days he wasn't pissed drunk and Swanny wasn't sure whether that made Clinton *more* ornery or less. "You're blaming me, asshole?!" Clinton shouted. "Huh?!"

Swanny's glare drove knives into his brother. He wanted to shout, "Yes, *you* are the reason I'm in this chair." He wanted to spit it into his eyes and nostrils and frothing mouth. But he knew the uncontrolled rage that would unleash in Clinton who was already tense and bulging like a bodybuilder flexing at a competition. Instead, having learned from his mother when dealing with their father, Swanny dove into his reserve of restraint and said nothing.

Snorting like a bull, Clinton stomped past him as though he were leaving the grow room. And just as the lava pain and leg-shaking began to subside Swanny felt what he knew was coming. *Thwak!* Clinton smacked him hard across the back of his head. Swanny yowled, the pain like being slammed with a two-by-six.

"Fuckin' rights yer not blaming me!" Clinton spat. He looked around the grow room as though a wayward bottle of Jack might magically appear amongst the pot plants.

Swanny cupped the back of his head, then wheeled away.

Clinton was still seething. "And if yer too weak, too much of a pussy, too ungrateful for the traditions our father raised us with, to get back at Seeger, then I'm A-okay to do it by myself."

What traditions? Swanny wondered. Dispute resolution through savage brutality and gleeful revenge? Unquestioning respect for hierarchy? The greedy pursuit of money above all else? Unfettered misogyny? About women, their father used to love saying with a slippery diamond grin, "Can't live with 'em, can't make stew outta their bones."

Then in '96 the Hells Angels lost Swanny for good with their so-called traditions when a bunch of them had been partying at the Haney clubhouse. With bags of cocaine, Clinton had convinced two peelers from the Cadillac Lounge in nearby Maple Ridge to roll with them. Swanny had Jenna at his side; a sweet, witty, beautiful waitress he'd met a few days earlier. When a hammered Clinton ordered all the girls to strip naked and dance around to the Judas Priest that was blaring from the clubhouse sound system, Jenna flat out refused. Then Clinton decided that he wanted Jenna for himself because, as Swanny knew, his older brother was jealous of Swanny always scoring the more attractive women, and because as Hells Angels tradition dictated, Clinton, being senior to Swanny, could simply *take* her. When Jenna again refused, this time with "not if you were the last man on Earth," Clinton grabbed her hard by the arm, pulled her away from Swanny and threw the yelping woman to the ground. Swanny clenched Clinton by the throat but was met with a swift, hammering elbow to his face that sent him sprawling backward. With one hand Clinton gripped Jenna by the throat and picked her up off the ground, then brought his forehead smashing down onto the bridge of her nose. Clinton released his grip, sending the unconscious girl collapsing to the floor.

That had definitively done it for Swanny. Selling weed to the Angels was as close as he'd ever come again to the club. Now he leaned into a plant, grabbed a top cone and sniffed it. Clinton continued pacing the aisle of the grow room like a hungry wolf. For a long time, there was only the whirring of fans, buzzing halogen lights, the clop of Clinton's boots on cement, and Swanny spraying.

Eventually Clinton stopped, broke the silence. "How 'bout that kid of yours, huh? Too much of a bitch to demand to see him?"

Swanny gave Clinton the middle finger. "That's not our deal."

"Not your deal?" Clinton threw his head back and cackled. "Ha! Not your deal. You got a kid that you never met? Pretty fuckin' lame if ya ask me."

"No one's asking you. Besides, Ruby and I came to an agreement regarding the kid a long time ago. And I'm A-okay with it."

Clinton snorted. "Whatever. All this started with me tryin' to be nice to you. Ya want the cleaning chick to come by or not?"

"I'm not your charity case, Clinton."

Clinton laughed a choppy laugh. "Oh yeah?" He swept his arm around him. "Whose money got this place fired up, huh?"

Swanny stopped spraying, glared at his brother. He aimed for Clinton's maddening grin, but pathetically the insecticide bottle missed his face by a foot and hit one of Swanny's plants instead. "*Half* was your money—"

"And half, the old man's."

"I'm still planning to pay you back, asshole." Swanny wheeled past his brother. He didn't want anyone to feel sorry for him. He especially didn't want a girl paid to have sex with him no matter how lonely it got out there.

Clinton opened his mouth to say something just as a buzzer sounded. "The fuck's that?" He looked around frantically as though he spotted an annoying fly buzzing around the room.

"That's someone at the front door of the house, is what that is," Swanny said.

"Shit," Clinton spat. "Left my gun in the fuckin' truck."

***

After making sure the coast was clear, Swanny and his brother left the barn grow op and entered the house through the back door. Clinton now stood hiding on the hinge side of the front door, shotgun at the ready. Swanny was positioned on the other side of the door. "Who's there?"

He heard a chuckle, then, "It's… Freedomite Yuri."

"Who the fuck is that?" Clinton whispered.

Swanny exhaled relief. "My closest neighbour. My friend."

"Christ." Clinton didn't budge.

"It's okay, relax, he's harmless," Swanny said. "And try not to be a dick."

Clinton frowned and stomped back to the kitchen table, plopped down into a chair in the manner of a petulant child. He dropped the shotgun at his feet. Swanny unlocked the deadbolts and opened the door. A slight, scrubby man in his sixties stood grinning and holding up two Mason jars of soup, as if he'd won top prize in a raffle. Scraggly white hair poked from under his black Russian fur hat. An equally scraggly beard reached down to the collar of his oversized winter jacket from whose breast pocket stuck out a single white feather. On his feet were black rubber boots. If Tolstoy were alive today, that'd be him, Swanny thought whenever he saw Yuri.

"Well hey… I made borsch and t'ought I'd bring you a couple jars," Yuri said.

"Thanks, Yuri, come in," Swanny waved him in. Yuri stepped through the door, shuffled into the kitchen and stopped when he saw Clinton. He stared at him and after a moment, smiled. Swanny pointed. "This is my brother, Clinton."

"Hello, big fella," Yuri said cheerfully. "Nice to meet you."

Clinton eyed Yuri, assessing what type of man he might be. "The fuck ya smiling at?"

Swanny looked at his brother, shook his head, looked back at Yuri. "Our dad died. Clinton here is taking us to the funeral tomorrow."

"Oh, I'm very sorry to hear dat, fellas." Yuri shuffled to the kitchen counter and set the jars down. "Plenty of times I've felt the sting of a loved one's passing."

Clinton took a long pull from a new bottle of whisky he'd just cracked. He slammed it down on the table, startling both his brother and Yuri. "Why they call you Freedomite Yuri for?"

"Ah… I gave him that name," Swanny said. "I know more than one Yuri."

"I'm a Son of Freedom. Makes sense I suppose," Yuri replied.

"Oh yeah? Proud of that, are ya?" Clinton said.

Yuri pondered this for a moment. "The t'ings I've done in my life make me who I am. Some of them I'm proud of…" Yuri looked directly at Clinton. "Others not so much. Know what I'm saying?"

Clinton scoffed. "Think ya know me?" His voice was filled with scorn. "Maybe we should call you Burn-It-Down Yuri instead, eh? Fuckin' Douks."

"Jesus. Sorry, Yuri, don't mind him. He's not himself right now," Swanny said.

"Don't gotta speak for me," Clinton continued staring at Yuri.

Yuri turned and headed for the door, patting Swanny on the shoulder as he passed. He stopped and spun around, his finger in the air as if he just remembered something. "You know, in the Doukhobor tradition we say, *Vechnaya pamyat.* It means may the dead rest in our eternal memory. So, I say it now for your father… *Vechnaya pamyat.*"

"Don't bother," Clinton said.

Yuri shrugged and yielded with a bow. He turned to Swanny, smiled and gave him a wink.

"Thank you, Yuri, I appreciate it." Yuri shuffled out. Swanny locked the door behind him and wheeled around to his brother. "Yuri's a good man. My friend. He looks out for me."

"He's a Douk."

"So? In high school you used to be friends with Danny Harshenin. He was a Doukhobor. And you like my buddy Ryan Androsoff."

"Harshy never spoke Russian or talked about being a Douk. Coulda been Italian for all I knew. He was a regular Canadian. But most Douks are a bunch of fuckin' anti-war freeloaders who've never fought for this country."

Swanny laughed. "Right, and you really care about Canada and fighting for a government and its people that you rip off any which way you can."

"That's different."

"How?" Swanny asked.

"How? I don't parade around nude and burn my house down. Fuckin' freaks."

"That wasn't *all* Doukhobors. It was the Sons of Freedom. You know that. That was their form of protest."

"Exactly. Gandalf Twinkletoes there just admitted he was one of 'em."

"That was a long time ago," Swanny said.

"What was there to protest anyway?" Clinton looked baffled, raised his upturned palms in the air. "Canada gave 'em a place to set up shop when their commie homeland didn't want their fat asses. Far as I'm concerned, they're no better than a buncha Indians. There's a reason why people call 'em Dirty Douks."

"No one calls them that anymore," Swanny said. He slid his bandana off his head and ran his fingers through his hair. "Just like no one says *Indians* anymore."

"First Nations fuckin' blow me." Clinton took another swig of his whisky, wiped his mouth. "The old Douk thinks he knows me? You squawk about me to him or somethin'?"

Swanny was astonished. "No, of course not. I'm not an idiot."

"Yeah well, best keep yer mouth shut. Specially these days."

"Like I said, not an idiot."

"At least Douk food is delicious." Clinton smirked. "Let's crack open one of them jars of borsch—" He held up the bottle of whisky. "—An' I'll pour you glass of this here fine Irish nectar."

Their father's funeral couldn't be over soon enough for Swanny. The less he saw of his lunatic half-brother the better. And he sure as hell did not want any part of a revenge scheme against Jonah Seeger. Swanny would've done the exact same thing if he'd been in Jonah's place.

In 1924, George Love, American Legion commander and leader of the Eugene, Oregon Ku Klux Klan, warns an angry crowd in Junction City about the danger of allowing the communist Doukhobor invaders to establish colonies on land that Peter V. Verigin had purchased. Ultimately, a Doukhobor colony in Eugene fails due to an anti-radical and racialized atmosphere throughout the state.

In that same year, while travelling by train between Grand Forks and Castlegar, a mysterious explosion underneath Peter V. Verigin's seat kills the Doukhobor leader and eight others. Some Community Doukhobors suspect government agents, or possibly the Sons of Freedom, while the Sons of Freedom and the government point fingers at each other. Still others suspect Soviet agents sent by the Stalin regime.

A procession of seven thousand Community, Independent and Sons of Freedom Doukhobors from across the country march and sing psalms up the side of Mount Sentinel to Verigin's Tomb, the leader's final resting place overlooking Brilliant, BC.

Camp Fallujah, Iraq, December 2004

Jonah sat cross-legged on a cot in a compact room, writing a postcard to his old skate buddy Cedar. One exposed bulb hanging from the ceiling lit the room. Outside, a sandstorm shook and pelted the portable with infinite grains of sand; the sound like bacon frying. Lewis sat on the floor across the room, shuffling a deck of cards. He'd invited Private Sadie Ellard, a twenty-year-old recruit from Mississippi, to play Blackjack with him. They'd met her and a few other searchers at a checkpoint when the female Marines would catch rides back to camp with Jonah and the fireteam. Now they were at Camp Fallujah, a former Mujahideen training compound of one-storey cement buildings on the outskirts of the city. Windows had been covered with blankets and sandbags; in other rooms Marines listened to music, played cards, talked about home, avoided talking about home, tried to sleep.

Jonah passed Private Ellard the flask of bourbon he'd been sipping from as she examined her cards. She thanked him. Jonah glanced at her, considered her all-American looks: straight little nose, thin lips and round cheeks in a compact face. Her sandy-blonde hair was in a ponytail so that every tiny movement of her head caused her bunched locks to bounce and quiver. Jonah considered her athletic frame, a reminder that cheerleaders weren't his type. He recalled that the few times he'd seen Private Ellard, not once had he returned her smile.

He wondered what she saw when she looked at him. His brown eyes once clear and confident, now distant and tired? His toned frame depleted from lack of appetite? He wore a green sleeveless shirt and a black bandana around his neck. The tattoos that dotted his arms seemed to be his only outward signs of intensity.

"Been a rough couple weeks?" Sadie asked Jonah in her thick southern drawl.

He remained focused on his postcard.

Sadie tapped the floor and Lewis gave her another card. "Haven't really been in the thick of it yet like y'all have. Mostly just pattin' down haji women at checkpoints."

"Uh-huh," is all Lewis could muster as he dealt himself a new card.

"But when I get in a funk I think of home. Biloxi. Noodlin' for catfish in the delta." She passed Lewis the flask.

"Thinking too much of home can get you in a deeper funk, Private," Lewis offered. He nodded at Jonah and snickered playfully. "Especially this sucker when he thinks of Ruby... his good girl gone bad."

Jonah looked up at Lewis and scowled. "Man, why you gotta ...?" He shook his head.

"Got yourself a funky fiancée, Corporal Seeger?" Sadie said.

Lewis laughed. "Damn, girl, gonna call you Saucy Sadie. Only been here a few days and look at your jealous ass."

Jonah stopped writing, glanced at Sadie. Behind her quick blue eyes he sensed genuine curiosity.

"Pfft. He wishes." Sadie smirked at Jonah. "This Ruby, she dump yer ass or what?"

Jonah was silent.

Sadie's smile faded. "Sorry boss, none of my beeswax."

Jonah slumped. "She's gone is all." He placed the postcard down on his lap. "Why you visiting us?" he asked, unable to conceal his annoyance.

Sadie pointed to Lewis. "Cuz I have a rare moment away from my unit and because Lewis here invited me." She tapped the floor. "Hit me."

"True story." Lewis dealt her another card.

She thumbed behind her. "Plus, the jerkoffs in the next building are havin' a fartin' contest. And in my building the ladies are talkin' about their husbands and boyfriends. An' across the way they're listenin' to nothing but shitty metal. You'd think they'd never heard of Tim McGraw or Shania Twain."

"You're welcome here with us, Sadie." Lewis threw down his cards. "Aw hell, bust." He passed the flask to Jonah. "Don't mind the grump. We've been through some intense shit lately."

"Lucky," Sadie said.

Jonah stopped writing again, was about to address what he considered her naïveté, then thought better of it.

"Speakin' of Shania Twain. Word 'round here's yer a Canuck," Sadie said to Jonah.

"Mhmm… half. My father's American. I was raised in Canada."

"Whatcha doin' fightin' for Uncle Sam then?" she asked with a smirk. She peered at Jonah sidelong. "Aren't y'all a bunch of peace lovers up there?"

Jonah met her eyes. "A mighty southern observation of you, Private Ellard. You're totally right, every single Canadian is a hippie. So, I guess that makes me half into this war."

She shook her head. "Ain't no room for freakin' peaceniks in the Marine Corps, boss."

"Shit, girl, that eager for combat?" Lewis said.

"Jonesing for your *fix*?" Jonah added sarcastically.

"I don't know 'bout no fix." Sadie dealt two cards to Lewis.

Jonah considered the situation. He was living with the daily threat of violent death, a lonely Marine who missed the touch of a woman. Given her naive, patriotic warbling, Sadie was not at all his type. Yet… her spunk reminded him of Ruby.

"All I know is I wanna see combat. To kill the freakin' enemy," she said.

"Easy, tiger." Jonah laughed. "You can't even *freakin'* swear properly."

Sadie presented her middle finger to Jonah. He knew the ritual. They'd all acted tough at first despite having "scared shitless" tattooed across their foreheads.

"We chomped at the bit once too, hey bro?" Lewis asked as he tapped the floor.

"Yup we sure did. Let me guess," Jonah said to Sadie, "you were playing *Halo* when the Marine recruiter phoned. And because you wanted to find some meaning in your life, make a big decision on your own for once, maybe get away from whatever depressing little shithole you grew up in and whatever douchebag boyfriend you couldn't let go of, you believed the recruiter when he said, 'join the Marines, you could be the best.'"

Sadie puffed hard through closed lips, glared at Jonah, gave him two middle fingers.

"You know, first time I killed a man..." Lewis shook his head, looked down at the cards in his hands.

Unconsciously Jonah started rubbing his knuckles. A shadow flickered in the corner of his eye. He swivelled his head, blinked hard, was about to ask the others if they saw what he was seeing. Fresh-faced and smiling at Jonah was Mason sitting on the gear bags piled against the closet. Since the incident in that Fallujah alley not a day had passed without a visit from Mase; the way he prayed into his wrists, went on and on about his fiancée, how he looked to Jonah and Lewis to guide him in combat. Jonah squeezed his eyes tight, shook the kid from his vision.

Sadie threw her cards down, looked at Lewis. "I don't need to hear yer sob story, Lewis. Besides, they're the freakin' enemy. They hate us!" she hollered. "They hate 'merica an' everthin' it stands for. What's so hard about killin' them bastards? It's what I'm here to do."

Jonah was confounded. He'd heard plenty of good ole boys in the Marines talk the way she was talking. And as far as he could remember, none of the women he knew ever uttered the desire to harm anyone. Even if, like Ruby, they had cause to.

"You think it's that cut and dried, Private?" Lewis asked.

"Yeah, I do."

"You're such a boot." Jonah air-poked his finger at her. "Everything we need to know about being proud warriors you've already learned back at Parris Island."

"And now I'm gonna use that boot camp trainin', kick some freakin' I-raqi ass," Sadie said with forced bravado, "and make darned sure America stays safe."

Jonah offered her a slow clap, then said, "Cut the hero crap, Ellard. That'll just get you ... *killed.*" Jonah emphasized the word as though he were shooting it from his mouth. Its vibration in his skull suddenly changed the channel. Just like that, he was back in the Fallujah alley next to Mase who was frozen, staring at the startled insurgent in the baggy blue sweater as the young Iraqi opened fire on him. Mason was flung backward and in a split second Lew would be next. In a heartbeat Jonah peppered the insurgent's torso with dark crimson bullet holes. Lewis lifted Mase over his shoulder and ran. For weeks Jonah had been trying to remember what happened next and now it suddenly came to him. As he passed the Iraqi insurgent sprawled on his back on the ground, Jonah paused. He noticed the soldier was around Mase's age. Bleeding out, he stared at the crisp blue Autumn sky above the shadowed alley. In less than a minute he'd be dead. Just before Jonah turned to follow his team to safety, he heard the young man call for his mother. He delicately said, "*Umi ... umi,*" and then he was gone.

"Ya hear me, Seeger?" Sadie said. "I'm all-American, Captain Canuck. Ready to die for *my* country."

Jonah finished off the last of the bourbon in the flask then stared Sadie in the eye. "I'm sure you are all-American," he snickered, "but you're all-naive too."

"An' I reckon you're a bit of a *pussy,*" she said in the most condescending tone she could muster.

Blood rushed to Jonah's face on the double. He blinked hard and felt the snap come on; his vision blurring, growing shadowy around the edges, his heart punching. He clenched his fist hard around the flask and slammed its metal into the floor in front of Sadie, sending it bouncing an inch from her face and clattering into the opposite wall. "How dare you?" Jonah leaned into Sadie, teeth bared like a wolf. Her smugness rapidly gave way to shock.

"Dude, take it easy," Lewis said.

Jonah bore into Sadie's surprised eyes with all the conviction he could summon. His arms trembled. "I've pulled mangled children from rubble," he spat. "Think it mattered to me that they were I-raqi? Huh? I've seen grandmothers dying in the street in front of me, watched people blow themselves up for their stupid God ... I've killed men," Jonah said, jabbing himself hard in the chest. "Men who have children, who are loved, who believed, like we believe, that they're fighting the good fight. So don't you dare call *me* a pussy."

Jonah's chin quivered. Sadie's eyes softened with realization. She opened her mouth to speak. "Shut the fuck up," he barked. Even as he was saying it he knew it was the war talking. Up until that point he hadn't realized just how much he'd been suffering. Especially from what happened that day in the Fallujah alley. It wasn't even post-traumatic stress that was eating at Jonah, it was now-traumatic stress. But he couldn't stop himself. He pointed at Lewis. "Me and Lew here watched Mason, a good gentle soul bleed out in front of us." Jonah's eyes welled with tears as the previously blacked-out memory came into sharp focus. "I held his hand and ..." The anger suddenly ran out of Jonah. He spoke quietly now. "I leaned in close to hear him whisper a dying message to his fiancée. 'Tell Jenny,' Mase said, 'tell her I'm sorry I left her. Tell her I love her.'" Jonah tugged at his hair, closed his eyes tight. "You could get your pretty cheerleader face torn apart by shrapnel tomorrow, Sadie." He opened his eyes, looked up at the ceiling. "And you'd just be another in a long list of horrors."

Jonah's words had performed their intended lobotomy. All colour had drained from Sadie's stunned face as though she had not once considered the repercussions of being a Marine, until that very moment.

"Chill, brother. That's enough," Lewis said.

Jonah hadn't even noticed that Lewis was crouched beside him, hand on his shoulder, gently easing him back onto his cot. Jonah slumped and buried his head into trembling hands. Sadie got up and quickly walked out into the passing desert storm.

It's 1925 and both the Community and Sons of Freedom Doukhobors continue to refuse to send their children to public school, which they consider a breeding ground for militarism and capitalist greed.

In Grand Forks, British Columbia, eight hundred Doukhobors demonstrate outside the house where visiting British Columbia premier John Oliver is staying. In a heated exchange they tell Oliver that their laws are better than those of Canada, to which he furiously replies, "The laws would be more right if you were dead than as you are now!"

Spokane, Washington, February 2005

At the Big Easy that night the band's stage volume was ear-splittingly loud. Tomás was spitting all over the mic, sing-yelling at the audience as though they'd done something wrong. But they hadn't. They'd shown up in droves to the cavernous music hall and were singing along with the band. Now as Caravana neared the end of their show and were playing "All Freaks Calling," their impassioned ode to nonconformity, Ruby's ears were worn and ringing, spells of dizziness coming and going. As they entered the song's bridge, the quiet part where Ruby's voice could truly shine, she sang flat, and her guitar strumming was sloppy. She could feel the spiral coming on. Always the signal that more drugs needed to course through her bloodstream.

They had agreed not to drink too far past tipsiness prior to performing, but as the tour rolled on, the line between tipsy and hammered became increasingly blurred. Ruby recalled how the after-party following the previous night's show at the Hard Rock in Vegas was the most decadent yet. So, earlier that afternoon after finding a decent Thai restaurant Alice had offered Ruby some of her cocaine stash to help her deal with her monumental Vegas hangover. Before hitting the stage, she'd cut a fat line on the back of the green-room toilet and snorted it all in one go. Then chased it with a vodka Red Bull. She knew her high school crew of Nadya, Bobbie and Delia had braved snowy roads to get to Spokane and she absolutely did not want to suck.

But she *was* sucking, lacking composure and dignity, and now she craved the upthrust of more cocaine. She'd already messed up the intro to "Start Wearing Magenta" earlier in the set and forgotten some lyrics in their fiery cover of Fleetwood Mac's "Landslide." Up next was her song, "Spirit Wrestlers."

Ruby could feel the crash happening, like it always did at various points throughout the night. She strummed on autopilot, closed her eyes and saw herself floating in the blackness of deep space. In front of her was a distant, flickering star, a small beacon of hope, while behind her was the voracious appetite of a black hole. She knew that if she consumed more drugs she could lift and spring toward the light. But the drugs were draining from her, she was hurtling toward oblivion, and panic was choking her like a python coiling around her neck, squeezing tighter and tighter.

"Freaks" couldn't end soon enough. The crowd roared. Ruby opened her eyes and swivelled to Alice, caught her eye, pointed up at her own nostril and flicked her eyebrows. Alice nodded. Ruby staggered over to her as the band tuned and Tomás engaged with the crowd. She tried not to get her feet caught up in the various cords strewn about the stage and stepped behind Alice's multi-level keyboard set-up. There she bent down and, as covertly as possible, snorted what Alice had presented to her, a tiny pile of powder on a beer bottle cap. She winced at what felt like battery acid singeing her nostril. What the fuck was that? She staggered back to her amp from where she picked up her shot of vodka and downed it. She dropped the glass onto the stage and stepped back to her mic.

Tomás droned on at the crowd. A group of female fans pressed up against the stage, loudly professing their love for Ruby as she slung her acoustic over her head. They wore bright-coloured face paint that gave them a pixie-like appearance, and multicoloured bandanas around their necks, and cleavage-revealing fatigues. Ruby blew a kiss at them, prompting loud screams of adoration. By now she knew she should be feeling the effects of the cocaine; thin beams of clarity, a much-needed zip of energy. But at that moment she was starting to feel relaxed. Too relaxed. Soupy. Did Alice mistakenly give her oxy?

Ruby scanned the audience again for her friends and thought she caught a glimpse of Nadya up in the balcony VIP section. She wasn't sure it was her but waved anyway which produced some claps and cheers from the audience, and a bemused look from Tomás as he segued from banter to his gracious introduction of her. Ruby giggled, swayed in place, bobbed her head to a beat that only she could hear. She mumbled, "Thank you," closed her eyes and was transported to the last time she'd made the trip south from the Slocan Valley to Washington State... That must've been what, seven years ago now? She and Nadya... and Jonah had been day drinking at Troup Beach, a long slice of sand jutting into the middle of Kootenay Lake and... then what? Distantly, Ruby felt herself strumming her guitar. Was she playing it on the beach that day? Was she playing it now on stage? They were jonesing for good Mexican food, so they packed up, jumped in her Honda Civic and drove south. They were spontaneous, they drove through Colville and—

—*Thwak!* Ruby felt a smack to her ass. She opened her eyes and whipped her head around, prepared to hurl eye daggers at Tomás when she realized the band had already started "Spirit Wrestlers." Ruby's face flushed as she turned to the audience. She lifted and strummed her guitar high beside her head in rocker pose and threw herself into the song with more juice than usual. Way too much juice. Something was wrong. She hadn't tuned. Was she even singing the right part? Her voice sounded horribly discordant alongside Alice's warm Wurlitzer tones and Vlad's piercing violin. She blinked her eyes hard and looked at Tomás. He blurred in and out, his eyes wide and imploring, mouth melting. Ruby was so tired. Her lips moved but she had no idea what she was singing. She began scream-singing, which surprisingly felt good, cathartic. Somehow, she'd managed to lift her guitar, strap and all, above her head, then dropped it on the stage with a glorious screech and clang. She grabbed the mic attached to its stand and dragged it, stumbling toward her amp. She bent over and continued scream-singing at the amp as though it were responsible for all the wrongs that had ever been done to her. Most of the band had stopped playing now as Ruby continued to vent her fury. It was when the drums finally cut out, and the entire venue was deathly silent that she noticed blood dripping onto her forearms. She felt suddenly sick and dizzy and incredibly sleepy. What the hell was happening?

She shakily stood upright and in a split second of returned clarity, that's when she saw them side stage: her mother with her hands over her mouth, Dad beside her, stock-still, eyes pinned to the floor in front of his feet, and Sasha in between them, hands cupping his ears, looking scared and bewildered. Ruby closed her eyes and saw a beautiful summer day at Crescent Beach, Sasha's arms wrapped tight around her neck, worried that she might drop him into the cool river. She pretended to and he screamed and giggled and they both laughed, and she kissed his cheek, and he rubbed the tip of his nose against hers and that day she had no thoughts of escaping the Slocan Valley, of running off to join the freak circus. She only desired to be with her son, a desire that came flooding back in an instant.

Ruby opened her eyes just as her world tilted sideways and she slammed onto the stage floor, a blurry panic of feet and faces swirling around her.

All she ever craved was escape—from her mother and the Kootenays, from the boredom, from the bruised memories and the scars etched into her soul. But not like this. If she had to wonder whether death was on its way, then she knew she'd finally gone too far. Ruby tried but failed to lift her hand and reach out to Sasha. As the stage lights dimmed her last thoughts were of how much she loved her beautiful son. She thought of Jonah, too; not as a soldier but as the teen skater boy she'd adored. And how sorry she was that she'd lied so profoundly and unforgivably to him.

In 1927, following the death of his father, the newly anointed Doukhobor leader Peter "the Purger" Verigin arrives in Canada. In front of thousands of his followers at Brilliant, BC, Verigin gives the type of sermon he is known for: rambling, colourful, tinged with mysticism and sloganeering. It is here he shouts that "Sons of Freedom cannot be slaves of corruption." Far from being corrupt, he says, with their enthusiasm the Freedomites are the ringing bells that will keep the ears of other Doukhobors open to truth. The Sons of Freedom, misinterpreting the speech as endorsement, are emboldened. With their zealotry reinforced, and with many more of Verigin's speeches misinterpreted thereafter, decades of protest, guerilla warfare tactics and terrorism follow.

Fallujah, Iraq, December 2004

On overcast days Jonah found that the desert and sky in Iraq often merged into one dull, beige moonscape. But its monotony that crisp February day was pierced by a brilliant sky, cloudless and powder blue. Jonah and his fireteam, plus Sadie and her fellow searchers, were in the back of a seven-ton, a tactical workhorse truck that rumbled along the potholed highway out of Fallujah toward the village of Al-Karma. Jonah peered out the back: a few wild oak trees and short palms were scattered in the desert, and a column of black smoke spiralled on the distant horizon. Sitting beside Jonah, Lewis bounced his tree-trunk legs, the heels of his boots creating a nervous rhythm on the metal floor. Between them was where Mason would've been sitting, should've been sitting. Next to Lew, Sergeant Cafferty was finger-drumming on his chest along to Ozzy Osbourne's "Crazy Train" blasting from the one speaker that had been jerry-rigged in the upper corner of the back compartment. Across from them sat Sadie and three other female Marines, searchers assigned to a checkpoint outside Fallujah. Jonah, Lew and Sergeant C. would be dropped off near the village of Al-Karma to team up with another unit.

Jonah focused on Sadie, who was looking out the back at the Iraqi landscape. She had that rookie grin plastered on her face, like a nervous prom queen trying her cheery best for the camera. As usual she was pining for some action to go down at the entry control point where she'd be patting down Iraqi women for another day. She clutched her rifle to her chest and bobbed her head along to the music. Jonah was already looking forward to a quiet night with Sadie back at camp, far more than he was looking forward to the day's mission. It was how he knew, had known for quite a while, that he was ready to go home.

Jonah had enjoyed the war zone love affair he and Sadie had been engaged in for the past month. He thought back to the day after his freak-out at her, how she'd slipped into his portable and jumped him on his cot. Afterward they sat opposite from one another, against the humid vinyl-panel walls of the portable, staring at each other like two caged apes having just satiated their feral needs. Apologies were made; Jonah for flipping out on her, Sadie for calling him a pussy. He couldn't get enough of her warm belly and her breasts that pressed against him that day. Or the desire to bite into her neck and grab a handful of her hair. He wanted her cherry-lip-balm mouth and the tongue that she never once offered. It was on that day too, when something Sadie had said caused an internal shifting and cracking, like an iceberg about to calve. She'd inquired about his silver crescent necklace. He'd told her that it was from the seventeen hundreds, belonged to his great-grandfather times six, the first Cossack in his family to renounce militarism and become a Doukhobor. He told her what little he knew of the pacifist sect and of his mother's family; the nude fire-starting terrorists known as the Sons of Freedom.

"How messed up is that?" Jonah had said to Sadie. "Staunch pacifists using violence to get their point across."

"Jesus." Sadie snickered. "You're a freakin' weirdo Christian terrorist from Canada fighting weirdo Muslim terrorists here in Iraq."

He hadn't connected the dots before that moment. Suddenly he felt... exposed. Foolish even, for being in Iraq at all. He came from a people that at one time *were* considered terrorists, fighting against people that *are* considered terrorists, for a nation that those people considered to be the biggest *terrorist* of all.

"My grandpa was a Vietnam vet," Sadie said to Jonah, "and he used to always say, 'It's insects we should be fightin', not each other.'"

Jonah rubbed his Cossack crescent earring between his thumb and forefinger, continued to scan the scene out back of the seven-ton where ragged Fallujah evacuees lined the road, making their way slowly back toward what was left of their homes. He expected some of them to be defiantly, pathetically throwing rocks at them as they passed. But the citizens just looked on impassively, with sunken faces and hollow stares. On one side of the battle were the insurgents; on the other side, the coalition forces, the infidels. The locals had been battered from all angles. The spark was almost all gone. Except for the lunatics whose misguided spiritual terrorism reminded Jonah of what he knew of his uncle Yuri. An unsettling heaviness came over him. He hadn't even noticed that he'd been pinching his bottom lip with tented hands until Sadie piped up.

"Oh Jesus, can you just..." she said above the growl of Humvee and the din of music.

Jonah pointed out the window. "Look at those poor people. Do they even need us? Like, what the hell are we doing here?"

Lewis looked over at Jonah with a blank stare. Jonah caught Sergeant C.'s scrutinizing sidelong glare. The female Marines around Sadie impassively watched the exchange.

"Can we just be guilt-free Marines for one day?" Sadie returned her gaze outside the back. "Jesus."

"Guilt-free Marine?" Lewis scoffed. "Ain't no such thing, Momma."

Sergeant Cafferty couldn't help himself. "Everyone just shut the fuck up, will ya?" He leaned forward to address Jonah. "Private Ellard is right, Seeger. What's gotten into you?" Jonah frowned and shrugged. "And besides," Sergeant Cafferty continued, "even if we were here just for the oil, wouldn't that be reason enough? Huh?" He pointed his finger piously in the air. "Bet your sniper ass it would be. Take oil away from America and whaddaya think'll happen?" He continued to stare at Jonah.

Jonah wasn't stupid. They all knew why America was there. But being a warrior, being part of a brotherhood—oorah—thinking you were helping people, getting a paycheque... it just wasn't worth it anymore, was it? Jonah noticed he'd been rubbing his knuckles again. He stopped when the seven-ton slowed and swerved erratically. His helmet slammed into Lewis's muscled shoulder then he straightened himself. He got up, grabbed a strap fastened to the inside of the compartment near the back opening and swung his torso out of the truck to have a look. Up ahead a herd of goats was being ushered onto the road by an adolescent boy in sandals.

The seven-ton pulled onto the shoulder of the road, slowed to a crawl and finally stopped.

Sadie smacked her thigh at the sight. "Little fucker." She and her fellow searchers laughed.

Still clutching the strap near the open back of the truck, Jonah locked eyes with the boy who glared back at him with contempt. His black hair was cut short, bangs just touching thick eyebrows. A stained beige puffy jacket and baggy beige pants matched the desert terrain around him. Just as Jonah was about to spin around and rejoin Lewis on the bench, the boy turned and ran to the other side of the road. His goats didn't follow. If they were his to herd, Jonah thought, wouldn't they instinctively follow the boy? Jonah leaned farther out the back and noticed that the kid was reaching into his pocket. From the outside Jonah banged the side of the seven-ton.

"What's going on?" Sadie said.

Jonah yelled at the driver over the music and engine rumble. "Possible IED, let's go!" He kept banging the side of the truck. "Step on it!" Both Lewis and Sergeant C. were at Jonah's side now. Jonah watched as the boy pulled out a cellphone from his pocket.

Sergeant Cafferty tilted his head down and spoke into the radio receiver attached to his tactical vest to alert the driver. "Jiminez, you seeing this goat herder kid with a cellphone?" Sergeant Cafferty's radio crackled with the driver asking whether he should go forward or reverse.

The boy was behind them across the road. Jonah surmised the explosive would be somewhere up ahead, or directly underneath them. But the driver had made his decision and was now rumbling forward through the parting goats. "Reverse! Reverse!" Jonah shouted, his nerves raw and his chest tightening. Sergeant Cafferty echoed the command into the radio and motioned for Jonah and Lewis to take their seats. Just as Jonah and Lewis took their places on the bench the driver slammed on the brakes and shifted into reverse. Sadie's panic-stricken eyes met Jonah's. He breathed out, tried to surrender to the moment. He reached out to grab her hand—blissful scenes of home flashed through him: his mother and father dancing together in the living room, Ruby's little gap in her front teeth as she leaned in to kiss him. Jonah focused on warm feelings of love. He grazed the tip of Sadie's fingers just as the seven-ton lurched backward and an explosion ripped up through the back, launching the truck off the ground and sending chunks of metal slicing through Jonah's legs. White-hot pain seared through him. Broken bodies slammed into one another mid-air amidst sounds of twisting, groaning metal. Gasping for breath, Jonah's lungs were instantly choked with diesel smoke as the truck landed hard on its side.

As the world faded Jonah heard hissing, the faint bleating of goats, and the groans and cries of pain of those around him. He felt his outstretched hand holding Sadie's hand… or was it Ruby's? His mom's? Mason's? Jonah was clasping a prayer rope fastened to someone's slender wrist. The blurry figure was drifting away, the prayer bracelet elongating like taffy being stretched and stretched… until finally it snapped… and Jonah plunged into a welcome opiate darkness.

II

Love and Consequence

By the end of May 1932, 745 Sons of Freedom men, women and children are held in detention camps in Nelson. They are arrested for nude marches protesting their expulsion from the Doukhobor community by Peter "the Purger" Verigin over their refusal or inability to pay their community dues. By the end of June, six hundred adults are sentenced to three years imprisonment at the Piers Island Penal Colony (built solely for Doukhobors) for the crime of public nudity. Their children—365 in total—are sent to orphanages and provincial industrial schools where many suffer physical and emotional abuse.

Moscow, Russia, May 1996

The vodka was working its magic, warming Ruby on the chilly spring night. She tilted her head back, exhaled and watched her breath rise in a column, forming a wispy mushroom cloud above her head. Screw the jet lag; she was giddy, thrilled to be in a real cosmopolitan city. Ruby, Nadya and a few Doukhobor girls from Mount Sentinel High and schools in Castlegar and Grand Forks were in Red Square. For the last hour they'd been strolling with Moscow boys they'd met at a bar in the colossal Soviet-era Rossiya Hotel; their home for the next three nights. Peter, the tall blond twenty-year-old who'd glommed onto Ruby when she ordered a vodka tonic at the bar, was now fondling the small of her back underneath her jean jacket.

St. Basil's Cathedral, with its candy-swirl cupolas, was a trippy fairy tale gleaming in the night, while farther beyond was the three-thousand-room Rossiya. Clusters of people were ambling arm in arm through Red Square.

Ruby laughed at the thought of how easy it had been ordering drinks at the Rossiya. Initially the other girls—even normally sassy Nadya—feared being ID'd and getting in trouble. But when Ruby stepped out of the bathroom in the suite she and Nadya shared, looking all gorgeous in her silky black dress, with makeup liberally applied, the girls quickly fell into line. Their chaperones, Ms. Voykin and Mrs. Popoff had retired for the night and in the end none of the bartenders had even blinked an eye at sixteen-year-old girls from America ordering drinks.

Ruby and the girls were speaking Russian with Peter and his three friends; the guys occasionally having a laugh at the girls' Canadian-accented Doukhobor dialect.

"We should get back to the hotel, it's getting late," Nadya said to the girls. A mostly sober girl from Grand Forks named Jenny, who wasn't paired with one of the Russian boys, agreed.

"No hotel," Peter said bluntly in English, his Husky-blue eyes sparkling in the night. "We party at club now." He twirled Ruby around and kissed her on the lips. Momentarily dizzy, Ruby playfully pushed him away. He pulled her back in and brought his hands way up her back underneath her jean jacket. Nadya caught Ruby's eye and gave her a stern look that said, "It's time to go back." Ruby wanted nothing more than to experience a Moscow club. It was so adult and would be a great story back home. She glared at Nadya, gave her a what's-your-problem look.

Now Peter twirled Ruby again so that he stood behind her, pressed up against her ass, his hand on her stomach, slowly sliding up. "*Davay devochki*," Peter said, "*davayte veselit'sya*."

"We cannot go party with you," Nadya replied in Russian. "Our chaperones will be checking on us. If we're not in our rooms we'll get in trouble. But… tomorrow night we can meet up."

Ruby opened her mouth to refute Nadya's lie when she felt one of Peter's hands cupping and squeezing her breast, the other circling her stomach. Before she could even react, Nadya had grabbed her by the hand and yanked her away from the drooling Russian.

"Do you want us to yell for the police?" Nadya said sharply.

Peter snickered and backed away. "Let's go boys." He motioned to his friends. "These are just little girls."

On the walk back to the hotel, Ruby made Nadya promise to continue getting drunk. No way their first night in Moscow would end like *that*. Nadya and the rest of the girls agreed. At a packed bar on the fifth floor of the Rossiya's east wing Ruby tried to avoid the leering eyes of chain-smoking men, downing one vodka after another until her memory of Peter was that of a tall, handsome Russian, and not of a lecherous creep. After two more rounds Ruby led the girls around the impossibly long corridors of the hotel. They sang '80s pop songs at the tops of their lungs, collapsing in laughing heaps on the faded carpets, stopping in at every bar in each wing of the massive Rossiya until Ruby was as drunk as she ever remembered being.

Sometime before sunrise she woke up with her head throbbing, pleading for her to not exist, her sour, sticky mouth begging for water. She looked around. What the hell? She was in a... cabinet of some sort, dim light seeping in through cracked open doors. She kicked them fully open, saw she was still in her black satin dress, hugging a dirty mop, sitting on a bucket that reeked of pee. Last night she must've thought that she was in a bathroom stall instead of a janitor's closet tucked in the corner of a foyer. She crawled out, had no idea what floor she was on or how to get back to her room, just as Ms. Voykin the chaperone rounded the corner with hotel security. Ruby spun around, vomited into the bucket, wiped her mouth and knew there was no way she'd be allowed to join the group for the day's itinerary. She vomited again and realized just how much shit she was going to be in once word got back to Virginia and Big Nick... her *perfect* Doukhobor parents.

In 1938 during the Great Depression, trust and mortgage companies foreclose on and seize six million dollars' worth of Doukhobor community property throughout the West Kootenays of British Columbia for unpaid interest payments on a debt of three hundred thousand dollars. The courts refuse to offer special protection on cooperative enterprises. A perfect storm of Doukhobor financial mismanagement, decreasing membership, the Great Depression and the destruction caused by the Sons of Freedom results in a collapse of the communal experiment. At the time it is the largest communal enterprise undertaken in North America.

A year later on February 11, Peter "the Purger" Verigin dies in Saskatoon, Saskatchewan, aged fifty-eight, of liver and stomach cancer misdiagnosed as an ulcer. His body is transported to British Columbia and laid to rest alongside his father at Verigin's Tomb five kilometres east of Castlegar. His son, Peter "the Hawk" Verigin is elected leader, but he is in Stalin's Russia and is only years later found out to have died in a Soviet gulag as an enemy of the state.

At the outset of World War II, Peter "the Purger" Verigin's seventeen-year-old grandson, John J. Verigin, assumes leadership of the Community Doukhobors.

Shoreacres, British Columbia, July 1996

"The *last* time we were here was summer 1986," Jonah's mom said, forcing more cheerfulness than necessary into her lilting voice. "It was the *last* time you saw your Uncle Yuri, the *first* time you met Ruby..." Her voice lowered. "And the last time I saw her mother, Virginia."

Jonah's leap from the old train bridge into the cool emerald waters of the Slocan River a few moments earlier was exactly what he'd needed on this sweltering day. He patted down his long hair and board shorts with a towel and spread it next to his mom who was splayed in her pink one-piece swimsuit. Jonah had reluctantly joined her at the little sandy beach which sat under slices of afternoon shadow created by a train bridge at the north end, and a vehicle bridge that abutted it. Behind them up a small embankment was grassy Shoreacres, the rural neighbourhood where Jonah's mom had rented them an old mobile home.

"Remember?" Sharon asked above the boisterousness of a beach full of families, their screaming kids, and packs of teenagers. "The *whole* family was here? The last time we were all together."

A few feet away from Jonah, two muscled, twenty-something jocks with 'dos exactly like Chandler from *Friends* drank cans of Kokanee beer, frowning at the scene around them. Especially at Jonah and his mother.

Three weeks earlier they'd moved back to the Kootenays from Kelowna; in Jonah's eyes a proper city of a hundred and fifty thousand, a popular summer vacation town and British Columbia's wine-producing capital which sat along the eastern shores of Okanagan Lake three hundred kilometres to the west. Since then, Jonah had spotted an endless parade of bland dudes sporting hockey mullets. He bunched his long, grunge-rocker hair into a ponytail as the jocks zipped up their cooler bag, stood up, wiped sand off their shorts and the back of their legs. The blond jock glanced Jonah's way. "Let's jet, Taylor. Zero hot babes here, just a bunch of long-hairs... and well-fed Douks." They both snickered.

Jonah's mother pretended not to hear them. With years of kung fu classes under his belt, Jonah knew exactly what he was capable of. But instead of roundhouse kicks and lightning-fast punches to their heads, he offered them his middle finger as they cackled, turned and walked away.

Why the hell did she drag him back to the Kootenays anyway? Because he was running from the cops now and then with his skate crew? Big deal. He was six when he left and didn't know a soul now. Not even Ruby. They'd been back only a few weeks but already he knew he hated it there. From what he could tell Castlegar was a long strip of cheap motels, gas stations, a shopping plaza with empty stores, a few gritty pubs and a pulp mill that made the air hazy and ripe with fart. Trail to the south was even worse with its giant Cominco smokestacks and hordes of Italian kids always looking for a fight. Their trailer in Shoreacres was flanked by a cow pasture on one end and a mobile home inhabited by an unfriendly logging truck driver on the other side. Thankfully Nelson, with its indoor skatepark, artsy freaks and a decent mall, was only a fifteen-minute drive east. Jonah exhaled heavily. At least the move back to the Koots had gotten Sharon away from the string of terrible assholes she constantly dated. There was that too.

"Do you remember my brother, Yuri?" Jonah's mom asked as she propped herself up onto her elbows with great effort.

"Kind of like an elf with a bushy beard and eyebrows like little moustaches stuck onto his forehead?" Jonah thought for a moment. "And a tattoo of a... a guy's face on his chest?"

"Mhmm. Dima, Dimitri, Yuri's... his friend. He died when they were both around your age."

"And I remember you and Uncle Yuri and Grandma Polly arguing about something and then Grandma swimming across the river to visit her friend's house on the other side."

"You thought she was like Superwoman for jumping into the current. Shortly after that is when you met Ruby. Remember?"

"Of course." His dad had him in his arms flying him around the beach when all of a sudden Jonah's ears perked up at the sound of singing. His dad stroked his Tom Selleck mustache, cupped his ears and said it sounded like someone's radio. But even as a six-year-old Jonah new better. His dad plopped him onto the ground, pulled a can of beer from the pocket of his shorts, cracked it open, took a big sip, then watched as Jonah set off to investigate. At the south end of the beach Jonah spotted her squatting, scooping sand into a bucket, singing "May There Always Be Sunshine," but in Russian. Her voice was warm and made Jonah's stomach tingle. When she saw him staring at her with mouth open, catching flies, she stopped singing, stood up and stared back. He followed Ruby's blonde hair, which was the colour of sunshine, down to where it ended just below her shoulders. Jonah remembered liking the little space between her front teeth and her tanned skin. She fearlessly walked up to him, held out her hand and said she was Ruby. He said he was Jonah, took her hand, then followed her pull. They laughed and made sandcastles together for what seemed like forever. Sharon and Virginia were both shocked when they found Jonah and Ruby with each other, giggling and covered in sand. It would be years later before Jonah found out the story of Sharon and Virginia's broken friendship.

"Why did you and Ruby's mom let us play if you two weren't friends anymore?"

"Because you two were adorable." Jonah's mom reached into the small plastic cooler next to her and pulled out a two-litre bottle of Pepsi. She filled a plastic cup and handed it to Jonah, then poured herself one. "And because it'd been eighteen years since I last saw Ginny." Sharon slumped. "Back then your father used to say I could've been in the *Sports Illustrated* Swimsuit Issue," she said flatly. "Ginny looked as good as ever. She hugged me and even asked how Yuri and your Grandma Polly were. I guess she was in a good mood."

"But then?"

Jonah's mother pulled a bag of Doritos out of the cooler, opened them, stuffed a handful of chips into her mouth and passed the bag to Jonah. In between crunches she said, "Then… your sleepover happened… where she called you a… a little Svobodnik. Don't you remember…? Who says that to an innocent child?"

Like any kid, Jonah had wanted summertime to last forever, much like his sleepovers in Ruby's awesome tree house. It had been built high up in the muscular limbs of a weeping willow in the Samarodins' backyard overlooking Virginia's garden. Its walls were painted green, had two small windows with shutters and a roof capped by cedar shingles. Inside, a Persian rug covered the floor, big fluffy pillows and fuzzy blankets were scattered about, a small wooden table sat beside a little bookshelf filled with comics and dog-eared paperback novels, and in one corner was an antique lamp topped with a frilly beige shade. Jonah remembered it all like it was yesterday. That final sleepover, Ruby had tried to teach Jonah "Walk Like an Egyptian," which she'd strummed on her ukulele as he sang along with her. Then they'd scared each other with ghost stories and ate way more chocolate bars than Virginia allowed. That night they slept intertwined with each other, snug and safe until birdsong woke them.

The next morning, just before his mother picked him up, ended up being a terrible morning. Ruby had wanted to play a game of "you show me yours and I'll show you mine" as a way of ensuring they were boyfriend and girlfriend now. They were giggling and pointing at each other's junk, their pyjamas down around their ankles when Virginia—apparently having crept up the stairs—flung the tree house door open.

Jonah would never forget the look on Virginia's face, beet red as though someone had slapped her, shocked as though she'd never once before seen a naked body. And then Ruby, the little liar, she pointed at Jonah, said he'd *forced* her to pull her pants down. Jonah's whining protests fell on deaf ears though. Virginia's perfect daughter of course could do no wrong. Ruby's mother shook her head, wagged her finger at him and called him a "rotten little Svobodnik." On the car ride home Jonah regretted telling his mother what had happened because after dinner he watched in horror as she laid into Virginia on the telephone.

"What did you say to her on the phone?"

Sharon chased her Doritos with a gulp of Pepsi. "I told her that she hadn't changed a bit and that she should be ashamed of herself for making a little boy cry like that."

"Will you ever tell me why the Sons of Freedom subject is *sooo* taboo for you?"

Jonah's mother looked around to make sure no one had heard. She held out her hand for Jonah to help her up then started packing up her things. "You're sixteen. I suppose it's time I told you a few things. Let's go for a little drive."

After four years of relative peace and unity amongst the Doukhobors in British Columbia during World War II, acts of resistance once again ramp up. At the end of 1943 selective service is introduced, in which authorities are given power to make anyone do any job for the war effort under the National Resources Mobilization Act. On December 12, Major J.B. Cowell is in Brilliant, BC to present an ultimatum to 3,500 gathered Doukhobors. But before he can speak, the crowd parts and John J. Verigin emerges, clearly and loudly telling the major, "The answer of the Doukhobors... is no!"

That evening the Brilliant Jam Factory—once the crown jewel of Doukhobor enterprises and now in government hands—is burned to the ground by the Freedomites. Both the meeting with Major Cowell and the jam factory arson serves as a warning to the government to back away from the selective service program. Which they do. Nonetheless, as World War II nears its end, a new wave of Sons of Freedom terror begins.

Castlegar, British Columbia, July 1996

With her scarred left hand, Sharon clutched the Volvo's grab handle; with her right hand she held the top of the open driver's-side door and squawk-groaned as she pulled herself to standing. Under a hot July sun, and with no air conditioning in the car, Sharon's many pits and folds were pooled with sweat. She could feel her heart beating dangerously fast.

Jonah helped his mother to the edge of the embankment overlooking Verigin's Tomb, the sacred Doukhobor site below. Sharon hadn't been there in decades. A freshly mowed lawn stretched to the edge of another embankment. A row of flowers in the centre ended at a small set of stairs that led up to a white slab of concrete the size of a backyard swimming pool. The slab was surrounded by more lawn, flowers and small bushes with a low railing bordering it all. Big, leafy trees ringed the edge of the park. The whole area was enclosed by a head-high chain-link fence. Past the white slab, a rocky cliff dropped to a bridge that crossed the turbulent Kootenay River. To the left of that bridge was a bridge of rusted iron and rotting wood that Sharon recalled was built by the Doukhobors around 1913. Farther on was a plateau, on top of which was the West Kootenay Regional Airport where her ex-husband Roy used to fly in and out for work. Behind them, looming over it all, was the granite face of Mount Sentinel.

"What is this?" Jonah asked.

"Verigin's Tomb. It's where the Doukhobor leaders, the Verigin family, are buried." She exhaled wearily. Why couldn't Sharon have groped past decades of grief and shame to impart the good and dignified aspects of Doukhoborism to her sons? Because there was plenty to celebrate, wasn't there? Community for one. Such a cozy, simple, friendly, idyllic term. Rarely used unfavourably. Except when it came to her Sons of Freedom community. Even through the thick fog of fanaticism that Sharon grew up with, she could occasionally glimpse authentic, unfettered Doukhobor culture as though she were gazing skyward to catch sunbeams trying to pierce the fog. Culture was rich, buttery food. Culture was a connection to the land and its bountiful harvest. It was solace and strength found in prayer, song and laughter. It was resilience cultivated in the face of hundreds of years of oppression. It was community. Sharon could grasp it intellectually, yet the ability to feel it in her bones, to feel it course through her veins and pump through the ventricles of her struggling heart... remained elusive.

This was why Sharon had never brought Jonah here before. He knew this much: that she was raised in the radical, Doukhobor sect called the Sons of Freedom. That the most fanatical of them used arson and bombing as a form of protest. It was why the Sons of Freedom were called Dirty Douks and terrorists. It was why regular Canadians had often hurled these same insults at the non-Sons of Freedom Doukhobors. It was why Virginia and her family despised the Freedomites so much. They hated being guilty by association.

One time in elementary school in Kelowna Jonah had let it slip that his mother was a Son of Freedom. He'd come home that day crying because his teacher had made fun of him. Jonah had asked why the Sons of Freedom burned and bombed, and Sharon had said, "Because they're crazy Christians. Crazy about being pure and holy." And then Sharon told him to never again tell anyone she was raised as one.

Jonah was a teenager now and deserved to know more. But how much was too much? Sharon closed her eyes. She'd always told Jonah she was born with a scarred hand. When she opened her eyes, she offered the truth. "I was six years old..." she began. She told him how she was clutching a doll next to her naked mother and father. There were men, women, children and teenagers from her Krestova village all in varying stages of undress standing amongst household items scattered throughout the yard as though they were part of the set of a theatre production: bedding piled into and spilling overtop of a crib; a dresser lying on its side with a kerosene lamp and glass jars from a medicine cabinet gathered on it; leather suitcases with straps unbuckled and clothes spilling out; lampshades here and there; a bedside table draped with an embroidered doily, a fedora on top and a fishing rod leaning on the side. Against Sharon's will, her mother had forced her to unbutton her top and pull it down to her waist. She'd refused initially but when her father smacked her across the back of the head, she knew she'd better comply. Then all at once she felt the heat. Her mouth fell open as flames engulfed her home, the only home she'd ever known, still full of her toys, books and dresses, and everything she loved. Her mother snatched Betty from her hands and threw her favourite doll toward the flames. Her father bent low and whispered in her ear in Russian, using her Russian name. "Don't worry Stasya," he'd said, the smell of alcohol on his breath stronger than usual, "the flames are how we cleanse ourselves. It's how we remind ourselves and our Doukhobor brothers and sisters that material possessions are not what matter most. Owning stuff doesn't bring us closer to God. Being naked and holy as the day we were born does."

Jonah wore a look of bewilderment as Sharon continued. "The gathered began singing a solemn Doukhobor hymn and all I could think was, Where would we live now? I was confused, sad and angry." Sharon looked at Jonah. "As an adult I understand why they burned homes—it was a way of saying, 'All we need is God and God is within us.' But as a child our parents are supposed to be protectors, our home is a sense of security. And so, when my parents burned my home—more than once—my sense of security was shattered, the rug was ripped from under me." Sharon told Jonah how she loved her house, and her toys, and especially Betty, who her mother had snatched from her. Sharon hadn't taken her eyes off the doll; Betty hadn't yet caught fire. There was still time to save her. Sharon broke away from her parents in spite of the spanking she'd suffer afterward. Free of her mother's grip, she bolted for Betty.

Jonah shook his head. "So that's how you burned your hand? Trying to save your doll?"

"No, no, of course not, we never got that close to the flames. I didn't get far. I tripped and Dad clutched my hair and dragged me back in line. But in the days afterward when he and my uncles rebuilt our home, a shack really, I was so nervous and traumatized I spilled boiling water from the kettle all over my hand."

Jonah gently took Sharon's scarred hand in his as her painful memory faded. She squeezed his hand, let go, then wiped her sweaty forehead with her sweaty forearm. "Are you okay, Mom?" he asked.

She was forty-three years old and nearly a hundred pounds overweight. No, she definitely wasn't okay. "It's just the heat."

"I can't believe Grandma Polly made you strip naked and watch your home burn? That's wack."

"Mhmm. But don't think less of her. Those were the times we were living in. The next day the cops came for… They raided our village."

"Huh? Why?"

How much should she tell him? With a distant stare she said, "Because there were hundreds of Freedomite kids not attending public school, which was against the law." Sharon's chin began to tremble, her chest tightening. "So, cops snatched them up in nighttime raids, sent them to a terrible prison school in New Denver. Similar to the ones First Nations kids were sent to. Stealing the children was a way for the government to punish the Freedomite parents for their protest actions." Sharon swallowed her grief; she didn't have the strength to tell of the horrors that transpired there. "Your uncle Yuri had already been there two years the day I burned my hand and spent three more years there after that. Shortly after the kids were released in 1959—some of them your age—they came here and…" Sharon pointed. "Blew this tomb to smithereens."

Jonah's eyes bugged out; his jaw dropped. "Uncle Yuri?"

Sharon slumped. "I don't know." She looked Jonah in the eye. "It was terrible, caused a lot of grief. No one knew exactly who was involved and as a result the entire Freedomite community suffered. My dad couldn't get work for years. He drank more. Basically, drank himself to death. And the terrorism didn't stop there. The hardcore

Freedomites went nuts, burning and bombing. Lots of young men went on the run, into hiding. I didn't see Yuri for nearly a decade."

"Why target such a sacred spot?" Jonah asked.

"Because terrorists love to feel holier than their targets. Because... whoever did it was caught up in the fever of the '60s, like so many self-proclaimed revolutionaries around the world were. And because the Sons of Freedom believed that the Doukhobor leaders shouldn't be treated special, that we're all equal in the eyes of God. And this tomb didn't reflect that." Sharon's voice went quiet. "And because whoever blew the tomb up had likely been imprisoned in that school and lived through things no kid should *ever* have to live through."

Sometimes Sharon felt as though she would never recover from the wounds of the past. She looked around, was suddenly thirsty. "Don't go talking about this," she said to Jonah. "The community here, especially Virginia and her mother, they don't need to have any more ammo for their... prejudice against us. Understand?"

Jonah nodded. Sharon wiped her forehead, reached into her purse and pulled out her car keys, handed them to Jonah. He was perplexed. "I haven't taken my test yet. You know that."

"I know Julian taught you to drive this old girl." Sharon patted the roof of the Volvo as she opened the passenger-side door. "I need to rest." Jonah helped his mother into the passenger's seat then ran around the front of the car and settled in behind the wheel. Sharon already knew she'd be raiding the fridge once she got home. But after that... "Starting tomorrow—" She pinched the tire-tube rolls of her stomach. "—it's crucial I try a new diet."

At the start of the 1950s, around 2,500 people in British Columbia's West Kootenays identify as Sons of Freedom Doukhobors. Of those, eight hundred are under constant surveillance by the Royal Canadian Mounted Police for using public nudity and the arson of their own homes as a means of protesting materialism and assimilation into Canadian society. Of those eight hundred, around two hundred are active in what the Freedomites refer to as black work—acts of terrorism in which non-Freedomite Doukhobor homes are set alight, and schools, railway bridges and other public property are burned or dynamited.

In 1953 the conservative government in BC invokes the Protection of Children Act, making state-run education mandatory for all children. By that point the Community Doukhobors had for nearly two decades accepted public schooling, and the Independents for four decades. But on September 9, 148 Sons of Freedom adults are sent to Oakalla Prison for parading nude, and 104 children are forced from their homes by the RCMP. The children are taken to a prison school—the same facility used to imprison Japanese Canadians during World War II, in the remote mountain town of New Denver, BC.

Slocan Valley, British Columbia, August 1996

Ruby alternated between watching Swanny—who was swimming in the Slocan River with his gross older brother, Clinton—and scribbling ideas for lyrics in the little black notepad that went everywhere with her. She studied the joint burning between her fingers and debated whether she needed to get more stoned than she already was. She glanced at Clinton eyeing her from the river, then looked down at her way-too-exposed boobs and pulled up her black bikini top. Avoiding unnecessary eye contact with the biker, Ruby adjusted her mirrored aviator glasses and looked over to Nadya, who sat beside her wearing a stylish, wide-brimmed straw hat and an oversized t-shirt that covered the bubble butt she was shy to expose. They were in Swanny's tricked-out Chevy van, chilling at the open side doors. It was parked under the shade of poplar trees next to the gently flowing river. A cool breeze drifted off the water, making the scorching day more bearable. Guns N' Roses's "Patience" played on the van's stereo.

Nadya snatched the joint from Ruby and puffed hard to keep it alive. Behind them on Slocan River Road a vehicle honked, presumably at them, as it drove by. Ruby instinctively recoiled. Since her debauched school trip to Russia, when her furious mother had punished Ruby with three months of grounding, she was being extra cautious. No way she'd withstand the monotony of watching movies and listening to music all alone in her bedroom yet again. Luckily, she had her Visine on her to mitigate red-eye, and Dentine for smoker's breath. She could hear her mother now, ragging on her, sermonizing a long list of her friends' kids that had started out as model Doukhobors regularly attending *molenya*, and choir practices, and Festival, before dope—as her mom ridiculously called it—had ruined their lives. Jesus, it was only weed. Ruby laughed to herself knowing Virginia would have a shit fit if she knew that Ruby and her friends had already experimented with shrooms, LSD and ecstasy.

"I get to proof anything you're writing about me," Swanny said as he crawled out of the river.

"Don't kid yourself, bro," Clinton said as he bobbed in the middle of the river, "the Douk hottie's writing about me." He laughed wildly.

"Ew. In your dreams," Ruby said. Clinton's face immediately flushed red. God, why'd Swanny even invite him? He was old, like, thirty-something, smelled as though he sweated whisky, said *fuck* every second word, loved talking shit about Doukhobors, and even more shit about anyone who wasn't white. On top of it all he couldn't keep his filthy eyes off Ruby's boobs. She knew now it had been a terrible mistake laughing at one of his stupid jokes. She ought to have known better; a laugh from a girl, in a dude's mind, usually translated to, "I like you, you're hot, I wanna jump your bones."

She closed her notebook and happily watched Swanny drying off in the sunshine, a steady stream of water running down the loose threads of his cut-off jean shorts, pooling in the dry, dusty ground at his feet. He leaned sideways and rung out his long hair. Ruby had used the puffy bruises under his blue eyes and the ten stitches holding his fat bottom lip together as lyrical inspiration in her notebook just moments before. She was amused that Swanny was still buying that she was two years older than her actual age—sixteen. With her tree-tall height and full figure (and stupid, wide shoulders) and a touch of makeup, she'd found that she could easily pull it off. Unfortunately, Ruby thought as she glanced at Clinton now doing push-ups at the river's edge, her looks also attracted the vile ogling of apes like him as well.

Ruby recalled that it was just over a year ago, as she and Nadya were sipping tangerine Zimas on the patio of Nadya's brother's house, when Swanny made his grand entrance. He growled in on a shiny black Harley, like a biker version of Eddie Vedder, his brown hair flowing down to a black leather vest that he wore overtop a red and black checkered jacket. When Ruby noticed that he was wearing cut-off jean shorts and black Chucks—a bold move considering he was riding a motorbike—she decided that she needed to know him.

He wasn't at all like *anyone* from the Valley. No, that dude had been places and seen things, she'd thought.

"No more smoke for you?" Swanny asked Ruby.

"Nope. Can't be stoned around my parents."

Nadya held the joint out to Swanny. He waved it off. "I gotta pop the hood, the Blue Beast hasn't been starting properly lately."

"What the hell happened to you anyway, Swanny?" Ruby pointed at his face. "Why won't you tell us?"

"None of your business is why." Swanny walked to the front of his van.

"He got bitch-slapped by his boyfriend," Clinton said as he towelled off on the beach.

"Come on, we're practically your girlfriends," Ruby said, thumbing at Nadya.

"Don't you trust us?" Nadya snickered.

Swanny laughed from behind the popped hood. "Teenage girls? Yeah, no."

"We promise we won't tell," Ruby said.

He poked his head from around the hood. "I went through a..."

"An initiation," Clinton said as he pried off his beer's bottle cap with his teeth.

"Initiation?" Nadya and Ruby said in unison.

"Yeah. I mean, it's no secret..." Swanny gestured to Clinton's Harley.

"For the last six months he was a Prospect," Clinton said. "Basically, a bitch to a senior member of the club."

"Now I'm a full member." Swanny disappeared behind the hood again.

"What kind of lame initiation makes it look like you enjoy it when your face meets a fist over and over?" Ruby asked.

"A biker kind." Clinton glared at Ruby. "And watch your pretty little Douk mouth. Nothing we do is lame."

"Is that right?" Ruby said.

Swanny emerged from behind the hood, stepped in between Ruby and Nadya, climbed into the van, sat behind the driver's seat and tried to start the engine. Nothing but repeated clicks. He hit both hands on the steering wheel, cursed and made his way back to the engine with Ruby in tow. She poked her head under the hood.

Swanny laughed. "What, you a mechanic now?"

Ruby rolled her eyes. "Guys are all the same." She stepped around Swanny and peered at the van's battery, then pointed at the white corrosion coating the terminals. "It's not rocket science. Clean your posts, doofus."

Swanny leaned in to have a better look. "Shit. Who taught you that?"

"Big Nick makes sure I know how to do all the things guys do: change oil, chop wood, swing a hammer." She stepped closer to Swanny. A Ford F-250 on the road behind them slowed as it approached.

Swanny glanced at the truck. "Who's Big Nick?"

"My dad." Ruby grabbed Swanny by his shoulders, pulled him toward her and planted a kiss on his lips, something she'd wanted to do since she first met him. She glanced to see if Nadya had seen them, but it was Clinton instead who'd noticed the kiss. He glowered for a moment then offered a mocking smile as he took a pull from his beer, tossed it back over his shoulder into the river and mounted his motorbike.

Swanny gently pushed a blushing Ruby away and shook his head. "You're trouble." He gestured at the female driver in the Ford F-250 that had now slowed to a crawl.

Ruby looked over her shoulder as the truck picked up speed again. Was that her mom's friend Carol? Shit, she hoped not. She stepped around Swanny and rejoined Nadya who was spreading tobacco on a rolling paper. Swanny followed. He opened the passenger-side door, opened his glove compartment, shuffled around in it, pulled out a small baggie, and handed it to Nadya. "Sprinkle some of this in there."

"What is that?" Ruby asked.

"Coke." Swanny sat down beside Ruby, pulled a set of keys from his pocket, dipped the end of a key into the flap of white powder, brought it up to his nostril and snorted loudly.

Ruby gestured at Nadya. "I've only ever seen her brother doing it at his parties."

"It's a fun high," Swanny said, sniffing loudly. "It's the Energizer Bunny compared to weed. That's why it's so popular in the cities." Swanny wiped his nostril with his thumb. "Around here it's like *Dazed and Confused*, a bunch of country bumpkins just toking up all day. Coke's great if you're too drunk, too. A fat line'll sober you up lickety-split."

For a moment Ruby imagined she was not hanging out next to a lazy river in a lazy Canadian valley but was instead on a road trip with Nadya and Swanny through California, en route to San Francisco or Los Angeles. God, at this point even Spokane would be a relief. "Can I try?" Ruby asked.

Swanny pointed at the joint Nadya had just rolled. "Smoke that. She sprinkled it with coke."

"Why not how you did it off your key?" Ruby asked.

"Oh, so now you're Ruby Escobar?" Nadya laughed.

"I need to sober up before heading back home," Ruby pleaded.

Swanny thought for a second. "Yeah, I don't wanna be that guy. Stick with the coco-puff. You won't get blasted, but you'll get a taste of the high," he said as Clinton's Harley growled to life. "You off already?" Swanny called over the rumble.

Clinton put his leather vest on over his bare torso, slipped on his wraparound shades and strapped a German, SS-style helmet to his head. "I got important club business to do." He scoffed. "Unlike you, I don't got time to be hangin' with *teenagers*." He revved his throttle and sped off in a cloud of dust.

Ruby's whole body relaxed. Good riddance, creep. Nadya lit the joint, took a drag and passed it to Ruby. The smoke smelled sweeter than weed usually did. She took a big, long pull, winced and nearly coughed up a lung. She checked the time on the dash of Swanny's van and shot up. "I gotta go." She stuffed her notepad into her Jansport backpack.

"Chill, Rube," Swanny said.

"Her mom micromanages her life now, since she pissed herself on our school trip to Russia."

"Shut up! Did not!" Ruby's face blushed red as Nadya launched into a laughing fit and Swanny bit his lips in amusement. "I'm late for dinner." Ruby gave Nadya the middle finger. Before slipping on her backpack, she fished around inside, pulled out a cassette tape and handed it to Swanny. "Made it for you. 'Summer Vibes '96.' Let me know what you think."

"Thanks. Oh, hang on a sec." Swanny jumped into the van. When he re-emerged, he had two Ziploc bags full of marijuana and passed one each to Ruby and Nadya. "On the house."

Virginia had just gotten off the phone with her friend Carol, who had seen Ruby and some sort of greasy hippie kissing in front of a van next to the river. She turned the pot of spaghetti down to a simmer, then stepped out onto the patio. She explained to her husband, who was up a ladder picking peaches off the tree, what Carol had seen. Nick only grunted. Virginia sat down on a deck chair where she'd wait for her daughter who would no doubt try to quietly enter the house through the basement door. Ruby had made a fool of herself *and* the good family name with her antics on the school trip to Russia. There'd be no more of that.

Sure enough, fifteen minutes later, Ruby came around the side of the house, peering into and shuffling around in her backpack. She glanced up at her dad humming to himself on the ladder then started to tiptoe down the stairs to the basement door.

"Where are you coming from?" Virginia said in a loud, sharp tone.

Startled, Ruby dropped her backpack, spilling its contents down the stairs. "Jesus. What, you're just sitting there like a hawk waiting to pounce on me?" She turned around and crouched down. "I'm like, five minutes late for dinner. Big deal."

Virginia quickly walked down the patio stairs and strode to the far side of the basement stairwell to see exactly what Ruby was frantically trying to stuff back into her bag.

"Nick," Virginia called, "get over here." She descended the steps and snatched Ruby's backpack from her.

"Mom, you can't just go through my stuff like that," Ruby said.

Virginia unzipped it, fished around inside and pulled out the bag of weed. She handed it to Nick, turned back to Ruby and glared at her. "Yes, I damn well can. You live under our roof, young lady." Nick held the open bag of weed up to his face, his big nose stuffed into it, sniffing loudly. Incredulous that he seemed to be enjoying the pungent aroma, Virginia snatched it away from him, spilling marijuana throughout the stairwell. "Carol saw you at the river with some hippie guy…" Virginia waved the nearly empty bag of pot in the air. "*Kissing*," she hissed as though the act were the pinnacle of depravity.

"Is that a sin?" Ruby asked. "That's not how babies are made… or did you forget?"

Virginia chose to ignore the slight against her and Nick's muted love life. "Is that who you got the marijuana from?"

"No."

"*Ne breshai, mne.*"

"I'm not lying." Ruby looked to her father for support. "Dad, what's the big deal?"

Without looking at him, Virginia knew that he'd shrugged his shoulders and held up his hands in surrender. "It's your mom's… it's our rules, Luba," her dad said, using her Russian name. "No drugs, no drinking and no Angliki boys trying to… you know what."

Ruby groaned, dramatically rolled her eyes then glared mockingly at Virginia. "I've been following your stupid archaic rules since coming back from Russia. Christ, it's just some weed. It's not a gateway drug. I'm not onto cocaine next."

Ruby reached out and grabbed her backpack, yanked it from her mother's clutches, stunning Virginia with the aggressive gesture. "I *hate* it here," Ruby said loudly. "I can't wait until I'm old enough to move the hell away from you. You're turning into what Baba Mary was to you when *you* were a teenager… a Douk tyrant."

Without hesitation Virginia smacked her daughter hard across the face. Ruby's jaw dropped open as she placed her palm over her crimson cheek. Tears welled in her eyes.

"Jesus, Ginny, what the hell's gotten into you?" Nick stepped to Virginia's side and glared at her.

Virginia's heart sank, knowing she'd crossed a line. She was about to apologize when Ruby screamed, "Fuck you!" The shock of it—something Ruby had never done before—was like a smack to her own face.

Virginia spoke through clenched teeth. "Go to your room and do not emerge until I tell you to."

Still holding her cheek, Ruby turned and walked down the steps.

"And you can forget about your band practices for the next month," Virginia added.

Ruby stopped with her hand on the doorknob, hesitated, turned around and gave her mother the middle finger. She opened the door and slammed it hard behind her as she walked in.

Virginia shooed her husband away as he tried to follow her out to the garden. Once hidden in between rows of tall corn stalks, she wept freely. She'd railed against her own mother when she was Ruby's age. Up until Nick, her boyfriends were never Doukhobor enough, her skirts were too short, her love of secular music vulgar, her use of English in the home met with scorn, her teenage friendship with Sharon heavily frowned upon. But she'd never sworn at her mother or lashed out aggressively or implied that she'd hated her.

Softly, under her breath Virginia began to utter, *Doukhoborits Tot* (What Is a Doukhobor?), for prayer had always brought her back to understanding, to holiness, hadn't it? Whenever she recited the words that her ancestors had recited for centuries, those words came alive inside her like scurrying T cells battling infection. They became powerful, forward-moving blessings that enabled her to add to her moral tower, to feed her sacred engine, to allow her passage through heaven and Earth where she could commune with the divine, always leaving her feeling cleansed and delicate afterward.

She emerged from the corn rows nodding, satisfied with the punishment dealt to Ruby, clinging to the belief that through atonement her daughter would eventually see the error of her ways.

Slocan Valley, British Columbia, September 1996

Jonah was at his new school, standing at the bathroom mirror obsessing over his hair in a bid to try to mentally calm his stomach before first class. He thought the ten-minute bike ride from Shore-acres would do it. Or that morning's sesh on the scrap plywood quarter-pipe he'd nailed together in the carport—practice for the upcoming competition in Nelson. He re-envisioned his imaginary girlfriend, Phoebe Cates, revealing her boobs to Judge Reinhold in the swimming pool scene of *Fast Times at Ridgemont High*, which he'd watched the night before on the little black and white TV in his little room. But none of it had calmed him, because Jonah knew at some point he'd be running into Ruby Samarodin. A neighbourhood skater named Ferdy had told him that unless wild child Ruby was being sent to private school after all, she would be at Mount Sentinel for grade eleven. Also, Ferdy let it be known, Ruby was the singer in a cool band called Jet Poison and looked like Patricia Arquette in *True Romance* except with longer hair. Jonah already had a boner.

He ran his fingers back along his scalp, tousled his mane. He splashed water over his pimpled forehead, down his skinny face and looked himself in the eyes. "It's all cool," he said to his reflection. "You're a city boy, these Kootenay hicks don't know what's up." He stepped back from the mirror and with eyes still fixed on himself, threw a combo of left and right hooks and delivered a flurry of quick uppercuts. "Besides," he continued, "no one…" Right hook, left jab. "Not even a grade twelver… " Right jab, left uppercut. "Is gonna mess with me."

"You sure about that, Karate Kid?" A voice said over a flushing toilet from the farthest stall.

Jonah spun around as the stall door flung open and a tall, gangly boy with a bleached-blond mohawk walked out clasping a skateboard under his left arm. He wore a Skull Skates t-shirt and the same baggy faded jeans as Jonah. He dropped his skateboard in front of Jonah and carefully zipped up his fly.

"Got my dick caught once when I was eight. Ever zip up your pecker?"

Jonah shook his head.

"Cedar," he said, offering his fist to Jonah.

Jonah fist-bumped him back. "Jonah."

"My buddy Ferdy said you skate."

"Rides a Powell-Peralta?" Jonah asked.

"That's him. Meet us out back by the auto shop at lunch. Got a doobie for us."

"Uh... sure."

"You *do* blaze don't-cha?"

"Of course," Jonah said. Cedar spiked his mohawk in the mirror, then kicked his skateboard's tail, popping it up into his left hand. He gave his back wheels a spin then strode out of the bathroom as cool as if he were Danny Way himself.

In the hallway a tingling sensation formed in Jonah's groin. He recognized the sensation: excitement mixed with anxiety. The tingle rose into his stomach, then further up it poked at his heart, causing it to beat faster. He usually wasn't this nervous in *any* situation, let alone standing in a school hallway. The bell rang. He gave his head a shake as he walked toward class. When he got there a girl—much taller than him—was holding a door open. She was looking away from Jonah, waiting for a man-sized boy approaching from down the hall. Jonah's heart began beating faster. The more he thought about how fast his heart was beating, the faster it beat. It beat so fast he thought he might die. In a matter of seconds, he was sweating profusely. He suddenly had to crap. He turned the opposite direction, clenched his butt, slapped himself across the face, then wiped the sweat from his brow. He spun back toward the girl. Nothing about her seemed familiar except for her long blonde hair. And yet... Jonah was sure it was Ruby.

Ruby was holding the classroom door open for Dallas, the backwards ball cap–wearing hockey star she despised. His biceps, big as softballs, spilled out of his t-shirt, on the front of which was a feisty Yosemite Sam character wielding a hockey stick. But Ruby couldn't have been more pleased to be holding the door for him. She'd bargained with her parents—her mother really—to please, for the love of God, not send her to a private school; promising them straight As, no more partying of any type, and an earnest attempt to try find a good Doukhobor boy to date.

Ruby heard someone approaching from behind her and turned around to see a cute boy with long hair eyeing her up and down. Must be a new kid, she thought. He stepped closer to her, leaned in slightly and sniffed. She frowned, puckered her face and drew her head back. Weirdo. She turned back to Dallas shuffling up to her. "You're welcome, Dallas."

"Such a gentleman you are. Say my name again," Dallas said. "I can't get enough of your sexy Demi Moore voice."

Ruby rolled her eyes.

"And I see you're dressed for... success," he snickered.

Ruby gave herself the once-over: black Doc Martens, a jean skirt that hung just above the knees of her long legs, a fluorescent-pink t-shirt that poked from underneath a black cardigan: an ensemble that mercifully distinguished her from all the unexceptional girls at school. She offered Dallas her middle finger.

"Why don't you take a picture, it'll last longer, faggot," Dallas said to the new boy still standing behind Ruby. Dallas towered above both of them. Ruby turned to face the new kid again. He stared up at the jock and smirked. Dallas glowered down at him as if he were a sub-human species best suited for kicking around. The new kid quickly glanced at Ruby. Those eyes. She squinted and stared at him.

"Hey." He smiled.

"What are you smiling at, loser?" Dallas said.

"I'm smiling at... Fuck. You," the new kid said calmly.

Dallas's jaw clenched as though he were imagining chewing him apart. Ruby smiled back at the new boy, who was now grinning ear to ear.

"You're dead meat ya little prick," Dallas seethed.

"Chillaaax," Ruby said to him. The cute new boy was a good foot shorter than Dallas. She admired him for standing up to the jock. Few kids at school ever did, considering he practically lived in the gym.

"Ladies and gentlemen of the doorway," Mr. Swetlikoff's voice bellowed from the far end of the classroom, "stop admiring each other's summer fashion purchases and come in and take your seats please." Dallas did as he was told.

The new kid stared into Ruby's eyes, then said, "Still tempting boys... or girls... to strip naked for you in your tree fort, Ruby?" He wore a broad, glinting grin.

Ruby dropped her jaw ever so slightly and smiled. As if. "Jonah?"

Jonah sat four seats behind Ruby and one row to the left, staring at her as though she were on fire and only his longing could extinguish the flames. Distantly he registered the faint staccato of a summer squall showering the classroom windows, and the spitball that splatted on the back of his head, no doubt courtesy of Dallas the hockey jock. Whatever. None of it mattered. Jonah shifted in his seat and continued staring at Ruby the way only a teenage boy could stare at someone he suddenly longed for: slack-jawed and feverish, as if that person alone held the key to a boy's life-long happiness.

Mr. Swetlikoff droned on about how modern sewage systems and the invention of cement was all thanks to the Roman Empire, while the chubby boy sitting in front of Jonah twisted in his seat and glared at him for presumably being the source of the spitballs that peppered him as well. None of it mattered, none of it existed. What did exist was Ruby's long, neon-blonde hair, how it splayed over her broad shoulders and fell down the middle of her back, a lock of it dangling over her chair's backrest. And her pencil rotating in between the thumb and forefinger of her hand. Those things existed. And both her legs lightly bouncing on the balls of her Doc Martens. And how she bit the corner of her bottom lip when she turned her head just the right amount for Jonah to notice her pretending to look at something of interest out the window. Only once did Ruby look over her shoulder, amused when she caught Jonah staring. He'd blushed and quickly turned away, pretended to take notes.

He thought now of that summer with Ruby, when they were both six. It was quite possibly the best year of his life; his parents still together, he and Julian running wild and free in the outdoors, watching Saturday morning cartoons, all his meals cooked for him, hanging in Ruby's tree fort. Not a trouble in the world. It'd been a decade since Jonah last saw Ruby. It might as well have been a lifetime ago. What could a sixteen-year-old possibly have in common with his six-year-old self? Zits speckled Jonah's face now. Muscles had formed where before there was just plywood flatness. The first pubic hairs of manhood sprouted from his balls. Grunge music made his brown hair bangin'—long, messy and usually tucked under a Skull Skates ball cap. Skateboarding ruled his life. And Ruby? Holy wow, Jonah thought. She was hotter than he could've ever imagined. A full-grown, fully developed, fully gorgeous babe.

As Mr. Swetlikoff, the spitballs and everyone in the classroom except for Ruby faded into white noise it dawned on Jonah that she'd been with him all along, living in a secret attic bedroom at the top of a set of stairs, next to his heart. Throughout his childhood, months and eventually years would drift by without thinking of her. But once in a while if he was bummed about school bullies, or his mother's weight battles or her shitty boyfriends, he'd think about that final summer he'd spent with Ruby in her tree fort: singing and dancing with her, eating piles of junk food, curled up next to her, the chirp of crickets lulling them to sleep. The spark that was ignited at Shoreacres Beach as they made sandcastles, and was enflamed during those sleepovers, had been dormant for years. But now, like a buried World War II land mine unwittingly stepped on, it blew Jonah's chest clear open. It sent his heart running the moment he stepped up to Ruby in the classroom doorway and realized that it was her. Just like that, he realized, Jonah Seeger was in love with Ruby Samarodin.

By the end of the 1950s, over two hundred children aged seven to fifteen have been incarcerated in New Denver, British Columbia, because of their parents' refusal to send them to public school. During RCMP raids of Freedomite villages, terrified children futilely hide in crawl spaces, hay lofts, washing machines and even cemeteries. At New Denver they are denied their language and culture. Some suffer mental, physical and sexual abuse. Parents are allowed one-hour bimonthly visits through a chain-link fence while half a dozen RCMP officers look on.

In a May 11, 1957 Maclean's *magazine interview, New Denver school superintendent John Clarkson says that being separated from their children does not bother Freedomite parents because "they're not like us." His matron at the school, Frances Sinclair, adds, "If the kids never saw their parents at all, they'd be a happy band of children."*

On August 2, 1959, after Freedomite mothers sign an agreement to send their kids to public school, the final seventy-seven children are released from New Denver.

Slocan Valley, British Columbia, February 1997

Ruby pinched the little baggie of cocaine and flapped it in the air. "Ladies?" The chipped black polish of her fingernails was on full display. Maybe she'd touch them up later.

On the stereo, PJ Harvey implored a boy named Billy to come back to his lover's bed. Ruby stood amongst swap-ready clothes splayed all over the carpet of her bedroom. Hole, Nirvana, the Smashing Pumpkins and Bikini Kill posed with attitude, staring at Ruby and her friends from the posters that hung on her walls. Purple velvet curtains hanging over the basement window blacked out the snow falling over the backyard.

Nadya fussed with her new choppy bob haircut while she talked to a boy on the phone. She cupped the receiver, shrugged at Ruby's coke offer… then scrunched her nose, shook her head and resumed her conversation. Bobbie was in an electric-pink bra and underwear that matched the colour of her hair, selecting clothes from Ruby's sizeable closet. Ruby didn't mind. Bobbie's mom only worked part time so most of her decent clothes she had "borrowed" from Ruby. Bobbie glanced back at her. "Where'd you get that?"

"Where else? Swanny," Ruby said.

Bobbie fully turned to Ruby, her ponytail bouncing as she did. She bent down and fished a baggie full of pink pills from her jeans lying at her feet. "Baby brought the E.'"

Ruby looked down at Delia sitting on the floor against Ruby's bed, going through a pile of CDs. Delia looked up. "I'll stick with these." She rattled the twelve-pack of Smirnoff Ice her brother had bootlegged for them, then held up a No Doubt CD. "Can we put on something more lively?"

"Give 'er," Ruby said. Fine, she thought, cocaine was still pretty taboo amongst her friends. She had no problem doing a line in the bathroom by herself before the evening kicked off. She'd just have to make sure she scrubbed the sink and counter with Ajax before her parents returned from their dinner party.

Nadya hung up the phone, sat down in front of the glass-topped coffee table and started sprinkling marijuana into a rolling paper. "Bitch, you doing that shit every weekend now or what?" she asked Ruby.

Ruby tucked the baggie of coke back into her jeans. "No," she said defensively, then lied, "I've had it for weeks." Having coke felt sophisticated, like what people in a big city would always have on them. She knelt down beside Nadya and rifled through a pile of clothes laying in the middle of her room. Delia adjusted the volume on the stereo. Gwen Stefani started singing about taking a pink ribbon off her eyes and being exposed. "So, where we going?" Ruby asked Nadya.

Nadya rolled the joint, then licked the length of it to seal the paper together. "Looks like Cedar and Jonah and the guys are going to the Boiler Room."

"Thank god," Ruby said. Since spending the Christmas holidays with her brother in Toronto—shopping on Queen Street West, going to U of T parties with Alan and his girlfriend, eating delicious foreign food in Kensington Market—the Kootenays, and especially the Slocan Valley, were sucking big time. The Boiler Room, the only decent night club in Nelson, would have to do.

"Any takers?" Ruby said holding up a t-shirt.

"You're giving away your Bikini Kill tour tee?" Nadya blew smoke rings and passed the joint to Ruby.

Ruby cupped her breasts. "They won't stop growing and it's too tight on me now. Tired of the hallway catcalls, and gross old Mr. Lewinski drooling over me in economics class."

"Dibs." Bobbie snatched the shirt from Ruby and slipped it on.

"No bitching at me two days from now," Ruby said, "because the lettering on the front of the shirt is all stretched and wonky." Ruby took a toke then passed the joint to Bobbie.

Bobbie looked down and patted her chest. "Give me a set like yours and I'd handle the attention, nooo prob."

Sure, Ruby thought. But not if Bobbie had been getting unwanted attention since she was twelve when her breasts first appeared. She initially noticed it when her dad took her to the mill one day and his gross co-worker kept ogling her. Then at fourteen, wearing a bikini at Crescent Beach, a group of grade twelve boys purposely kicked sand at her so she'd need to wash herself off in the river. There was Peter the Russian creep in Moscow who copped a feel. And the one time she decided to get a gym membership, the muscled jocks gave her unsolicited pointers about sets and reps, sweating overtop her as they showed her how to lift properly. It was suffocating to smile and thank them, to not ask them to stop or complain to management because she didn't want to seem like a bitch. Sure, if Ruby could pick and choose who drooled over her it'd be fine; tall, swarthy Ward Jackson in PE class, Swanny the odd time she did see him, and Jonah… but not every day like he'd been doing since they'd started hanging out six months earlier.

Ruby pulled a short denim skirt from the pile, turned it in her hands. Some days she couldn't figure out whether to say, "Screw it," and dress how she really felt—like a Riot Grrrl in a black baby doll dress, torn fishnet stockings and combat boots. Or should she get all costumed for attention in a tight t-shirt and miniskirt because that's what passed for attractive in small towns? Or should she dress down in baggy jeans and a prudently frumpy sweater because she *didn't* want any of the sidelong glances she'd otherwise receive from insecure peers and puritanical adults?

"Ugh, every single guy gets fixated on my big, round ass." Nadya gave her bum a good smack.

Ruby smacked Nadya's ass too which produced a squeal from her. She motioned for Delia to pass her a Smirnoff Ice. "Why are guys so fixated on looks anyway?" she said. "Like, a perfectly symmetrical face."

Delia lifted her t-shirt and pinched her squishy belly. "Allison loves it." She slipped out of her jeans. "Being with girls is *sooo* much easier." She pointed to Ruby. "Pass me that black dress."

"We're just a far more advanced species, right?" Nadya said.

"Hells yeah we are." Ruby took a sip of her drink. "For one, we bleed. We're tough. It's biology."

"True," Delia said, slipping into the black dress. "Whereas the boys? They bleed because of stupidity." The girls laughed.

"I love a guy with big knuckles, and a sharp jaw line." Nadya held up her empty bottle and waved it at Delia.

"Personally, I think it's the hottest when a girl can teach me things." Delia passed a Smirnoff Ice to Nadya.

"Give 'em to me tall, dark and handsome. Sorry ladies, I'm a traditionalist," Bobbie said.

"I like a confident guy who can make me laugh," Ruby said. "He's got to have interests beyond sports and video games. Got to be smart, worldly, you know?" Ruby picked up a lighter from the coffee table, lit the joint that had gone out. "*And* he's gotta be a bit of a bad boy." Ruby exhaled and woody, skunky smoke wafted through her bedroom.

"Ah, that's why you hang with that older biker dude," Bobbie said.

Nadya took the joint from Ruby. "Come on, Rube, Swanny's hot but I still think he's *way* too old for you.

"Wait, have you done it yet?" Bobbie asked. "Or are you still the big *V* amongst us." She quickly pointed to Delia. "Sorry Dee, lesbian sex doesn't count." Delia flipped Bobbie the bird.

"We've... almost done it?" Ruby said.

"Girl, this isn't the 1950s," Bobbie said, "you need to get some vitamin D-I-C-K in you."

Ruby squealed and blushed. After the girls stopped laughing, Delia said, "How about Jonah? He ticks a bunch of your boxes. And you guys have been like, hanging out at least once a week since he first drooled over you. Plus, he's Doukhobor."

"Half-Doukhobor," Nadya said.

"And from the wrong side of the tracks," Ruby added. "Doesn't give two shits about his heritage. Plus, I don't know, my mom and baba don't have anything good to say about Jonah's family, so... I don't know."

"So what?" Delia said. "You guys are great together. Who cares if he's not as tall as what's-his-name from PE class, or as *dangerous* as Swanny. Or a perfect Doukhobor, if there even is such a thing. Jonah treats you like gold, and that's way more important. At least it should be."

"Two weekends ago he chose to play D&D and PlayStation with Cedar and Ferdy and his skate crew instead of hanging with me," Ruby said.

"I'd be sketched about hanging here too," Nadya said, "if Virginia didn't like me and your mountain of a dad barely acknowledged my existence."

"And you *still* haven't made him a mixtape after he made you two," Bobbie said.

"Remember at my place, he showed you his sweet kung fu moves and all you did was yawn?" Nadya said. "Could be why he's been taking little digs at you lately."

"Blue balls," Bobbie said, laughing. "He loves you and you're just teasing the fuck out of him. Don't you have the hots for him even a little bit?"

"It's gotta go deeper than just horniness, Bobbie," Ruby said.

"Wouldn't it be the biggest *F*-you to Virginia," Nadya said, "if you started dating a dude who came from a Sons of Freedom family and who lives in a trailer with his mom who used to be friends with your mom?"

Ruby had never considered it. But Nadya was right. Virginia would be deliciously livid. "While that's a valid point, it's not the sole reason to jump Jonah's bones."

Bobbie snickered. "How about popping your cherry? Valid enough of a point?"

Ruby winced. "There's just one problem. A few weeks ago, I *may* have told him he was like a brother to me."

The girls all made sour faces and collectively said, "Ooooh shit."

Nadya shook her head and flipped her palms up. "Why would you say that?"

Because he's too into me, Ruby thought. Because he's kinda geeky sometimes. Because I feel more than just lust for him. "Because… I don't know why."

"Do you love him?" Delia asked.

Ruby jerked her head back. "No… No. I… Er, I mean, I… want something better than just having sex with him."

"How would you know?" Bobbie said. "Gotta get laid first to know if you even like him."

Ruby traced her forefinger over lips. "Pretty sure he's a virgin too."

"It's settled then." Nadya stood up and raised her Smirnoff Ice. Ruby, Bobbie and Delia stood up too. "You're going to pop mutual cherries with Jonah Seeger." Ruby blushed and giggled. The girls clinked their drinks together.

"Then make him your boyfriend and royally piss off your mom in the process," Delia said.

"We'll see. No promises," Ruby said, even though she was damned well determined to get the deed done with. No way she was going to be last virgin standing amongst her peers.

Slocan Valley, British Columbia, April 1997

"You ever..." Ruby's eyebrows peaked at their limit. "...Done it before?"

Jonah rubbed his knuckles. "Of course I have. Plenty. Back in Kelowna." Even as the words tripped out of his mouth Jonah knew by the way Ruby squinted at him that she could tell he was lying.

They were sitting on Ruby's bed—gigantic compared to his own—drinking cans of Nelson beer. The Fugees' "Killing Me Softly with His Song" played on her portable CD player that was tucked into a lower ledge of a bookshelf towering next to the bed.

Ruby hadn't seen Jonah for weeks. She'd stepped way back, focused on her songwriting and rehearsals with her band for an upcoming wedding gig. She cooled it with Swanny too. Her friends were right; he was too old for her. And what was a supposedly good Doukhobor girl like her doing with a biker anyway? If Virginia had found out that Ruby had continued to hang out with Swanny she'd have grounded her for life. At school Ruby tried to imagine herself with anyone other than Jonah. But they were all too boring, too into partying, not into partying enough. Too into hockey, too into playing video games, too Doukhobor, too redneck, too rich, too hippie-dippie. They smoked too many cigarettes, had bad taste in music or a terrible sense of style. Too fake, too macho, too feminine. In the end she always came back to Jonah. Plus, she was lonely. Would he ever stop looking at her like she was the last girl left on Earth, though? Did she want him to? Would he be a good kisser? A good lover? Whatever *that* meant. Her only gauge had been Swanny and what friends had said, if they were even telling the truth in the first place.

Earlier that day, just before last class, Ruby left a note for Jonah tucked into the vents of his locker.

JRS.

My parents are in Grand Forks to check on my Baba Mary (broke her hip). Come over at eight. I miss you.

xo Ruby

When she'd opened the front door at exactly eight p.m., Jonah stood there grinning like an idiot. A really cute idiot. He seemed to have grown an inch too since they last hung out. Miraculously he'd washed and combed his hair. Like her Baba Mary would sometimes say, "The fish had whistled on the mountainside." And even more miraculously he was without his skateboard. That banged up thing went everywhere with him. He'd worn perfectly broken-in combat boots, new faded jeans, a black and red plaid shirt, and what must've been his brother's black leather jacket.

The first thing Jonah had noticed was Ruby wearing red lipstick, which he'd never seen on her before. And he'd never seen her in a dress quite like the one she was wearing. It was black and fell to just above her knees. The type Winona Ryder wore, with pink and grey flowers, in that movie he forgot the name of. She stood barefoot, smiling back at him. When he walked up her driveway, Jonah had been wondering why Ruby had been avoiding him. But he knew why. Ever since he'd been friend-zoned, he'd been a dick to her. It didn't help either that he'd been losing a fresh battle with acne, and that every time they hung out, he'd crush on her like a puppy. She could probably always smell how much he wanted her. And now, standing there, admiring Ruby in her dress, he was reminded that she was light years away, galaxies away from any other girl he'd ever known. Always would be. She was his type. She was, in fact, the blueprint for his type: witty, smart, wild, devastatingly beautiful and a freak in the best way. He didn't care at all that she outsized him. She was everything he wasn't, too: from a solid family who lived in a big house and were proud of their Doukhobor roots. Ruby was perfect and Jonah was determined to keep punching above his weight class.

"You okay?" She asked. Jonah had been standing there with his mouth open, staring at her in awe as though she were Wonder Woman fresh from battle.

Jonah blinked and gave his head a shake. "Sorry, yeah, uh this is for you." He produced a book from behind his back. "*Shampoo Planet* by Douglas Coupland. Guy that wrote *Generation X*. Julian recommended it, said it was good."

"Thank you." Ruby bounced on the balls of her feet.

"Also, you look ... uh, totally amazing," Jonah said.

Ruby's cheeks suddenly warmed. "You too. Love the boots. You look ... you look hot."

Jonah's world tilted on its axis.

They hugged each other longer than usual. To Jonah she smelled of fresh flowers after a rainstorm. To Ruby, Jonah smelled like Jonah: woody, a little sweet like the first day of spring, a hint of salty man. She led him by the hand into the house.

Now there they were, on her bed, Ruby sitting cross-legged, Jonah next to her, stretched out, propped up on one elbow. She knew even before asking that he was a virgin. High school kids talk after all. Plus, she could tell; she almost still felt like a virgin herself.

She and Swanny had done it a month earlier, in March. Jonah was being a jerk; she'd had enough chiding from Bobbie. She just wanted it over with, and Swanny was there. A night of coke and vodka had built up her courage enough to do it. She wished now that she hadn't. Swanny was sweet enough about it. But during the first attempt on the thin mattress in his van she'd laughed so nervously and awkwardly that she laughed him right out of her vagina. After more liquid courage they went for round two. Swanny was drunk by then, calling her a dirty girl over and over for some reason. Was it supposed to be that rough? Like a train being forced into a tunnel made only for cars? Afterward she kept thinking, what *was* that? It was like some of her friends said it would be, and not like she'd imagined it should be based on the rom-coms she'd watched. She didn't really enjoy it. She knew that much. And now, there on her bed with Jonah, it would be like the blind-in-one-eye leading the blind.

In the background Lauryn Hill sang about someone strumming her pain with his fingers. An empty six-pack was scattered across the bed. The roach of a joint still smouldered in a glass ashtray sitting between Jonah and Ruby.

"How about you?" Jonah asked. "Did you and… Swanny do it?" He laughed nervously.

Ruby leaned over and punched him in the arm. "I don't kiss and tell," she said coyly.

Well, that answers that, Jonah thought. He could feel himself starting to sweat. He swallowed hard, wished they had more beer. Wished he wasn't a virgin.

"Are you mad at me?" she asked.

"For what?" For losing your virginity with… not me? he thought.

"For avoiding you the last few weeks," Ruby said.

"I'm sorry…" Jonah looked away from Ruby. "I just… really like you, always have and… when you put me in the friend zone… I just didn't know how to react. I was a royal ass."

"You kinda were but… no biggie." Ruby looked down at her hands. "I was being a freakazoid and needed time to figure some stuff out."

Jonah sat up now, moved closer to Ruby, crossed his legs. "And? What did the freakazoid figure out?"

Ruby looked up. "That I missed you… a lot." She fearlessly stared into Jonah's eyes.

Jonah froze. He wanted to look away but fought hard not to. Ruby usually wasn't one for mushiness. He knew he had good timing when it came to sticking a Frontside Air. And he knew exactly when to pull the trigger when hunting out in the woods. But when it came to girls, he always seemed a millimetre off. He didn't read the signs, or would make a move a minute too late, or in the case of Ruby, be too scared to make a move at all. Not this time, Jonah thought. Not going to screw this one up. He took a breath and leaned into her. To his surprise... she didn't back away.

Ruby parted her lips and their tongues met. A shudder ran through both of them.

They'd known each other since they were six years old, Jonah thought, and *finally* they were kissing.

Whenever Ruby had imagined what it would be like to kiss Jonah, never did she think it would feel like this. He was actually a *good* kisser. Better than Swanny who'd had plenty of practice. Where Swanny grabbed her by her hair and shoved his tongue down her throat in a bid to swallow hers, Jonah was slow and searching, allowing the electricity to spark naturally. He gently bit and pulled her lips, his hand gripping her jaw. Her heart raced as though she'd just sprinted a mile... or done a line of coke.

Jonah felt like the first time he'd gone hunting, the buck fever messing with everything—tight chest, adrenalin spiking. Beads of sweat trickled down his forehead even as they kept kissing. Save for a soft moan, Ruby was silent. Was she being timid, Jonah wondered? His blood surged even more.

Ruby wondered if Jonah was mistaking her stillness for insecurity.

Jonah tried unbuttoning Ruby's dress but all of a sudden it was as if he was wearing mittens. She continued the unbuttoning. He pulled the dress down over her shoulders. "Is that okay?" he asked.

Did he just ask that? Ruby melted. Her heart easily surrendered. It felt light, as though doors had opened in it letting a fresh, soothing breeze flow through. She bit her bottom lip, nodded, then undid her bra and let it fall.

Jonah slipped her dress all the way off. He would've been lying if he'd said he hadn't imagined Ruby's magnificent nakedness on dozens and dozens of occasions. He was definitely, not in a million years, absolutely *not* disappointed. He lifted his shirt over his head, then frantically pulled his jeans off. No time to worry about the socks.

Ruby leaned across her bed and clicked off a lamp on her nightstand. Candles on her dresser were all that illuminated the room now.

In one efficient sweep of his arm, Jonah cleared the beer cans and ashtray off the bed. Ruby giggled as the items tumbled onto her carpet with a clatter. This time Ruby moved in to kiss Jonah, then pushed him back and down onto the pillows. They both frantically slid their underwear off. Jonah stared up at Ruby who was straddling him now. She leaned down, pressed her warm breasts against his pounding chest. They both breathed hard as they kissed. Jonah grabbed himself and tried to guide himself into Ruby, but she let out a quick yelp, backed away from the kiss and looked at Jonah with wide eyes.

He froze.

Ruby had curled her lips in and was biting them, smiling, a twinkle in her eye. "Wrong door, babe." She giggled. Even in the dim light she could tell Jonah flushed red.

He laughed nervously. "But... bum sex is all the rage these days."

Ruby slapped him playfully, then slowly guided him into her. They clasped hands, each gripping with strength like rock climbers scaling a cliff face...

Very soon afterwards, they lay under Ruby's covers, both their heads on one pillow. She lit a freshly rolled joint, inhaled and passed it to Jonah.

"I'm... I'm sorry it didn't last so long..." he said. "It's just, you're so hot and I've wanted this for..."

Ruby placed her finger over Jonah's lips. "It was perfect." For the first time in Ruby's life, she felt that it was possible there was a soulmate for her, that another person could be the missing part of her that she didn't even realize she'd been searching for.

Jonah toked on the joint, inhaled deeply, then blew the smoke out. It *was* perfect. He'd never felt anything quite like it. Never in a million years had he thought such a bond with another person was possible.

Throughout the night, in between making love, Jonah and Ruby smoked joints, repeatedly raided the meagre Samarodin liquor cabinet and excitedly talked about a future together. That summer they decided they would camp at Troup Beach on Kootenay Lake, and

Bannock Point on Slocan Lake; they'd secretly plant some marijuana seeds in between tomato rows in Virginia's garden just to confuse and irritate her; they'd road trip to the Gorge Amphitheatre for Lollapalooza, and from there maybe even drive down the Oregon coast to the California Redwoods. Jonah would enter and win skate competitions throughout British Columbia and Ruby would be there to cheer him on; Ruby would play as many shows with Jet Poison as possible and Jonah would be there to cheer *her* on. Whatever they chose to do, they decided they'd do it together, because they were young, wild and free; teenagers without a care in the world.

A sixteen-year-old Sons of Freedom boy is killed and four accomplices are badly injured on February 16, 1962, en route to destroy a government facility in Castlegar, British Columbia. A bomb they're carrying accidentally explodes in their car as they drive down Columbia Avenue. The teenager is in the rear seat holding the bomb in his lap when it prematurely detonates, shattering windows of nearby houses and blowing the roof and doors off the 1958 Chevrolet.

Nearly six months later in Ootischenia, a village on the outskirts of Castlegar, a group of young men set twenty-six Doukhobor homes and buildings on fire in the middle of the night. Forty people narrowly escape injury or death in what is the single largest act of arson ever by the Sons of Freedom.

Slocan Valley, British Columbia, December 1997

Like everyone around the dinner table that evening, Virginia sat frozen, unable to say or do anything, watching Sharon with a look of horror as though Sharon had just doused herself in gasoline and was about to light a match. Except Jonah—he wasn't frozen. After calling Virginia's mother a cow, he bolted to standing, toppling his chair backward, and frantically searched for anything he could drape over his mother's shoulders.

Christmas dinner with Virginia's family and Sharon's family, a notion previously inconceivable to Virginia, had turned out to be the disaster she suspected it would be. But she never imagined to what extent. Ruby, damn her, had insisted, had threatened to move out, to live with Jonah in Sharon's trailer at Sharon's invitation, if overtures weren't offered to make Jonah feel welcome.

Earlier that evening when Virginia led Sharon, Sharon's mother, Polly, and Jonah's brother, Julian, through the house and into the gigantic, high-vaulted living room for pre-dinner cocktails, she tried not to but definitely did take a small amount of pride in the setting. A tall, majestic Christmas tree stood in the far corner, wound with a string of glowing lights. Underneath were heaps of presents. A flickering, crackling fire warmed the home from a stone hearth. Christmas music played on the stereo. Big Nick was kneeling in front of the sound system, leafing through records, while Virginia's parents sat on the enormous leather couch chatting in Russian with her clean-cut son, Alan, a successful lawyer home from Toronto. And unlike the trailer that Jonah and his mother lived in, the three-level, five-bedroom Casa Samarodin was full of modern furnishings and appliances, and when not imbued with the delicious aromas of fresh-baked bread, *pyrahi* frying in butter, and creamy, vegetarian borsch—as it was that night—Virginia's house was the precise scent of Pine-Sol, sterile and pathogen free.

Virginia knew that she and Nick had not made it easy for Ruby and Jonah. Over the past several months that they had been dating, Big Nick hadn't grunted more than a handful of words to Jonah. When Jonah offered to mow the lawn or shovel the snowy driveway, Nick would nod and bring out the appropriate tools for him. Virginia hadn't been much better. She forbade Jonah to sleep in Ruby's bedroom with her and preferred he didn't spend the night at all. When he and Ruby helped with weeding and harvesting in the garden, Virginia would occasionally ask about his mother. Beyond that, she paid Jonah little attention, except to suggest it was high time to learn a few words of Russian and even higher time for a haircut. When a month earlier Ruby had threatened to move out, Virginia agreed to their Christmas dinner plan, which, while well intentioned, Virginia knew to be naive and doomed from the get-go.

Introductions and greetings between the two families were cordial but terse. And in the case of Sharon's mother, Polly—a staunch and once militant Freedomite—and her own mother, Mary—proudly Doukhobor and fiercely anti-Sons of Freedom—the greeting was non-existent.

Virginia was genuinely happy that she'd get to reconnect with Sharon, and even though she'd heard from Ruby and others in the community that Sharon had gained weight, Virginia never would've imagined it would've been to such a worrisome extent.

Throughout their teenage friendship in the '60s, and whenever she'd seen Sharon in the subsequent decades, Virginia always thought Sharon to be well proportioned and pretty in a plain way. But as Sharon waddled into Casa Samarodin that snowy Christmas Eve, Virginia was flabbergasted at what she saw. Her old friend was now morbidly obese, her breathing laboured from the seemingly great effort of having climbed the seven front steps. And even though Sharon's hair was styled and shiny, and she'd opted for a chic, burgundy blouse and dress, which she complimented with golden hoop earrings, it was precisely this attempt to blunt her eating disorder with fashion sense that caused Virginia's former animosity toward her old friend to quickly evaporate.

Virginia had made sure to seat her parents as far from Sharon and Polly as possible, but it was futile; her mother's innuendos and insults crawled across the table anyway. Her blue-grey hair was freshly permed for the occasion; her hands were clasped together in front of her. She wore a cream polyester blouse and green cotton slacks. A tight smile constantly pulled at her lips. Virginia's father, God love him, sat as obediently as ever next to his wife, his belly threatening to pop the buttons on his dress shirt underneath his brown tweed suit.

In her thick Doukhobor accent, Virginia's mother first admonished Jonah for his long hair, his inability to speak a word of Russian and for spending too much time riding, as she called it, his skating board. Ruby's rebuttals of her boyfriend having good grades, being eager to help around the yard and winning skateboard competitions fell on deaf ears. Then, as Virginia had feared she would, her mother rerouted her disdain for Jonah onto Jonah's grandmother, who had entered the Samarodin home with head held high, moving with ease and grace, and at nearly seventy years old, still wearing her silver-streaked black hair youthfully long and braided.

By this point everyone, except Virginia's mother of course, had been enjoying festive drinks. Even Virginia had poured herself a second glass of wine in order to mitigate the growing tension. Sharon was the visible outlier. Having barely touched her plate of food and having polished off four glasses of expensive Burgundy, she was simultaneously growing more comfortable with herself and more agitated at the dinner conversation as time went on. Everyone was mid-sip when Virginia's mother spoke.

"Jonah?" she'd said in a forcibly sweet voice.

"Yesss?" he'd said tentatively.

"You hardly know your baba there beside you. Why's that?"

Oh, here it goes, Virginia had thought. Her chest tightened. She peered at Nick at the head of the table. Her husband met her eyes and offered her a knowing frown.

"More desert for anyone?" Virginia said, trying to deflect the conversation.

Jonah stammered. "Uh, I… I guess…" He'd trailed off. He leaned forward, grinning nervously, and looked to his mother.

"It's none of your business why, Baba," Ruby said. Ruby's grandmother was taken aback at her granddaughter's insolence.

"Ruby, mind your manners," Virginia said, then looked to her own mother. "Mom," she said sternly, "not tonight."

"It's just a simple question," her mother had said, folding her napkin more than she needed to. "I know my daughter and her children very well. It's how a good Doukhobor family should be, if you ask me."

Sharon had finally spoken up. "Well M-Mary, it's probably my fault," she said, her speech starting to slur. "I didn't stay in touch with Mom as much as… I could've over the years and—"

"Oh, I don't know, Sharon," Virginia's mother interrupted. "I think you had good reason to run away from the Svobodnik life. It must've been unbearable."

Ruby gulped down the last of what Virginia assumed to be vodka-spiked orange juice and slammed the glass onto the table, startling everyone. "Baba, please. It's Christmas dinner." She looked to her dyeda for help but Dyeda John, as usual, just shrugged and frowned.

"That was a long time ago, Mary," Sharon's mother said. "I made mistakes and—"

"Good of you to admit it," Virginia's mother interrupted at the exact moment the Christmas music went silent in the living room.

Jonah hiccupped. "I don't know what the big deal is. What's done is done. Right?"

"Hear hear." Ruby had lifted her empty glass in cheers.

"Well, you can make light of it all you want, you kids," Virginia's mother said. "You didn't have to live through those times. Guarding your house so—" She jabbed her finger in Polly's direction. "—lunatics don't come and burn it from under you." Dyeda John placed his hand on his wife's forearm to calm her.

"I don't think we need to be calling anyone a lunatic, Mary," Polly had said calmly. She looked unflinchingly into Mary's eyes. "And my daughter and I have since made amends..." They'd moved forward, she concluded in Russian: "*Mi prodvinulis vpered.*"

"Per-perhaps you should t-too," Sharon said to Virginia's mother as she downed her wine and gestured with her glass for someone, anyone, to pour her another.

An awkward smile crept over Jonah's lips; it looked to Virginia as though he couldn't quite believe what was happening, but was perversely interested in seeing how it all played out. Ruby tugged on his arm and shot daggers at him when he looked at her.

"See?" Virginia's mother pointed at Jonah. "He thinks it's somehow *funny*."

"No, no." Jonah waved the notion away. "Not funny as in ha-ha. I... I just think it's a little silly." Jonah exhaled heavily and shook his head.

Virginia's son, Alan, and Sharon's eldest, Julian, stood and retreated to the kitchen.

"Can we please change the subject?" Big Nick said calmly in his deep voice. He got up and walked to the stereo.

Virginia's mother pointed at Polly while looking at Jonah. "What she and her cronies did to our community, is *greshniy*, it's sinful." She wagged her finger in the air as a preacher would, then glared at Polly. "Especially Yuri, that, that deviant, queer, devil son of yours. Me and John lost *everything* when he burned our house down."

"Baba!" Ruby had raised her voice.

"Jesus." Jonah turned to his mother. "Uncle Yuri burned down Ruby's grandparents' house?"

Virginia's father finally spoke up. "That *was* over thirty years ago, Masha," he said to his wife. "And we had home insurance, dear."

With great effort Sharon had stood up, her chair toppling backward as she did. Ignoring the clatter, she adjusted her glasses and laughed. "I think ratting on our family to the media and authorities made up for that."

Ruby turned to Jonah and whispered, "That's not fair is it? Your uncle burns my grandparent's house down, they go to the cops, and your mom says they *ratted* on your family?"

Jonah did nothing more than frown and shrug in response.

Virginia stood up, her chair scraping across the hardwood floor. "*Gospodi,*" she'd said, exasperated. "Can we all just stop? Please? No one's a devil and no one's a rat." Virginia sat back down in a huff and downed her wine in one gulp.

From the living room came the sounds of Bing Crosby and David Bowie's duet of "Little Drummer Boy."

Virginia watched her mother press her lips together tightly. She examined herself, adjusted her blouse, then looked up, pointed at Polly and Sharon and announced to the room, "Once a Svobodnik always a Svobodnik, in my books."

Sharon wobbled, steadied herself on the table then seemed to examine what she was wearing. Virginia noticed tears had welled in her eyes. "Why... why hang on to all this, this, this ssstrife?" Sharon slurred.

"Because the past is always just an eyelash away," Virginia's mother had said, wagging her finger in the air.

"Oh, Jesus, Baba, we're all Doukhobors here. Why can't you see that?" Ruby said.

"Uh, no we're not." Jonah pointed at himself. "I mean, I'm certainly no Douk." Ruby kicked Jonah hard under the table. "Ow." He flinched and looked at her with confusion.

"How many times have I told you not to say *Douk*? It's derogatory," Ruby said.

Virginia, Big Nick, Baba Mary and Dyeda John nodded in agreement.

"But I'm *not* a Doukhobor," Jonah had continued. He eyed Baba Mary. "Especially if it means being a judgmental *cow* and thinking you're better than everyone else."

Ruby had smacked Jonah across the back of the head and then sat frozen, watching as Sharon began doing something so shocking that time froze, and a deafening silence descended on the entire house.

Sharon positioned her fingers on the top button of her blouse, tears rolling down her cheeks as the delicious alcohol coursed through her veins. She didn't know what exactly she would do or why, except that maybe it would be a tiny act of anarchy against Virginia and her clan. A pathetic act or a righteous one, she knew not.

She peered at Virginia who had just finished her glass of wine and was staring at Sharon as though she'd just shape-shifted into a wild boar or an ogre. It was easy to see where Virginia got her loyalty to Doukhoborism from, Sharon thought, her air of piety, her goody two-shoes routine. Her mother, Mary Kalesnikoff, was like so many of that generation: desperately clinging to an ideal of what it meant to be a Doukhobor, unable to surrender to or be open to change. As if their stubbornness and crotchetiness alone could right the rusted, listing ship that was Doukhoborism. But, even if Mary reminded Sharon of the closest thing Doukhobors had to clergy, up until that evening she'd still managed to hold on to some admiration for the woman. Which, over the decades, Sharon had struggled to feel for her own mother. Sharon had mostly forgiven Polly for all the bonkers Sons of Freedom lifestyle choices she'd made, had slowly been growing closer, but still, the wounds were there. And those wounds would tear open a little every now and then.

Sharon had invited her mother to join them for Christmas, their first one together in three years. Roy's parents were long gone, and Jonah had only met his grandma Polly twice before, both times when he was very young. Two days later her mother made the three-hour journey from Creston. That afternoon while Julian and Jonah were shovelling snow off the mobile home's roof, Sharon and her mother had rehashed familiar, frustrating territory. Everyone in the Kootenays seemed to know everyone else's business when it came to the tight-knit Doukhobor community, so when word spread to Creston that Polly's grandson Jonah had been getting into fights in Kelowna and was en route to juvenile delinquency had the family not moved back to the Kootenays, Sharon's mother couldn't resist getting into it.

Sharon scoffed as she handed her mom a cup of coffee. "Ah, you're one to talk about violence."

"No one died, Sharon," her mother said flatly. "What we did, sure it was a little ... misguided, but—"

Sharon laughed at her mom having the audacity to preface her actions with *a little*.

"But we did it in the name of God," her mother continued. "You know that. What Jonah was doing in Kelowna, trying to fix his problems with his fists, injuring people, that is not our way."

"Ach, go on." Sharon backhanded the air. "Not this again. Yes, Jonah was wrong to hurt people, but he was standing up to bullies and—"

"Just like we Svobodniki were. The government, the police, the—"

"Your own people?" Sharon raised her voice. "Were they bullies, too, that you were standing up against? Just because they wanted to live like regular Canadians? No, you were nothing but *razboyniki*."

"Really, Sharon," her mother said, "hoodlums?"

"Absolutely. I've said it a million times and I'll say it again, what you and Dad, Yuri, Uncle Fred, the Harshenins and Perepolkins, what you all did, every single one of you, was *terrorize* in the name of God. Nothing less. And that caused a lot of harm to a lot of people."

Sharon's mother looked down into her coffee. In the ensuing silence came the sound of shovels scraping the roof. Polly took a sip of coffee, stared into it some more.

Finally, she said quietly, "We never meant to hurt anyone."

"But you did, Mother. You hurt me." Sharon lay her palm over her heart. "A child can't comprehend why you did the things you did." She lifted her scarred left hand to show her. "And then we paid the price in New Denver. And Yuri?" Sharon looked sidelong at her mother, shook her head. "*Ohn byl ozhasen*, just terrible. Why do you think a whole generation of us ran away from the Kootenays?"

"We were caught up in the times," her mother pleaded. "It was the '60s."

"The '60s were about peace, love and happiness. The Sons of Freedom sure as hell were not. You were caught up in *madness*. Just like those Muslim terrorists today."

"*Och*, Sharon, you can't compare us to them."

"Maybe not... but I know how regular Muslims feel these days. I still don't tell people I'm a Doukhobor. Because when I do, you know what they hear? They still hear nudity, arson, bombings, stolen children... terrorists."

"I get it too."

"But the difference is *you* deserve it, and *I* don't. You don't know what it's like trying to hide behind booze and pills, while stuffing a barnful of food into your mouth every day," Sharon said, gripping and rattling her double chin. "You have to understand that what you did, that hurt and shame, it trickles down. I'm only now starting to care about my culture. My sons could give a rat's ass. Which is sad because I'm sure there is a lot to be proud of."

Jonah walked in with Julian behind him. They stomped the remaining snow off their boots on the door mat. "Mom, why the long face?" Jonah asked.

"...Mom!" Jonah yelled, clutching her shoulder. "What the hell are you doing? Sit. Down."

Sharon looked around. She wasn't in her trailer arguing with her mom; she suddenly remembered she was at Virginia's for Christmas dinner. Her scarred left hand was trembling on her chest. Everyone at the table was standing now; Virginia was looking at her with tears in her eyes, while Mary's face was stone cold, her lips quivering in disgust. Ruby was covering her mouth as Julian and Alan ran in from the kitchen to see what all the commotion was about. Big Nick was red in the face and utterly confused. Sharon looked down at herself as Jonah frantically removed his hoodie. Her blouse was unbuttoned and hanging around her waist. Her frayed bra was dangling from her left elbow, boobs spilling over the thick rolls of her stretch-marked stomach.

In 1964, Vancouver Sun *reporter Simma Holt, known for her malicious, anti-Doukhobor newspaper articles, releases* Terror in the Name of God, *a one-dimensional and sensational book about the Sons of Freedom Doukhobors. While quickly becoming a bestseller, Holt's portrait is mocked by many at the time and long afterward for its inaccuracies, tactlessness and anti-Doukhobor bias. It becomes part of a long list of careless, headline-grabbing media that portrays all Doukhobors as terrorists based on the radical actions of a small splinter sect.*

Slocan Valley, British Columbia, July 1998

Ruby was aware of herself on stage, drenched in sweat, beaming at the audience. Her entire body from her groin to the crown of her head tingled as though she was high on coke. But better. She'd never felt anything like it before. This was the biggest, most appreciative crowd Jet Poison had played in front of. Now her bandmates were tuning and adjusting for their final song. Ruby's smile grew wider at the scene in front of her. There must've been a thousand partiers on the grounds of the Slocan Valley Give'r Fest; its grassy field, bone dry from the summer sun, sloped gently down to a shallow, lazy bend in the Slocan River where people swam and floated on inner tubes. Others lounged on the yellow grass, drinking and smoking pot. Some escaped the sweltering heat under the forest canopy surrounding the field. After an unusually cool and wet spring, everyone was celebrating the arrival of summer.

At the front of the crowd were Jonah and a hundred or so people—many of them close friends—gathered to watch Ruby and Jet Poison perform. Finally, Jonah would see what she did best.

They'd been struggling the past few months. Every weekend he'd been away at seemingly every single skateboard competition between the Kootenays and the Coast as far down as Portland. At the first competition she'd been to in Nelson back in the fall, the girls had swarmed all the skaters afterward—including Jonah, who seemed to enjoy the attention. At the following competition back in April, Ruby had been making her way through the crowd to congratulate her boyfriend for his second-place finish when she saw him sitting up at the top of the half-pipe a little too close to the cute skater girl from California who had just won the female event. They were smiling and chatting with each other as Ruby approached from below. Jonah just glanced down at her, said, "Oh hey, Rube, be down in a sec," then continued talking with the girl. No introduction, no mention that Ruby was his girlfriend. Nothing.

Ruby had needed her and Jonah to re-spark their romance somehow. Lakeside camping and road trips together like the previous summer. Or just a weekend laying around listening to music would've done the trick. Anything. But instead... she fucked up.

Ruby shook the guilt from her head and turned her attention back to herself on stage. Her voice, as usual, had been on point. She loved her stage outfit too: itty-bitty red roller-derby shorts; a white ringer t-shirt with rainbow edging, cut short to expose her flat stomach; hair in pigtails; eyelashes extended; gold sparkles spiralling around her eyes like shimmering galaxies. She'd moved and danced around with ease and confidence. The crowd had loved it, especially the boys. With Fleetwood Mac's "Rhiannon," she'd ripped the audience's hearts out. Then, a few songs later, during the band's rendition of Beck's "Where It's At," she had them—especially the dreadies—grooving and twirling, arms above their heads twisting in figure eights. God, she loved it. Too bad no amount of practice could've made Jet Poison sound any better than they were. If her bandmates had been as talented as she was, that entire party would've been pinned to Ruby's performance.

She stepped up to the mic and asked the audience how they were doing. Hoots and whistles came in response. Ruby smiled at Jonah, who winked back at her. He was sunburnt, wearing only board shorts and skater shoes, clutching a six-pack of Kokanees. She couldn't tell what Jonah thought of the show. In that moment she wondered if her stage outfit was maybe too much?

Ruby looked to see if the guitarist was ready for his solo intro. Behind him, down off the side of the stage in the VIP section, was Swanny. She'd managed to avoid eye contact with him the entire show. He was with Clinton and their biker buffoons. Hanging off of Clinton was a girl with teased and hair-sprayed black hair, wearing a neon-yellow bikini. Clinton puffed on a cigarette, paid the girl no attention, ogling Ruby instead. He brought his thumb and middle finger to his lips, whistled loudly and yelled for Ruby to show him her tits. What a dick. God, how she despised his gross, bugged-out eyes on her.

In response, Jonah yelled from the audience, "Shut the fuck up, douchebag!" Their friends laughed and whistled in support. When Clinton spotted that it was Jonah who'd said that he flicked his cigarette and made a move to go deal with him. To Ruby's great relief Swanny grabbed him by the shoulder, pulled him back and stuck a placating bottle of whisky in his hand.

The guitarist stepped to the front of the stage and began strumming his drawn-out intro to what would be their last song, a cover of the Fugees' "Killing Me Softly with His Song," amped up in rock 'n' roll style.

When Swanny caught Ruby's eye he smiled and gave her two thumbs up. She ignored him but couldn't ignore the guilt that burned in the pit of her stomach whenever she thought of that night in May. She'd woken up in Nadya's bedroom with daggers being driven into her temples, her mouth pasty and her lips desert dry. When she heard a rustling beside her, followed by a prolonged yawn, she rolled over… but it wasn't Jonah she saw lying in bed. Swanny was propped on one elbow, shielding his eyes from the crack of light that sliced in from the window. She sat up and inspected herself; naked save for her panties. Her pink, traditional Doukhobor dress and embroidered shawl were on the floor at the foot of the bed. She'd been mad at Jonah for refusing to go to Festival with her that weekend, instead choosing to go on a stupid hunting trip with his dad. She still harboured anger at him calling her Baba Mary a cow at Christmas dinner, and at his mother for failing to apologize for her disgraceful behaviour. And then there were all the skate competitions and all the attention he was loving from the female fans. Ruby felt like a jilted lover. So, when Swanny showed up at the Festival after-party at Nadya's place, offering MDMA, she gladly partook. And because the drug softened the edges of life and gave Ruby a deep and highly sensual sense of connection, when Swanny offered to massage her in Nadya's bedroom she easily said yes. And when he whispered slippery sweetness in her ears, she easily wriggled out of her dress.

But exactly what happened that night was fuzzy the next morning.

"Wait a minute… did we fuck?" Ruby asked as she put her bra on.

Swanny rubbed his eyes. "Uh… yeah."

Ruby pulled on her dress. "You gave me E."

Swanny sat up and looked around for his underwear. "Yeah, you wanted it."

"I was drunk."

"You weren't slurring or stumbling." Swanny pulled on his underwear.

"I have a boyfriend, Swanny. Fuck."

Swanny was up now. He pulled on his jeans, t-shirt. "Jesus, don't piss on me because *you* feel guilty."

Ruby stopped folding her shawl, stared at Swanny. "You better not have had sex with me without a condom."

Swanny finished tying his red bandana around his head. "Don't worry. I was mostly pushing rope. Too fucked up."

"You know I have a boyfriend. Why did you let me do it?"

Swanny threw his hands up in surrender. "Let you? In case you forgot, you… you said yes."

"I trusted you."

The guitarist strummed the last chord of the intro. Ruby fought back her welling tears and plastered on a fake smile. The drummer clicked his sticks four times and Jet Poison launched into "Killing Me Softly with His Song."

The praise Ruby was getting from Nadya, Bobbie, Delia and her friends was genuine. From Jonah… it wasn't what she'd expected from the boy who loved her. He gave her a quick hug, handed her a can of beer.

"Probably time to change outta the… rock star clothes, eh?" Jonah eyed her up and down.

Ruby's black bra and overflowing cleavage *were* showing under her soaking-wet, midriff-exposing t-shirt. But it was the slightly snide way Jonah had said *rock star* that pissed her off. Like being one was somehow beneath her.

Ruby deflated. "Thanks a lot, Jonah." She thought his digs at her were a thing of the past. She saw the chip on his shoulder for what it was. Since the contentious Christmas dinner, and the skate competitions with all the adoring female fans, then her massive misstep with Swanny—which caused her to push Jonah away—the dynamics of their relationship had been shifting back and forth as if they were opponents in a tennis match. Maybe he sensed that she'd for real outgrown the Kootenays, had one foot out the door?

"I was singing that set for you, you know," Ruby said. She popped the beer tab and took a big gulp. Her girlfriends exchanged glances.

Jonah frowned and tilted his head. "Whaaat? You were great, okay?" He took her hand in his. "Really. All that choir you go to has really paid off."

"Come for a swim when you guys are ready," Nadya said.

Ruby watched their friends head down toward the river. Nadya turned back and yelled, "You're a rock star, babe!"

Ruby gave Nadya a little wave then looked at Jonah. "At least *someone* thinks so."

Jonah groaned.

"I'm gonna go side stage for a sec."

"Why?" Jonah squinted. "For what?"

"Help pack up."

Jonah glanced side stage. "They're pretty much done."

"Jonah what's your problem? You're such a fucking downer right now."

"Why do you need to see Swanny so bad, huh? Party treats?" He stared at her unflinchingly.

Ruby shook her head. "Look, I just played a great show. I'm sorry if you can't see that and feel like you need to bring me down and keep tabs on my every move."

"Huh?" Jonah was taken aback. He looked genuinely puzzled. He threw his hands up in surrender. "Whatever. Go, if you need to party with your bikers so bad." He turned and walked toward the river.

How easily Jonah had erased her gig high. Ruby made her way side stage desperate to keep the feeling going. "Got a bump for the rock star?" Ruby said, approaching Swanny. He was talking to his red-faced and shirtless brother. Clinton's bikini-clad girl was twisting a strand of chewing gum from her mouth, feigning interest in everything around her.

"Heyyy. Nice to see you, you look great," Swanny said. "Great show, Rube. Who knew?"

"I knew," Ruby said flatly. Clinton laughed the raspy, grating laugh of a lifelong partier. Bikini girl popped her bubble gum and looked away from Ruby. Ruby easily stood a foot taller than Clinton, but his reputation more than made up for the deficit. Somehow, he managed to puff a cigarette through clenched teeth while grinning like a maniac. He was fidgety, bobbing his head to a beat only he could hear. Clinton sniffed and pinched his nose, pulled off his sunglasses. He dropped his bugged-out eyes to Ruby's sweat-soaked chest.

"Shit, damn, you got a set of lungs on you, girl." Clinton laughed like the creep he was. "Screw that slag from Hole," he continued, "Cobain's bitch has got nothin' on you. A regular ole Douk diva we got here." Clinton raised his beer in salute to Ruby.

"Bumps eh? I'm out, but..." Swanny looked at his brother.

"Glovey of my truck," Clinton said. "An eight ball for you. On the house." He raised his finger. "On one condition."

Ruby raised one eyebrow. Her gig high was almost completely gone now. It took everything for her not to turn around, hide in the forest and cry. Whatever Clinton's condition, she'd agree.

Clinton's grin got even greasier. "I get to do some lines with the Douk diva later."

Ruby looked back toward the river. Jonah was wading near the shore with their friends, watching her. She turned back to Clinton and shrugged. "Sure."

"Follow me," Swanny said to Ruby.

Clinton and his girl headed toward the river. Ruby followed Swanny behind the stage, between the rows of vehicles, toward the edge of the forest.

"I gotta use the can," Swanny said to Ruby. They were sitting on the bench seat in Clinton's truck. Swanny had turned the stereo on. Slayer's "South of Heaven" crackled from the speakers. Swanny reached over Ruby's legs and opened the glovebox. "Help yourself. I'll be back in a flash. Outhouses are just there in the woods." Swanny nodded out the back window of the cab. "Glad you found me, Rube. I was meaning to talk to you. I've missed you. And I wanted to… I wanted to apologize, in person." He'd been thinking of her a lot since that night back in May. There were things he needed to get off his chest. "I screwed up. I care about you, a lot. I just…"

Ruby softened. "Go, we can talk about it when you get back."

Maybe she'd forgive him? Maybe there was a chance they could still be friends? Swanny nodded, opened the door and jumped out.

* * *

"You deserved way better than that." Swanny said aloud to himself. She had looked so prim and proper in her pretty Doukhobor dress. Swanny stepped out of the porta-potty in the woods. Only one other person was waiting to use it. "All yours, buddy," Swanny said as he passed the guy. He continued to rehearse what he wanted to say as he walked through the forest. "Look, Ruby, I'm sorry for that night. I care for you, I really do. The first time I ever saw you, at Ryan's party, I… I fell…" Swanny tripped on a root, steadied himself. One too many beers. "What happened back in May was wrong," he continued. "It was my fault. Instead of looking after you, making sure you were okay, I acted like all the assholes I ever grew up with. Clint, my old man, all the bikers. It's all I've ever known. I'm truly sorry. But listen, I don't want to be like them. I swear. I wanna be a better man. That's why I'm going to leave the club. I have a plan. I want to be with you and I—" Swanny's rehearsal speech was cut short by what he saw as he emerged from the forest: Clinton crawling into his truck, alone with Ruby. Worse than that, at the edge of the parking lot, Jonah had just spotted Clinton, too.

"Let's please wait for Swanny." Ruby did *not* want to be in the truck alone with that hopped-up, bugged-out gangster.

Clinton's eyes darted around, searched outside the cab. "What for?" He grabbed the baggie of coke from Ruby, poured a small pile of powder onto the back of his hand, and greedily sniffed it up into his flared nostril. He wiped his nose and looked around again. He turned up the stereo, then poured another little pile onto his hand and brought it up to Ruby's nose. His face was close to her. She could smell his rank cigarette and beer breath. It was when she shook her head, refusing to snort the powder, that she felt his big, meaty hand slide in between her legs. She squeezed her thighs together, balled her fist tight like Jonah had showed her to, and punched Clinton in the mouth as hard as she could. His eyes turned to stone and like a chameleon his puffy face instantly flushed dark purple. Dread spiked through Ruby as he cursed a curse Ruby could not understand, spittle flying out of his mouth. Clearly the bastard did not respond well to a woman saying no to him. Clinton reached behind him and locked the doors, then unzipped his shorts.

Ruby's voice trembled. "What the fuck do you think you're—"

With his scarred, meaty forearm Clinton pushed Ruby down hard onto the seat. She hit her head against the passenger door. Clinton clawed at her shorts, started pulling them down. Ruby screamed from depths she did not know she possessed.

Swanny ran up to the jacked-up Chevy, peered through the driver's-side window and saw to his horror Clinton pushing Ruby down. The truck rocked back and forth. Muffled sounds of struggle came from inside the cab. Swanny glimpsed a look in Ruby's eyes, a look he'd seen in his mother at the hands of his father, and in Jenna at the hands of Clinton: pure terror, as though those moments might be their last.

Swanny pulled at the door handle. Stupid idiot. Swanny had the keys. His hands were trembling; he fought to get the right key into the keyhole as he heard Ruby gasping, screaming no. Finally, Swanny flung the door open to see Ruby red-faced, squirming underneath Clinton. Worse, Clinton's hand was shoved in between her legs. Swanny climbed into the cab, scrambled on top of his enraged brother, grabbed him by his shoulders and tried with all his might to pry him off of Ruby. He screamed Clinton's name just as he was yanked hard out of the cab.

Jonah didn't know exactly what was happening. But when he saw figures grappling inside the cab of Clinton's Chevy he was thankful he'd grabbed his skateboard from the car. And the instant he heard Ruby's blood-curdling scream above the din of blasting metal music, he saw red and bolted toward the truck's open driver door. Martial arts muscle memory took over; dozens of fights under his belt, guiding him, giving him strength. Jonah threw his board to the ground, planted his feet, reached in, clutched a fistful of Swanny's hair and grabbed him by the arm. Fuelled by adrenalin, he effortlessly yanked Swanny back out of the cab and threw him to the ground.

"Get off of her!" Jonah commanded. By the tattoos he could tell it was Clinton. He was about to fully climb into the cab when he felt Swanny grab his shoulder.

"No, let me, I can—" Swanny yelled but was cut off mid-sentence by Jonah's elbow. Instinctively Jonah thrust it back, felt it connect with Swanny's skull, heard him yelp. Jonah spun around and with the distance he'd just created, was able to take one step forward with his left foot and plant a solid front kick to Swanny's chest with his right foot. Ruby's former lover was forcefully propelled backwards, slamming with a loud thud and crack into a parked car.

Jonah spun back around to the cab to see Clinton twisted back, glaring at him over his shoulder with unfiltered hatred. He released his chokehold on Ruby. She gasped for air as the biker scrambled out of the truck awkwardly like a dog walking backwards.

Clinton reached under the seat. "You're fucking dead," he spat at Jonah between gritted teeth.

Jonah frantically looked for where he'd thrown his skateboard and spotted it near the truck's back tire. He took a step toward it, reached down and grabbed it just as Clinton emerged from the cab with a revolver in his right hand. He slammed the truck door behind him.

Jonah froze. Icy adrenalin rocketed through his entire body. With the look of a man possessed, Clinton raised the barrel, pointed it up at Jonah's head. He grinned a devil grin and squeezed the trigger...

But nothing happened.

In the split second that it took for Clinton to click off the safety, Jonah made his move. With a two-handed grip on the board's deck above the back trucks, Jonah positioned his skateboard to his side and slightly behind him. He lunged and swung it hard, slamming the skateboard up into Clinton's hand as though he were batting for a home run. The crunch of metal trucks on bone as the gun flew out of his hand, was unmistakable. Clinton's face turned an impossible shade of magenta, his eyes bulging and about to burst.

Jonah guessed what a gorilla like Clinton would do next. He'd trained for it with Julian, over and over in dojos and backyards. But that didn't make the moment any less terrifying. Clinton let out a primal, guttural roar and stepped to Jonah, faked with his right hand, then threw a ham-fisted left that smashed Jonah square on the jaw. The oily copper taste of blood filled his mouth, bits of teeth and blood spraying out, skateboard dropping to the ground as he stumbled backwards. His brain threatened to explode. It had been a long time since he took a punch to the head like that. Jonah shook the worst of the pain away just as Clinton lunged at him, both hands aimed for his throat. This time Jonah would not make an error. He dropped to his knee and spun around in one fluid motion, thrusting his knuckles hard into Clinton's ribs, producing a wincingly loud crack.

As Clinton doubled over, Jonah returned to his feet behind him. He spotted his skateboard, bent down and grabbed it. The sound of Ruby calling his name momentarily startled Jonah. He glanced back to see that she'd opened the door and was pulling her shorts up, tears streaming down her face. When Jonah spun back around Clinton was coming at him again, his right arm cocked. Jonah ducked to the right, but Clinton's massive fist clipped him above his right eye socket. The skateboard slipped from his hand again. Luckily, Clinton's momentum carried his wide, bulky frame stumbling forward. Jonah easily moved out of the way, twisted around and steadied himself. Clinton swung around, glanced at Jonah then spotted his gun a few yards away. If Clinton were to get that gun first, Jonah was a dead man. He took two quick steps toward Clinton, swung his arm out wide, and landed a furious right hook to the side of the biker's head, square on his ear. Clinton roared in pain, stumbled and fell.

Jonah looked around, trying to catch his breath. A crowd had gathered; his buddies amongst them. Everyone had looks of horror on their faces. If they had been saying or shouting anything since their arrival, Jonah hadn't noticed. Clinton grunted and crawled around to face Jonah. He was breathing hard, wincing in pain. The muscled goon managed to raise himself up on one knee. The gun was now within reach to both of them. Suddenly the Slayer music that had been the battle's soundtrack cut out. Ruby slammed the driver's-side door shut. She was standing in front of it. Clinton glanced at her as she yelled, "You fucking pig!"

Seeing his opening Jonah sprung at Clinton and slammed his elbow and forearm into Clinton's nose with all his might as he landed. Globs of blood spattered from Clinton's face. The biker toppled to the ground. Jonah straddled him and began punching his face quickly, relentlessly, with as much force as he could muster. He stopped only when Cedar pulled him off.

"The bikers are coming," Cedar warned.

III

Fallout and Fate

In 1967 as Canada marks the hundredth anniversary of Confederation, efforts are made to portray harmony within the Doukhobor communities across Canada when the first ever unified choir of Sons of Freedom, Independent and Community Doukhobors performs at the Expo 67 World's Fair in Montreal.

Slocan Valley, British Columbia, February 2005

"Virginia, please, my love... get up." Nick stood over his wife who was curled in fetal position in their bed. "You can't sleep this away." In his slow, deliberate way, her husband turned, stepped to the sliding glass doors of their patio and flung the curtains open with his long, solid arms. The sobering silver light of winter flooded in behind him. Virginia winced and looked away. Just as she'd been trying to look away from what the doctor in Spokane had confirmed for her at the hospital; Ruby's concoction of alcohol and a drug called oxycodone had caused her to overdose on stage that night. She was lucky to be alive.

What was meant to be a surprise—her, Nick and Sasha watching Ruby perform with her band—had turned into a disaster. Two days later the three-hour trip from Spokane over winding, snow-covered highways had been sombre. Ruby sat in the back seat of the Suburban next to Nadya, with Sasha between them, while Nick drove. Everyone looked as worn out as Virginia felt from the forty-eight hours they'd spent in the city. She mostly stared out at the passing winter scenery, sick to her stomach wondering what was next for her daughter, whether Sasha needed to know the full story, and how Virginia and Nick would keep it from their friends. Occasional small talk was of home and which high school friends were doing what, and of Sasha's adventures in kindergarten. When Ruby inquired about Jonah, neither Nadya nor Virginia had anything to report.

As soon as they pulled into the snowplowed Samarodin driveway, Ruby took her mother aside and said they needed to talk. Virginia's heart sank a little more.

Everyone helped carry Ruby's guitars and amplifiers and luggage while Sasha came alive again, stomping through the snow in his cowboy boots, asking his mother questions about her guitars, and the tour bus, and Los Angeles, and why the singer, Tomás, was sad in the hospital room, and whether she was friends with Conan O'Brien, and whether she was sad that she was leaving her band. On and on it went. He might as well have been in the throes of a sugar high. In the kitchen Ruby couldn't take it anymore. She exhaled deeply, gently placed her hand on Sasha's shoulders and kneeled down in front of him. With her gaze cast to the floor, she rubbed her eyes with her palms and breathed slow and deep, actions Sasha had seen before, actions which made him finally hush.

"What's wrong, Momma?" he asked.

She looked deep into her son's eyes, smiled, and with a clarity that Virginia hadn't seen in her daughter since she'd decided to move to LA in the first place, told Sasha she would never leave him again.

"Okay," he said, seemingly unsurprised. Or unbelieving. Virginia couldn't tell.

"I promise." Ruby stood, scooped Sasha up and showered him with kisses. He giggled and tried to duck his mother's affection. She put him back down, nodded at Nadya—a signal for her to ask him if she could see his Lego creations in his room.

Over a steaming cup of coffee at the kitchen table, Ruby made her emotional confession. Her chin quivered as she cupped her mug with both hands. With tears streaming down her cheeks, she said bluntly, "I'm an addict. Have been since I was… sixteen." Nick groaned and creaked as though her were a giant tree bending in a vicious storm. He got up from the table, walked to the patio doors, opened them and in his woolen work socks stepped out onto the snow-covered deck. Speechless, Virginia clutched her mug hard enough that she thought she might crush it. Her daughter's admission was a punch to the stomach. How could she and Nick have possibly failed her? Weren't they good role models for Ruby? They rarely drank, hadn't even so much as smoked a marijuana joint. Virginia stared slack-jawed at her daughter.

"Say something, Mom," Ruby implored as she watched her father standing with his back to her on the patio.

Virginia wiped away her own tears. "Nick, get the hell back in here." Avoiding eye contact with anyone, Nick stepped back into the kitchen and with soggy socks sat back down at the table. Virginia took her daughter's hands in hers. "I love you. We love you." She turned to her husband and glared at him. He got up from his chair, lumbered around the table and sat down beside his daughter. He wrapped his long arm around her, hugging her into his protection. Ruby collapsed into her father in heaving sobs. Virginia was frozen, unsure whether to join the embrace, unsure what if any comfort or answers she could provide. In that moment she felt as hollow as an old log, beyond tears as the realization came quickly that she'd failed as a mother. "We, we'll figure it out, honey," she stammered.

When Ruby eventually stopped heaving, she looked up and peeled away from her father. She swiped at her tears with the sleeve of her hoodie. "I need help," she said matter-of-factly. "Professional help."

"Whatever it costs, honey," Virginia started to say, "you don't—"

"No." Ruby shook her head. "You and Dad have done more than enough." She looked at both her parents, sniffled and said, "This is on me."

* * *

Later, when Ruby was in her old room with Sasha and Nadya, Virginia walked upstairs in a daze and, without taking her clothes off, crawled under the covers. She slept fitfully throughout the rest of the day and through the night. She stayed in bed well into the afternoon of the following day. If it were up to her, she would never get up. But her own mother had taught her to always be on, to be of motherly service. That was the Doukhobor way after all, wasn't it?

Now there was her dear husband, casting shadows over their bed. "This doesn't happen to..." She trailed off.

"What? To good Doukhobor families?" Nick scoffed. "And you believe there's still such a thing? Our daughter had already run off and left Sasha *years* ago," he said, casting a thumb behind his shoulder.

When Ruby first went to Los Angeles, Virginia had been naive in thinking that she and Nick were helping raise Sasha while Ruby pursued her dreams, regardless of how ill-advised they believed those dreams to be. When she stopped coming back home every month, and then every three months, and then not at all for six months at a stretch, Virginia knew something wasn't right. But a drug addict? The Makortoffs' son, Ivan, was addicted to heroin, the Plotnikoffs' grandson had died from some sort of overdose, Nick's stepfather, Alek, was an infamous abusive alcoholic in their village in Grand Forks. The list went on. But she and Nick had always imagined they were raising their family to the highest Doukhobor standards: hard-working, vegetarian, pacifist and vice-free. Their son, Alan, was engaged to a beautiful obstetrician and had a successful law practice in Toronto. Apart from some rebellious missteps in high school Ruby had excellent grades and had been a lauded soloist in the Doukhobor youth choir; Virginia and Nick, for the most part, could talk with pride about their children to their friends.

Virginia petulantly threw her covers off. "How, Nick? We'd talked to our kids their whole lives about not turning into so-and-so from this family or that. We led by example. Not once have we been drunk in front them. My parents aren't drinkers. Ruby had good friends growing up. Even Jonah didn't seem like he partied too much. I don't get it."

Nick groaned. "I don't know how these things happen." He eased himself down onto the bed and gently placed his hand on his wife's clammy forehead, stroked her hair, the calloused roughness a comfort. "But I guess now we know they do. Remember what Tolstoy wrote in *Anna Karenina*?"

Virginia thought for a moment. "Happy families are all alike; every unhappy family is unhappy in its own way."

"Aha. We're not so unique," Nick said. "Maybe... maybe we tried *too* hard."

Virginia strained to raise herself, her muscles stiff from inactivity. Nick helped his wife up into sitting position, encouraging her in Russian. "*Woht tak*. Ruby's going to rehab in a few days," he said. "We need to be strong. I don't know what to say to her. You know how I am when I'm upset. So… you need to pull yourself together for all of us."

Virginia leaned toward her husband. Nick hugged her into him. She began to sob softly, her tears soaking his collar. After a few moments she looked up at him, noticed the purple under his eyes. He hadn't been eating or sleeping well either. He looked like he'd aged ten years overnight. Yesterday, after fixing breakfast for the family he'd retreated to his shop to tinker on who knows what, not returning until dinner time. "I don't feel like I'll ever be the same again." Virginia wiped tears from her cheeks.

Nick nodded slowly, spoke in Russian. "I know. This isn't something that will be fixed in six months either, my dear. It could go on and on."

Virginia's eyes widened with shock. "Don't say that, Nick."

Nick held up his palm, closed his eyes, turned his head down and to the side; always his gesture for when enough was enough. When he opened his eyes, his gaze was stern and unflinching. "Enough lying to ourselves. This is a wake-up call. We are *not* perfect. Our daughter is *not* perfect. She's in for one *hell* of a fight. Now get up, dear, clean up, and phone Doris. Your sister always makes you feel better. Sasha has been asking about you, too. I told him you had a cold. But we need to sit down, all of us as a family, and *finally* explain to the boy in a way that doesn't scare him, that his mom is home to… to get better."

As Nick stood and helped his wife up, a panicked shout from Ruby came from downstairs. They'd made their way out into the hallway when Ruby, calling to them all the way up the stairs, stepped onto the landing with phone in hand, hyperventilating and trembling. Sasha, woken by the commotion, stepped out of his bedroom down the hall, rubbing his eyes.

"My God," Virginia said. "What's wrong?"

"Olga… Olga Makayev just phoned." Ruby looked at the receiver in disbelief. "She thinks Jonah is dead."

Swanny honked his horn, three short bursts. Apart from the smoke swirling up from the chimney, the log cabin was as still as the forest that surrounded it. He was glad to see that a path to the front door had been cleared of snow. Three more short honks… A few seconds later the door creaked open and Yuri peeked his head out, tufts of white hair in an uproar as though he'd just crawled out of bed. He squinted at Swanny's van, then quickly shut the door. Steak-sized chunks of compact snow slid off the cedar-shingle awning over the door. Swanny kept the engine running and the heat cranked. Yuri moved at his own pace; Swanny knew this could take a while.

He'd just come from his home, sparkling clean courtesy of Brandi, the attractive yet uncouth housekeeper Clinton had paid for. After she'd finished, she stood there with her long brown hair and her tanned Italian features, wearing a curve-hugging pink Adidas track-suit, gesturing, with spray bottle in hand, at his groin. Swanny had jokingly asked if it was time to clean his crotch.

"Suppose you could say that," she replied. She seemed genuinely upset and perplexed as to why he wouldn't want to take her up on her crude offer of fellatio. When she asked, he told her, no, it wasn't because he was gay, and when she pointed to his midsection, raised her finger skyward in mock erection and asked if it worked, he adjusted his red bandana on his forehead, cleared his throat and assured her that it did. Why did people always think it was okay to ask that? He wasn't like his brother, he'd told her. He didn't expect (demand) sex from a woman. And when she told him he was cute for an older guy in a wheelchair and that she was good at BJs… he just slumped. It had been years since Swanny felt the intimate touch of a woman. He so desperately wanted it. But Brandi would just be doing it because she was paid extra to, not because she wanted to. The whole experience made him thirsty for drink. No one to better share one with than Yuri.

Where the hell was the old Freedomite anyway? Swanny looked down at his useless legs. It had been years since he'd felt sorry for himself, but he was feeling it now. He couldn't help but wonder... had his mother not met his father at a party in San Francisco back in '69, then Clinton would've never been his brother, and that brother never would've forced himself on Ruby, and Swanny never would've been in that goddamned wheelchair. And maybe, just maybe, in another life he would've met Ruby, and they would be together. The last time he felt that much self-pity was a few months ago when he'd driven to the Samarodins' place to foolishly see if he could catch a glimpse of Sasha.

Just as Swanny was about to put his van in reverse and leave, the front door of the cabin opened. Yuri stepped out dressed in his winter usual: black toque, ratty wool winter coat overtop an old dress shirt, faded blue jeans held up with purple suspenders and his new dark-green gumboots. Swanny rolled down his window, told Yuri it was about goddamned time, and teasingly waved a bottle of Stoli. None of that Smirnoff crap, Yuri told him once. He only drank true Russian vodka. A figure appeared behind Yuri; a muscled and much younger man with shoulder-length brown hair that Swanny had seen leaving Yuri's place once before. The man pulled on his coat as he and Yuri chatted closely for a moment. They hugged quickly, then the man stepped around Yuri and gave Swanny a small nod as he walked past him down the driveway.

Yuri shuffled up to Swanny's window, took the bottle, turned it in his hands, admiring it. In his pronounced, croaky Doukhobor Russian accent he asked, "What's this for, Michael?"

Besides Swanny's mother, Yuri was the only one that called Swanny by his given name. "For being a good neighbour." Swanny pressed a button and his van's side door slid open. "Mind grabbing my wheelchair?" Swanny gestured to the vodka. "I'm gonna come help you with that."

"Should have told me you were coming, Michael."

"Yeah, sorry, didn't know you had company over."

Yuri reached into the side of the van. He grunted and pulled the folding manual wheelchair that Swanny used for outings to the snow-covered ground with a clatter. "No, it's not that. I could have had borsch ready for you."

"Well, now you can teach me to make it like you've always been promising."

Yuri pointed at Swanny. "Deal."

Swanny gestured with his head back down the driveway. "That one a keeper?" he asked, knowing full well what the answer would be.

Yuri shrugged, shook his head. Swanny knew that none of them would ever be keepers.

Swanny had never been inside Yuri's home. He'd been invited plenty but the twenty minutes of wheelchair prep for a forty-second drive wasn't usually very appealing. But his friend and neighbour had brought him home-cooked Doukhobor food so many times, Swanny felt he owed Yuri a visit and a bottle of vodka.

Inside, Swanny took note that Yuri's place was just like the old man himself: small, rustic and spartan. A wood stove sat crackling in one corner of the cabin. In the opposite corner a plastic standing fan blew air on low. Between them was a well-worn La-Z-Boy recliner; beside it a reading lamp on a small, lacquered table. Separating the living room from the kitchen, where Swanny sat at a turquoise 1950s Formica table, was a tattered green sofa of the same era, with curved arm rests. Several framed black and white photos of family members hung on one wall. Two small, wood-framed windows let in meagre winter light on either side of the cabin. In the sill of one of the windows was a Mason jar with one lone white feather poking out, sitting next to a black and white framed photo of Yuri with his arm around Dimitri. On top of an old yellow fridge beside a gas-powered stove, 1950s rock 'n' roll crackled out of a vintage transistor radio at low volume. Yuri stood next to the stove, stirring in a cast-iron pot the vegetables that Swanny had just chopped: onion, garlic, carrot and green pepper. "Yuri, you own anything manufactured in any of the decades *after* man first set foot on the moon?" Yuri pointed at the fridge, which looked to be from the '70s. Swanny laughed and began chopping cabbage as Yuri had instructed. "Why no modern comforts? No stereo, no TV, no computer?"

Yuri stopped slicing potatoes and beets and, with knife in hand, waved the notion away as though it was obviously preposterous.

"Ah yeah, it's a Sons of Freedom thing, eh, living simply like this?" Swanny poured each of them a shot of vodka. He passed a glass to Yuri, clinked it, then they both downed their shots.

"It *was* a Sons of Freedom thing to live simply, like I do," Yuri said. "Forty years ago *all* Doukhobors lived simply. For the simple reason that materialism is bleak and destructive." Yuri moved on to chopping celery. "Parasitic."

Swanny pursed his lips and nodded. "Yup, suppose it can be."

Yuri stopped chopping, swivelled around, grabbed the vodka, opened it and poured them two more generous shots. He slid one to Swanny. "Your brother, that big, angry fella I met, would you say he's a troubled soul?"

Swanny raised his eyebrows, scoffed. Where did that come from? "Clinton? Hell yeah. But his troubles go way beyond buying motorbikes and Hummers and all sorts of toys."

"Yes, of course, but it's all related you see. Materialism is a sister of greed, and both are cousins to violence. I'd bet Clayton—"

"Clinton."

"Clinton lives in a world where these things can only ever offer saltwater to the thirsty. The spiritually thirsty. Which is what we all are."

Classic Yuri, Swanny thought. Give the old guy some vodka and he loved to wax mystical. "My brother... He's actually my half-brother. He wouldn't even understand what spiritual thirst is... because sometimes I think the devil has his number. His soul is *way* beyond repair."

Yuri lifted his glass, winked at Swanny. "Here's to being spiritually thirsty." They both threw their heads back and downed the shots. "That's too bad about him." Yuri gestured at Swanny. "If he was a good man like yourself, he'd be just my type." Yuri winked and chuckled.

"I don't think he's anyone's type. In fact, I've never known him to have a girlfriend."

Yuri continued stirring the contents of the cast-iron pot. "Ah well, that might explain why he's so angry. Maybe he's been barking up the wrong types of tree."

"Yeah maybe." Swanny took a deep breath, let the sting of vodka wash through him. It felt good to be in Yuri's cozy cabin, breaking bread with him, forgetting his sorrows. "I can give you a small TV in exchange for this borsch-making lesson. I have an extra one."

"*Och.*" Again, Yuri waived the preposterous notion away.

Swanny gathered his chopped cabbage into a bowl, handed it to Yuri. "Suit yourself," he said as a quiet thud sounded against the front door. Swanny looked at Yuri. "Your friend come back?"

Yuri stopped scooping boiled slices of potato from a pot, shook his head. "Probably just the wind." He plunked the potatoes into a large metal bowl, then handed it, along with a masher, to Swanny.

Swanny began mashing the potatoes. "Oh hey, speaking of TVs, remember I mentioned to you a while ago that my mom's uncle died? That sleazy American televangelist?"

Yuri looked up toward the ceiling, right eye squinting, lips puckered, the way Swanny always saw him do when he was searching for answers. "Rings a bell."

"Bobby... Pope? His stage name apparently. I think Popoff was the actual surname."

Yuri asked, "Are you sure?

Swanny squinted in thought. "I think so?" He shook his head. "I'll ask my mom."

"Because if it's Popoff, it's likely a Russian name."

"*Reeally*. Well get this, my mom went down to the funeral in LA and she said they served borsch at the service, similar to the kind we're making." Swanny continued mashing potatoes. "Turns out my great grandparents on my mom's side were Russian."

"*Very* interesting." Yuri smiled coyly at Swanny. "There were small groups of Doukhobors that went to California and Oregon to try to set up colonies." Yuri added the chopped cabbage to a cast-iron pan for sauteing. "Might explain why I like you and allow you into my house."

Swanny laughed. "Apparently he was a shyster, like all those televangelists—" Swanny was about to continue when out of the corner of his eye he noticed movement outside the small window in the middle of the room. He swung his head toward it and swore he saw the tail end of a shadow.

Oblivious to what Swanny had seen, Yuri said, "I sometimes drive to that small Selkirk College building down the valley to use their computer. I will investigate this Bobby Pope-slash-Popoff for you."

Swanny turned his attention back to Yuri, pointed at him. "Freedomite Yuri uses a computer?" He laughed. "The internet?!"

Yuri raised his eyebrows and looked around as if it was obvious. "I don't have room for all sorts of books like you do. So… I learn from the internet."

"Damn, Yuri, you never cease to amaze me. Ever wish you'd had kids instead of a life running from the cops? Some little Freedomite tykes you could've passed along all your life lessons to?"

Yuri laughed. "Yes, many lessons on what *not* to do."

Swanny heard the faintest crunch of snow on the front doorstep just as Yuri's phone started to ring.

Unaware, Yuri gestured for Swanny to pour them another shot, but Swanny was already wheeling toward the door. "But I do have two nephews to whom I can pass on any wisdom I do have," Yuri said as he walked to the living room and picked up the phone.

"Hello… Sharon, Sharon slow down," Yuri said loudly into the receiver. "Who? Jonah?"

Swanny stopped in his tracks, spun his chair to face Yuri.

Yuri cupped the receiver, looked at Swanny, his face scrunched in confusion. "My… my nephew… he's a soldier. Uh… apparently…" Sharon's voice crackled through the phone. Yuri returned to the call. "I'm here, I'm here… Uh-huh, oh *Gospodi*… Okay, I'll call Mom."

Swanny's heart started knocking and sprinting, just as the front door burst open, slammed against the fridge, and Clinton lurched in.

Nelson, British Columbia, February 2005

It all happened at once; a knock on the front door and the phone ringing incessantly as Sharon was on the living room floor, half-naked, frantically packing, wondering what to do about the grief that was eating at her soul. Sharon suddenly remembered that her eldest, Julian, would arrive soon with his father, Roy. Luggage sat open on the couch, clothes overflowing. It was a bright, sunny day outside, but inside the shuttered house it might as well have been the middle of the night. Frozen with indecision, she first looked at the phone ringing on the kitchen counter, then over at the front door. Knock, knock, knock.

"Sharon?" a woman's muffled voice called.

Still on all fours, Sharon swept the pile of take-out containers, empty chip bags, candy bar wrappers and various two-litre pop bottles under the couch, then groaned and struggled to a standing position. Sharon grabbed her coke-bottle glasses that were sticking out from between the couch cushions and slipped them on.

"Sharon, I'm on my way," came her mother's voice from the answering machine. "Be there by five. *Och, dotchka,* I can't begin to..."

Three more knocks. "Oy," Sharon said quietly, "go away." In the dim light she found her sweatpants bunched up near the television and with great effort slipped them on as far as her knees, then stumbled, wobbled and toppled to the floor with a loud bang.

"Sharon, are you okay?" came the muffled voice from outside, followed by three more knocks.

With sweatpants around her knees Sharon rifled through her open luggage for a top and settled for one of Jonah's old skater hoodies. The sight of it made her heart sink as she pulled the pants up around her waist, got up and waddled to the front door.

Since the terrible phone call early that morning Sharon had been in shock, as though stumbling through the aftermath of a tornado that had ripped through a trailer park. Sharon hadn't realized exactly how rough she looked until she slowly creaked open her front door and watched both Virginia's and Ruby's faces sink, and their bodies deflate.

When Sharon had given birth to her sons all those years ago, it was only the physical links that were severed with their umbilical cords. Her motherly intuition instantly told her something terrible had happened when the phone rang that morning at five a.m. And in that instant, she began shaking and sinking as though she were plunging on an old wooden rollercoaster. She had bolted upright and yanked the phone out of its base on the third ring. "Hello," she'd said timidly.

"Hello, may I speak to Sharon Seeger, please?" the serious male voice said.

Tears poured out of a face that twitched uncontrollably. Her hand quaked; the phone threatening to drop from her numb fingers. "This... this is her."

"Mrs. Seeger, this is Sergeant Peter Ogden from Headquarters Marine Corps—"

"Oh god, oh god, oh please no..." Sharon couldn't hold in her pain any longer. She began to sob as the man continued to speak.

Now, standing in the doorway, Ruby looked as rough as Sharon felt; under bunched red eyes Ruby's puffy bags were black as though she'd messily applied thick eye shadow. Her lips were dry and cracked, her cheekbones protruded from a gaunt, ashen face. Standing slightly behind her, Virginia didn't look much better. Without a word Ruby wrapped her arms around Sharon and cried into her neck. Virginia stood holding a grocery bag full of food, eyes welled with tears. Sharon stayed still, surprised to see them both, unsure what to do, ashamed at her grumbling, distended belly and the grief-induced chaos partially hidden in the living room behind her.

In Russian, Virginia offered their wishes for Jonah's eternal rest in the Kingdom of Heaven. "*Tsarstve nebesnom yemu.*" She sniffled. "We're so sorry for your loss."

Ruby sob-spoke words into Sharon's neck that she couldn't understand.

"My… my loss? Oh God… no, Ruby, Ginny, no, no… Jonah's alive."

Ruby jerked away from Sharon, clutched Sharon's upper arm, and blinked rapidly at her with an open mouth. Through heaving sobs on the phone to Olga, Sharon must've said "roadside bomb" and her old friend must've inferred instant death. Oy, how easily rumours could spread in that community.

"But we'd heard… *Och, Gospodi,*" Virginia said. "*Slava Bohu.*"

Yes, Sharon thought, thank God. Thank all the gods, the Universe, anyone and anything responsible for bringing her boy back home.

Ruby swayed and faltered for a moment. Virginia steadied her. "He's alive?" Ruby said still in open-mouthed disbelief.

Sharon nodded. "He is. In critical condition, but alive," she said as Ruby hugged her again. "He's at the US Army's medical centre in Germany."

When the man from the Marines had informed Sharon of the news, the phone had slipped from her hands. If she had looked in a mirror that second, surely, she'd have looked as white as her bed sheets. Why did she ever let Jonah join the military? she'd thought. Why did his damned father allow him to? They'd failed their son. She'd crawled out of bed and stumbled to her bathroom, her own life feeling as though it might be near the end. She scrambled through the medicine cabinet and found the Xanax she kept in case of emergency. She dry-swallowed two pills, then propped herself up along the hallway walls as she wobbled into the kitchen. She'd flicked on all the lights, phoned her neighbour who was an old high school friend and asked her to pick up the hundred dollars worth of food she'd just ordered from A&W.

Sharon knew she should invite Virginia and Ruby in, but she couldn't bring herself to. "I'm just…" she looked back over her shoulder, "I'm just getting ready to fly to Germany tomorrow with Julian and Roy."

"Oh, of course, dear." Virginia handed the bag of food to Sharon, gave her shoulder a gentle squeeze. "Just a few things we thought you might like. Some of my veggie soup, and veggie chili, and some homemade *pyrahi*." Virginia wiped her eyes and smiled.

"*Spasibo*," Sharon said. "It was so nice of you two to come by. I'm sorry you'd heard such a terrible rumour." It hadn't even registered that Ruby was back in the Kootenays until Sharon was about to close the door. "Ruby..." she said, eyeing her up and down. "Is everything okay? You're back now?"

Ruby wiped her hair from her forehead. "At my last show in Spokane I—"

"She's come home," Virginia interrupted. "To be with Sasha." Virginia and Ruby exchanged glances. Ruby blinked slowly, forced a smile and nodded.

Obviously, Sharon knew there was more to the story. But now was not the time. Sharon needed to clean herself up, finish packing and prepare to be by her baby boy's hospital bedside.

Slocan Valley, British Columbia, February 2005

"Who would've thought you and ole Freeeedomite Yuri," Clinton slurred with eyes shut, "had Jo-Jonah *Fuckface* Seeger in common, eh?"

Back down at Swanny's place, Clinton was splayed on the couch. The bottle of vodka Swanny had given to Yuri was in Clinton's clutches, hugged close to his chest as if he were a child and it was his teddy bear. Clinton raised his head and opened one bleary eye, grunted as he sat up. "You knew."

"I told you already," Swanny said. "I had no idea."

"Uh-huh. I need to crash here for a bit." Clinton slowly unscrewed the bottle's lid and free-poured vodka in the vicinity of his mouth. "They're closing in."

"Cops?"

Clinton nodded. "And fuck… fuckin' UN too."

Swanny had always found that gang's name so unthreatening. Not anymore. "Great, so you put *me* in danger?"

Clinton's face flushed redder than it already was as he roared. Drunkenly he lobbed the open bottle of vodka at Swanny. It landed and splashed at Swanny's feet, rolled up to the right wheel of his chair. "We're Angels, fuck. We're in this together."

"Asshole, *I'm* not the one that killed those innocent people." Swanny glared at his pathetic brother.

Clinton slumped over, put his head in his hands. "I'm sorry… sorry. Jusss until I get my shit together and… and head to Mexico… or Bol… Bra… Brazilvia."

What an idiot. "Bolivia? Brazil? Either way, first thing you're going to do tomorrow is get rid of your Hummer and get something less conspicuous."

"Conspic…" Clinton pointed at Swanny. "Good idea… Say, Swan… why were you at Freedomite Yuri's anyway? You two…"

Clinton cackled. "You two lovers now? Huh? Always thought you might be a fag."

Half an hour earlier Swanny had faked accidentally falling out of his van. Coupled with that and the entire experience with Clinton and Yuri, Swanny was still reeling. But it was either take a hard fall or Clinton's drunken rage toward Jonah would've redirected and slammed fist first into Yuri's slender frame. After Clinton had burst into Yuri's home he'd swayed in place, surveyed the modest dwelling and slurred, "He's Jonah Fuck-Fuckface Seeger's Dirty Douk uncle *and* a fuckin' hermit." He pointed around the room. "Look at this shithole."

Yuri had looked to Swanny for help... then back at Clinton whose bleary eyes had spotted the bottle of vodka. Swanny wheeled himself toward the door. "Clint, let's go."

Clinton swiped at the bottle like a grizzly swiping at salmon leaping from a river, missed, swiped again and finally caught the prize. He brought the bottle close to his face, his eyes crossing as he read it. "Ah, Stoli, the good shit."

Outside, Swanny had hoisted himself into his van while Yuri lifted and shoved his wheelchair through the side door.

"The hell were you two lovers doin' anyway? Hmm?" Clinton had asked as he stepped out the front door.

"What friends do," Yuri said. "Talk about life, you know? Shooting the shit, as the youngsters say."

"He was teaching me how to make borsch. What are *you* doing here?" Swanny had said, unable to conceal his annoyance. "How did you know I was here?"

"Saw your van tracks. How else?" Clinton had stepped out the front door, stumbled and toppled into the snow, somehow managing not to drop the bottle of vodka. He laughed and grunted as he shimmied himself upright. "Can't a man visit his li'l bro?" Clinton had gotten back on his feet, his face red from effort. "Can't a man get in on the shit shootin' you old pals were doing?" He took another swig. "Hey Yuri boy?" Clinton stepped toward Yuri at the side door of the van, pressed in on his face. "Was my goody two-shoes little brother here tellin ya *all* about my... line o' work?"

Yuri shrugged, looked at Swanny, back at Clinton. "No, like Michael said, we were talking about life and—"

Clinton let out a forced, comical, laugh, then said, "Michael?" Clinton had looked at Swanny, who glared back at him. "Michael is it? Ha ha ha!" He swivelled his head back to Yuri as Swanny started his engine. "Know what I am, Yuri boy? Know what I *do*?"

Yuri shook his head. "I, I was just teaching him to make da borsch, when my sister called about my nephew..."

Swanny raised his voice. "Clint, let's go. Yuri has nothing to do with anything."

"How do you know Jonah?" Yuri asked Clinton.

Clinton swayed, starred at Yuri. He brought his head back, eyebrows nearly touching each other, frowning like a clown. His head quivered there for a second, turned to Swanny. "Wait..." Clinton stepped even closer, his fist on Yuri's chest, pinning him against the front of the van. "He never told you that your fuckin' nephew—"

A clamorous thud caught Clinton's limited attention. "Ow! Shit," Swanny said, having launched himself out of his van to land on Yuri's driveway. Theatrically, Swanny howled in pain, which achieved his desired affect; Clinton's drunken train of thought was diverted. For the moment. "Get me home. I need my pain meds."

Now back at home, Swanny watched Clinton lean forward to reach for the bottle of vodka he'd thrown, then tumble onto the living room floor in the process. Clinton laughed and lifted his head. "Ahh shit," he said, with one eye open and trained on Swanny. "Ole Freedomite Yuri... Seeger's blood..." Clinton banged the back of his head on the floor. "Perrrfect," he said, then passed out.

Landstuhl, Germany, March 2005

Jonah struggled to sit up, his chest quaking as he did. His head throbbed from concussion. He made the best fist he could with his sprained left hand, pushed into his mattress, grunted as he heaved himself upright with all his strength. His right hand was in a cast up to his elbow and only good for a bit of balance. He took a breath as deep as his punctured lungs would allow. What a mess he was. A tube stuck out through his ribs to help his lungs drain air. Other tubes were inserted into his left forearm. He threw off his blanket to stare, yet again, at the stump of his right leg, amputated just below the knee. His left hand was involuntarily tapping his left thigh, the *SKATE OR DIE* tattoo inked on top of his left hand teasing him. Up until that very second, he'd given it zero thought, and only found it mildly amusing that he felt nothing when it dawned on him: bye-bye skateboarding.

It had been a week since the surgery, and he still couldn't stop running his hands over his stump's puckered skin no matter whether it was throbbing, aching, cramping or felt like it was burning. Jonah had *never* been in so much physical and emotional distress. He deserved it. Savoured it.

The doctors had assured him they'd done a fine job of removing his lower leg; there were no signs of bone spurs or nervous-system tissue growth on the stump, which they'd called a neuroma. Even still he'd wake nightly, sweating in agony from acute phantom limb pain, a sensation like getting stabbed in places where the leg used to be. It was on those nights he'd hear it, the *whup-whup-whup-whup* of the Black Hawk medevac, and see them, the dark figures gathered around two body bags that lay on stretchers next to him. His vision had been blurry, but he'd known the figures were there, could feel them staring, smirking, taunting him: Blue Ball Cap, the young insurgent in the Fallujah alley, all of them, all of his kills. Even Mase was there, whispering into his prayer ropes.

In a moment of panic Jonah checked to see that Mason's prayer rope was still around his wrist. It comforted him to know that his best friend, his brother-in-arms, Lewis, had the black prayer rope around the wrist of his new prosthetic arm as he lay in his own hospital bed in another wing of Landstuhl. Jonah didn't know what he would've done if Lew hadn't survived too.

He let out a heavy breath, then gazed outside the hospital room window at the brown German winter. Small clumps of week-old snow clung to scraggly, naked branches. The sky was grey like one of those old television sets. He looked back at his leg and felt nothing. One day it was there, and the next it was simply gone. Poof, just like that. He could've woken up that first time there at the hospital with *both* his legs amputated. His arms too. His head. He supposed it would've evened the score with all that had gone down on the field of battle since he'd become a Marine. He tilted his head back and gave it a shake, scoffed. If Lew had known what Jonah was thinking in that moment, he would *not* be impressed. "Oh hell no, bro," Lewis would say, then playfully smack Jonah upside the head. Jonah closed his eyes and saw Lew sitting beside him in the rumbling Humvee, mouth agape, staring back at him with a "holy shit" look seconds before the roadside bomb ripped them all apart. And Sadie. Poor Sadie. If she were there, she might call Jonah a pussy. Sergeant Cafferty would just hiss and tell him to shut the fuck up. What had his friends back home heard? Ruby knew. How about Uncle Yuri? Swanny and Clinton? His dad had told him that Ben Whitewolf wanted to call, but Jonah wasn't ready to talk about anything with anybody just yet.

Jonah kept his eyes closed, started slapping his stump. All he had been able to think of for that past week as he'd lain suffering in his shiny, annoyingly spotless hospital room was that his life had already been lived. What more could there possibly be?

Slap.

Nothing had ever been as satisfying and essential, and full of love, vitality and promise, than the years he'd spent with Ruby.

Slap.

Nothing would be as gratifying, invigorating, important or life-affirming as the bonds he'd developed with his fellow Marines.

Slap.

It had been agonizing to leave the love of his life behind... for good.

Slap.

And there would be never be anything worse than what Jonah had already lived through—watching those you love die beside you.

Slap slap.

Or killing men, some close enough that you could see the same look of adrenalized terror in their eyes as you had in yours; most, though, not even shooting at you, completely unaware that you even had them in your crosshairs. They were all ghosts now, and they tormented Jonah.

Slap slap slap. Each hit harder than the one before.

Jonah winced, turned his attention back to his stump; rubbed his palm over its puffy redness. Soon he would be fitted with a prosthetic limb. And then what? He wondered if he could find a sympathetic soldier there at the hospital, suffering just as he was, to scour the hallways, sneak him some heavy drugs, or perhaps a sympathetic nurse who could slip him some potent pills? How he would gladly take *way* more than was recommended.

Jonah wished his family hadn't come to be by his side, and then felt a twinge of guilt for wishing that. His father did the best he knew how, his big, rough hands perched at the edge of the bed while he told terrible dad jokes. His brother offered small talk about music and movies, and once asked if Jonah wanted to talk about... *it*, lowering his voice, as though a two-letter word could sum up all the horrors of war. Jonah's chest had been squeezed like it was in a vice, his heart heavy as lead when he thought about Sadie. Or when his mind hamster-wheeled the pros and cons, the weight of killing the "bad guys."

Just that morning, before his family went to town for lunch, his mom gently rubbed ointment on his scars. She spoke without making eye contact. "Healing has its own timeline," she said gently to Jonah. "The places where we keep our deepest wounds and sorrows are the same places where our biggest treasures lay. Take your time, Jonah… When you're ready you'll find those treasures." Mom, Jonah thought, with her own scars and healing.

Their efforts were little balm for the pains that burrowed to the very core of Jonah's being. His dear family had no clue, they didn't understand that Jonah felt permanently stained with sadness. He balled his fists under the hospital-green covers and willed stinging tears to surface. But they were hiding in his soul caves along with all his other sorrows. The last time Jonah cried was at his father's place on the phone with Ruby when she'd told him they were finished and she was having Swanny's baby.

Jonah fingered the silver crescent earring dangling at the end of a gold chain necklace. He thought of his mother, Uncle Yuri, Grandma Polly—they were his Kazakoff side. They were once Cossacks. He thought of the night before when, in a rare offering of Doukhobor pride, Jonah's mother sat at his bedside and told him a story.

"It was 1895," she'd begun. "In a dismal Siberian village teetering on the shores of the Arctic Sea, Doukhobor leader Peter V. Verigin sat in exile, thinking that it was high time to stop paying lip service to Doukhobor ideals. It was time for action. Time to refuse military service. Time to quit the killing because killing is not… Christ-like. Tsarist Russian authority was fuming about this, of course, because there was no place in the empire for radical pacifism. Easter Day arrived and, heeding his leader's call, would-be colonel Matvei Lebedev," Jonah's mother said as she made a show of clutching at her shoulders, "defiantly ripped his epaulettes from his uniform. His Doukhobor comrades followed his lead. To the judge, Lebedev was unrepentant, declaring that the only ruler he would serve was the Tsar of Heaven. That he would sooner take death by firing squad than take another person's life."

Jonah had exhaled deeply and looked out at the bleakness.

"I'm sorry Jonah, is this too much?" his mother had asked.

He shook his head. "It's okay."

Jonah's mother continued, "More Doukhobor soldiers laid down their weapons. They were imprisoned for this and endured medieval punishment: acacia-thorn floggings, starvation, cold, dark cells. Flog, starve, repeat. Further defiance followed. 'No to war,' the Doukhobors said. 'No to violence and the corrupt power of the state.' One summer night in the hills above villages throughout the Caucasus, bonfires were lit. Firearms were collected. Doukhobors gathered in their masses and unquestionably, brazenly, joyously offered their weapons to the flames."

"The Burning of Arms," Jonah said. His mother's eyes were saucers as her mouth dropped open. "Ruby told me the story once. Virginia said it's the greatest moment in Doukhobor history."

"She's right," Jonah's mother continued. "A policy of terror and repression followed. Cossacks beat and killed men, raped women, exiled leaders. Still, the Doukhobors would not budge. Morals for miles," Jonah's mother said, pawing the air above her head. "Tough as nails. The government thought, 'Surely a decorated general could talk some sense into the pig-headed, rebellious sect?' I forget his name, but like most generals who lie when they say they long for the day when there is no more war, General so-and-so told our ancestors that day had unfortunately not yet arrived. The Doukhobors' response? 'The time may not yet have come for you,' they said to the general, 'but it has come for us.'"

A nurse popped her head into Jonah's hospital room, brought him back to the present. "Bath time in ten." Jonah realized he was still rubbing his Cossack earring heirloom. He brought it up to his lips and kissed it. It had kept his great-grandfather (times six) safe when he was a Cossack, before becoming a Doukhobor, and Jonah supposed it had kept him safe too. Like his ancestors, Jonah thought, the time had now come for him to lay down his weapons. There was just one problem. One more battle awaited him at home.

What he wouldn't give to have Ruby there, Jonah thought. Her breath on his neck, singing silly pop songs to him, her fingers through his hair, tracing the contours of his bruised face, her smooth, warm nakedness soft against his... That'd make him slow it down... want to keep on going. Would he give his other leg to have her by his side? Jonah threw his head back, cackling, slapping his fingers on the end of his hot, throbbing stump. Yes, he would.

Slocan Valley, British Columbia, March 2005

Jonah picked up on the fourth ring, said hello in a tepid, strained voice that sounded like an old man version of himself. Ruby was freshly showered, in a robe, pacing her bedroom. Her small window was open a crack letting crisp early March air in. She'd rehearsed exactly what she would say, even scribbling some talking points on a piece of paper that she now held out in front of her. But as soon as she heard Jonah's raggedness, she let the paper slip from her fingers. Without even so much as a hello, she began, "Jonah River Seeger, don't you dare die on me, you hear?"

On the other end of the line Jonah snorted and let out a restrained laugh. "Ah, ow… Ruby… Sarah… Samarodin, as I live and breathe… albeit with punctured lungs."

Ruby laughed and cooed tender sympathy. She bit her lip to keep from betraying how easily she could cry. Why had she been so stubborn about not contacting him all those years? "Jonah. It's so good to hear your voice, babe."

Jonah sighed into the receiver. "You too." His voice was warm and gravelly. "I'm so, so glad you called, Rube."

"I wanted to call earlier…" Ruby said. She should've called years ago. Once a year. Every few months. "But word from your mom was that you weren't up for talking until today, I guess. How are you, babe?"

"I'm… well shit… I've been better." Jonah snickered. "I'm a right mess."

It was pointless; Ruby's eyes overflowed with tears. She sniffled, wiped her cheeks. "Me too. But at least I still have both my legs." They shared a laugh, and Ruby could hear how it pained him to do so. Jonah coughed a deep, phlegmy cough. "Our mothers have talked," Ruby said.

"Yes, our mothers have talked," Jonah echoed. "You're back home, apparently done with rock 'n' roll and the… rock-star lifestyle, eh?"

"Mhmm... Working through a mountain of crap," Ruby said. One day the mountain would seem insurmountable, the next day it might feel scalable, more like a hill.

"Yeah, oh yeah... I'm climbing Crap Mountain myself."

Ruby laughed and sniffled. "How much does it hurt?"

"It... I... hurt so fully, and so deeply, and *so* far back that I don't even know..."

"Yeah..." Ruby's voice was a quiet murmur full of sympathetic pain.

"The doctors have me hopped up on a cocktail of drugs." Jonah continued as though reading from a grocery list, "Fentanyl drip for pain, clonazepam for anger, citalopram because of adrenalin deficiency, hydrocodone for headaches, Ambien to help me sleep, and prazosin... for the... for the nightmares."

Ruby swiped at her tears. Her bedroom door creaked open and Sasha clomped in wearing his pyjamas and the cowboy boots he never seemed to take off. Her mother and father stood in the doorway, blocking the fluorescent light of the laundry room. Behind them, underneath the stairs, a washer swished and a dryer hummed. Ruby's pacing increased as her heart started pounding. She brought her forefinger to her lips, gave Sasha a stern look so he knew to keep quiet. He stopped in his tracks and looked expectantly up at her. She willed herself to calm down, to breathe. She eased down onto the edge of her bed and patted a spot for Sasha at her side. She looked to her parents for reassurance. Her mother smiled and nodded. Her father offered a thumbs-up.

"Ruby?" Jonah said.

"I'm here, babe."

"I feel like you should know," Jonah said. "If you hadn't called... I mean, it's getting a bit better now that I'm on all these drugs. But... there were some days I didn't know how... I didn't know how I would go on... you know?"

Oh, Ruby knew. It's also why she knew he needed to hear what she was about to tell him. "Okay, Jonah River Seeger, you listen to me now," she said as calmly, sternly and affectionately as she could in that moment. "Listen to me *very* carefully. I called to check on you, yes, but I called mainly because I have something important, life-changing to tell you. Something I should've told you a long time ago. But ... I ..." She sighed deeply. "I had my reasons, and when you think about it all ... I think you'll understand."

"Jesus, Rube, what is it? You're scaring me. Are you sick or something?"

"No, no." For an instant Ruby questioned whether this was a good idea.

Sasha tapped her on her leg, looked up at her. "Soon, Momma?"

Ruby cupped the receiver. "Are you ready?" she asked Sasha. Sasha looked at his grandparents, then back to her and nodded. "Remember what I told you?" Sasha smiled and again he nodded.

"Before I tell you, I'm going to put you on speakerphone, Jonah. There's someone here who wants to say hello."

Ruby handed the phone to Sasha. He held it up near his mouth and spoke. "Hello Mr. Jonah, this is Sasha."

"Oh ... umm ... Hi Sasha, it's nice to talk to you." Jonah was surprised, his voice suddenly an octave higher as though he were unsure how he should sound speaking to a child.

"Uh-huh. Momma says I'm supposed to ask two things."

"Okay, go ahead," Jonah said.

"Are you ..." Sasha stuck his finger in his nose and fished around. Ruby lightly swatted at it and shook her head no. "Umm ... are you finished being a soldier?" Sasha bounced the heels of his cowboy boots on the carpet.

"I ... Yes ... I am totally finished being a soldier."

"Okay, and question number two ..." Sasha looked up at his mother. She nodded. "When are you coming home?"

"Good questions, Sasha. I'll be back there soon." Jonah took a big breath. "Like, a month or two maybe?"

"How many sleeps is that?"

"How many sleeps? Let me see ... like, around fifty?"

"It's when the snow is all gone and the spring birds are chirping again," Ruby said to Sasha.

"Oh, okay," Sasha said. "I'll show you my favourite Lego and we can play Tonka trucks in the sandbox."

"Sounds like a plan, Sasha," Jonah said.

Ruby bent down and kissed Sasha on the cheek. "You did great, Sash. I'm proud of you. Now back upstairs, okay?" Ruby's mother waved Sasha toward her. Ruby turned speakerphone off and brought the handset back up to her head when Sasha and her parents were gone.

"Jonah," Ruby said.

"Wow, what a nice son you have there, Rube. Thanks for that. I'm sure he's stoked to have you back. Is Swanny in his—"

Ruby cut Jonah off. "Jonah. This is why I called. To tell you..." Ruby blew out a massive breath she'd been holding in. "To tell you that Sasha is *your* son."

Jonah immediately launched into a strained coughing fit. When he finally spoke again his voice was hoarse. "*My* son?" His voice was now two octaves up from his regular pitch.

"Yup. Me and you, we made Sasha together, one sexy night." Sheepishly, she said, "Swanny was a lie... sorry."

For a long time there was only the sound of Ruby and Jonah breathing. She understood why there was a canyon of silence between them. He was likely tense with the need for answers and she was tense with the need to offer them. The telephone was no place to talk about the detachment and secrecy all those years, or to rediscover each other, or to confess their sins, or to be angry with each other, or to shed more tears, or to try to forgive. There would be a time and place for all of that.

Jonah finally broke the silence. "Does Sasha know?"

"He knows. Me and my mom and dad sat him down a few days ago. You should've seen how excited he was, running in circles, stomping his feet."

Jonah spoke with joy in his voice. "I'm glad, I'm thrilled actually. And... yeah," he continued, his voice growing more serious. "I definitely have a bunch of questions."

"Yup. There's lots and lots to talk about. But first things first, Jonah. You heal yourself. Understand? That's what I'm trying... That's what I'm doing back home here. And I don't just mean, physically. Sasha... *Our* son..." Ruby teared up again. Her voice quivered. "He deserves that. Okay?"

Jonah breathed deeply. "I know. Absolutely. On it. This... This changes everything."

"Good. Then, and *only* then... you come home, and you come to me, and you meet your boy."

In 1979 John J. Verigin, Community Doukhobor leader and 1977 Order of Canada recipient, is indicted as the mastermind behind the Freedomite arson of the Grand Forks Post Office, and the town's Doukhobor Community Centre, following several years of relative Freedomite peace. The RCMP raid his home and office, confiscating boxes of documents. A highly publicized trial follows, in which several Sons of Freedom accuse Verigin of ordering them to carry out the arsons, lest they suffer a seven-generation curse. In the end, John J. Verigin is acquitted. Many fear the irresponsible government actions and Freedomite accusations will result in renewed animosities. Remarkably, the trial has the opposite effect. It initiates the Expanded Kootenay Committee on Intergroup Relations, a Canadian precursor to the South African truth-and-reconciliation process, in which rival Doukhobor factions are given a venue to air decades-old grievances.

In 1987, following five years of exhaustive talks, a landmark agreement is signed in which the Sons of Freedom thereafter reject arson, nudity and violence as a means of protest.

Spokane, Washington, May 2005

Jonah's knuckles were blistered and stinging from obsessive rubbing. Knowing it was his turn to speak he took a big breath, raked fingers through dishevelled hair and stroked his neglected beard. Both needed a wash. It was a warm spring day and he'd decided to wear shorts, unashamed of his prosthetic leg. He liked the way it looked; from the middle of where his shin would've been there was a shiny silver precision-made alloy post. For the first couple weeks the whole contraption felt so heavy and awkward, and because he had no toes or ankle bend, he was constantly being thrown off balance. Driving his father's truck had been a comical, jerky, lurching affair.

Jonah's dad's old friend Ben Whitewolf, sitting a few chairs away, gestured to Jonah. Jonah shuffled in his seat, took another deep breath, forcefully exhaled, then began. "A few weeks ago, I hobbled my ass into Egger's, the butcher shop on East Sprague—my dad likes their sausages—and soon as I make it through the door, whammo… I was back in that twisted, smoking Humvee outside Fallujah. Even just that slightest scent of raw meat in the butcher shop had me hightailing it out of there. I mean, as fast as a dude with a robo-leg could hightail it." He looked up from the grey carpet. The vets in the Wounded Warrior peer group sitting in cheap plastic chairs in front of him were all uttering solemn sounds of acknowledgement, including Ben and Lewis. The group was in a featureless, yellow-walled room in Spokane's West Central Community Center. Way-too-bright panel lighting buzzed overhead.

Jonah looked over at Lewis. Unlike himself, Lewis had kept his hair tightly cropped. He wore a tight-fitting white t-shirt, his prosthetic arm lighter in colour than his muscled bicep. Jonah was relieved Lewis had said yes to coming from Buffalo for a visit. His battle buddy's presence, as usual, calmed and reassured Jonah.

And then there was Ben Whitewolf leading the support group. Had it been anyone else Jonah might still be trying to deal with it all by just writing in a journal or listening to advice from friends who had no bearing, or by going to the strip bar, looking for fights, drinking himself to blackout. If it weren't for Ben, Jonah might still be staying silent at these meetings like he had the first week he attended them.

Ben's dark eyes were flanked by deeply etched crow's feet that curved down the side of his face. He smiled and gestured for Jonah to continue.

Jonah resumed the knuckle rubbing. "I couldn't handle crowded places either, man. A mall? Forget it. My anxiety would ramp up, I'd be on high alert, my head on a swivel. My temper would flare at the littlest things, too: if I bit my cheek while chewing gum, if a waiter got my order wrong, if a kid skateboarded by me too close on the sidewalk. I had horrible, debilitating recurring nightmares. Well, you guys know the kind." Jonah looked around the room full of nodding heads. He pressed on. "I'd wake up from one of those nightmares and instantly came the teeth-gritting need for booze. Ride it out with painkillers was all I could do."

Jonah sucked a breath in through his teeth, winced and searched for some kind of answer in the featureless walls and ceiling of the room around him. He rested his elbows on his thighs, rocked back and forth, then turned to Lewis, who hadn't been suffering as much as Jonah had. "How do you do it, bro?" he asked. "Already prepped by East Buffalo, eh?"

"Hell yeah." Lewis said. "The hood is real. I seen photos of your Kooties—"

"Kootenays," Jonah corrected.

"And those whatchamacallit googly web pics you showed me. Shit, Nelson's some sort of idyllic little cowboy town with cute little stores selling crystals next to a sushi joint across from a store for ski bums next to a hippie weed shop. Reminds me of one of them Upstate New York towns all them white folks can afford to live in."

Jonah nodded. "Yup." He knew Lewis grew up seeing neighbourhood kids killed by gangbangers, cousins shipped off to the pen, teenage girls selling themselves for a hit.

"Word. Ain't no secret," Lewis said. "I went into Afghanistan and Iraq already fucked up. Just a different kind of fucked up than you, man."

Jonah admired his friend's ability to deal with his own shit. Lewis was never as disturbed by what they did in combat as Jonah had been. And even though Lew knew his country was messed up, he'd joined after 9/11 because he loved it enough to defend it, thinking it was under imminent attack. Jonah had joined for very different reasons. "Did you ever think you'd had enough of all the crap we went through in Iraq?" he asked Lewis.

Lewis frowned and looked down at the grey carpet. "Well yeah, I'm still a human being," he said. Sounds of acknowledgement from the group followed. He looked up at Jonah. "Did we kill bad guys who deserved it? Hell yeah we did."

Jonah scoffed. "Yeah, and did we also kill men that were better, godlier men than us?"

Lewis nodded slowly. "Damn straight. But that's what we signed up for, man. You were running from some legit fucked-up shit to fight for a country you never grew up in when you joined. But me? I'm proud to have served the US of A. Feel me?" A chorus of *oorahs* went around the room.

"Would any of you do it again?" Jonah asked the group.

"Not sure," Ben Whitewolf said. Others around the room shrugged or shook their head no. A few nodded yes.

"Oh *hell* no, bro," Lewis said. "Not me. But then I wouldn't have met you, and we all wouldn't have had each other's backs out there." Lewis tapped Jonah's chest with the back of his hand. "Especially *you*, Jonah Seeger. I'll *never* forget what you did for me, brother. Mad, deep respect. Us lookin' out for each other? *That's* what I'm most proud of, bro." All in the Wounded Warriors group nodded and offered words of agreement. Lewis continued, "You and I made it back home in one piece, bro."

Jonah laughed, looked down at his leg and tapped his metal shin. "Well, almost in one piece."

Amidst the chuckles Ben stood, walked over to the craft table and poured himself a coffee. "You've been with us a few weeks now," he said as he took his seat again. "Can you share with us the moment when your ship stopped sinking? When a life preserver was thrown to you?"

Jonah rubbed his knuckles again, peered down at his feet. "Sure. The real kicker was when my mom and grandma came down from BC to visit. We were sitting on lawn chairs in my dad's backyard, roasting some wieners and marshmallows over the firepit. It was a clear, crisp, starry night. I was sitting next to my mom, enjoying a beer. I hadn't seen her that happy in years, man. So thrilled that I'd be going home to meet my son soon. Thrilled that she had a grandson. My grandma Polly had just brought out some snacks from the kitchen. My dad was across the fire from me, inspecting Lewis's robo-arm with Ben. I was smiling at my ma, about to tell her how nice she looked in her new contacts—her thick glasses always made her eyes so gigantic—when... *bam, bam, bam*! The neighbours' kids blow off some firecrackers. That was it. I lost it. The channel changed—" Jonah snapped his fingers. "—Just like that. Backyard campfire scene, gone, and I swear I'm back in Fallujah. I went into full infantry mode." Jonah sat up in his chair and started miming his actions. "I sprang up, pounced on my mom and tackled her backwards to the ground. She screamed, her cup of tea flying out of her hands. I hunched over her to shield her, while yelling for all of us to get down. I looked insane. I searched for Lewis, spotted him hunched over in his chair, hugging his knees. I couldn't understand why he wasn't moving. Frantic, I reached for my grandma while still shielding my mom, and I ripped away her tray of snacks and scratched at her pant leg, screaming, confused, trying to yank her down to safety, and then more firecrackers, and I'm not in my dad's backyard anymore. I'm in the thick of battle. The absolute thick of it..." Jonah slowly stepped back and sat down in his chair. His thousand-yard stare hushed the room.

After a while, Ben unbuttoned his medal-adorned Vietnam jungle camo, shuffled in his seat, then broke the silence. "Should've seen. I had to pull Jonah off his mom myself. Poor woman, she was so utterly shocked. Just frozen like a deer in the headlights. Roy and I pinned Jonah to the ground, but he was still at war... bucking, and spitting, growling and moaning, nostrils flared, face red as a ripe tomato. At least five or six times I had to yell, 'Marine, stand down,' my nose an inch away from his, getting sprayed with spit, smelling the fear on his breath. A hard smack across his face finally snapped him out of it."

Jonah rubbed his palms into his eyes and slid them down over his face. He blew out a big breath, shook his head. He slapped his thigh. "And that, folks, is when I knew... That's when I *really* knew I needed a shrink *and* these group sessions." Had it not been for both those remedies that past month, especially the support of the Wounded Warriors, Jonah knew with absolute certainty the PTSD would've killed him. Knowing he had Sasha wasn't enough like he thought it would be.

"But check this y'all." Lewis looked at Jonah. "Bro, what your granny did next... Reminds me of my own granny back in Buffalo. Mad tough, no nonsense, man. Ladies of faith. Know what I'm sayin'?"

Jonah smiled and nodded. "Yup. Grandma Polly. Didn't really know her that well growing up. Had last seen her the Christmas before I deployed. But she's in my life now. Happy for it too. She still has this thick long hair, barely gone grey..."

"Could've sworn she was an old Indian woman when I first saw her," Ben said.

"Yeah, at that point I'd hugged and apologized to my mom, made sure everyone was okay. But I'm still kinda in shock, you know? Pacing around the backyard. Well, my granny, she methodically ties her hair back, steps around the fire, calls me by my Russian name. 'Vanya,' she says, loud and clear. She's only called me that once before, when I was a kid, so it stops me pacing. Grandma Polly slowly, resolutely approaches me. She puts her hand on my chest, tells me to take this off." Jonah lifted the necklace from under his shirt, showed it to the room of vets. "Got it from her before I went off to war. Cossack earring, family heirloom. I do as Grandma Polly says, hand her the necklace. She bunches it together like she's about to chuck it away, but she brings it up close to her mouth as though she's gonna eat it instead. But she closes her eyes and starts whispering into it. And all of a sudden the neighbour kids on the other side of the fence stop their jabbering and yelling, even the fire stops crackling. I swear the entire city goes silent for a few moments..."

"True dat," Lewis said.

"Old-world magic," Ben added.

"Grandma Polly's whispering gets louder and louder. An ancient Doukhobor prayer, I find out later. She translated it into English for me afterward. I only remember parts of it and I'm no God and Jesus believer, but I tell ya, it felt good to hear the words." Jonah unclasped his necklace, bunched it up in his palm in front of him as his grandma had done, and stared at it while speaking. "Lord, protect and have mercy on this servant of God, Jonah Seeger of the Kazakoffs... Mother Moist Earth, all the sacred places, you were created simply, so forgive us simply, too. Forgive, Mother Earth, with body and deeds, with all thoughts. Forgive..."

For a few moments Jonah remained staring at the necklace bunched in his palm. He looked up around the room and continued. "When my grandma finishes her prayer, she fastens the necklace around my neck, then pulls my head down close to hers, kisses me on the forehead. She glances at my mom who's sitting back by the fire, Lewis's arm around her, and she glances over at Ben and Dad, both their faces shadowy and glowing orange from the fire. Then she pats me on the chest, stares *deep* into me, man, *deep*. Grandma Polly says, 'You are going to learn to forgive. You are going to learn to forgive your mother for the shame she passed down to you, because of the fanaticism I passed down to her, because of the turmoil my parents passed down to me. You are going to forgive your father for leaving you. But most of all my dear Jonah, you are going to learn to forgive yourself for the things you saw, and the things you did and *all* the things you could not do.'"

Nelson, British Columbia, May 2005

The looming mountains of the Kootenays were thick and broad, impenetrable like ancient fortress walls. And just because she couldn't *see* the mountains around her, didn't mean she wasn't feeling them closing in. Ruby and her father had been on the move for fifteen minutes now, Big Nick marching his bulk slowly and methodically a few feet in front of Ruby, both their headlamps casting long, wild shadows through the woodland. For as long as Ruby could remember, mountains had made her feel hemmed in and claustrophobic, leaving her craving open skies and all-day sunshine. During the winter months, weeks would pass in grey faded light and a nightfall that would come way too soon. The need to rid herself of the deep valley gloom made running off to Los Angeles not quite easy, but easier. Since returning home, that old familiar restlessness had been getting into her bones like a creeping, invasive vine. At the Kootenay Holistic Rehabilitation Centre in Ainsworth, Dr. Edler had suggested Ruby go on long walks while there; they'd proven good for clients in the past. She did, and soon found that she yearned for a long afternoon stroll. It didn't matter where, she just needed to move. To sift through her thoughts. To let shit go. This had become Ruby's simple, Dr. Edler–approved mantra: Let shit go.

Day by day Ruby was falling in love with the Kootenays again. The valleys that followed the various rivers—Slocan, Kootenay, Columbia—didn't seem as sun deprived and claustrophobic as they had before. She took a deep breath, reminded herself that she'd made the right decision to come home. To get clean. To be a proper mother to her son. To reconnect with Jonah at long last and offer him the chance to be the father he should've known he was for the past six years.

"Let shit go," Ruby repeated to herself as she traipsed along, swatting wildly at what turned out to be a falling pine cone that bounced off her head. But why for the love of God had her dad insisted on starting the hike while it was still dark? She remembered Big Nick hitting the trails when she was a kid and teenager, and always refusing when he'd ask if she wanted to join. "It'll be good for you," he'd say, stuffing his Thermos and some devilled-egg sandwiches into his pack. "It'll give you that prairie view," as he called it. She could never see the point in walking up a mountain. Walking to meet up with friends after school, to go for a swim at Crescent Beach, to go to band practice, sure. But walking just for the sake of walking, especially when she was a teenager, seemed utterly pointless. And what did a "prairie view" have to do with a mountain valley anyway? The only other hike she'd been on was ironically not in the outdoor enthusiasts' paradise that was BC but in the dry, scrubby hills above Hollywood. The band members in Caravana thought it would be a good bonding experience to do the Runyon Canyon loop alongside LA's finest and fittest, and all just for a view of Hollywood's toniest homes. Turned out they couldn't see jack shit through the smog, and ended up sitting in a circle, plotting their next tour, laughing about their past antics, draining their flasks of vodka and whisky in the process.

Left foot, right foot, left foot, right foot. Ruby was in step with her father's march. How did Big Nick keep such a solid pace? she wondered, her headlamp beam sweeping the root- and stone-strewn path in front of her. Her dad had suggested the Pulpit Rock hike overlooking Nelson a few days earlier when he and her mother and Sasha had come for their thrice-weekly visit to the rehab facility. She was granted a day away as long as she was supervised. Her dad had picked her up at four in the morning. After forty-five minutes of dark winding road from Ainsworth to Nelson along the North Shore of Kootenay Lake, they parked on Johnstone Road across from downtown, the city's glimmering lights stark against the night. In the chilly pre-dawn Ruby regretted not wearing a warmer outfit than her runners, yoga pants, t-shirt and hoodie. Her teeth had clattered as her dad handed her a wool toque, then strapped a Petzl headlamp around her dishevelled blonde head. Big Nick was wearing what

Big Nick had always worn, first as a logger, then later as the logging company manager, or when he was gardening with Ruby's mom in the backyard, and even out for a family dinner at a nice restaurant: leather lace-up boots, denim overalls, and a red and black plaid mac jacket.

"Dad... Uhh... Why are we hiking so early again?" she'd asked him before they'd set off.

"To properly welcome a new day," he'd said as he adjusted the intensity of her beam. "It's a blessing." He'd squeezed her shoulders, clapped his hands together, and waved for her to follow. Then he turned and headed into the pitch-black beyond.

Now, twenty minutes up the mountainside, Ruby's thumping heart and wheezing lungs were both begging for her to stop. But she kept pace with the seasoned mountain man ahead. The farther they hiked up the narrow path, the more the city lights shrank below. It wasn't long before Ruby needed a sip of water. She stopped, slipped off her small day pack and retrieved her water bottle. Sweat trickled down her back. As she sipped, she took in a crisp lungful of earthen, dewy forest air. She closed her eyes and enjoyed just breathing for a moment.

"That's a mix of cedar, pine and Douglas fir you're smelling," Ruby's dad offered. "With a mix of sprouting undergrowth, and spicy tree resin." He lifted his head and sniffed the air. "Strong hints of sweet Cottonwood budding down at the lakeside as well. All together that's the sweet scent of springtime in British Columbia, honey." In Russian, he asked her if she had missed it. "*Skuchala?*"

Ruby nodded, hadn't realized just how much she'd missed the fresh scent until that moment. How did she ever adjust to LA's smog? Or taking two hours to drive somewhere half an hour away? All the people, everywhere, all the time, too. Ruby scoffed to herself at the thought of them. God, some Angelenos were so disingenuous. At parties, as soon as they found out she was in a band they'd heard of, they'd be nice to her, try to cloak that they wanted something from her with shallow conversation. Ruby kept her eyes closed, crisp air

cleansing her of LA. She'd gotten lucky, she supposed. She was invited and thrust into the city's music scene without having to sell herself on the way up. So many women that she knew in the biz weren't so fortunate: sex in exchange for a record deal, and copious amounts of drugs to try to erase memories of those transactions. But the forgetting never lasted too long, did it?

A hollowness the size of a peach pit formed in Ruby's stomach. She knew now that she'd fooled herself into thinking that when she left the Kootenays six years ago, she was so cool, authentic and sophisticated, so liberated. She'd been so full of herself because, she thought, there's nothing quite like looking back on the small town you've left behind.

Ruby closed her eyes, could see Dr. Edler at rehab writing in his notepad, adjusting his black, thick-rimmed designer glasses, then tenting his hands in front of his chin in a stereotypical psychiatrist pose. "What were you really leaving behind? What were you running from?"

The hollowness in Ruby's stomach was now the size of a fist as she hiked on. She'd thought that by running away to Los Angeles all her needs would be taken care of: for freedom, for a like-minded music community, for safety and self-sufficiency. The need for true love. "I was just running away from myself," she'd told Dr. Edler, "and stumbling right back into the fucked-up Ruby I had been since I was fifteen."

According to Dr. Edler people much like herself commonly bundle all their needs into a single, monolithic need... the need for a drug. For her, cocaine. The memory of that rehab session now had Ruby's entire stomach hollowed out with grief. A gust of cool wind blew down the mountain and soothed her flushed face.

She'd told Dr. Edler during that session that the drugged-up version of herself ran away to a fake-ass city to pursue a dream. "I could've pursued my dreams from here," she'd said, jabbing at the floor, "supported by family and friends in this beautiful part of the world where my ancestors have lived for a hundred years. And most

importantly, I wouldn't have been a shitty-ass mom who broke a little boy's heart over and over again."

"Let shit go," Ruby mouthed. Let shit go. She took off her toque and stuffed it into her pack.

Ruby's dad had been glancing back at her that whole time. He stopped, turned, tilted his headlamp skyward. "How are you doing... with everything?"

Ruby peered off the path, her headlamp's beam illuminating the steepness of the mountainside. "It's going. One month clean and sober, Dad."

"Not even allowed a beer or glass of wine, eh?"

"It's not advisable. Being drunk, especially on tour, always, without fail, put me in the mood for... worse."

Nick squinted with concern. He nodded slowly. "You ever get that urge, honey... I didn't know how to handle it properly when we first brought you back home. But now... I can do my best to talk you off that ledge."

"Thanks, Dad." She'd be going to him daily if that were the case. Ruby slung her pack back on and gave her father two thumbs up.

It was twenty minutes later, when they were on a steep section of the trail, that sustained gusts of wind blew up from the lake. Ruby looked up from the mesmerizing path. Faintly, the deep blue of a new day was emerging. Her father was far ahead, almost out of sight. The rushing blast of wind through the trees whipped up Ruby's hair, drowned out her breathing, her rapidly beating heart. But the wind couldn't silence the nagging thoughts that, like clockwork, had started minutes earlier. On tour, if she was ever up this early it was only because the night's party was still raging. She'd be drunk, blasted on blow, sometimes mixed with oxy, wanting the night to last forever. "Let shit go," she yelled to the wind and swaying trees. But just the mere thought of cocaine teased her with tiny flickers of arousal. The wind died down. She laughed a choppy laugh. She could hear her dad calling from up ahead. She set off again, watching one foot stepping in front of the other, left, right, left, right, onward, upward.

By coming back home, Ruby had been able to apply pressure to the wound. But she knew she had a lot of walking to do, plenty of amends still to make before she could fully stem the bleed. Drugs equalled freedom, excitement, self-worth and escape for her. This was etched into her orbitofrontal cortex. At least that's what Dr. Edler had kept telling her. The bliss of dopamine could still be sparked in her ventral striatum, wherever the hell that was. Those were the conditions of her nervous system now.

"But not forever," she said, spotting the beam of her dad's headlamp. "I can do it. It is possible. I *will* do it." She'd do it for herself. More importantly, she'd do it for Sasha.

Ten minutes later Big Nick was drinking from his Thermos, sitting, waiting for Ruby on the sloping face of Pulpit Rock. She walked up to him, eased down beside him. She caught her breath and let her aching leg muscles rest. The shimmering lights of Nelson hundreds of feet below were flickering away as the first powder-blue smudges of dawn traced the mountains behind the town. Ruby's dad pulled out a devilled-egg sandwich from his pack, unwrapped it from its plastic wrap and gave Ruby half. They ate in silence, a light breeze on their faces, birds chirping to each other in the forest as the dark receded.

Ruby's dad finally spoke. "First time I came up here was for an evening snowshoe with a couple friends and my Uncle Ivan leading us. Must've been oh… '62, I think. I was barely thirteen. It was a cold, clear night, endless stars twinkling above. We were sitting pretty much in this exact same spot, drinking hot chocolate, when all of a sudden we hear a faint explosion down in town. Few minutes later we can see the Nelson courthouse is on fire… Svobodniki."

"Oh yeah, I heard about this from Baba Mary."

"Tried to destroy it. Beautiful old stone building, like some little European castle."

"Why exactly?"

Ruby's dad shrugged. "Freedomites being Freedomites. They were mad as hell over what happened up in New Denver, I guess."

"The school their kids were sent to?"

"Mhmm. Crazy times those were. Crazy times." He glanced at Ruby. "I don't wanna come off as sounding like your Baba Mary, but your Jonah there has some of that Svobodnik blood in him you know."

Ruby frowned and glared at her dad. "And?"

Ruby's dad placed his hand on her hand that rested on her thigh. He spoke in Russian using the tender version of her given name. "Luba, I'm just saying, he's been a soldier. You yourself said he was suffering from the shell shock—"

"—PTSD, Dad. It's called PTSD now, and he's been working really hard at feeling okay again. Just like I've been."

"Look, all I'm saying is Sasha has been through a lot. And there's no way on God's green Earth me and your mother are going to let him get hurt..." He looked away. "More than he already has."

Ruby swallowed a lump of sudden grief. Fair enough, she thought. "I know, Dad, I know." Ruby looked away. "It's all my fault."

"That's not what I'm saying."

"But it's true. You and Mom, you've been... There's nothing I could ever do to show you how thankful I am that you guys stepped up when I wouldn't... couldn't."

"It takes a family, a village, as they say, to raise a child. Just like it was back when I was a kid. Raising a family was a community effort. You never have to thank us for giving us that special boy. Just... don't run off again."

Some days it was easy to make that promise. Some days, not so much. Because it was a promise that felt as fragile as if she were crossing a raging canyon river on an old wooden ladder whose rungs were threatening to crack. It would be a struggle. She'd likely lose her footing now and then. She'd stumble. She'd fall. But in her heart, she knew she would never leave Sasha again.

The first beams of sunlight crested over the eastern horizon. Ruby and her father welcomed the warm radiance on their faces. The surrounding mountain peaks were touched by a peach glow while wispy orange clouds slid across the sky.

After a while Ruby's dad continued. "Me and your mother, we just don't want Jonah around so much if he's not… if he's not right in the head. *Ti ponimaesh?*"

She understood. Ruby slid closer to her father. "Dad, just like raising Sasha is a family effort, and me getting better is a family effort, it's the exact same with Jonah getting better, too. Yeah, he made a bad decision to run off and join the Marines—"

Ruby's dad scoffed lightly. "That's an understatement, honey."

"Yeah, it was dumb… and tragic… and painful. But we've all done stupid shit, Dad."

"Not *that* stupid, Ruby." When matters were serious her father spoke in Russian. He asked her what kind of man Jonah was. "*Ohn kakoy chelovek?*" Switching back to English, he said, "He's no Doukhobor."

"Fuck, Dad." Ruby squeezed her eyes shut and balled her fists. "Stop it." She peered at her father who was looking down at his palms, tracing lines with his thumb. "I've always looked up to you. Don't spoil that for me."

He opened his Thermos and took a sip, handed it to Ruby, who shook her head. "Me and your mother just want what's best for you."

"Jonah is *family*, dad. He's with us for the rest of our days. And he's going to need our help too. We need to welcome him back into the community, not *shun* him, not make him feel like a pariah."

"Well I'm certainly not going to treat him bad. I'm not going to shun him."

"Do better than that."

"He doesn't care about his Doukhobor roots," her dad said.

"Maybe. Maybe not. We don't know. Lots of our ancestors were soldiers at one time too."

Big Nick's face was orange from the sunrise. He squinted and nodded slowly, looked at Ruby. "Okay… *dochka*. He's family now, yes. But I need to see him face to face. I need to see how he is with Sasha and how Sasha is with him before I fully approve."

"Fair enough." Ruby slung her arm around her dad, hugged his bulk into her, and watched the unfolding beauty in front of them. As sunbeams climbed down the sides of the mountains, the morning breeze died away. Far below, the lake began sparkling silver. Steam rose from the rockface around them. Cheery birdsong grew louder.

"That's the prairie view you always talked about?"

"That's it. When you can see for miles and miles... that's a prairie view. And the only way we can get that around here is from up in the mountains."

Ruby took a big, easy breath. For the first time in days she felt light and hopeful. "I get it now."

"I know you always felt... hemmed in here, even as a kid. Maybe now though, try to think of the mountains like I do. As protectors."

Ruby looked at her dad when he said *protectors*. She smiled wide, grabbed his hand and stood up. "Check it out. My new mantra." Like a wizard casting a spell, she burst her arms out in front of her and flared her fingers. "Let shit go!" she yelled to the bright, sunny morning.

Ruby's dad looked surprised, impressed. She gestured to him with her chin. "My turn?" he said, eyebrows raised.

Ruby nodded. Big Nick copied his daughter, thrust his long thick arms out in front of him. Like a bear up on its hind legs, protecting its family, he roared, "Let shit go!"

Ruby laughed a joyous, freeing laugh at her father until her stomach muscles hurt. Together they burst out their wizard arms to the world and in unison shouted her new mantra over and over.

Sharon was tickled pink to have Jonah's friend Lewis and her family in her home: her eldest, Julian, the boys' grandma Polly, and her brother Yuri. Everyone except for her was seated at the table about to enjoy the dinner she and her mother had specially prepared. She was too nervous to sit, instead flitting about between the kitchen and the dining room making sure everyone had what they needed. The house was filled with the fragrant aromas of baking, melted butter and creamy vegetarian borsch.

Sharon had set the table with a seating arrangement in mind, but when it came time to eat, Jonah had insisted that not only would he and Lewis sit facing the window, but the blinds throughout the house would be drawn, as well. At first perplexed at her son's insistence, it was when she noticed him scanning the neighbourhood through cracked open blinds, then recalled the SUV with tinted windows that she saw parked in front of her place back in November, that she understood.

"Thank you, ladies." Lewis leaned into his food to closely inspect it. "This all smells *so* delicious. Mm-mm."

Jonah and his brother, Julian, had spent the morning catching up, playing video games with Lewis downstairs while Sharon had vacuumed her area rugs, dusted her antique lamps and chosen which of her favourite spring dresses to wear now that they fit her again. The boys' grandma Polly had travelled over a mountain pass from her home in Creston to help prepare the meal. The compact kitchen in Sharon's Victorian-era heritage home, while stocked with decent appliances, could be claustrophobic. But Sharon had enjoyed toiling over the stove again with her mother, who at seventy-five was a better cook than ever. Yuri as usual had arrived late. He'd come in through the back door moments before. Stepping into the kitchen, he removed his ball cap, curtsied ever so slightly and, as though Jonah's homecoming dinner was news to him, asked what was happening in Doukhobor slang. "*Noo chewoh?*"

Lewis reached into his pocket, brought out his cellphone, and began taking photos of the feast. "What y'all call these again?" He hovered the camera phone over his plate piled with food.

From his place at the head of the table Yuri undid the top button of his butter-coloured dress shirt, adjusted his purple suspenders and pointed at the small heap of dumplings. "Most people know those as perogies, but the Doukhobors call them by their proper name, *vareniki*."

Sharon hadn't seen Yuri since the fall, her mother in even longer. First her mother, then Sharon hugged Yuri at length. And after introductions to Lewis and a quick hug for Julian, Sharon steered Yuri's attention to Jonah. "He's grown up since you last saw him, eh Yuri?"

Yuri had eyed Jonah up and down, then levelled a friendly gaze at his nephew. Along with Sharon, Jonah and Yuri shared the dark, almond-shaped Kazakoff eyes. And for the first time Sharon saw that the similarities went beyond genetics. Jonah and Yuri both had the sharp, vigilant look of men who'd lived scrappy, unconventional lives, parts of which were spent on the run. Sharon knew her baby boy had seen and done more than most twenty-five-year-olds. As Jonah peered into Yuri's lucid, musing eyes, could he see that his uncle was truly an old soul? Since she was a child, every now and then Sharon would look at Yuri and see someone who had returned for one final incarnation to impart a few more secrets to life. She knew that Yuri, like herself, like Jonah, like so many people, had regrets. But unlike most people's, Yuri's eyes rarely betrayed any traces of them. Like his uncle had learned to do, perhaps one day Jonah would also learn how to make peace with himself.

Uncle Yuri had shaken Jonah's hand firmly, held his gaze sincerely and with just a hint of a smile said, "Welcome home."

Now sitting at the head of the table, Yuri was explaining to Lewis that, much like for the French, the secret to Doukhobor cuisine was lots of butter. Across the table from Jonah and Lewis, Sharon's mother was staring at Lewis as she had done periodically since she'd arrived. Sharon laughed to herself; her mother had likely never spent so much time with a Black man, and certainly not one as gigantic as Lewis.

Sharon's mother spoke. "And… and those oval tarts are called *pyrahi*." She pointed at a glass oven dish in the middle of the table. "We made four different kinds."

Sitting next to his grandmother, Julian scratched his chin and rubbed his hands together. "Definitely my fave."

Sharon found it amusing that technically Jonah was the little brother. Julian wasn't shaggy haired and bearded like Jonah was and his lankiness compared to Jonah's filled-out frame made *him* seem like the younger one now. Not only in stature. Julian's forehead wasn't etched with deep lines; he didn't have the faraway, haunted eyes that Jonah sometimes did now, and all his limbs were still intact. Julian, God bless him, lived a regular life in Castlegar, managing the Lions Head Pub, dating Cassandra, one of the waitresses.

Sharon wiped her hands on her apron and continued the food tour. "Those *pyrahi* are filled with mashed peas, those ones with mashed beans, cottage cheese over here, and these are with beets." Sharon grabbed the cup of melted butter. "Now be generous with the butter on the tarts, Lewis, and make sure to add dollops of sour cream.

"This salad here," Yuri said, pointing, "is my mother's specialty."

"It's called vinaigrette," Sharon's mother said, "made with beets, kidney beans and pickles. And if you like things hot add this home-grown horseradish to it."

"And this." Sharon scooped a ladleful of soup into Lewis's bowl. "*This* is Jonah's favourite… creamy potato and cabbage borsch."

"Everything here is a vegetarian Doukhobor specialty, hand-made by Mom and sister," Yuri proudly announced as he twisted his beard.

"So, eat up." Sharon's mother gestured with her chin. "Looks like you can fit a lot in there." She laughed and Lewis nodded vigorously. Grandma Polly pointed at Lewis. "You know, many of our Doukhobor men are like your people…"

Oy, *your people*? Sharon thought. Where was she going with this? Jonah glanced at Sharon with furrowed brows. She held her breath…

"Big, strong…" Grandma Polly said. "Proud."

Lewis smiled. "Yes ma'am. Only way we could've survived all these hundreds of years."

"And faith?" Sharon's mother asked.

"Mhmm, whole lotta faith, too… and… caution," Lewis said.

"Caution?" Yuri asked, taking a sip of his beer.

"Yes, sir," Lewis said, putting his phone down on the table. "I don't know what it's like up in Canada. I mean, on the drive here from Spokane, not a Black man in sight, but in the US of A, I know where I'm welcome… and where I am not."

"Welcome?" Sharon's mother said. "But segregation is over… thank God."

"Yes ma'am, technically. But not in reality. Let me put it this way, when I knew I was joining Jonah out here in the honky-tonk west, and I seen how close we was to Idaho, I said to myself, I gotta make sure I bring a pistol."

"A pistol? What on Earth for?" Sharon asked.

"Sorry," Lewis said, taking in everyone at the table, "I know all y'all is pacifists but… as a Black man in America I know *exactly* where I ain't wanted in America. And northern Idaho…" Lewis pointed toward the back door. "Like Montana, and Wyoming and all those Republican cowboy states… Northern Idaho is one of them places."

Jonah nodded. "Hmm. Yeah, I'd heard stories when I was a kid about neo-Nazis and KKK compounds in northern Idaho."

"Oy," Sharon said with a smile, "well good thing this isn't Idaho. You're safe here, Lewis." Her smile instantly vanished though as she thought of the Pritchard brothers and the troubles Jonah potentially still faced. As if picking up on Sharon's thoughts, Jonah and Lewis glanced at each other.

"You're in Doukhobor country now," Sharon's mother said. "You didn't actually bring a pistol with you, did you?"

Both Jonah and Lewis shuffled in their seats and again glanced at each other. "He didn't, Grandma," Jonah said. He turned to his mother who was still hovering around the table making sure everyone had what they needed. "Anyway… *spasibo,* Mom… Grandma. You can't imagine how much I've missed this food."

Sharon and her mother raised their eyebrows at each other. Jonah speaking Russian? Sharon stepped behind Jonah, leaned down and wrapped her arms around him.

He smiled. "Little by little I'm trying to learn the language. It means *thank you,*" he told Lewis.

Sharon was infinitely relieved that her baby boy was home, safe and sound. She hugged him even tighter and gave him a peck on the cheek. And even though she still needed to keep it a secret, she was thrilled too that little Sasha Samarodin was blood, that Jonah could experience the joy of being a father, and that she, finally, could be a grandmother.

Lewis echoed Jonah's appreciation for the feast. "*Spa… sibo.*"

* * *

After dinner Yuri was standing at the head of the table gesticulating, telling one of his stories to a rapt audience. He caught Sharon smiling up at him and gave her one of his mischievous winks, which caused the past to hurl itself at her, to thrust Sharon back to a cold, blustery winter day in New Denver. She was just seven years old, Yuri around twelve. They were standing behind a chain-link fence visiting with their mother and father for their allotted hour. Sharon was so small and frail, shivering uncontrollably. Her little fingers clutched the frosty fence. She still couldn't understand why she and Yuri and all the other kids had been sent to that old prison camp by the lake. She cried and cried because she couldn't go home with her parents. Her mother was unable to embrace her and wipe her tears away. Instead, Yuri did it, like he always did when he spotted her weeping in her bunk bed or outside a classroom. At that godforsaken prison school

Yuri was always there for her, even when *he* was suffering from getting picked on for being different, a "limp-wristed queer," as the other boys would say. Even when he was ghostly pale, stone-faced and distant from the abuse he'd suffer at the hands of that devil Ms. Clarkson, Yuri could still find it within himself to wrap his arm around little Sharon.

"Mom, you're not gonna cry *again* are you?" Jonah's voice mercifully brought her back to where she was sitting opposite Yuri at the dinner table. Perhaps one day, she thought, when he was himself again, she'd tell Jonah the whole story.

"Ah, let her," Lewis said. "My momma cried for a week straight when I got home."

Sharon dabbed at her tears now. Her emotions were welling from thinking about her past, from knowing her baby boy had his own trauma to deal with too. And she could do very little to help relieve him, which made her suddenly feel thin and skinless, her emotions raw and muddled and flowing in such a way that she didn't think she could stop them. The price for not popping a Xanax. She glanced down at her plate of food which she had barely touched and all at once felt the urge to scarf it down as quickly as possible, to eat all the leftovers on the table, then cook the entire feast again and consume it all by herself. Sharon closed her eyes and took a big breath instead. "You fellas don't know what it's like to have children." Sharon glanced at her mother. "From the first second we cradle you and set eyes on you, our hearts are filled with worry." Sharon considered Jonah now, fidgeting in his chair. Years of nightmares—when she could even sleep—agonizing about his safety, surfaced unstoppably now like a venting volcano. Her voice quivered when she continued. "Especially if you go off to fight in some, some… stupid war." She pawed at the air.

Yuri placed his elbows on the table, clasped his hands and rested them against his white whiskers. He peered at Sharon with an uneasy look she remembered well from when they were adolescents and she was about to get into it with their parents. "Please don't go there," it said. But Sharon couldn't help herself. In place of the need to binge, a need to vent took over.

Jonah exhaled heavily and looked at her with the same tilted-head, droopy-faced way he had as a teenager.

"I may not be the most devout Doukhobor," Sharon said, "but I sure as hell did not raise you to be a soldier, Jonah." She looked to Lewis. "I'm sorry, Lewis, I mean no disrespect to your American traditions." Sharon swiped tears from her cheeks.

Jonah tried to look anywhere but at his mother. Agitated, he said, "Okay, okay, Mom, now's not the friggin' time."

"Mhmm," Yuri, Julian and Sharon's mother agreed in unison.

Sharon ignored them. Lewis's chair creaked as he shuffled his big frame. Sharon placed her hand over her heart, looked down around the table as though she were searching for something. "The whole time you were deployed I just couldn't… I couldn't stop thinking of all those poor mothers out there… and their sons… *killing* each other." She looked at everyone around the table, then rested her gaze on Jonah. "And for what? Hmm? For what?"

"Mom…" Jonah looked up at the ceiling. He winced, groaned and shook his head like someone who'd just swallowed some rancid food.

"Stasya…" Grandma Polly leaned forward, used Sharon's Russian name, glared at her. Julian placed his hand on his mother's shoulder in an attempt to calm her.

"Look at you boys." Sharon pointed to Jonah and Lewis. "Missing limbs, metal plates keeping your bones together, scars for—"

Bam! Jonah's palm slammed on the table, sending silverware clattering against dishes, and everyone flinching in their seats. Jonah's eyes glazed over, cold and distant. Sharon's hands started shaking as she leaned into Julian, the memory of Jonah throwing her to the ground in Spokane all too fresh.

Lewis put his hand on Jonah's back, causing him to recoil. "Breathe, bro. Chill."

Grandma Polly eased herself up to standing. Jonah glanced at her sidelong with a look of shame. She poked repeatedly toward his chest.

He looked at her, down at his chest, back at her and then seemed to understand. He lifted his Cossack earring necklace, rubbed it between his fingers, took big breaths.

Grandma Polly glared at Sharon, asked her in Russian if she was finished. "*Zakonchila?*"

Jonah slowly pushed his chair back and stood. He covered his face with his hands and wiped them down to his chin. "I'm sorry. Please, Mom. It's hard enough as it is." Yuri scooched his chair in as Jonah stepped around him. Jonah helped his mother stand, then gave her a tight, reassuring hug. "I'm sorry I scared you. It's, it's just … Remember in the hospital when you said healing has its own timeline?"

Sharon nodded. Yuri stood and walked to the kitchen. Julian joined him.

"I'm still at the beginning of mine."

"It's just … I feel helpless," Sharon said, looking into Jonah's eyes.

"This …" Jonah swept his hand over the table. "You guys here, home-cooked meals, that's enough … for now."

"How about Ruby … and Sasha? Are you ready?" Sharon asked.

"*Och*, he's ready." Sharon's mother raised her hand in front of her. "Just stop pestering him, for God's sake."

Yuri and Julian returned with beers, and tea for Sharon and her mother. Jonah pointed to the ceiling with both forefingers and moved them around. "Feeling ready is the goal … but the goalposts keep moving." He returned to his seat beside Lewis. "All I know is I need more than anything to see them … They're family now."

Yuri eased into his seat then shot right back up again as though he'd sat on a pincushion. Sharon watched him take a swig of beer, clear his throat. His face was flushed pink from the booze and that sparkle was in his eye. Sharon knew what came next. Yuri pulled at his beard and nodded at everyone at the table. He began to speak in his wise, measured voice that had a way of drawing people in. "We Doukhobors … We have a saying … '*Vce khorosho v svoye vremya*.'" Yuri lifted his beer in front of him. "It means, 'Everything … good …

in… its… own… time,'" he said, punctuating each word with little nods of his bottle. "Let's drink to that, eh?"

Sharon lifted her mug and along with everyone else reached to the centre of the table and clinked their drinks together. Yuri's keynote was clearly not done though. He spun around to face the front door and raised his beer in toast. "To the Kootenays out there, to my fellow citizens, to my Doukhobor brothers and sisters; I have not always been good to you… And for that I am very sorry." Yuri turned back and cast his eyes next toward Sharon. She forced a smile, unsure of what was coming. He raised his beer to her. "Sister, my actions in the past have hurt you, and I wasn't always there for you like a big brother should have been…" He bowed his head ever so slightly. "And for that I am truly sorry."

Sharon's chin quivered as she nodded at him.

Yuri turned to face their mother as a sadness washed over her face. "To you, my dear mother…" Yuri raised his drink. "I am deeply sorry for causing our family more grief than we needed."

Grandma Polly was momentarily frozen in place. She wiped her eyes, then gently clasped her tea and raised it ever so slightly. "M-me too." She glanced at Sharon, then back at Yuri. "I'm sorry."

Yuri smiled, leaned forward slightly. To Julian, Jonah and Lewis he said, "I'd like to get to know you boys better if that's all right with you." They raised their glasses to him. Yuri eased down into his seat then shot up to standing yet again. "Oh, one last thing if you'll allow. I want to thank everyone. I'm glad we're all here, alive in this moment, sharing a beautiful meal together as family. And can I suggest we let the past go as though it were unwanted luggage? You just put it down beside you." Yuri mimed placing luggage on the ground. "And walk away." He wiped his hands together. "Then let come what may, hm? We'll face the future together, striving to be better. How does that sound?"

Lewis clapped his hands. "Hear, hear, my little white elder. You wise like Gandalf." Lewis giggled. Sharon, her mother, Julian and Jonah laughed heartily. Yuri chuckled, twisted his beard and took a bow. Everyone stood, clinked their bottles and glasses yet again, then drank. Jonah stood and made his way around the table hugging everyone, saving the last one for Lewis. They bumped chests, and whispered, "Oorah."

Sharon felt bad for pressing her baby boy, for triggering his PTSD. She imagined most soldier's mothers would tell their sons how proud they were of them for their service. But Sharon's unending relief that he'd made it home alive was still muddled with the shame she felt that he'd gone in the first place. Welling tears stung her eyes. She reached out for Lewis's hand and her mother's hand and gestured for everyone to grab the hand of the person next to them.

"Now what?" her mother asked.

Sharon closed her eyes and in her rusty, halting Russian, began reciting the Doukhobor prayer, *Dom Nash Blagodatniy*, Our Blessed Home. Her brother and mother joined her, helped her carry the incantation along almost to its conclusion. But the prayer was cut short by the sound of tires screeching to a halt on the street outside the dining room window, followed by the blat of a revving diesel engine.

Jonah's heart leapt as he unclasped prayer hands with Lewis and Yuri. Something about the revving diesel engine didn't feel right. Both Jonah and Lewis stood, their chairs scraping against the hardwood floor. Jonah immediately started rubbing his knuckles as Lewis reflexively opened and closed his prosthetic hand over and over.

"What's wrong?" Sharon asked.

Grandma Polly leaned forward. "What, did someone hear something?"

"I'm... sure it's nothing," Jonah said, his voice betraying anxiety. He automatically reached to his waist for his Marine-issued M18 Sig Sauer handgun that wasn't there. Jonah's eyes darted wildly as he moved quickly to the living room. He gestured to Lewis. "Back door." Julian and Yuri slowly stood.

"What's going on?" Grandma Polly said. Jonah assumed that his mom had told her why Jonah fled years ago and joined the military, but doubted she would've divulged exactly how bad the situation was then... and possibly still was now.

Jonah moved to one end of the living room window, cracked the blinds and squinted out into the rainy night. Across the street from the house a black Hummer H2 with tinted windows sat revving its engine under the orange glow of a streetlamp. Rain lashed its windshield. There were no houses on that side of the street, only an elementary school. From behind the Hummer's rain-blurred windshield came the flick of a lighter sparking up a cigarette. It momentarily illuminated the large man behind the wheel, wearing wraparound shades. "Everybody downstairs," Jonah said. "Now."

Half a minute later, with his family safely locked in the basement spare bedroom, Jonah and Lewis were crouched in the stairwell outside the basement door. What had started as a light shower before dinner was now a monsoon, but neither Jonah nor Lewis had time to don any rain gear. Jonah's nerves were thin, jagged-edged panes of glass. He was still rubbing his knuckles hard as he gulped deep breaths to try and calm himself. Lewis handed him Tupac.

The day before, they'd been waved through the Frontier–Paterson Border Crossing south of Rossland, BC. Lewis was sitting rigidly, sweating profusely, having just produced a metal container from under his seat, then fished a small key from his pocket. He unlocked the case, looked around suspiciously, then lifted the lid. Jonah's eyes popped. He reflexively checked his rear-view mirror. "What the hell? Duuude. What if we'd been searched at the border?"

In the black metal case sat two identical handguns inserted into grey foam slots. "Got all the papers, bro," Lewis said. "Both is Dan Wesson Specialist .45s."

"Lew, it's illegal to bring handguns into Canada."

"Duh, That's why I hid 'em. Besides, these is to protect your ass." With his prosthetic fingers Lewis lifted one of the guns out of its slot and plopped it flat onto the palm of his left hand. "Single amber tritium dot in the rear sight and a green lamp with white target ring in front. Ambidextrous thumb safety. Extended magazine release and detachable two-piece magwell. Duty-black finish." Lewis was beaming as though he were showing off his newborn. "Mine's Biggie, yours is Tupac." After their last Wounded Warrior group session in Spokane, Jonah confessed to his friend that he never wanted to fire a gun again, never wanted to kill another living soul. "With everything you told me 'bout them Hells Angels," Lewis had said. "Shit, bro... You be *dreamin'*."

Now outside the basement door, Jonah reluctantly took the handgun and tucked it into the front of his jeans waistband, then covered it with his hoodie. They crept up the back stairs and through the slanting downpour scanned the tree-lined backyard dimly illuminated by dappled light from neighbours' houses and streetlights. Jonah's heart rate spiked as he caught glimpses of figures in the shadows at the edge of the yard. He ducked and Lewis followed suit. But when Jonah squinted and looked closer, the figures were gone.

"I don't see anything, bro," Lewis whispered.

"Eyes are playing tricks on me," Jonah whispered back. He pointed up the sloped backyard. "I'll head up there and face him from the front of the house. Lots of street light." He gestured with his head down toward town. "You head into the alley and sneak up from behind, keeping in the shadows of trees at the edge of the school. We engage only as a last resort."

"Copy." Lewis nimbly crouch-ran across the lawn, hopped over a wood-slat fence then disappeared into the alley. Jonah slinked around the back of the house, keeping tight against the wall, then stepped over small bushes and planters along the street-facing side of the house. He crouch-walked through the narrow yard, around the trunk of a maple tree, and stepped out onto the sidewalk in full view of the Hummer. By now he was thoroughly soaked. The Hummer revved its engine. Shadowy figures emerged from the schoolyard treeline behind the Hummer. Jonah was about to retreat when he saw that the figures were Sadie, Mason and Sergeant C. Their blurred forms pulsed in and out.

The Hummer's tinted passenger-side window began to slowly descend. Jonah reached down to his waistline and lifted his hoodie high so that his gun's rear slide, hammer, grip and magazine were clearly visible. The unmistakable, party-worn cackle of Clinton Pritchard discharged from the now fully open window at the same instant that Jonah spotted movement in the treeline behind the vehicle. This time it wasn't ghost traces of dead comrades… It was Lewis. He stealthily descended the embankment twenty metres behind the Hummer. In a bid to distract Clinton, Jonah gripped his handgun and removed it from his waistband just as Lewis snuck up behind the SUV. All at once, sirens sounded from cop cars approaching down the steep street in the distance. His mother must've made the call, Jonah thought. They'd have to make this quick. Getting caught with the handguns—especially for Lewis—would be disastrous. Just then Lewis popped up alongside Clinton's driver's-side door, and, rain-soaked and grinning maniacally, tapped the window hard with his gun's muzzle. The glow of flashing red and blue lights emerged from the bottom of Josephine Street. The Hummer's tires spun on the slanted street, over which a shallow creek rapidly flowed. Once the tires caught, the Hummer peeled away, screeched around the corner and sped west to wherever Clinton had come from. Jonah watched as the ghost traces of Mase, Sadie and Sergeant C. turned, moved a few steps and dissolved into the night's torrential rain.

Throughout the final year of the twentieth century the Doukhobors commemorate one hundred years of life in Canada (1899–1999). To help celebrate the occasion the Canadian Museum of Civilization in Ottawa runs a two-year exhibition titled The Doukhobors: "Spirit Wrestlers."

Slocan Valley, British Columbia, May 2005

Jonah clicked off the Jeep's wipers as the light May rain subsided and beams of sunlight broke through the couds. It had been nearly seven years since Jonah was last in the Slocan Valley. With the threatening appearance of Clinton the night before, Jonah knew there was little time to waste. Head properly sorted or not, he'd called Ruby early in the morning and arranged to meet.

Now as Jonah turned off Poplar Ridge Road onto the familiar hedge-lined driveway, his heart was beating so loud it drowned out the Jeep's engine, and his racing thoughts. He relaxed his grip on the steering wheel as he rolled to a stop. His mom had trimmed his hair and his beard, and even though he'd showered that morning, nervousness still wafted from his underarms. With the Jeep parked next to Big Nick's Suburban, Jonah leaned over and opened the glovey, fished around for some pit stick, applied it liberally and smelled himself. He quickly checked the rear-view mirror: freshly trimmed hair had exposed his first few greys jutting out at his temples. Would Ruby think he looked seven years older? Or, like he thought as his eyes stared back at him, an entire lifetime older? He peered out the window. There it was, the big, timber-frame Casa Samarodin he knew so well. It was both familiar and strange to him, just like being back in the Slocan Valley, and back home in general, was. He took a big breath and blew it out forcefully, like he used to before the start of a skate competition. He grabbed the grocery bag full of gifts from the passenger seat, crawled out of the Jeep and hobbled to his new life.

The ring of the doorbell made Ruby jump in her chair. Sasha shot up from his own chair. "Is that him?" His eyes were as big as saucers.

Ruby held up a stop-sign hand meant to calm him. "I'll go see." She gestured to her mom and dad to take Sasha into the living room. "You wait with Baba and Dyeda like we said, okay?"

Ruby hadn't been that nervous since her first show in LA with Caravana six years earlier. Her palms were cold and sweaty. She rubbed them on her jeans as she made her way to the front door. She stopped in the hallway and studied herself in the mirror, picked pieces of lint off the deliberately frumpy sweater she wore. She ran her forefinger underneath her eyes. The purple bags she'd had the first weeks she was home were gone thanks to a combination of helpers: the proper sleep she'd been getting; being with Sasha, her parents and old friends; her mom's home-cooked meals; Sunday service; the rehab; the long walks and hikes with her dad; all the love she'd been getting from everyone. All of it was a big motley remedy helping her to step into a new version of herself. Her twenty-five-year-old face glowed with youth again. She adjusted her bangs and blew herself a kiss. At the front door, she took a big breath, then opened it.

Ruby wrapped her arms around Jonah how he imagined weary World War II soldiers were hugged fresh from the trenches of the Western Front—urgently and generously, with passion and necessity. For what seemed like an eternity in that doorway they were the only two people on Earth.

Jonah's heart swelled knowing that after all that had transpired between him and Ruby time had not curdled his love for her one bit. Quite the opposite. To Jonah, Ruby still smelled like she did when they were teenagers—a fresh, flowery spring rain. Jonah smelled like a man to Ruby, with the faint scent of a warm, musky cologne.

The long embrace was heaven to them both.

Eventually Ruby pulled Jonah inside, shut the door behind him and took his leather jacket.

The familiar scent of disinfected house and home cooking had the peculiar effect—opposite to when Jonah was a teenager—of putting him at ease.

Even as thoughts of that terrible afternoon at the music festival threatened to surface for Ruby, with Jonah's strong arms wrapped around her they were washed away. She melted into the familiarity of his steady, warm heartbeat. How and why did she ever put up with a man-child like Tomás? Ruby hung up Jonah's jacket and turned back to him. "Look at you." She was grinning ear to ear. Lightly she tugged on Jonah's beard, then ran her fingers playfully through his hair. Her eyes filled with tears. Jonah was alive, standing in front of her. Her heart surged and offered itself like it only ever had with him. She wiped her cheeks. She'd rarely seen Jonah in anything but skater clothes. But he'd arrived wearing a designer leather jacket, a white Henley that hugged his muscular chest, blue jeans and brown leather Blundstones. Ruby levelled her gaze, studied Jonah's eyes. The same, she thought, but much sadder. Even though he was grinning ear to ear too, his eyes couldn't hide all that he'd seen and been through. She wondered if hers told a similar story.

To Jonah, Ruby looked as though she were two people at the same time. She'd lost her baby fat, her face was more defined, and her eyes were lightly, attractively lined now and a little wiser. But underneath that face, as though it were translucent, were traces of teenage Ruby as well; cheeky, always stoked for some new adventure, a bit of a freakazoid.

"I love the beard." Ruby squeezed his shoulders and biceps. "You're … you're a man, Jonah."

He laughed. "About time, eh? The Marines fed us well and worked our asses off."

"I'll say." She glanced down at Jonah's legs. "You almost came home in one piece."

Jonah nodded. "Yup. Almost. A little damaged … inside and out."

Ruby pulled Jonah toward herself, wrapped her arms around him again. "Me too, babe."

He looked her in the eye. "Knowing that you were out there somewhere, Rube, and remembering what we had … That got me through it."

Ruby's lips quivered. She sniffled, let her tears surface. "Come in," she said. "We can get into all that later. Ruby breathed a smile back onto her face. "Time to meet someone who's *extremely* excited to meet you …" She glanced back over her shoulder. "Aren't you, Sasha?"

"Yes," came a shy voice as a head full of brown curls vanished behind the wall at the end of the hallway.

Jonah and Ruby both giggled. Jonah wondered if Ruby could hear his heart knocking loudly in his chest. She led him by the hand down the hall into the living room, where her mother and father sat on a big leather couch anxiously waiting. Sasha rocked back and forth on his heels, floppily swung his arms around him.

There was his son: sturdy, shy, perfect... wearing the cowboy boots Ruby had told Jonah about. Sasha was the most beautiful thing Jonah had ever seen. Jonah grinned, if only to keep the stinging tears at bay. This wasn't the place for him to sob. Not yet. If the love he'd felt for Ruby had been bona fide and golden, then in that instant what Jonah felt for Sasha was love transmuted into an elixir, a potion of limitless joy and wonder. It was a feeling he never even knew existed, let alone—it suddenly dawned on him—one he'd needed his whole life. It was a love that was effortless, in the way that smiling when hearing good news was effortless or how the simple act of breathing was. Yet, Jonah considered, at the same time, it was heavy with the unending weight of responsibility.

Jonah raised his hand and gave Sasha a little wave. Virginia patted Sasha on the bum, nudging her grandson forward. Sasha shuffled toward Jonah, arms again swinging back and forth, his gaze anywhere except directly in Jonah's eyes.

It was May of 1995 the first time Virginia encountered a soldier in real life. Nick was at the Kooznetsoffs', next to the river below the Samarodin house, sweating in a t-shirt and overalls, passing sandbags in a line of a dozen soldiers deployed to the valley to help stave off the rapidly rising spring flood waters. Virginia had brought snacks and refreshments to the polite, appreciative young soldiers. They weren't hard, scowling, foul-mouthed men like were depicted in Hollywood action movies. Each could've been a neighbour, someone selecting diapers in a grocery store aisle, an elementary school teacher. And now, a decade later, a soldier who had recently been in combat, who had likely done terrible things, had seen terrible things, and was the father of her beloved little Sasha, was standing in her home. Jonah was still the Jonah she knew as a six-year-old, and as a teenager. And he was not. One look in his eyes and Virginia could tell, twenty-five-year-old Jonah had been profoundly altered. She'd seen the same shipwrecked look in the eyes of young Freedomite boys and girls after they were released from New Denver, and in the eyes of her parents after they'd lost it all to Sons of Freedom arson.

Jonah squatted in front of his son. Sasha's mouth was hanging open, "catching flies," as Virginia would always tell him. Ruby crouched down now too. "Well, what do you say?"

"Hey," Sasha said shyly.

"And?" Virginia said.

Sasha tried not to look directly into Jonah's eyes. "I'm Sasha… Baba told me to say, um… It's nice to meet you." Sasha was relieved when Jonah held his hand up for his preferred high-five instead of a handshake which he always said felt too icky. Sasha smacked Jonah's palm and smiled shyly, finally felt brave enough to look his new dad in the eyes.

"It's *super* nice to meet you too," Jonah said, his chin quivering.

When Virginia had thought of Jonah in her home, she'd imagined she would keep her distance, imagined that if she were to pass him on a sidewalk, she'd give his soldier-tarnished soul a wide berth, as though he were a leper. The thought of giving him a hug had initially repulsed her, which in turn made her feel ashamed. For it was a similar, yet lesser feeling of repulsion she'd had after Ruby confessed her drug addiction.

As Virginia watched her innocent Sasha falling in love by the second with his not-so-innocent father, she shuddered at the thought of how much she'd allowed herself to see imperfection as something beneath her. In her dogged pursuit of Doukhobor excellence, integrity and purity, Virginia had not always been a good person. As a result, she'd been imperfect in her own way, allowing these imperfections to rule her life. She'd allowed fear to steer her impulses. And that fear—which squashed vitality, expression, beauty, respect, integrity… love—had damaged her daughter. And to some extent, she now realized, had damaged Jonah too.

Virginia had rarely seen Jonah be overly emotional when he was a teenager, even when she and Nick didn't treat him as kindly as they should've and he'd had every right to be upset. But now, watching him try to contain what Virginia could only imagine was an intense mix of emotions at meeting his son, made Virginia swallow the sudden need to weep.

Sasha glanced at his mother, then looked at Jonah still squatting in front of him. "Momma Ruby said, she told me, she said that you used to be umm, like boyfriend and girlfriend, and because of that it's how come you are my dad."

Jonah smiled. "That's right." For the first time since he arrived Jonah looked at Virginia and then at Nick. He smiled and nodded at them.

"Sasha, *kotyik*," Virginia said. "Can me and Dyeda say hello to Jonah for one quick second?"

The night before Virginia had phoned her cousin J.J. Verigin Jr., the next in line to be the leader of the Doukhobors, to ask him his opinion about Jonah having served in the military. At forty-seven, J.J. was several years younger than Virginia and had adopted a more progressive, magnanimous, cosmic view of life than she had. She knew J.J. as someone who'd perfected the art of sprawling oration, so it was after twenty minutes of sermonizing that he finally arrived at his point. In his typically effervescent manner he had said, "War makes us sick, but malice makes us sicker."

Virginia got up from the couch, stepped toward Jonah and for the first time ever, hugged him. Then Nick stood and shook Jonah's hand and said it was really good to see him and good to have him back. Virginia hoped Nick was being sincere. Yesterday during supper when Sasha yet again asked—as if still not quite believing the lie—if it was true that Mr. Jonah being a soldier was the reason they couldn't tell Sasha about him, Nick had gone quiet, then eventually just said, "*Da*, Sasha."

With hugs and handshakes done, everyone sat down on the living room couches. Sasha plopped between Jonah and Ruby while Virginia and Nick sat across from them on the sectional. Jonah reached into a paper bag and brought out a present for Sasha. A set of Lego, his favourite.

Sasha thanked Jonah, shook the Lego box and looked at him. "Are you still a soldier?"

"Sash, remember we said we weren't going to ask about that?" Ruby said.

"It's okay," Jonah said. "I used to be a soldier, Sasha. But I'm not anymore."

"Does that mean you can be a Doukhobor like me and Momma Ruby and Baba and Dyeda?"

"Well... I don't know." Jonah glanced at Virginia, then looked at Ruby. "I'm not sure exactly how it works... but I'd like to try."

Sasha spilled his Lego box out onto the carpet. He slid off the couch and sat with the blocks scattered around him. He looked up at Jonah. "How long will you be my father?"

Virginia's heart sank. Jonah wore a look of confusion. Unsure what to say he quickly looked at Ruby, then at Virginia and Nick, and then back at Sasha who patiently waited for an answer. Jonah finally spoke. "I'm going to be your father... from now on."

"Forever?" Sasha asked.

Jonah nodded eagerly. "Forever."

Sasha smiled as wide as the morning Ruby told him that his real dad was coming to meet him, then connected a bunch of coloured blocks to a robot foot piece. "Okay." He pointed at his grandparents. "But Baba and Dyeda made an agreement with Momma Ruby that they will always be like my parents too. Mmkay?"

Jonah swiped at his welling eyes. "Yes, yes of course. We're all going to be with you, and, and to help you grow big and strong and learn things, to play games with you, to help you with your homework, to do all sorts of things with you. We're all going to make sure you're healthy, and happy."

"And safe," Virginia said, eyeing Jonah.

"Yes, and safe," Jonah said, glancing at Ruby, then at Virginia and Nick.

"Mr. Jonah, can I see your special leg?"

Jonah rolled up his jeans. Sasha's eyes went wide. He reached out and gently traced his fingers up and down the shiny metal shin. "Cool," he whispered.

"Yeah, I think so too," Jonah said.

"It happened because of war?" Sasha asked. Jonah nodded. "Does it hurt?" Jonah pursed his lips and shook his head.

"Sash, when you feel ready, you can stop calling him Mr. Jonah," Ruby said with a giggle. "You can just call him Jonah."

"Or... Dad," Virginia said.

"Yes, or Dad," Ruby repeated.

Sasha was handing Jonah the Lego robot foot piece he'd just assembled when Virginia heard a helicopter flying low over the house.

"Look what I made. Mr. Jo— Dad."

Jonah reached out to examine the Lego but stopped before it was in his hands, as if he'd just been zapped and frozen.

* * *

"Jonah...? Babe... are, are you okay?" Ruby's hand was on Jonah's shoulder.

Poor thing, Virginia thought. They were all staring at Jonah as though he'd transformed into someone else right before their eyes. Sasha was protectively holding his Lego robot close to his chest. Jonah's hand was still frozen mid-reach, shaking as though his circuitry were glitching. Eventually he drew his hand back and shook his head while Ruby continued to rub his back. Virginia poured Jonah a glass of water which he drank all in one pull. "Sorry..." Jonah said, almost out of breath, "the sound of the helicopter took me..." He pointed to the sky.

Sasha looked to his grandmother. "Baba, what happened? Did I say something wrong?"

Jonah was mortified. He reached toward Sasha. "No, no, Sasha, it's nothing you did or said at all. It's... When I heard the helicopter, I was reminded of... of being a Marine... and sometimes those memories are like a bad dream."

"A bad dream but instead of sleeping you're awake?" Sasha asked.

Jonah nodded. "Yup, exactly. Eventually they'll... they'll stop happening. But..."

Virginia got up and gestured at her husband. "I'm going to start dinner now. Jonah, you'll stay and join us?"

Jonah looked at Big Nick. Nick considered him for a moment longer than was comfortable, then finally nodded. Jonah looked over at Ruby, who smiled reassuringly. "Thank you, Mr. and Mrs. Samarodin. I'd like that."

Sasha's eye's sparkled and he grinned as though he'd just been given a shiny new bicycle. "Yes!" he said victoriously, then held up his little hand and high-fived with his new dad.

Later in the evening, Jonah was watching Sasha sleep between him and Ruby on the big leather couch. Before falling asleep Sasha had told him all about his protectors. Jonah watched in wonder, candles lit around the room, as Ruby, Nick and Virginia recited the long list of those that are called upon to safeguard the boy's precious soul. Afterward, Virginia had brought a blanket and pillow down from Sasha's room and now he was curled up, breathing peacefully.

The evening had grown chilly and Big Nick had lit a fire before he and Virginia went off to bed. It crackled now from the stone hearth as rain pattered against the living room's bay windows. Jonah sipped his tea while Ruby played her acoustic guitar and sang softly.

Where do you go with your broken heart in tow?

What do you do with the leftover you?

And how do you know when to let go?

Where does the good go?

Where does the good go?

Ruby strummed the song's final chord as Sasha stirred.

"Beautiful... Yours?" Jonah asked.

She leaned her guitar against the couch beside her. ""Where Does the Good Go,' by Tegan and Sara. Canadian twin sisters. They put out my favourite album of last year."

"Where *does* the good go, Rube?"

Ruby nodded slowly. "Caravana were set to go on tour with them in the fall."

"Having second thoughts? Regrets?"

"Nah. The road is risky, that whole lifestyle can be unhealthy." Ruby looked around the living room. "Home is where I need to be right now. Besides, I've been getting calls and emails requesting interviews from all these mags—*Rolling Stone, Fader, Spin*—and radio stations about why I quit Caravana and asking about the rumours of drug abuse and all that shit. I don't miss the circus at all."

"I don't miss my circus either. I mean, a lot of guys after they get home just freak the hell out and can't deal with civilian life. They buy racing bikes to replace the rush of war, stuff like that… not me. I'm never going back." Jonah cast his eyes down as soon as he said that, knowing full well his combat days were not exactly over.

In spite of all there was to say, neither said anything for a long while. They watched the soft rise and fall of Sasha's chest. The fire popped and crackled. Ruby reached out and ran her fingers down the length of Jonah's forearm draped on the back of the couch.

"The few things you told me about your time over there…" Ruby said as she ran her fingers down to Jonah's palm. They clasped fingers. Sasha rolled over and made a soft groaning sound. "I'm really sorry about… the friends you lost," she continued, "and… what you witnessed…" Ruby looked at the crackling fire. "And what you had to do."

Jonah squeezed Ruby's hand and stared into the flickering flames for a long while. There would be a time and place to talk about it. He lightly brushed Sasha's hair off his forehead. "God, he's so smart, and handsome… such a little angel." Jonah grinned. "We made him. Can you believe that?" Ruby's bottom lip started to quiver. Jonah continued. "He's got your eyes, my nose and… maybe your mouth?"

Tears spilled over and streamed down Ruby's face. She whispered, "Your mouth… Jonah, I fucked up."

Jonah slid closer and put his arm around Ruby, touched the side of his head against hers. He spoke softly into her ear. "Everyone fucks up. We've both made some pretty doozy mistakes. I mean. It couldn't have been easy…"

Ruby pulled away. She knew Jonah well enough to know what that meant, and he knew right away that he'd overstepped. But, looking at Sasha now, Jonah knew that it could *not* have been an easy decision to leave him.

Ruby scrutinized Jonah as his eyes searched the living room. It actually was easier than one would think. She'd been barely out of her teens, Ruby wanted to say to Jonah. He'd been gone and Ruby had still been messed up from everything that happened to her, confused as hell, no one to turn to. And then along comes a baby? The burden of being a good mother was too much. After Sasha's birth, Ruby had resumed partying, tried to drink and snort all the trauma and responsibility away… And what about her dreams of being a musician? They didn't just vanish. So, when she got the call to join an amazing band whose lead singer she was smitten with and who, she naively thought, she could use to fill the void left behind by Jonah… she went for it.

Ruby finally spoke. "Back then it was easier to leave him in good hands… than for *my* hands to raise him."

"I'm sorry, I didn't mean…"

Ruby frowned and shook her head. "It's okay. Anyway, we've got here and now to deal with." Ruby cast her eyes on Sasha who remained sleeping. She took Jonah's hand in hers and regarded him for a moment. She tilted her head down, looked at Sasha again, brought her eyes up to Jonah. She levelled her head at him, her face full of worry.

Jonah understood. "He's already here." The blood drained from Ruby's face. "Paid a visit to my mom's last night. Just sat idling in his douchebag Hummer, staring at the house."

"Oh god… Oh god." Ruby tried to remain quiet as Jonah squeezed her hand.

He and Ruby sat and considered each other. For a long while there was only the crackle of the fireplace, the patter of rain and between them, the pure, effortless rise and fall of Sasha breathing. Finally, Jonah spoke. "There's no running away for me this time."

Ruby further hushed her voice. "Do you think he'd use me… or Sasha, or any of our family… to get to you?"

"Can't rule anything out with him, can we? You and I have both heard the rumours of what he's capable of."

"They're not rumours," Ruby said.

Jonah whispered now. "The idea of any harm coming to you or Sasha or anyone we love…" Jonah shook his head.

"Remember Ron Finney from our history class?" Ruby asked. "He's a cop in Nelson now. Let's call him."

Jonah's eyes widened. "And tell him what? That seven years ago Clinton Pritchard tried to..." Jonah made sure Sasha was still sleeping. "That he... raped you, and I accidentally caused his brother to become a paraplegic while trying to save you? And that Clinton wants to *maybe* still kill me?"

Ruby deflated. "Well, what *do* we do?"

"Even if they were able to charge him with something and it *did* end up in court and he *was* convicted... What do you think his Hells Angels buddies would do to me?"

Ruby felt the sting of tears welling again. Sasha stirred, barely opened his eyes. He saw his mother and father, yawned and lazily drifted back to sleep.

"So, what are you saying?" Ruby asked.

Jonah shook his head, looked away from Ruby. "I... I don't know exactly."

"If you... do something to him and the Hells Angels or the cops find out..."

"I know. Damned if I do, fucked if I don't."

Another canyon of silence. Ruby and Jonah were lost in what-ifs, ideas racing around their heads. After a while Jonah spoke. "Remember that one morning sitting in the kitchen, your mom forced you to rehearse some lesson plan for Sunday school?"

"Yeah."

"And you talked about Tolstoy and about the bonfires for the guns?"

"The Burning of Arms."

"I get it now," Jonah said.

Ruby was confused. "Get what?"

Jonah sat upright and looked her in the eye. "Why the Doukhobors burnt their guns, why they vowed not to kill again. Every day I painstakingly relive all the terrible shit because I can't find meaning in what I did there. Sure, the Iraqi insurgents were supposed to be the bad guys but, in the end, I couldn't justify any of it other than just… staying alive. And without being able to justify it, I look in the mirror now and I see…" Jonah heaved, swallowed a sob, slapped his palm over his eyes. He didn't want to say it out loud. Murderer. Government-sanctioned murderer.

Ruby got up carefully from the couch so as not to disturb Sasha. She sat down on the other side of Jonah, put her arm around him as he continued to swallow his pain. He removed his hand from his red eyes that were welled with tears. He stared at Sasha. "For some guys war was fine. For a few it was even an urge, a need. For me it was duty and then it quickly became repulsive. And now it's just a stain."

Ruby looked at Jonah's profile for a long time. He watched Sasha but was clearly visiting somewhere she could not, nor did she want to imagine. She got up and started pacing around the living room. She sat down on the opposite couch and beckoned to Jonah. He carefully got up and joined her. Ruby searched the room, her hands up in front of her, fingers spread as though she were an idea-generating machine. "I know what we do. We can, we can talk to Swanny. Maybe he can mediate, maybe we can even speak with Clinton…." Ruby was growing frantic. "Make a deal. I'll borrow money from Dad, we can pay Clinton off? Or, or tell him I won't tell the cops that he… raped me… in exchange for leaving us alone? Or maybe we—"

Jonah put his hands on Ruby's shoulders, turned her to face him. He was shaking his head. "You really think he'd go for any of that?"

"It's worth a try," Ruby pleaded.

"And we'd trust him to keep his word?"

When no answer came, Ruby deflated and dropped her head into her hands. She drew her hands back through her hair, sighed deeply. She got up, checked to see that Sasha was sleeping. She gestured for Jonah to follow her, then walked into the kitchen. She crouched and opened the pantry cupboards next to the fridge and thrust her arms toward the back. She fished around, then pulled out a bottle of red wine.

"Is that a good idea?" Jonah asked.

"Booze was never my problem," she said as she uncorked it.

"Yeah, but—"

"Jonah, I don't need a lecture right now. This is fucking stressful. I just need to take the edge off. If I had some pot, I'd use that, but I don't." She poured herself a generous glass. "Don't worry, I'm not jonesing to get high or anything like that." But she was, wasn't she? Just a little?

Jonah opened the fridge, took out a beer and twisted the cap off. He nearly drank it all in one pull. There were bigger issues at hand than Ruby drinking alcohol. Jonah started rubbing his knuckles hard. Even though the kitchen was fully reflected in the patio windows and he couldn't see out into the night, Jonah knew they were out there, standing on the deck, taunting him. "Fuck," he said under his breath. He started nodding his head as though it was suddenly all so clear. "I, I can't see any other way." The safety of his home and his family were under threat, which meant he would eventually lose control. He'd relinquish control of his life to Clinton. The world would be robbed of meaning; he wouldn't be able to comprehend it, or cope with it. What would that make him? He'd lose his mind faster knowing there were a constant threat out there, than he would if he just eliminated that threat himself.

Ruby took a big mouthful of wine. "I can't condone—"

"You don't have to..." Jonah stepped around the kitchen table and flicked a light switch on the wall. The patio lit up. Empty.

"Did you hear something?" Ruby asked with concern in her voice.

"No, no, it's nothing. I just sometimes, I see..." Jonah walked back to Ruby. He placed his hands on her shoulders, squeezed them gently. He peeked behind her to make sure Sasha hadn't gotten up and wasn't watching them, listening to them now. Ruby put her wine down on the counter.

"I love you, Ruby. I always have and I always will."

She knew that. Even if it was hard for her to say it out loud sometimes, she felt the same.

"And now I have Sasha," Jonah continued. "You don't need to do anything or condone anything. I wouldn't put that on you. Your Doukhobor soul can stay intact."

Ruby knew what was coming.

"Laying in the hospital in Germany I made a vow to myself." Jonah's eyes suddenly grew cold and distant. "I see now it wasn't a very realistic one."

God, did it really need to come to that? Ruby wondered. No. No, no, no. It did not. Jonah had once come to her rescue, now she would come to his.

Beams of moonlight and the soft glow of a little flame-shaped night light gently illuminated the interior of the tree house. Ruby had suggested they sleep up there for old times' sake. Jonah eagerly agreed. Now, unable to sleep, Jonah decided to write a letter to Sasha, for when he was old enough to understand. He sat cross-legged against a wall with a notepad in his lap, watching his beautiful son as he lay on a faux-fur rug, surrounded by fluffy pillows, curled into the warmth of Ruby's belly. Their chests rose and fell symbiotically, the sound of their sleeping breaths a comfort to Jonah. He thought of something Lewis had told him once, something Lewis's grandmother passed down to him, a quote from American abolitionist Frederick Douglass: "It is easier to build strong children than to repair broken men." Jonah brought pen to paper and began to write.

> Sasha. One day you will read this. Maybe it'll be 2013 and you'll be fifteen years old, or maybe you'll wait until you're twenty-two and it'll be 2020. Either way you'll be on the road to manhood.
>
> It was hours ago that I met you. Unquestionably, fully and completely, with heart-bursting, galaxy-forming, nuclear-fusion love, it was the greatest day of my life. A father appeared, a new character on your favourite TV show, limping onscreen, stepping into the narrative, twisting the plot for all remaining episodes.
>
> You shied away from too much eye contact, preferring your shuffling feet instead, offering a quick measuring glance and a nonchalant *hey* when I introduced myself. You were six. Lego ruled. Your hair was like mine at your age, full of commotion. Totally free. I learned that you could eat spaghetti every day. Before bedtime you whispered a secret to me; you had protectors, who you offered to me for protection too.

Thank you. If I'm still around when you read this, then it worked.

Is this how you remember our unification?

If you're reading this letter far enough in the future, perhaps society by now will have robot maids, jet packs and hoverboards, like we were promised. I hope so. On the flip side, are the summer temperatures unbearable? Has Kokanee Glacier all but melted away? Are Vancouver and New Orleans and Amsterdam partially submerged under the sea? Has a new pandemic ravaged the land? I'd like to hope not.

Wherever you are, and whatever you're doing, and whoever you're with, I trust you are safe, healthy, happy and loved. By now you know the story of why you were mostly raised by your grandparents for the first six years of your life and why I wasn't involved. I was wounded, a Marine, a war hero, a son, a half-Doukhobor, a nobody, a dead man walking. I was just dust swirling through space. Then I careened into you, and we spun together. And here we are. I trust that my love and guidance and your mother's love and guidance and your grandparents' continued love and guidance has been the gravity that held our galaxy together. I trust that it's been enough to steer you through a world that may not always be kind and understanding and forgiving to you.

Your mother and I have both seen and done things we wish we could go back to unsee and undo. Just like our parents before us and their parents before them. Ad infinitum. But that's not how life works, Sasha. You're starting to see this though, aren't you? Because all those unsavoury, swear-at-the-top-of-your-lungs, terrible moments, fused with all the big breaths of kindness, tenderness, love and forgiveness, are what forged us into who we are now. If you've rummaged through our treasure chest of keepsakes, photos and memorabilia, and if you've absorbed the raw stories of our exploits, our shortcomings, missteps, fuck-ups, tragedies and victories (both big and small) that we've surely been telling around the family dinner table, on hikes with Dyeda, on weekend camping trips, drives into town to get groceries, and in fist-clenching moments of disagreement... then you'll already know this.

Undoubtedly, you'll have heard this too, and likely on more than one occasion. When I was a Marine there were many times when I should've died. Many times when those beside me did. And seven times too many when my finger pulled the trigger. And after each time, little by little, life began to lose its meaning and importance. Until I met you. Until, like the Kootenay River had always been destined to join the mighty Columbia, me and your mother met at the confluence and we became a family.

So, for that very reason, every single day I will drape my arm around your shoulders, pull you in, embrace you. I'll kiss your forehead, and tell you that I love you, and for many many years you will likely gripe and recoil whenever I do. But maybe as you now read this, the day has come when you appreciate that I did that. Because believe me, there will also come a day when you'll wish I was still around to do that some more.

Know this, Sasha, my son, my sun... whatever funk you may have gotten yourself into, whatever rut your wheels are temporarily stuck in, whatever shit-storm life decides to sling your way, whatever ignorant, fearful bullshit people will spew at you... you keep your galactic spark alive, pry your cosmic heart open when

> it threatens to collapse, laugh loudly like a supernova about to expire, continue to quench your blazing thirst for life, be ferociously proud of who you are and where you come from, and always, always, my boy… hold your beautiful head high.
>
> Love eternal,
>
> Your—

—The faint sound of creaking wood coming from the back deck of the house sent icy spikes of adrenalin shooting through Jonah's body and his heart leaping into his throat. He swore at himself for leaving Tupac in the Jeep as he placed the pen and notepad down beside him. He quietly got up, tiptoed to the door, looked back to make sure Ruby and Sasha were still asleep, then slipped out of the tree house. A lone figure stood on the back deck looking up at him, backlit by a faint orange glow from the kitchen. Whoever it was gestured with a wave for Jonah to come to them.

As he crossed the backyard it became increasingly clear that it was Virginia on the back deck, wrapped in a light blanket. She held a glass in her hands filled with… juice? Jonah wondered. She gestured for Jonah to sit next to her as he walked up the stairs.

"Did I startle you?" she asked. "I just couldn't sleep a wink."

"Me too."

"Would you like some… wine?" Virginia asked, looking at her glass and shrugging her shoulders.

"No, thank you."

Virginia held the glass close to her lips as she stared at Jonah for an unsettling length of time. It was the same scrutinizing look she'd given him as a teenager at the breakfast table every time he'd stayed the night, supposedly in the spare bedroom. She likely knew that Jonah would sneak down to Ruby's bedroom for the bulk of the night, then slip back into the spare bedroom before sunrise. Just as she likely knew now that Jonah's bliss at having met his son was proportionate to the dread he felt at needing to protect him at all costs.

Virginia took a generous sip of her wine and broke the silence. "Of course, Nick and I know about the Pritchard brothers. Ruby has told us everything right from the beginning."

Jonah rubbed his tired eyes. "Okay."

"And while I've thought about this scenario a lot over the years, it never really hit home until last night."

Jonah foraged in his beard. "I don't think anyone, apart from Ruby maybe, has thought about this more than me." Jonah looked at the tree house across the yard. "I don't know how he knew I was home but… Clinton's in the area now."

Virginia closed her eyes slowly, lowered her glass of wine, started whispering what Jonah could only assume was a prayer. She opened her eyes and placed the wine on the table beside her. "You know our family's—our people's beliefs…"

"I do."

"And now you want to try embrace your Doukhobor heritage? To be able to cleanse your soul and begin walking the path of a Spirit Wrestler?"

Jonah closed his eyes, exhaled deeply, opened them. "More than anything."

"I can't begin to imagine what you went through and what you… had to do." Virginia reached for Jonah's hand, took it in hers. Her eyebrows drew together. She leaned in and made pleading, unflinching eye contact as only a concerned mother could. "My dear, listen to me very carefully. It's all well and good to believe as the Doukhobors do when you live here, a peaceful region of a peaceful country. And we Doukhobors love to talk about pacifism as though our resolve in this matter has been greatly tested. I mean, in many ways it *has*… but not quite like the test you face now. I love Sasha more than life itself…" Virginia cleared her throat again and squeezed Jonah's hands tight. Tears welled in her eyes. "If anything were to happen to him as a result of this mess you're in…" Virginia choked up, swallowed hard.

She kept her gaze steady. "I saw you with Sasha. It isn't possible to not love that little boy with all your heart."

"He's absolutely everything to me now," Jonah said, lightly squeezing Virginia's hands back.

"Tomorrow is the start of Festival weekend. You'll come to that. Both our families together. United. And then after… because you… trained for it…" Virginia yanked her hands out of her clasp with Jonah's as if his hands were suddenly scalding hot. She looked away, curled her fingers into fists, drew them close to her chest in a gesture of self-preservation. Unflinchingly she looked Jonah in the eye. "You'll do what's necessary to keep him safe."

Castlegar, British Columbia, May 2005

The curtains slowly opened to a packed Brilliant Cultural Centre and a boy and girl stepped from the wings to the front of the stage. The boy began reading a poem in English as Ruby straightened her silky blue traditional dress and adjusted her hand-embroidered white shawl. She wondered how the crowd would react to the youth choir—at her friend Nadya's passioned request—breaking from tradition tonight. Ruby caught the eye of Nadya standing at the far end of the front row of women in the forty-person-strong youth choir. Her friend winked and offered a reassuring smile to Ruby.

At least people weren't scrutinizing her as much as they were Jonah, Ruby thought. Many in the crowd were still glancing sidelong or sneaking peeks at him and his entourage, as they'd been doing since their arrival an hour earlier. Ruby couldn't tell if it was Lewis—Jonah's six-foot-four Black friend that sat next to him—who stuck out more, or Jonah himself—a wounded war vet and son of a mother whose family members were infamous Freedomites. Or was it his Uncle Yuri, the man responsible for much of that infamy, a rumoured gay man who hadn't shown his face in the Doukhobor community in nearly thirty years?

Ruby looked at Jonah, handsome in the navy-blue suit he'd bought for the occasion, sitting next to Sasha, Lewis, his Uncle Yuri, Sharon and Grandma Polly on his left, and Ruby's mom and dad to his right. Jonah spotted Ruby and pointed at her for Sasha's benefit. She smiled at them both. Sitting in the front row, as they did every year during Festival, were Ruby's Baba Mary and Dyeda John, chatting with a slender, moustached man in a black suit—future Doukhobor leader J.J. Verigin. Baba Mary had refused to sit next to Jonah's family, the memories of that uncomfortable Christmas dinner seven years ago apparently still fresh for her. J.J. paused his conversation with Ruby's grandparents, turned fully back, seemingly to examine Jonah, Lewis and the family. Was J.J. concerned that Jonah's Uncle Yuri was there? Yuri would've cut a peculiar image even without his infamy in tow. Ruby couldn't help but giggle when she met him for the first time in the parking lot earlier that day. He'd slowly exited Sharon's Volvo, head held high, surveying his domain like an elder statesman, albeit one that looked like he'd recently been homeless. He had a white beard that crawled down to his collarbones and a thinning head of grey hair slicked back and glistening with Brylcreem. In his oversized beige suit—which he paired with black sneakers—Yuri had curiously tucked a white feather into his breast pocket.

Or perhaps it was the presence of Jonah that had caught J.J.'s eye? Ruby scanned the crowd and recognized several people from high school, all of whom she knew Jonah to have been friendly with. Most acknowledged him with a nod and a smile, while a few glanced at him with cold stares, and frowns, for what Ruby could only assume was a distaste for Jonah's military service.

The young girl at the front of the stage completed her poem in Russian and both her and the boy exited to the wing. After a young female emcee standing at a podium at the side of the stage introduced Ruby in Russian, her male counterpart introduced her in English. "Brothers and sisters, tonight, the Doukhobor Union of Youth Choir will be presenting an original song written by Ruby Samarodin, which she performed around the world with her former band, Caravan… excuse me, Caravana. The song is titled "Spirit Wrestlers—"

Hoots and whistles came from the crowd.

"—and for the first time in the Festival's history, we have allowed a choir to be accompanied by musical instruments." A discernable murmur spread throughout the crowd. A whistle came from the balcony.

Ruby stepped out from the bottom row of the choir. Stagehands removed a small, standing curtain to reveal a grand piano and acoustic guitar set up at the side of the stage. More murmurs in the audience as she walked toward the instruments. Since coming back home she'd had zero desire for any of the crap that was part and parcel of the music biz, and little desire to play rock 'n' roll. And although she'd continued scribbling down lyrics for possible songs she'd write later, she hadn't even really wanted to *listen* to music. In its place she had turned to singing the old Doukhobor hymns, psalms and folk songs, harmonizing with her peers in the youth choir like she had as a teenager. It felt natural to her. Just her voice. A primal connection to her ancestors. A human's voice was the purest connection to the spirit, Baba Mary would always tell her. One of the few things Ruby agreed with her on. But then Baba's preaching would go too far. She'd piously wag her finger. "That's why we don't use instruments or play rock 'n' roll. It's the devil's music. It corrupts your soul." Ruby would nearly roll her eyes out of her head, baffled at how that generation could still hold on to such a silly, arcane belief.

Now, as Ruby picked up her acoustic guitar, she could feel her baba's eyes on her from the front row. Ruby brought the strap over her head. The choir director, old Mr. Samsonoff, took his seat behind the piano. Ruby looked out at the packed hall, her heart beating hard, her palms clammy. She dragged her stool to centre stage and made herself comfortable on it. The stage lights dimmed. A soft spotlight illuminated Mr. Samsonoff's head of thick white hair behind the piano, while a brighter one washed over Ruby.

Ruby took a big breath to calm her shaky hands. "Hello everyone," she said into the mic. She cleared her throat and forced herself to speak with confidence. "I'm Ruby Samarodin... I've spent several years away from the Kootenays, away from home. You could say I was running from who I was, messing up along the way... a lot." She laughed nervously. "But no matter where I was in the world, whenever I sang this song, it always brought me back here, back home to all you beautiful folks. This song's about standing up for what you believe in, staying strong, no matter how much of an outcast you are. It's as much for our Doukhobor ancestors as it is for those still living on the margins today—people of colour, the gay and lesbian community, Jewish people, Muslims, women." More crowd murmurs accompanied by a few whistles from Nadya and the choir behind her. Others in the crowd clapped their approval. Ruby smiled. "It's called 'Spirit Wrestlers' and I hope you enjoy it."

Ruby closed her eyes and started strumming, the piano behind her tinkling and accentuating notes. She sang the first words of the verse, "Look at the long march from cruelty," her voice fragile and vulnerable as though she might cry mid-lyric, "look at the strength and the grace..." Ruby's thoughts went back to childhood and the times she was made fun of by jocks and rednecks for being a Doukhobor, for being different, something other. But harmonizing with her people had provided solace; it made life feel like it fit together and made sense. No one could make fun of Doukhobors when they stood and sang together. No one in any audience anywhere could escape the solemn hymns, the sound of hundreds of years of tragedy and sorrow, of being an exile... and the sound of hope in the face of it all. "... looking back at everything you've left behind..." It flowed through Ruby and her people. You couldn't mess with that. "...looking to promises of freedom, deliverance from pain..." As the verse ended, she sensed the choir behind her, ready to add its power to her song of rebellion. Try and hold back the tears, she thought, as she and the choir launched into the chorus.

... Spirits wrestle, we see it clear
Long life of running, the end is near
Rebels from the beginning, rebels fleeing fear
It was a long time coming... And we're still here...

Jonah inhaled a big lungful of fresh air. The evening had cooled considerably. The performances had finished and people were streaming out of the hall, many stopping to congratulate and shower praise on Ruby.

"Rube, you've expanded your fan base," Jonah said. "Totally deserved, babe."

"Really? You liked it?" Ruby reached for his hand, her post-gig high starting to wane.

Jonah was surprised. "Babe, are you kidding?" They moved off the bustle of the concrete walkway onto the lawn to wait for their families to finish saying goodbye to friends. "It absolutely floored me. Everyone loved it." Behind them Sasha was laughing, riding Lewis's neck as he ran in circles on the lawn. "That was a good minute-long standing O you and the choir got."

"Well, not everyone stood. You know, in the six years I was with Caravana, I rarely performed sober."

"Did today feel strange?"

Ruby let out a satisfied sigh. "Yup, a little. But mostly it felt great." Half an hour earlier when she'd stepped off the stage, she felt light, as though she'd shed several pounds. But now as she looked around, the sprawling Cultural Centre lawn seemed a little less green. The red-brick walls of the hall were a faded brown. The cloudless skies above, not quite so blue. The high of having performed on stage was nearly drained dry. The days ahead suddenly seemed overwhelming. A terrible, shit human had to be dealt with. The warm ball of wonder that she'd felt since she'd gotten home, gradually growing in her belly like a newborn, had gone cold. She felt empty, and scared. Damn, she needed to walk, to go on another hike with her dad. She glanced at Sasha riding Lewis's neck, then at Jonah holding her hands. She tried to conceal the shame that was suddenly welling in her. Why couldn't her boys be enough? She needed to stop the spiral. Let shit go, she began silently repeating to herself. She took long, measured breaths. You can do it. It is possible. You will do it.

Jonah leaned in and kissed her. "You okay?"

Ruby nodded.

"I'm really proud of you."

"Thank you," Ruby said, mustering as much genuine appreciation as she could. She hadn't been triggered in a while, but her post-gig comedown and thoughts of Clinton mixed into a potent cocktail. Her belly tingled, but not from wonder, newness or hope. For the first time in weeks, she needed some drugs.

A middle-aged lady and a guy Jonah recognized from high school approached them. Like Ruby, the lady was in traditional dress; an ankle-length skirt and white shawl wrapped around her head. The rosy-cheeked guy stood smiling beside her. Jonah couldn't remember his name. Gary something? With a tight smile the lady told Ruby she and her son had loved her song and the quality of her voice, but that none of it needed accompaniment by guitar or piano, or a dedication to people other than *nashi*, "Our people," she repeated in English, glancing at Jonah. Ruby forced a polite smile. Before Festival she had explained to Jonah the traditional Doukhobor belief that the truly purest connection to God, to one's spirit, was through the voice only. He didn't understand why. Now he came to Ruby's defence.

"Don't all the great traditions and faiths of the world use instruments to accompany the voice?"

The lady's thin smile tightened further as she turned her attention to Jonah. "You are Sharon Kazakoff's boy. From the army?"

"The one and only." Jonah knew there was no point in explaining that the Marines weren't the army, or that his mother's last name was now Seeger.

The lady's son glanced back at the hall, then at Jonah. "I didn't think we let military people into the *dom*. Lucky you."

Jonah shrugged. Without another word, Ruby took his hand, turned and led him deeper onto the lawn. "So that's how it's going to be for me then?" Jonah said.

"No, no. I mean, yes, *some* people are judgmental like Gary Hadikin and his mother, but... It won't be easy for some in the community to accept you. Your family has... history, and you *were* in the military, Jonah. What do you expect?"

"Yeah, I guess I... Hey..." Jonah pointed at Yuri and Grandma Polly. "Who's that guy?"

"With the 'stache, nice suit, looking our way now?"

"Yeah. Inside, he kept looking back at me and the fam."

"That's J.J. Verigin Jr., next in line to be leader—or Honorary Chairman as they like to be called now—of the Community Doukhobors. He's a relative of mine. Why?"

"Damn, here he comes," Jonah said, looking away.

"A real character. *Loves* to chat. Get ready."

J.J. skipped toward them, arms outstretched in greeting. His wispy moustache was spread wide across a genuine smile. "Right on guys, so glad you could make it," he said enthusiastically. He gave Ruby a hug, his smaller frame momentarily dwarfed by hers.

Ruby put her hand on Jonah's shoulder. "This is my... boyfriend... Jonah Seeger."

J.J.'s squinty eyes were warm and steady as he took Jonah's hand in both of his and shook heartily. "I know!" J.J. said. His constantly moving hands animated everything he said as though he were signing for the hearing impaired. "News travels fast around the Koots, eh?"

Great, Jonah thought. He towered over the future Doukhobor leader, but J.J.'s vibrant energy and undeniable presence made him seem the bigger man.

J.J. shifted his attention back to Ruby. "Ruby, cousin..." J.J. bowed to her with his arms in the air. "We're not worthy," he said, laughing.

Ruby blushed, put her hand on her chest, nodded and bowed her head slightly. His praise boosted her self-esteem, stopped her post-gig blues from spiralling out of control.

"No, but seriously," he continued, "that was right on, fantastic. Just what we Doukhobors need..." He leaned in close to Jonah and

Ruby. "To shake things up a bit," he said conspiratorially, "get some of these old timers to loosen up, eh?"

"Could you please tell that to my baba Mary?" Ruby said.

J.J. clapped his hands together gleefully. "I already did, during the standing ovation. I'll tell ya, your baba, and especially your dyeda, were genuinely impressed."

"I hope so. Mrs. Hadikin and her son Gary just stopped to let us know how much they did *not* like the choir accompanied by instruments." She nodded to Jonah. "And… didn't make Jonah feel welcome here *at all*."

J.J. looked around as though he were about to divulge a long-held family secret. His smile waned. "Young man," he said to Jonah, "you're not the first soldier to come to one of our events. We've had Native American Vietnam vets from Washington State here, and a group of Canadian military once at a peace conference I organized. I got shit for embracing them. But I fought for their inclusion. I asked our people to remember our Doukhobor history and how we were once shunned." J.J.'s arms were spread wide now, as if in sermon. "We've had a Muslim group request permission to use one of our prayer homes up in Ootischenia during Ramadan. I always get flak from certain…" J.J. looked around again and hushed his voice. "From the more staunch, holier-than-thou of the community." J.J. sighed and shook his head. "Drives me nuts how those who were once harshly judged throughout their history themselves become harsh judges, you know? Unfortunately, you'll face some of that here."

"Makes sense I guess," Jonah said.

J.J. continued, his hands tented in front of him as though in prayer. "I mean you are the first *Doukhobor* soldier to join us. And yes, that will make some in the community uncomfortable." J.J. looked back over his shoulder, gestured. "I was talking to your Uncle Yuri just now. His presence here makes some folks uncomfortable, too. Me and Yuri used to hang out together when we were kids, and then—" J.J. spread his hand out above him "—well let's just say our ideologies… diverged dramatically. I'm not talking about his… sexual preferences. I'm talking about the bad shit he did. I haven't seen him in decades. Point is, I've forgiven him and welcomed him back into the community. As for you," J.J. said, clapping his hands lightly, "I don't know how much of our history you know, but just over a hundred years ago back in Russia many of us were soldiers too. Soldiers that chose peace over war."

Jonah nodded. "Yes sir." He looked to Ruby and back at J.J. "Ruby told me about that years ago, the Burning of Arms."

J.J. raised his fists in victory. "Excellent. One of our greatest moments. Listen, Jonah, I look at you as a brother not a kil— Not a soldier, okay? The real Doukhobor way is to invite, to break bread. If I turned my back on you because of your past I am not being true to my calling as a Spirit Wrestler."

"Thank you, sir. I appreciate that."

J.J. put his hand on Jonah's shoulder. "Have you laid down your weapons, young man?"

Jonah's chest tightened. He suddenly needed space. He could feel Ruby's uncomfortableness come on as quickly as his own. J.J.'s hand on his shoulder was firm though. Jonah's eyes darted around. He spotted Sasha, now being carried under Lewis's arm toward them. He gestured to Lewis to give them another minute. Jonah took a big breath, looked back at J.J. and nodded. "I… I've absolutely had enough of being a Marine," Jonah said, feeling conflicted, knowing what he still had to do.

J.J. smiled and shook Jonah's hand again. "Good, good. Then I welcome you back into the Doukhobor community."

Jonah's chest loosened. "That means a lot."

"Do you know what *mujahedeen* means?" J.J. asked.

"Umm, warrior? Holy warrior?"

"Exactly. There's a Doukhobor song whose title translates to 'Sleep On, You Great Eagles Fighting,' and there's a line in that song that references *svetiya bartsi*, or holy warriors. Doukhobors are peaceful holy warriors. We practise jihad in the way jihad is supposed to mean, before the term was corrupted. Jihad is an internal struggle to stay true to values, to flush the garbage from our soul and to hang on to what is good." J.J. laughed and patted Jonah's shoulder. "I know, I have a tendency to ramble on. Forgive me."

"No, no, I appreciate it. Thank you," Jonah said.

"I should make my rounds. You kids behave," J.J. said as he turned to leave. He stopped, spun back around. Looking between Jonah and Ruby he stroked his moustache and squinted. "One more thing," he said as he stepped close to Jonah. "Remember… if there's no peace within, how the hell will there be peace without? The true temple of God is within. And that temple…" J.J. looked Jonah, then Ruby in the eye, then patted Jonah on the chest. "Even when broken… can be rebuilt." J.J. winked, smiled wide, bowed to Jonah and Ruby with hands in prayer, then walked away.

* * *

Sasha walked hand in hand between his mom and dad, looking up at both of them smiling as they made their way through the parking lot to the Jeep. "I know I already said it," Lewis said from behind them, "but damn, girl. You got some pipes on you. World class, Momma. And that men's choir, shee-it…"

Jonah glanced back at Lewis. "Language, Lew."

"Sorry, sorry," Lewis said as he trotted ahead of them, spun around and continued walking backwards. "What was that boat song the dudes' choir sung? Sounded like if "The Imperial March" from *Star Wars* was slowed down a thousand BPM?"

Ruby laughed. "'Song of the Volga Boatmen.'"

"Man. Powerful, powerful stuff. Hey, is it true, you're quittin' music?"

"Yeah. But… after tonight… I don't know."

Sasha suddenly looked up at her with concern. Jonah gave her a look. "I mean, I won't go back to the band or anything," Ruby clarified. She put her hand on Sasha's head. "I won't, I promise. But I love writing and performing," she said to Lewis. "I just gotta do it my way if I decide to keep doing it in some capacity. I don't know. Feels really good. Know what else might feel really good? How about we drop off..." She nodded at Sasha without him noticing. "...and stop by Nadya's place for the festival after-party?" She immediately regretted the suggestion as a memory of her cheating on Jonah flashed through her, filled her with regret.

"Why you so keen to go to the party?" Jonah asked, looking straight ahead. "I'm pretty beat."

"Forget I suggested it." Although, knowing what she was going to do tomorrow, even just one glass of wine would make her feel better, calm her nerves.

Jonah and Ruby said their goodbyes to their families, while Lewis flew Sasha through the air around the Jeep. A few minutes later as Jonah was about to climb into the driver's seat someone tapped him on the shoulder. He turned around to see his uncle.

"Jonah, want to meet up tomorrow?" Yuri asked.

"Uh, yeah, sure, that sounds good."

"Nine a.m. in the credit union parking lot at the Junction. Does that work?"

"Sure. And then what?"

"Then..." Yuri snickered. "Like your generation says, I'm gonna blow your mind."

In August 2001, Mary Braun, the sole remaining Freedomite practising confrontational protest, is caught attempting to burn down a Selkirk College community building in Slocan Valley, British Columbia. In court the eighty-one-year-old grandmother disrobes in the prisoner's box and is convicted of arson and given a six-year jail term. To the Globe and Mail *newspaper, her friend Sam D. states that "Mary believes the world is in a very bad situation and she feels she has to awaken the world to what is happening, that children are being killed by bombs. It is her way."*

Mary's conviction is her fifteenth for arson, and the last reported act of Sons of Freedom protest.

New Denver and Castlegar, British Columbia, May 2005

The Cape Horn Bluffs. The name made Jonah reflexively clench his ass and grip the steering wheel until his knuckles were bloodless. He and Yuri were driving along that part of the snaking highway that used to narrow to one lane, where a jagged, overhanging cliff face pressed in on one side, and a sheer, thousand-foot drop into the lake beckoned on the other side. As a kid, en route to camping at the north end of Slocan Lake, blood would drain from Jonah's face and he'd nearly crap his pants as his dad manoeuvred their truck through that terrifying section.

Jonah glanced far below at the lake made midnight blue by the shadow of the snow-capped granite peaks of the Valhalla Ranges rising like a medieval fortress from its shores. Beyond the peaks to the west, a roiling wall of dark-grey clouds loomed. For many kilometres Jonah and his uncle drove in silence, both admiring the remote, rugged beauty of the northern Slocan Valley. Eventually a semi-truck rushing past the Jeep in the opposing lane broke the trance.

"...you sing loud and I'll sing louder, tonight we're settin' the woods on fire..."

Jonah tuned back into the twang and country picking of the Hank Williams CD that Yuri had insisted on playing the entire drive thus far. They were winding their way through the mountains en route to the old silver-mining town of New Denver. Yuri turned down the stereo, glanced at Jonah and, out of nowhere, said, "Jonah, do you think you've... forgiven yourself?"

Jonah drew his head back, felt Yuri's forthrightness like a wake-up smack across the cheeks. Had he forgiven himself? Tasting oily iron blood in his mouth and not knowing if it was his own; feeling the hot rush of adrenalin as he took down an enemy at a distance; hearing the wretched screams of the dying; smelling the shit and blood and rotting flesh of the battlefield; feeling the precious life draining from

Mason's cold hand; seeing Sadie's dismembered form through the body bag in the helicopter; hearing the surprised insurgent go dead silent as Jonah fired a burst of bullets that cut him down five feet away; a swift, rage-filled, kick to poor Swanny's chest; abandoning Ruby. Had Jonah forgiven himself? Despite his best efforts he found he still despised himself at the drop of a hat. At times he was convinced that *he* was the enemy. Early on he'd done barbaric things that he'd excused too quickly and too easily. He'd killed men that if he otherwise had not, the war's outcome would not have changed one bit. He'd survived when so many of his comrades did not. Yet despite all this, he was loved by a family he'd recently returned to. He had Ruby again. He had a beautiful, amazing son. Had he forgiven himself?

"I don't know," Jonah said, staring vacantly ahead at the winding mountain road.

"Are you sure you don't know?"

Jonah squinted, glanced at Yuri.

"We usually have the answers to our every feeling, desire and motive," Yuri said. "If we're willing to look deep enough."

"Then … no, I have not forgiven myself. Not fully. Not yet."

Yuri asked why. And because he was blood, and because of the impression he left on Jonah at dinner the other day, Jonah felt comfortable laying it all out for Yuri. For the next half hour Jonah spoke uninterrupted about everything he'd done and seen and experienced since the fateful day that he'd fought to protect Ruby by beating the shit out of Clinton Pritchard. At this part of the story Yuri groaned almost imperceptibly, to which Jonah asked if Yuri was okay. He nodded slowly and gestured for Jonah to continue. When he was finished speaking, Jonah had formed blisters from white-knuckling and rubbing his steering wheel the entire time. Yuri sat silently looking out at the passing forest for a long while until he finally spoke. "I know just how difficult it is to rehash the past. *Spasibo* … Thank you for sharing." Yuri leaned forward, turned to Jonah and seemed to want to say more … but then he sat back.

"With certain people I don't mind talking about it. It helps," Jonah said.

"Have you let your tears flow over all this?"

Jonah frowned and shook his head. "Kinda wish I could. Almost did when I met Sasha, felt like it, but I also felt I needed to be strong in that moment."

"When the time is right," Yuri said, nodding, " your tears will flow... and afterward you'll be reborn. Trust me." He pointed out the window just as they were approaching the village of New Denver. "Turn left here, follow it to the hospital."

Thirty seconds later Jonah pulled into the parking lot of the Slocan Community Health Centre, what looked more like an '80s-era elementary school than a hospital. He put the Jeep in park. Yuri gestured for them to get out. Jonah followed Yuri as he walked around the building toward the lake.

"It was 1955, I was ten years old when the cops came to where your mom and I grew up in Krestova, and... abducted me and dozens of other kids. It was three a.m. 'Operation Snatch,' the authorities called it. They had police dogs barking by their side as they kicked in our door and dragged us screaming into the paddy wagons. Crying and screaming, sirens, dogs barking, parents pleading, cops yelling... it all echoed throughout the village." Yuri had stopped at the water's edge and was staring out across the placid lake. "The government ordered this operation mostly because our parents didn't believe in sending us to regular school, see? That had been a point of contention for decades, even amongst non-Freedomite Doukhobors. We were taught just fine in the Doukhobor schools in the villages. Our parents were afraid that in regular schools we'd learn the corrupt, greedy, war-mongering ways of dominant society. On another level though, the government and the Angliki—our term for anyone who was a native English speaker—were fed up with us Sons of Freedom. So, they hit us where it hurt most..." Yuri spun around and faced the hospital and pointed. "Between 1953 and 1959, they imprisoned over two hundred children between the ages of seven and fifteen... right here."

"A hospital?"

"Back before they renovated it, it was the New Denver Dormitory, a prison school surrounded by eight-foot-high chain-link fencing."

Jonah nodded. "Oh yeah... I remember now from history class; it was the former internment camp that the Japanese were held in during World War II."

"Exactly." Yuri slowly shook his head. "We were to pay for our parents' sins, you see. The government thought that this would be a definitive way to get the Sons of Freedom to send their kids to regular school, to stop the adults from burning the homes of materialistic Doukhobors, setting fire to schools, planting bombs on railway tracks, to stop the nude protests against government interference in our lives. I was locked up here for six years. I was a number instead of a name. Number seventeen. Forced assimilation. Just like all those poor Native kids in residential schools." Again, Yuri shook his head. "I haven't been back here since." He turned and walked a few metres along the pebbled beach, sat down onto a nearby log. Jonah followed. They both picked up small rocks and lobbed them into the lake.

After a while Yuri continued. "We could only see our parents one hour every other week, through the fence. We were given the strap, some of us beaten for speaking Russian, for practising our Doukhobor religion." Yuri looked over at Jonah. "Number seventy-six, your mother, she had a particularly difficult time here."

Jonah snapped his head toward Yuri, his eyes nearly popping out of his head.

Yuri seemed equally perplexed. "She never told you?"

Jonah shook his head vigorously. "No!"

Yuri frowned. "*Och...*" He tilted his head up to the sky, groaned, looked back at Jonah, shook his head. "Doesn't surprise me. She was barely seven. The cops snatched her up in one of the last village raids before the Svobodnik mothers signed an agreement to send us all back to regular Canadian school. New Denver was closed down half a year after your mother arrived."

Jonah glanced back over his shoulder, bewildered. "She was *here*?" It explained so much more about her reluctance to talk about her upbringing, about her shame, her morbid encounters with food.

Yuri rubbed the back of his neck as he continued. "I looked out for her the best I could, but especially at her tender age… to be forced from your mother and father, to have your culture and language shamed? Hey, come on, that's the devil's work. We got belittled by the alcoholic British headmaster. Bullied by one despicable matron in particular. And in turn some kids bullied each other. After we got out, your mother never mentioned New Denver again. Not once. It was like it never happened."

"*How* despicable were the matrons?" Jonah asked.

Yuri's forehead was glistening with sweat now. He stared at Jonah, stared through him with a faraway, damaged look that Jonah knew all too well. Yuri's neck tightened as he began to speak. "Ms. Clarkson. She was a big devil of a woman… She took grim pleasure in… molesting some of the boys…" Yuri fell silent, pulled on his lips, lost in thought. Even glancing at Yuri from the side, Jonah could tell his uncle's eyes were red-rimmed, welling with tears. Jonah suppressed the sudden urge to hug him.

"Not many people know this," Yuri continued, "but… I was one of those boys." He swiped at his eyes. "'Number seventeen, let's go,' she'd say. Then she'd grab the scruff of my neck and shove me into the janitor's room… press her thick, sweaty forearm into my throat and force me to… she'd force me to touch her." Yuri seemed as shocked to have admitted it as Jonah was to hear it. Tears trickled down Yuri's cheeks. He dropped his head to his chest.

An image flashed through Jonah's mind: Clinton on top of Ruby, choking her, and the look of terror in her eyes. He squeezed his eyes shut and shook it away. After a moment Jonah patted his uncle's back. "I'm really sorry you had to go through that, Uncle Yuri."

Yuri nodded, slowly raised his head from his chest, and continued. "From the age of ten to almost sixteen, I lived in hell." Yuri threw his thumb back over his shoulder. "When they finally released us from there, well… as you might imagine, many of us, myself included, were very damaged. We'd been thoroughly humiliated, marginalized, completely shamed. Yet…" Yuri grunted as he stood up and began pacing in front of Jonah, "At the same time we were prouder than ever to be Sons of Freedom. Right away certain… infamous, revered Freedomite elders in the community gathered with us and asked who amongst us would like payback and revenge. Those that raised their hands would learn the 'black work' as they called it; guerilla arson techniques and bomb making. It offered what was beaten and shamed out of us—respect and prestige. Me and my friends we were pent-up hormonal teens and we were angry as all hell. Of course, we signed up. And then…" Yuri threw his arms in the air. "We let the hounds loose from hell. We unleashed our vengeance, our Christian anarchy on a government that had locked us up and treated us like animals, and on the Doukhobors that we felt had abandoned us, abandoned their morals and virtues. We planted bombs inside the Nelson Courthouse, set fire to schoolhouses… We blew up railway tracks and hydro towers." Yuri stopped pacing and looked at Jonah. "And oh boy, one night alone in 1962, me and the boys—Harry, Ivan, his brother Serge, my Dimitri—we ran wild in Ootischenia. Wild, I tell ya. We brought hellfire to the Kootenays. Absolute, uncompromising hellfire."

Jonah peaked his eyebrows. "Jesus… what'd you do?"

Yuri shook his head and for the first time Jonah could see the look of regret in his eyes. "In one single night in Ootischenia, we burned nearly thirty buildings to the ground. Homes mostly."

"Whoa… anyone die?"

"Close… but thank God, no."

Jonah stared dumbfounded, unable to reconcile the slight, gentle, grey-haired man in front of him with the anarchic guerilla fanatic he used to be.

Yuri frowned, shook his head and shrugged. He motioned for Jonah to follow him. "Let's head back to Castlegar. Stops two, three and four on Yuri's-wild-years tour."

* * *

An hour and a half later Jonah stood at the edge of the parking area surveying Verigin's Tomb below. It was just as he remembered it from when he was last there with his mother as a teenager: a big white slab at the edge of a steep, rocky embankment, surrounded by trimmed lawn, rows of flowers and big leafy trees, all overlooking the Kootenay River. The afternoon had warmed considerably but dark clouds hanging over the Celgar Pulp Mill to the west were on their way. Yuri had gone on ahead and was now standing on the far side of the giant white slab with his head bowed, hands clasped together. Jonah walked down the dirt path that curved around a small rock outcrop, through the gates and onto the manicured lawn. A young female groundskeeper raking trimmings welcomed him with a smile.

Yuri opened his eyes as Jonah approached from the other side of the tomb.

"I've been forgiven," Yuri said.

"Oh yeah? The Verigin ghosts have spoken to you?"

"I've forgiven myself; they have no choice but to do the same."

"Didn't know that's how it works."

"Well, it helps that J.J. Verigin forgave me yesterday." Yuri gestured for Jonah to follow him as he walked slow circles around the tomb.

"The story continues here. After the night of hellfire in Ootischenia, you'd think we would've slowed down a bit. But me and the boys were full of red-hot hatred. We were like inner-city gang kids who felt they'd been disrespected by the whole world and needed someone to pay. And even though we had burning rage inside of us, our religious convictions were too strong to take that rage out on any humans. Objects still had to suffice. We thought of destroying the statue of John A. Macdonald in Nelson. Don't know if you knew this but Canada's first prime minister had a policy of starving the First Nations on the Prairies, he was the chief architect behind the residential school system, and he authorized what's known as the Frog Lake Massacre. But we wanted a target closer to home. So, one night

I came here." Yuri swept his arm around him. "To this very site... and carefully set a bomb with a timer. It wasn't a slab back then; it was a mausoleum with marble pillars. I must've been the third or fourth Freedomite to destroy it over the decades. We're all equal you see. That's what I was raised to understand. Doukhobors were equal. But the way me and my Freedomite comrades saw it, this tomb represented inequality, a privileged leadership who was buried in a fancy tomb away from the commoners." Yuri stopped walking, brought his hands up to his temples, shook his head. "I was *so* caught up in the fever of those times that I even believed that the Verigins were the ones that had sent the cops to our villages." Yuri peered at Jonah with narrowed eyes. "Can you believe that?" Yuri sighed and shook his head. "Our actions..." Yuri poked at his chest. "My actions, caused a lot of people a lot of pain and suffering."

Yuri let the memories hang in the air for a few moments as Jonah considered how so many of his own actions in his short life had done the same. Dark, angry clouds had slid overhead, churning with imminent rain. Then the realization came to him of why his mother withheld the full story of the tomb bombing when he was a teenager.

"We were kids, so naive, so stupid." Yuri looked up. "When we're young we don't know that we don't know everything." He gestured back up to the Jeep. "Let's go. Stop number three is in town. Let's see if I can find the spot... where death came to us... and everything changed."

Slocan Valley, British Columbia, May 2005

"Are you sure you wanna do this?" Nadya asked, sitting beside Ruby as she drove.

"We can still turn back," Delia said from the back seat.

Ruby stared ahead, her hands clutching the steering wheel of her father's Suburban. A light rain dappled the windshield. Ruby switched on her wipers.

"I have to try." Ruby turned onto the dirt road that led up the side of the mountain.

"What if *he's* there?" Nadya asked.

Ruby could hear the fear that they were all feeling in her voice. "That's the point. Maybe he can be reasoned with." Ruby came to a fork in the road. Could a man like Clinton Pritchard be reasoned with? The forest was thick on either side of the road, making the overcast May afternoon seem darker than it was. "You sure it's the first left off this road?"

"Yup," Nadya said, running a hand through her head of brown curls. "My brother visited Swanny last year. First left after Hummingbird Farm, then the first left after that, about three hundred metres. Go to the end of the road. House with a big barn behind it."

Ruby turned onto the driveway and drove along a narrow, bumpy track, crossed a small bridge. After a few moments the small, white-stuccoed house appeared, the steep roof of the barn visible behind it. Two family-style minivans were parked next to the house. Ruby pulled up next to them, then put the truck in reverse, backed up and positioned it so that the front end was facing the way they'd just come; a safety precaution in case they needed to make a fast getaway. Ruby put the Suburban in park and sat there thinking for a moment. Was this a stupid idea? Maybe. Could it make things worse? Yes. Could it possibly lay things to rest? God, how she hoped so.

Nadya looked at her. From the back seat Delia spoke. "Still not too late."

"This shit's gotta stop… for the sake of Sasha, and for the sake of his father." Ruby honked her horn three times, but it was for nothing. She turned to see that Swanny had already wheeled out of his front door… holding a shotgun. A large figure stood partially hidden in the shadows behind the half-opened door. Clinton. Who else? Ruby closed her eyes for a moment and whispered, "God, help me." Ruby glanced at Nadya, then back to Delia. "Ready?" Both friends nodded wearily. "Wish me luck."

Castlegar, British Columbia, May 2005

Yuri directed Jonah to drive along Sixth Avenue, past the hockey arena and the firehall, deep into the Castlegar neighbourhood of Kinnaird. Thick drops of rain started to pelt the windshield. Yuri craned his neck, scanning the area as they drove slowly along the street.

"Here. Stop here," Yuri said.

Jonah pulled over in front of a parked Ford Focus, turned off the engine. He waited for Yuri to get out, then followed. He looked around at the nondescript homes and manicured lawns and new cars parked in paved driveways. "Are we visiting someone?"

"A ghost." Yuri looked around him, looked up at a tree, muttered to himself. He pointed up ahead. "There, about twenty feet up. That's where it happened."

Yuri spotted a rose bush at the end of a driveway, walked up to it, and plucked a few bulbs. Back on the street he stood still and silent, staring at the asphalt for so long Jonah assumed that they were just going to get back into the Jeep and move on without any explanation.

Finally, Yuri spoke. "One day in '63, me and the boys had been instructed by elders to do some black work. We were to hit a bank. Blow it to smithereens. At the time we thought we were protesting against greed, corruption, land ownership. We thought we were protesting against the government who, like all emperors throughout time, unjustly took it upon themselves to rule us all, to rule everything." Yuri looked skyward. "To rule even the cosmos." He walked a few paces ahead, examining the pavement around him. "I was at the wheel in one car, with Ivan, while my... Dimitri was in a car ahead. He was in the back seat while John was driving, Frank beside him. The bomb was in a bag on Dimitri's lap. Why wasn't it in the trunk?" He shook his head. "Stupid. We all should've known better. *I* should've known better." Yuri walked a few more paces and crouched down, smoothing his hand along the wet asphalt. He placed the roses on the spot. "Right here. Dima was my first... and only true love." Yuri wiped his eyes. "I don't talk about him much. Folks around here know but... I keep—" Yuri pointed at himself with both hands. "—my ways to myself."

"It's okay," Jonah said. "No judgment here. It's 2005, Uncle. I'm sure not too many people, even here, care that much."

"You'd be surprised," Yuri said, glancing sidelong at Jonah. It's 2005 in the cities but..." Yuri waved his arm around. "In small towns like this, and especially for some in our Doukhobor community, it still might as well be 1965."

"I take it... something happened here?" Jonah asked.

Yuri nodded. "Dimitri's car hit a big pothole and..." Yuri burst his hands into the air. "I felt the heat of the explosion on my face. The car's roof, doors, front and back hoods were blown clean off. John and Frank fell out of the front, coughing, blackened, bleeding, stumbling onto nearby front lawns. Me and Ivan ran to try get Dima out, but... parts of him were everywhere, torso in the back seat, limbs spilling out the door, on the pavement around us. I'd never seen so much blood. Never in my life."

Yuri stared at the spot where the explosion happened. After a while he looked up at Jonah. "You know what that's like."

Jonah nodded.

"Right here." Yuri rubbed the pavement, then stood. "Well, I'll tell ya, the sight of Dima ripped apart like that—" Yuri snapped his fingers. "—it was like I'd been hypnotized my whole life right up until that very second. After that I went into hiding. For a decade I never showed my face in public. Ran around with stupid disguises. Became a recluse. Drank my pain away. But eventually..." Yuri stood and gestured toward the Jeep. "Last stop. Brilliant Cemetery. Let's go."

Slocan Valley, British Columbia, May 2005

Ruby stood in the middle of the driveway forty metres from Swanny. She clasped her leather jacket's zipper, unsure whether to undo it or not. A steady rain had begun to fall. Clinton still remained in the shadows of the doorway. Ruby took a big breath in a bid to control her skittishness and hammering heart. Despite this she made damned sure not to show any emotion. She stood with a clenched jaw staring into the dark entranceway behind Swanny; Nadya to her right; Delia on the left, slightly behind her. Swanny placed the shotgun on his lap and started to wheel toward Ruby. She trained her glare on him and shook her head. Swanny stopped.

"I'm not here for you, Swan."

"I figured as much."

Ruby's features softened for a moment. "I'll make time for you when it's right."

Swanny glanced at Nadya and Delia and then at Ruby. "This is a *baaad* idea."

Ruby hardened again. "I don't care." For far too long she'd let the shame caused by certain men bully her. Ogling gym rats, her father's co-worker, Peter the Russian creep, Clinton, even Tomás. Enough was enough. She gestured with her chin toward Clinton.

Swanny nodded, reversed his chair, turned it and parked in front of his van so that he was perpendicular to Ruby and his brother, and their inevitable face-off. Clinton stepped out of the shadows but remained just inside the doorway, holding himself upright against the door jamb. He wore his leather Hells Angels vest open, his distended belly spilling over faded jeans ripped at the knees. His untied running shoes suggested he'd put them on in haste. Ruby could smell the booze oozing from his pores even at that distance. Clinton had to be at least forty, Ruby thought, but the douchebag looked like he was pushing sixty. Even though he hid behind sunglasses, she could tell by his puffy, stubbled face that the bender he'd been on for much of his life was finally catching up with him. Ruby continued to stare at Clinton, who continued to stare back.

After a few moments of tense silence, Ruby spoke. "Afraid to come closer?"

"The hell you want? Some more blow… on the house?" he said, his voice even more haggard than she remembered.

"Prick. Take your glasses off."

"Beat it." He made to go back into the house.

She air-jabbed a finger at Clinton and took two steps toward him. "No, you do not get to tell me to leave, you pathetic *coward.*" Ruby made sure to emphasize the last word.

Clinton stopped, turned back to face her and stepped out of the doorway. Swanny inched his wheelchair forward. "Watch your mouth, bitch," Clinton croaked.

Many times, Ruby had imagined what she'd say to Clinton if and when she got to confront him; had nightmares about the scenario; imagined what it would feel like to receive an apology from the man, if it felt like anything at all. She even wrote a song about the confrontation that she had yet to play for anyone. Her plan now that it was happening was to see if she could appeal to any semblance of humanity clinging by a thread in Clinton's corroded heart. With Swanny's help maybe, just maybe, Clinton could agree to a truce. After all, Jonah had only done what any boyfriend would do to protect his love. What happened to Swanny was a deeply regrettable accident in the process. She'd beg if she had to. She'd confess to Sasha being Jonah's son. Please let Sasha have a life with his father. Maybe she'd even get an apology for the suffering Clinton had caused her.

But as soon as he fully stepped from the shadows and she heard his brute voice, Ruby was hurled back into his truck, choking underneath his bulging, sweating, stinking weight, his bloodshot and blitzed eyes pinning her down, his cock on her thigh and his thick fingers crawling inside her. The revulsion was instantaneous. As if her body were full of poison, her gut hitched and heaved, and it was all she could do not to vomit. Even behind dark glasses, she despised his eyes on her. Clinton stood there a wreck of a man, and Ruby understood with perfect clarity that his soul had been rotting away his entire life. Years of pent-up shame and anger abruptly altered her plans to plead with him.

"I want to know why you did what you did to me. Why you *raped* me."

Clinton scoffed. "Relaaax. I didn't *rape* you. I barely even finger-banged you, darlin'. We were just having some coked-up fun is all."

"You raped me, asshole." Ruby's heart was off on a sprint now. "You held me down against my will and jabbed your disgusting fingers into my vagina. That. Is. Rape. Doesn't matter how much booze or drugs either of us were on. Doesn't matter if I had played my gig that day completely buck-naked. You fucking raped me."

Ruby glanced at Swanny who was staring at the ground like a kid who was getting an earful from an angry parent. Clinton slid his sunglasses onto his forehead. His eyes were severely bloodshot, purple-black shadows sagged underneath them. He looked like he easily could've been a deranged guerilla commander from some long-forgotten jungle war.

"What we really should be talkin' about is yer little army boyfriend. You can still walk. You can still play rock star all you like." Clinton jabbed his finger in Swanny's direction. "But he's sentenced to that chair... for life."

Swanny raised his head and glared at Clinton. "Let her say what she came here to say," he said, his voice quivering.

Clinton scoffed. "You on her side now? Suppose you would be eh, baby daddy?"

Swanny said nothing. Nadya and Delia glanced at each other, then at Ruby, then at Swanny to see if he'd say anything. Clinton squinted as he measured his brother's response.

Would Swanny spill the beans, then and there? Ruby wondered.

Clinton needed to be distracted. He opened his mouth to speak but Ruby beat him to it. "Hey Clinton." Feeling emboldened, she took another step toward him. "What happened to you?"

Clinton closed his mouth, looked at Ruby. "The fuck you talking 'bout?"

Thunder rumbled in the distance. The rain falling on Ruby's head was cool and cleansing. "What happened to you in your life to make you hate and despise women, to despise me—" Ruby pointed to herself. "—so much that you felt you could degrade and violate and terrify me?" Clinton scoffed at this, but Ruby was far from finished. "Is it because I'm a Doukhobor, too? Huh? You hate us as much as you hate women?" Ruby pointed at Swanny. "I was your brother's lover, you goddamned pig. And still you thought you would fuck me. Have you no shame?"

Clinton lowered his head slightly. His eyes rolled up, still pinned on Ruby. His left eye began twitching. Clearly, he wasn't used to hearing the truth. He especially wasn't used to a *woman* talking back to him. He looked away slowly in a manner that suggested it was painful to do so.

"I think it's time for you and your little girl posse to get the fuck outta here," Clinton said, still looking away.

"Or what?" Ruby clenched her fists. She was shaking to her core. Her voice shook with a noxious mix of fear, righteous indignation and adrenalin high. Her heart was running wild. "You going to rape me again? In front of your brother? And my best friends?"

Clinton blinked purposely slow and levelled his gaze in Ruby's general direction. His chest was heaving as his tongue fished around and poked at his cheek. His bone-white knuckles threatened to tear out of his clenched fists. But he could not look Ruby in the eye. Rainwater sluiced off his bald head.

Ruby continued, her voice now raised. "I see your face all the time in places that should feel safe for me. Restaurants, bookstores, the grocery till … in bed with a lover."

Clinton snickered and smirked but still averted Ruby's gaze.

"Look at me," she demanded. "Look. At. Me."

Wearily, Clinton looked at her.

"Why can't you just admit that you did it, and say you're sorry for the suffering that you caused me? Hm? Or are you just a soulless piece of shit that's gotten too used to hurting people his entire life? Probably killing them too."

Clinton grunted, spittle forming at the corners of his mouth. "You wanna talk about suffering, huh?" Clinton pointed to his brother. "My brother can't fucking walk, bitch," he said with a raised voice.

Ruby shook her head violently, her soaked hair clinging to her face like webbing. "No!" She yelled. "You don't get to use him like that. Are you stupid enough to think that your brother is in that chair because of Jonah?"

Clinton's entire body went rigid. He clenched his neck. His face instantly blotched red. Nadya and Delia stepped back in unison, splashing through puddles as they scrambled to get into the Suburban. Ruby stood her ground.

Clinton bared his teeth and swore at the top of his lungs. His clenched fist was raised as he lurched toward Ruby. Swanny immediately wheeled his chair forward, causing Clinton to bash into it, nearly toppling both of them in the process.

Clinton looked at Swanny as though he were an alien life form. "The fuck you doing?"

"It's your fault, Clinton." Ruby's voice was calm and steady again. She poked at him in the air. "Swanny getting paralyzed is *your* fault."

Swanny clenched his brother's vest with both hands. "Ruby, leave. Now!"

The truck's engine roared to life. Nadya shouted for Ruby to get inside, but Ruby stood her ground even as every cell in her body screamed at her to run. Clinton yanked and yanked and eventually pulled free of Swanny's grasp. Ruby's bones rattled and shook as they had in the hours after her and Jonah fled an unconscious and bleeding Clinton, and Swanny unmoving, watching them run. Now Clinton snarled like a rabid wolf as he stalked toward Ruby with uncontrolled rage in his eyes. Ruby spat wet hair from her mouth and tightened her neck for what was about to come. Clinton held both his hands out in front of him ready to choke her. When he was nearly upon her, the shot rang out...

Clinton instinctively ducked and stopped in his tracks. Ruby jerked violently backwards into the grill of the truck. Still in a stooped position, Clinton twisted to face his brother. Swanny wheeled toward them with his shotgun pointed skyward. He pumped the handgrip, a spent shell ejecting from the chamber and dropping into a mud puddle.

Swanny lowered the barrel and pointed it at Clinton's knees, eyes trained on his brother. "Ruby, go now. Clinton, get the fuck back in the house."

Ruby walked backwards, feeling her way along the body of the truck, her eyes darting between Clinton and Swanny. She opened the passenger-side door. "I pray the devil has his way with you one day very soon," she said to Clinton before she climbed in.

The joker's grin stretched across his jaw. He spoke through gritted teeth. "He already has, baby. He already has."

Castlegar, British Columbia, May 2005

The clouds had dumped their rain and moved on in the ten minutes it took Jonah and Yuri to drive to the cemetery. Jonah was glad for the short drive, as his stump was beginning to ache from all the driving he'd already done that day. Yuri had informed Jonah that most of his ancestors on his mother's side of the family were buried in Brilliant, dating back to the early 1900s. His uncle led him through the wrought-iron gate onto the rough-cut grass. Jonah looked around to get his bearings. The rocky face of Mount Sentinel rose from the edge of Brilliant half a kilometre to the north. At the southern end of the cemetery the land dropped off down to a vast grassy plain at the edge of which was the confluence of the Kootenay and Columbia rivers. Straight ahead, Jonah noticed that nearly all the graves were just simple mounds of dirt or barren patches with small, squat, dark-grey headstones. A pine forest covered the original plots of the cemetery overgrown at the rear.

Yuri weaved through headstones pointing out distant relatives: a cousin twice removed here; a great-aunt there; Yuri's father, the grandfather Jonah had never met, there. They stood in front of the weathered headstone that read, *Sergei Kazakoff. Born 1925. Died 1977*. Strange, Jonah thought, his grandfather died at fifty-two, the same age his mother was now. Yuri closed his eyes, bowed his head and whispered a prayer. "He was a hard man. Drank too much. Abusive." Yuri opened his eyes. "Spent three years in Agassiz for arson and nudity. Came back from prison a haunted man. Died after his third heart attack."

Yuri looked up at Jonah. "You are haunted by war."

Jonah admired his uncle's ability to jump right in. "Some of it."

"Not proud of yourself?"

"Are you proud of the things you did?"

Yuri smiled wryly, subtly peaked his left eyebrow. Touché. "My ghosts don't follow me around much anymore though."

Jonah pursed his lips and dipped his head to the left as he considered how to answer. He nodded, then spoke. "In many ways I joined the Marines a boy and came out a man. For the first few years, I liked being a Marine. You're far away from home and missing the ones you love, so your fellow Marines become fast friends, and even faster family. No matter what, we had each other's backs."

Yuri nodded. "Mhmm. Like me and my comrades did."

"I loved my tribe like I've only ever loved Ruby. Oorah … that was our battle cry." Jonah looked at Yuri. "Plus, on plenty of occasions we improved the lives of the locals. We tried to do good out there. But …" Jonah looked away from Yuri, up at the imposing granite face of Mountain Sentinel.

Yuri motioned for them to walk. Slowly they snaked around headstones toward the forest at the back.

"I had to kill men," Jonah finally said. He stopped, lowered his head, closed his eyes and pinched the top of his nose. Then continued. "On top of that the Marine Corps is made up of some of the most messed-up dudes I've ever met. No joke. A lot of us were just a bunch of young dudes, boys really, who had no clue what we were fighting for, other than for country. Which wasn't the case for me. I'm no patriot. Most of the guys didn't even care if the war was about liberating locals, or if it was a war for the oil that ensured we could all keep enjoying the privileges that come with conquest. They'd say they had an opinion one way or another, but I usually called bullshit and they usually made fun of me for being Canadian." Jonah stopped again, turned to face his uncle. He narrowed his gaze and stared into Yuri's eyes. "I'm sure you can relate. Going into combat is the greatest rush on Earth. Nothing like it. I understand now how some people only find meaning in their lives through war. It's why a lot of us were over there."

Yuri gently tugged Jonah by the arm. The grass was tall now and they walked cautiously among the pine trees, mindful not to step on overgrown graves. Jonah breathed deeply. "I kinda feel weird now, to be honest, being back here in the Kootenays amongst the Doukhobors. The way some people have looked at me. Like... like I'm tarnished, you know?" Jonah scoffed. "People just assume that if you've been to war you've had to kill."

"Which you have."

Jonah nodded almost imperceptibly. "Makes me a bit of a black sheep here I guess."

"Welcome to the club. For some around here we'll always be black sheep. But those Doukhobors aren't true Spirit Wrestlers."

"How so?"

"Too easily they forget where we come from."

Yuri looked back out of the forest from where they came, then looked down at a chipped and moss-covered headstone he stood over. He trampled down knapweed and tall grass around it. He crouched and scraped away the moss, squinted at the Cyrillic lettering. Jonah could make out, *1882–1963*.

Yuri stood. "Do you know the story of me and your mom's great-grandfather Nikolai Cheveldave?"

Jonah shook his head.

"Back in Russia, in the Caucasus region, this would have to be in 1889 I think, Great-Grandpa Cheveldave was bringing the family sheep down from the hills. He was a young man, around sixteen maybe. A Tartar snuck up on him and tried to steal the sheep. The Tartars were the ethnic Turkic-speaking people that lived in the region. Great-Grandpa Cheveldave knew the Tartar language and tried to reason with the thief. 'Without the sheep my family can't make money; we'll be without food and warm clothes for the winter,' he told the man. But the Tartar didn't care. He said the sheep were now his. He started to draw his sword and Great-Grandpa Cheveldave thought that was it, the Tartar was going to kill him. But being younger and quicker, he pulled a knife from his belt, stabbed the thief twice in the chest, and killed him. Then he threw his body into the river. That story followed him all the way to Canada—" Yuri swept his arm around. "—to the villages here. And you know what? No one talked bad about him, nor was he ostracized, or looked down upon for having done that."

"Well, it's because he did it in self-defence," Jonah reasoned.

"Yes. But the Tartars were known to intimidate people with their swords; they rarely killed their neighbours, especially not over some sheep. Grandfather Nikolai was rash with his actions."

Jonah crouched and studied his great-great-grandfather's headstone. He traced his fingers across the lettering and numbers. "I wish I could've known him."

"I was eighteen when he died," Yuri said. "He was more gentle and loving than a man of that era could be. He wasn't a Freedomite, but he never said anything to me about the things I did." Yuri shrugged. "Maybe he didn't know."

Yuri whispered another prayer, then stood up and led Jonah out of the forest. "If Great-Grandfather Cheveldave and all the other Doukhobors would've stayed in Russia and kept up their rebellious resistance to the church and state, they would've died. Or they would've taken up arms again. Because just like a society that doesn't procreate, a society that vows not to kill when threatened dies out in a generation. But we were fortunate to have Tolstoy, and the Quakers put up money for our emigration to a country that—while at times genocidal in its own right—has never known war on its soil." As they emerged from the woods Yuri brought his palms up and looked around. "We were able to continue here with the lofty dream of pacifism."

"In some circumstances if we don't kill, we get killed," Jonah countered.

Yuri stopped in between two overgrown grave mounds and turned back to face Jonah. "In some cases, yes. But that's an untenable, zero-sum game. What we really should be focusing on is the question of how a person gets to the point where they're willing to kill in the first place." Yuri pointed at Jonah. "How do we curb that?"

By killing the killer? Since returning home, a constant, unstoppable stream had been running through Jonah's mind of all the reasons that justified why he would, for one last time, do what he vowed never to do again. It was the most fucked-up scenario he could ever imagine.

Yuri had led them back to the cemetery gates. He stopped, Jonah beside him, and turned to face the graves. "As a sniper, much of what you did in combat was from a distance? You weren't under direct threat?" Yuri asked.

"Yes and no."

"But… Clinton Pritchard is a different matter." Yuri looked at Jonah sidelong. "I've met him before."

Jonah shot Yuri a wrinkle-faced look of utter confusion. "What? How?"

"Swanny lives just down the hill from me."

Jonah threw up his hands. "What the hell?! Why didn't you tell me?"

"I'm telling you now. Swanny and I have become good friends over the years. I bring him borsch, he'll come up with a bottle of vodka, and we'll shoot the shit for hours. He's gotten me to help him now and then with his pot plants, and he'll help me with my vegetable garden. He's not at all like his brother."

"I know he's not."

"I can talk to him and see if there's not some sort of solution we can work out."

Jonah's eyes bugged out as he vehemently shook his head, his mouth forming the nos before he even said them. "No, no. Uncle Yuri, please, I don't want you involved. Clinton's here in the Kootenays. At Swanny's, I'd imagine. No, no. Do *not* go near him. That man is a Hells Angels maniac."

"I could tell he was bad news when I met him," Yuri offered. "Troubled soul."

Jonah scoffed. "Way beyond troubled. He's a murderer. What if he finds out you're my uncle?"

Yuri was silent.

"He knows?"

Yuri nodded.

Jonah's shoulders slumped. "You and Mom and Julian are going to stay with my dad in Spokane until this is all dealt with."

Yuri rubbed his chin in thought. "My days of running and hiding are long behind me, Jonah."

Jonah placed his hand on his uncle's shoulder, looked him in the eye. "Please, Uncle Yuri. Just one more time. Promise me."

Yuri forced a smile and nodded.

Jonah looked at his watch. Soon it would be time for him to pick up Sasha from school.

"One more thing before we go," Yuri said. "If you'll allow, I want to recite two very old Doukhobor incantations for protection. A mix of Christian and ancient Slavic traditions. When I was a kid every village still had healers, whose wisdom was passed down to them from their ancestors. My mother had some of that wisdom passed down to her."

Jonah nodded. "I know she did. But… I'm not a believer."

Yuri smiled. "Your grandmother said one of these protection prayers over your Cossack necklace before she passed it on to you." Yuri looked Jonah up and down. "And here you are back from a war, still alive. Either way, it doesn't matter. In your head replace 'Jesus' with the Universe, or the Creator, or Elvis Presley for all I care. Works all the same."

Yuri gestured for Jonah to stand close to him. He took his hand in his, closed his eyes and bowed his head. Jonah closed his eyes and bowed his head too.

"This one protects against the gun." Yuri's voice was low and sombre as he continued. "Christ was walking over eighty-one heavens, carrying his cross from Earth to heaven. With your iron pale, Lord, protect Jonah Seeger from the rabid blood, from the killing gun, from the cutting sword, from the Damascus steel, from the military spear. Amen. Amen."

Yuri let go of Jonah's hand. Jonah opened his eyes and followed Yuri to the ground where they knelt, and bowed deeply to the Earth, as a Muslim would during their prayers. When he stood Jonah felt lighter. He turned to his uncle and offered his hand to shake.

Yuri took his hand, pulled him close, hugged him, patted him on the back, then pulled away and looked Jonah in the eye. "You're a *maladyets,* a good man. Just like Great-Grandfather Cheveldave, no matter what's happened in your past, you can still become a Doukhobor. That choice is between you and your God."

Slocan Valley, British Columbia, May 2005

Clinton was red-faced, his jaw clenched, shoulders slouched, eyes locked on Swanny, as he paced like a wolf on the other side of the kitchen table from his brother. For a long time neither said anything as they stared at each other, waiting to see which wolf would make the first move. Swanny had removed the shells from the shotgun and had leaned the weapon against the fridge beside him.

Their relationship was doomed from the start. At the back of his mind Swanny had always known this. A boy who loses his mother at such a young age, raised by a hard-living, abusive gangster father? Even the love Swanny's mother showed Clinton would never have been enough to fix him and steer him onto a better path. Their father had ordained Clinton at too young an age, beating him for talking back when he was six, making him watch a Hells Angel snitch get knifed at a biker party when he was thirteen, forcing him to lose his virginity to a prostitute a year later. Swanny had it good by comparison. He had his mother, had tried to make smart choices, had kept the biker lifestyle at arm's length as much as he could. He'd stuck up for Clinton, made excuses for him all these years, felt compassion for him, knowing what a shit childhood he'd had. When Clinton had beat up Jenna in the Haney clubhouse though, that was the beginning of the end. And after he'd raped Ruby, and Swanny found himself on the wrong end of a powerful kick from a boyfriend just trying to protect her, Clinton came to mean something altogether different to Swanny. He became a half-brother in title only, a terrible human being who was surely beyond redemption.

Clinton broke the eyeball deadlock. He forcefully exhaled, shook his head, looked away and stopped pacing. He grabbed two glasses from the drying rack next to the sink, brought them to the kitchen table, and slammed them down next to a waiting bottle of Jack. Clinton opened the whisky, poured two large glasses and slid one to

Swanny. Clinton pulled out a chair and sunk into it. He drank the nearly full glass of amber liquid in one pull, wiped his lips, then broke the silence.

"Ya know, when I went through Dad's stuff after the funeral, there was a closet full of your shit: baseball jersey, trophies, graduation certificate, all sorts of crap... and only a shoebox for me."

Swanny wheeled to the table and reached for the glass of whisky. He downed it in two wincing gulps, eyeing at Clinton as he did. He didn't drink much anymore, and his body warmed instantly as the alcohol coursed through him. Swanny placed the empty glass back onto the table.

"What was I supposed to do?" Swanny said. "*Not* be me? Follow in *your* footsteps?"

Clinton poured another two glassfuls, slid Swanny's sloshing back to him. Clinton rubbed his eyes, kept them closed as he washed his hands back over his bald head. When he opened his eyes, he saw that Swanny hadn't waited for him. His glass was empty. Clinton gave him his best Robert DeNiro; eyebrows up, a comical frown, head bobbing.

Yes, Swanny thought, that was the way it was going to be. No respect. He was feeling light-headed now after the second quick glass in a row.

"Alright then," Clinton said, downing his glass. "Didn't realize until you had the shotgun pointed at my kneecaps out there... you actually loved the bitch."

"How could you? You only ever loved your mother, our old man and yourself."

Clinton shook his head silently for a long time. "Don't think I loved my brother?" he finally said.

Now it was Swanny who poured the next round. He capped the bottle and slowly pushed Clinton's glass toward him.

Clinton lifted it to his lips, then stopped. He squinted at Swanny. After a few moments he began bobbing his head slightly. "Kid's not yours is it... ?"

Swanny took a sip of his whisky while Clinton drank his shot, grabbed the bottle of Jack, opened it and took a long pull. He brought the bottle down hard onto the table, wiped his lips. "They thought I'd fucking hurt a kid to get to him?"

Swanny finished his glass, placed it back onto the table. He could see the hurt on his brother's face at this realization. "Can you blame her? Besides, Jonah never knew the kid was his either."

Clinton balled his fists. "You lied to me this whole time."

"Was the least I could do for her."

"You seriously think I'd fuckin' hurt a kid, Swan?"

Swanny shot upright in his chair. "You already did! That plumber's apprentice in Richmond was barely nineteen, asshole. Do you even *know* what you're capable of anymore?" Swanny reached for the bottle, missed it, swiped at it again and grabbed hold. He was suddenly feeling ballsy. Honest. He knew he was hurting his brother, but it felt good. Like what he imagined an inmate would feel like once released, at long last, from prison.

"It's only ever been about that… that fuckhead, Seeger. But…" Clinton pointed at Swanny and scoffed. "You never even really cared about that either, did… did you?" Clinton was slurring now.

"Maybe… at first… I wanted revenge…" Swanny had to speak slowly to form his words properly. "But I… I eventually realized it wasn't him that I wanted to… get back at. I was just pissed, and sad, that I…" Swanny looked down and slapped at his thighs. "That I didn't have the use of these anymore. Mad at *that* more than anything." Swanny could feel the neuropathic lava pain coming on now. "Don't you… don't you think it's time… to bury that hatchet for Jonah?"

Clinton cocked his back with a pinched look of total incomprehension. "Even if I could… I'd never forget where I buried it. Neverrr." He cackled, then poured two more glasses, slid one to Swanny, spilling half of it in the process. Swanny shook his head. "Drink!" Clinton shouted.

Swanny blinked slowly. He grabbed the glass and poured the whisky down his throat.

"Mad at *me*... more like it." Now it was Clinton's turn to slam his drink down his throat.

"I was ssscared of you... your reaction, Dad's reaction. I'm the fucking cripple now." Swanny's legs began to twitch. "You and him are the same. Club honour bulllllshit. Fucking monsters. You beat my girl Jenna right in front of me. Raped Ruby."

Clinton pushed himself up out of his chair, sending it toppling backwards, crashing into a cupboard. He stood, wobbling, staring at Swanny, tears rolling down his cheeks. He clenched his fists again. Swanny didn't care what Clinton might do to him. He wanted to feel the fury of his fists.

"Go ahead... do it. I don't fucking... I don't fucking care anymore." If booze wasn't coursing through him, Swanny's leg pain would be unbearable. "Go ahead, hit the cripple." Swanny looked down at his legs again and punched them repeatedly with all his might. He locked eyes with Clinton as he did. Clinton's bottom lip quivered. He turned an even deeper shade of red. Swanny reached for the nearly empty bottle, drank from it.

"You..." Swanny pointed up at his brother. "You only ever wanted to kill Seeger because you thought it would erase it. Him dead would mean you wouldn't be reminded... every... fucking... day..." Swanny's vision was blurred now. Two Clintons stood in front of him. "Reminded every day that this..." Swanny pointed all around himself, then smacked himself in the face with his free hand. The bottle slipped out of his other hand, thudding onto the linoleum, bouncing and clanging against his wheel. "That all this fucking... shit was all because of *you*..."

Clinton roared just as Swanny's phone started to ring. Clinton grabbed a kitchen chair and smashed it over and over on the sink.

Swanny laughed as he stared and pointed at Clinton. "Allll because of you, brother."

Clinton dropped what was left of the chair just as someone began leaving a message on the answering machine.

"Hey Michael, Yuri here. I think we should talk and..."

But Swanny heard no more as Clinton's fist slammed into the side of his head and his face hit the kitchen linoleum.

***

When Swanny came to, it was night. The house was dark. His mouth was dry, he could only see out of one eye and his head was filled with lead. He touched his puffy face and winced. He remembered Clinton punching him, knocking him to the ground, like he used to do when they were kids and teenagers. Like he always had when Swanny looked at him wrong, when Swanny got the attention from the cute strippers at the clubhouse parties, when Swanny, just a child, had asked Clinton once to tell him about his mother.

Swanny looked around. He was in his kitchen. Clinton had put him back in his chair. He called for Clinton, his head pounding when he did. He called for him again, louder. Again nothing. An empty bottle of Jack lay on top of the kitchen table. Swanny looked at the ground beside him. A bottle lay at his feet. A draft of cool night air suddenly blew in through the front door, as it swung wide open. Must drink water, Swanny thought. He wheeled past the kitchen table toward the sink and glanced at the nook next to the entrance to the living room where his answering machine sat. A wave of horror washed over him as he suddenly remembered Yuri leaving a message before Clinton knocked him out. In a panic Swanny reloaded his shotgun, grabbed his van keys from the kitchen counter and wheeled out the open front door.

In July 2006, to commemorate the roughly 125,000 Americans that resisted the Vietnam War by seeking refuge in Canada, the Brilliant Cultural Centre on the outskirts of Castlegar, British Columbia hosts Our Way Home, a Vietnam War resisters' conference. Speakers include former Democratic presidential candidate George McGovern, California Senate member and Chicago Seven activist Tom Hayden, four-time Emmy-winning investigative journalist Mark Nykanen, Mahatma Gandhi's grandson Arun Gandhi, Honorary Chairman of the Community Doukhobors John J. Verigin Jr., Vietnam War survivor Kim Phuc (informally known as Napalm Girl), Rabbi Michael Lerner and various US war resisters. Special musical performances are given by Woodstock alumnus Country Joe McDonald, as well as Buffy Sainte-Marie, the Doukhobor Men's Choir and Canadian punk rock legends D.O.A. A planned unveiling of a bronze statue of a Canadian welcoming two American draft dodgers is scrapped following US political pressure and negative US publicity.

The statue now resides in a private art gallery in Nelson, BC.

Slocan Valley, British Columbia, May 2005

"No answer at Yuri's." Jonah dropped his cellphone into the cup holder. He brought the Jeep to a stop, his headlights illuminating the road that twisted up the hill. Tall fir trees closed in on either side. Jonah rolled down his and Lewis's windows.

"Smell that?" Jonah asked.

Lewis sniffed the air. "Smoke."

Two hours earlier on the phone Ruby had told Jonah about her confrontation with Clinton. She was at Nadya's numbing herself with weed and wine. Given the circumstances, and knowing her recovery was a process, it was something he absolutely couldn't fault her for.

"Jesus, Rube, you're a fucking badass for going there," Jonah had said to her, "but... it was super reckless, eh? He could've hurt you."

"I just had to do *something*, you know? I thought... I thought I could talk some sense into him with Swanny there. I thought... fuck, I don't know what I thought. I was even going to beg but then the second I saw him all this rage welled up and it was like someone else possessed me. He had to know what he did. He had to feel my wrath."

"And did he?"

"Fuck yeah he did."

Before they hung up, Jonah asked for directions to Swanny's and Ruby made him promise her to come back to her and Sasha alive.

Jonah backed his Jeep onto Swanny's road, put it in park and turned the engine off. It was now in position should they need to make a quick exit. Or, if Clinton somehow managed to escape, it would block his retreat. Somehow Jonah didn't think fleeing was Clinton's style though.

"Locked and loaded?" Jonah asked.

Lewis nodded, brandished his gun, Biggie, and handed Jonah his, Tupac. Jonah inspected it, felt its weight in his hand, lightly placed his finger on the side of the trigger guard. He hadn't held a gun since

Iraq; it was a familiar and alien sensation at the same time. Goddamn, he wished it hadn't all come down to this. He closed his eyes and felt Sasha's warm hug, saw his exuberant wave goodbye to him and Lewis as they left, heard him asking if he'd see him tomorrow.

"You good?" Lewis asked.

Jonah nodded. He checked the gun's safety, then tucked it into his jeans waistband. They both exited the Jeep, quietly closed the doors and headed up the dark road toward Swanny's.

* * *

After surveilling the house from the woods, then doing a thorough search of the property, they determined no one was at Swanny's place. The smell of smoke was pronounced now. Through the woods came the faint sound of crackling fire. When they walked around to the back of the barn, they saw it: an orange glow seeping through the woods at the top of a slope. Jonah and Lewis both switched on small, tactical flashlights they'd brought with them. They aimed the beams low to the ground in front, then headed into the forest. Slowly they picked their way over roots, rocks and underbrush, as they climbed up the moderate slope. The crackling of fire grew louder, the smell of smoke stronger. Jonah stopped and turned around, a chance to rest his prosthetic leg. He raised the flashlight, clicked it to its most powerful setting, and swept the beam through the tall trees. Long, wild shadows jittered and swayed as he illuminated the way they'd just come. As far as Jonah could see, no one was following them. His stump started to throb from the effort of sneaking up a dark, sloped forest.

Several minutes later Jonah and his battle brother were crouched behind a large boulder at the edge of the forest, catching their breath. Their flashlights were off, tucked into their pockets. Their faces flickered orange from flames that were spitting out the windows of a small house. A minivan was parked in front of the house.

"Fuck," Jonah said, pointing to Yuri's truck parked perpendicular to the minivan. Jonah rose from his crouch and was about to run to the house when Lewis grabbed him hard by the forearm and pulled him back.

"Bro, Marine mode. We don't know who's around. Let's do this proper."

Jonah nodded, took a deep breath. "Got your fancy new cellphone on you, right?"

Lewis took it out of his pocket.

"Capture what you can. Try to keep our guns out of the shot. Let's move."

In unison they emerged in a crouch from behind the boulder, their guns drawn in front of them. They crouch-walked toward the back of the minivan. Lewis half turned and swept his gun behind them in case of a surprise attack. Once at the van they listened. Above the crackling fire came a grunting. Jonah raised his free hand and sliced through the air. Lewis crouch-walked around the right side of the van, Jonah did the same on the left side. At the front bumper Jonah stopped and stood up. Ten metres from the open front door Swanny was grunting, clutching a man's forearm with one hand while trying to manoeuvre his chair backwards on the rain-slick bumpy dirt driveway. Jonah couldn't tell who the unconscious man was. Swanny grunted some more, desperately trying to pull the man away from the flames. Intense heat from the open front door washed over Jonah. The entire inside of the house was engulfed in flames. He looked around to see if there was a third man anywhere. Lewis had his gun up and trained on the back of Swanny's head.

Jonah stepped out in front of the minivan. "Swanny!" Jonah called above the crackling din.

Swanny dropped the man's arm and spun his chair around. Jonah ran toward him, Lewis at his side. Swanny's face was smudged with ash, his eyes bloodshot and puffy. His chest was heaving as he tried to catch his breath. He wasn't surprised in the least to see Jonah.

Jonah peered around Swanny to see who the unconscious man was. Clinton. A bottle of booze lay a few feet away from him.

"Yuri!" Jonah called. "Yuri!"

Swanny stammered in between catching his breath, "I'm… I'm sorry."

Jonah stepped toward Swanny, glaring at him. He pointed at the burning house. "How the fuck did this happen?"

Swanny shook his head mournfully. "I… I don't know what happened. Ruby came, tore a strip…" Swanny gestured to his brother. "We were drinking afterward… a lot. Arguing. I told him… this—" Swanny pointed at his legs. "—was his fault. He knocked me out. When I woke up…" Swanny broke into tears. He pointed at the burning house then down at his brother. "I could barely see straight but I got myself in my van, drove up here, and… saw Yuri lying there, just inside his house. I called his name… I tried to go in but… but the flames…"

"Did you tell Clinton that Yuri was my uncle?"

Swanny's eyes bulged wide, ash-smudged tears streaking down his cheeks. "No! No. I tried to protect Yuri. He's my friend. I…" Swanny looked around as though Yuri's driveway would provide answers. "Clinton met Yuri a couple of times, didn't like him. He figured it out though. Maybe he was gonna use Yuri to get to you. I dunno how the fire started…" Swanny raised his hands in surrender. "I swear." Swanny dropped his arms and lowered his head to his chest. He ran his hands through his hair, shook his head. "Fuck. Clinton." Swanny raged at the top of his lungs. "Fuuuck!"

Jonah peered into the flaming house. From the moment he'd seen the orange glow through the woods and smelled the smoke he had feared the worst. Why did Yuri come home? He promised he wouldn't. Yet another tragedy at the hands of Clinton Pritchard. Jonah's vision blurred as he strode past Swanny toward the flames, his forearm shielding his face, the licking flames now suddenly not of a house but of an exploded Humvee. The smell not of burning wood but of burning diesel and seared flesh. Jonah was in a Black Hawk, its bone-rattling rumble a portent of the death that was all around him. Distantly, behind the kicked-up dust storm and *whup, whup, whup* of chopper blades, Lewis was calling for Jonah. Eyebrow-sizzling heat stopped him in his tracks. He coughed hard, stumbled backwards and tripped, falling back onto a body. He rolled off the body, up onto his knees. He stared at the form, blinked his eyes hard. It was Sadie in a body bag. It was two charred bodies in Fallujah clutching each other in the street. It was his first sniper kill in Bosnia, a blue ball cap flying backwards off the man's head in a burst of pinkish-grey mist. It was Mason, ghostly pale, calling for his fiancée. It was the teen insurgent, slumped in the alley, calling for his mother. It was mutilated Iraqi women and children. Everywhere the dead. He didn't need to look up to know they were there, standing all around him now, watching him, crowding in on him, a chorus of maddening moans. It was his own moaning. It was the moaning coming from the body in front of him. Jonah heard his name. He turned away from the body, looked back at the burning house. Yuri's house. His wise, kind, gentle uncle who, in just a few short days, Jonah had grown to love. The flames licked at the sky; large chunks of ash floated in slow motion by Jonah's head. His uncle was in there, charred, curled in agony. Dead.

"Jonah!" Lewis shouted. "He's waking up."

Jonah stood up. It was Clinton that he loomed over. The biker's eyes suddenly popped open like a Chucky doll. He lifted his head to see Jonah standing at his feet, gun in hand. Clinton was black-out drunk, his eyes bleary, trying to focus. Clinton looked around to see where he was, what was happening. He glanced at Lewis, then caught sight of his brother behind them. He coughed, squinted at Jonah. For the first time that night, Jonah saw Clinton clearly. His was the splotchy, puffy face of a lifelong alcoholic and drug abuser. His nose was mashed to the side; a long, wormy scar crawled diagonally up his right cheek, another across his forehead. Neither were there the last time Jonah encountered him. Clinton's white t-shirt was filthy with dark stains and streaks of ash, his jeans were torn nearly clean off at the knees. Large bleeding scabs dotted his arms. A filthy white bandage splinted together the forefinger and middle finger of his left hand. Clinton Pritchard was a mangled, rapidly sinking battleship.

Jonah looked at Lewis, who still had his gun trained on Clinton. In his other hand his prosthetic fingers clasped his phone with its swivel-screen camera still capturing the scene. Jonah gestured to the phone.

"You sure?" Lewis asked.

Jonah nodded and Lewis slipped the phone into his pocket. Jonah twisted back to Swanny. "This ends now." He faced Clinton again. Behind the biker were the dead, the blurry shadow ghosts of all Jonah's wars. Watching, judging him. "Swanny, go home," Jonah instructed, his eyes still pinned on Clinton.

Wincing, Clinton lifted himself up on his elbows. "Swan..." Clinton managed to croak, his voice far hoarser than Jonah remembered, as though he'd been gargling with razors. "Where am I?" Clinton shook his head and seemed to come alive. He took in Lewis as though he were nothing more than a statue. He looked back to Jonah. Of course the piece of shit would use the N-word when he asked if Jonah had brought Lewis to do his dirty work for him. He tilted his head back immediately afterward, spat the word, then cackled into the glowing orange night.

Clinton's racism had its intended effect. Further enraged, Jonah took a step closer to the biker, who warily levelled his head. Jonah raised his gun and pointed it squarely, confidently at Clinton's soot-covered forehead. In thirty seconds, Jonah would pull the trigger, and at close range, a man he loathed, a man he knew, would die. All of his troubles with that man would be extinguished and there would be one more ghost added to his dead.

Clinton spat weakly up at Jonah's face. A slow, greasy smirk curled his lips. "The old Douk begged for his life just like your bitch begged me to—"

Jonah roared a primal scream that was something far more ancient than he was. An explosion of molten rage ripped through him as though he'd stepped on a land mine. If he could've sunk his teeth into Clinton and tore his head clean off like a grizzly ripping into a salmon, he would have. He placed his finger on the trigger. Clinton's smirk disappeared. From in between the wall of ghosts standing behind Clinton, a small figure emerged. Jonah started to apply pressure on the trigger just as he could make out that it was… Sasha. He looked up at his son, at his innocent blue eyes. Sasha smiled and beckoned for his father to follow. In a lightning instant, Jonah knew what he had to do. The shot rang out, echoing throughout the surrounding forest, just as the faint sound of sirens wailed from down the Valley.

Ruby rolled a joint while Delia stood in the kitchen pouring drinks in the dim glow of the stove's hood light. Nadya poked her head out onto the patio, looked left and right, slid the door closed, then padded across the area rug and sat down on the overstuffed loveseat beside Ruby. On the CD player Peggy Lee watched the world go up in flames in a dreamlike malaise, asking if that was all there was to life, then seductively imploring the women to break out the booze and have a ball. Ruby and her girls had certainly drunk their share since racing away from Swanny's place hours earlier. But no one, as far as Ruby could tell, was having a ball.

"Maybe we should stop drinking, huh?" Nadya said.

Delia lowered a bottle mid-pour. Ruby looked at her and gestured for her to continue.

"I need to take the edge off. Today was fucked, and now Jonah's out there. Plus… it's not coke."

Nadya rubbed the small of Ruby's back. "You sure, babe?"

Ruby sighed and nodded. "Once this is all over, I don't know… I can go back to rehab for a week, or whatever." Ruby licked the rolling paper to seal it. How *would* it look when it was all over? What if something went sideways and Jonah didn't make it out alive? To have him back in her life, her heart opening to him again, and then to have him ripped away? What would she tell Sasha about how his father died and *why* he died? Would Clinton come after her? She shuddered and looked at Nadya with a lifetime of worry circling her eyes.

"He'll be okay," Nadya said, still rubbing Ruby's back. "Jonah can handle himself."

Delia set down the refilled glasses of wine on the coffee table. "Plus, he told you himself he has backup," Delia added as she eased down onto her knees.

"I know…" Ruby looked at the stereo's digital clock display. Over three hours had passed since she'd last talked to Jonah. "I just wonder what's taking him so long." Ruby lit the joint and brought it to her lips. She took a big toke just as her cellphone rang and rattled the glass-top coffee table, causing Ruby and Nadya to jump in their seats. All three girls leaned over the phone and looked at it as though it were a strange artifact. It was Tomás calling.

"That ex of yours?" Nadya asked.

Ruby nodded as she let the cellphone ring until it stopped. She passed the joint to Nadya. A few seconds later Tomás rang again. Again, Ruby didn't answer. A minute passed and a bleep alerted Ruby that she had a text message. She flipped her phone open and read Tomás's text aloud: "Hey Ruby. Miss you babe. Thinking of you lots. I guess you still don't wanna talk hey? Anyway, just thought you should know, 'Spirit Wrestlers' continues to climb the indie radio charts. It's in the top ten here in LA on Indie 103.1. Cool huh? The *Conan* people got back to us too. They really really want us and have rescheduled our performance for June. Two weeks from now. Do this one last show with us? For me and the band (they all miss you terribly)? For old times' sake? Love ya, T."

"*Conan*, that's pretty big-time, Rube," Nadya said.

Delia sipped her wine, then spoke. "Maybe wait until all this shit with douchebag blows over before you reply?"

Ruby took the joint from Nadya. Sucked long and hard, passed it to Delia. She reread the message, while drinking her wine. She chewed her bottom lip; her forehead's worry lines gradually softening. "Nah, I know already." She texted two words back to Tomás: "I'm in."

Thirty seconds later, Ruby's phone rang again. "Okay, Tomás," she said before answering it, "I told you I'm in, what more—" But it was Jonah. She answered right away. "Jonah, are you okay?" He was breathing hard, and she could hear voices in the background.

"I'm okay. Listen to me carefully," he said and then proceeded to give Ruby very clear and concise instructions.

The perky, early-morning song of chickadees and the chattering of sparrows flitting about seemed to mock the sombre mutterings of the curious crowd that had gathered. A cloudless, pale-blue sky stretched across the narrow valley. Golden beams of morning sunlight sliced through cathedral-like spires of cedar and fir, stippling the columns of smoke lazily rising from the still-smouldering ruins of Uncle Yuri's home. Jonah winced at the acrid, haunting smell of arson in the cool morning air. He eyed his and Lewis's handywork; Clinton slumped in a chair centre stage to it all, his hands and feet zip-tied, a black cloth covering his lolling head. It all had the air of a lynching or some sort of twisted medieval trial absurdly unfolding in broad daylight.

Lewis stepped up and slapped Clinton across the back of the head, then yanked off the black hood. His sweating dome, bruised and scratched as though a raccoon had attacked it, glistened in the morning sun. Clinton slowly peeled open his eyes and immediately recoiled from the sharp light, and from poisoning himself with blackout drunkenness for what Swanny had told Jonah was Clinton's fourth night in a row. The biker squinted to bring the scene in front of him into focus, his jaw immediately falling slack and his face twisting into an almost comical expression of bewilderment, for standing in a semicircle twenty feet in front of him was an audience of nearly two dozen people, holding hands or with arms crossed, sobbing, faces flushed with sadness and anger.

Directly in front of Clinton was Swanny, who had not yet looked up at his brother. Beside Swanny were Ruby and Jonah, holding hands reassuringly. Beside them was Jonah's mother, Sharon, with Virginia Samarodin next to her, arm around her, supporting her; Grandma Polly was beside them, with Julian holding her hand. Big Nick stood close behind all of them, a solemn, towering watchman. Fanning out behind them like a rearguard were Jonah and Ruby's friends: Nadya, her brother Ryan, Delia, Bobbie, Cedar, Derrick, Ferdy and Trevor. Interspersed with them were a handful of Big Nick's co-workers—for safety—and a few friends of Yuri's. Parallel to Clinton at each end of the semicircle and only a few feet away from his slumped frame, were Jonah's stone-faced, battle-hardened Marine brothers, Master Sergeant Ben Whitewolf who'd driven up from Spokane, and Corporal Lewis Robinson. Jonah had made it clear that no one was to bring any weapons onto Yuri's property. His uncle would've wanted it that way. Lewis and Ben agreed but not without grumbled objection.

A crisp morning breeze swept across the parking area where they all stood. Jonah glanced down at his prosthetic leg, exposed for all to see below the cargo shorts he'd found in his Jeep. The metal shin of his leg glinted where it was touched by rays of sunlight; the cool air was refreshing on his aching stump.

"W-water," Clinton croaked.

Lewis dug into a small backpack at his feet, produced a bottle of water and stepped to Clinton. Ruby let go of Jonah's hand and crouched beside Swanny, presumably to see how he was doing. Jonah started rubbing his knuckles at the anticipation of what was about to unfold, then abruptly stopped. He needed to stay present. But his twitching trigger finger pulled him back into last night, Yuri's blazing home hot on his face. In the instant when he'd decided to pull the trigger, realization came clear and profound as though he'd been in a dark room all those years and had only just discovered a door he hadn't even known was there. He'd adjusted his aim just a hair to graze Clinton's left ear. In doing so, not only did he cause the biker to piss his pants, but Jonah had opened the door to an alternate world illuminated by Sasha's innocence, Sasha's hope in him as a father, by Jonah's renewed forever love of Ruby, by the old Doukhobor wisdom shared with him by his family, his community, his Uncle Yuri. Jonah had looked up after the shot rang out through the forest… They were gone—Blue Ball Cap, Mason, Sadie, all of his ghosts. A dark, heavy shroud had been lifted. He hoped he would not see those phantoms again.

As Clinton took sips of water, Jonah turned to his right to see his mother and Grandma Polly sobbing. They were both heaving, arms around each other now, sheltered by the arms of Virginia, Julian and Big Nick. His Grandma Polly slowly lifted her head and began staring not at Clinton but past him at the charred remains of Yuri's home. Jonah's heart sank. His flesh and blood had spent their final, agonizing moments there. Was it right that Jonah called his mother and grandmother to this, his idea of communal witnessing? His mother had initially refused, thought it dangerous and grim. Jonah assured her that Clinton was securely restrained. Grandma Polly reminded her that if Yuri were to linger at his home like a confused ghost at the scene of their murder, then he'd need to be sent off properly.

Clinton wiped the corner of his lips with the backs of his bound hands. He hung his head and muttered to himself.

Jonah took a deep breath. He was exhausted from the previous night's events. They'd dragged Clinton into the back of the Jeep and drove him down to Swanny's. Less than a minute later two fire trucks, a cop car and an ambulance were at Yuri's. At Swanny's request, Jonah and Lewis begrudgingly helped him change Clinton's piss-stained jeans. Then Jonah got on the phone and like a political party whip, wrangled support for his cause well past midnight. Turned out to be an easier sell than he expected. A sober and sleepless night followed, in which Clinton would periodically grunt and groan. Swanny gave him a sleeping pill, after which he'd mumbled back to sleep and Jonah and Swanny could return to their awkward conversations. Then, hours later, just before first light, they'd brought Clinton back to the scene of his crime, dragged him out of the Jeep, and propped him on a chair to face Yuri's people.

Swanny hadn't mustered the courage to look at his brother, who surely by now saw him as just as dangerous as Clinton's enemies. If their father were alive, he might have Swanny killed for his sedition. At the very least he'd savagely beat him, then disown him.

Ruby's hand on his forearm pulled Swanny out of his gloom. Her touch had always felt good: warm, electric, genuine. She asked him if he was okay and he shook his head no.

"It's the best possible outcome," she said softly, squeezed his forearm, then stood from her crouch and returned to Jonah's side.

Swanny was a traitor to every Hells Angel that had murdered innocent people, raped women and extorted from the weak; he was a Judas to every brother who had bullied the people they were supposed to care for, who dished out beatings like they were handshakes, and mistook obedience and power for love. So, Ruby was correct when she said it was the best possible outcome, even if it didn't feel that way. But wasn't Swanny saving Clinton too, from what would surely be a gruesome way to die at the hands of the UN gang, his true enemies that were closing in? Word was that they were on their way to the Kootenays now. They'd chop Clinton's hands off, cut and peel his face to the bone, then set their pit bulls on him in the woods.

Swanny closed his eyes, his mind replaying the previous night. He was in his chair in the kitchen while Jonah was in the living room, his handgun on the carpet beside him. Jonah was leaning back against the window wall, staring at a bound Clinton who was sweating and convulsing on the couch, puking into a bucket every half hour before receding into unconsciousness. Next to Jonah was the hulking frame of his friend Lewis, who didn't once take his eyes off Clinton.

Swanny watched his brother's laboured breathing for a while, then broke the silence with a scoff. "With a father like ours," he said, "he was doomed from the start."

Jonah kept his eyes on Clinton. "We don't choose where we're born, or who our parents are, do we?" He looked over at Swanny, gestured at him with his chin. "But we can choose who we become." A small kindness, Swanny supposed. An acknowledgement.

"I'll never forgive Clinton for what he did."

"Like you never forgave him for what he did to Ruby?" Jonah said coldly. The moment of kindness had passed.

Swanny looked down at his legs. "I *didn't* forgive him for that. He's a monster, like our father was." He looked back up at Jonah. "You don't know what life under them was like. Like it or not I am his brother. Cursed to be an Angel. Best I could've done was take a shit-kicking for leaving the club, then move out here where they mostly left me alone." Swanny shook his head. "I kept Ruby's secret. *Your* secret. Least I could do. I'm not a brave man. I was late to the game when it came to doing the right thing. Not you though... you always did right."

Jonah looked down at his gun. "No, I haven't." He glanced at Swanny's legs then looked him in the eye. He shook his head slowly. His face softened. "And I sure didn't do right by you."

Swanny offered a nod of the head. That was apology enough from Jonah.

"Tell you the truth, I don't even remember what I did, that... that..." Jonah trailed off.

"Paralyzed me?"

Swanny rehashed the moments at the music festival that had shattered all their lives: Jonah's hard kick to Swanny's chest that had sent him flying backwards through the air, his upper back, neck and head slamming into a parked car where the bumper joined the front fender. He'd laid there unable to move, he told Jonah, helplessly watching his and Clinton's vicious battle. A small crowd of mostly Jonah and Ruby's friends had gathered to watch and were oblivious or didn't care that Swanny was splayed on the ground. Eventually Jonah was pulled off of Clinton, whose face was a bloody mess. "I tried to get up," Swanny said. "But my arms were weak, and I couldn't feel my legs. I spotted Ruby, terrified and sobbing, leaning back against Clinton's truck, her friends sheltering her. For an instant I'd hoped

Clinton was dead... because I knew that if he wasn't, you and Ruby would never be safe again. I hoped too that the paralysis in my legs would only be temporary. And if I had told Ruby that I couldn't feel my legs, that I needed help, she probably would've tried to help me. And you would not have left her side."

"Absolutely," Jonah said.

"I don't know if you remember but all I said was 'run.' And you grabbed Ruby's trembling hand and together you fled into the forest. And if you hadn't, Clinton's biker buddies would've beaten you and waited for Clinton to wake up and finish you off then and there."

After some time, Swanny said, "I loved Yuri like the older brother I wish I had." He looked up at Jonah. "You'd said that he'd promised to hide out for a while, but I think he understood the sacrifice he was making."

"What sacrifice?" Jonah asked.

Swanny wheeled to his answering machine and pressed play. Through his voice Yuri was resurrected. "Hello, Michael Swanny Pritchard. I just got home from a day spent with my nephew. He's told me everything, and he knows that we're friends and neighbours. Funny how time reveals all eventually, eh? Speaking of which, I think sometimes both you and Jonah wish you could go back in time and change what happened. But here's the thing, Michael, from what little I've learned in this strange, wonderful life... a person can either be time's victim... or they can be its master... In the mere week or so that I've gotten to know Jonah, my admiration and fondness for who he is and who he'll become has grown immeasurably. Very much how I feel about you, my friend. Like his girl, Ruby, you're all good people caught up in unfortunate circumstances. Anyway, here I am rambling on as I have tendency to do. The reason I called is to offer a way out of this pickle that you all find yourselves in with your brother. All of us really, little Sasha and his grandparents, sister Sharon, our mother, all of us, we're all caught in the web of Clinton's darkness. I promised Jonah that I wouldn't come home, that I would go hide in Spokane. But at this stage in my life I don't really feel like hiding any more. And

I have a feeling Clinton will be back anyway. So, here's what I propose: send Clinton up here… alone, and let's see if I can't somehow help resolve this mess we're in. I… I love ya, pal. Will you do that as a favour to me? Don't worry. I have a heart that's ready for anything."

Swanny pressed the stop button on the answering machine. The rest of Yuri's message could wait…

A morning ray of sun in his eyes, and the sound of Clinton hacking up a lung took Swanny away from his memories of several hours earlier in his living room and brought him back outside to the smouldering ruins of Yuri's place. Red-faced, still bound to a chair, Clinton looked up, spat weakly at his feet then levelled his confused, angry gaze at his brother. "Wha… what's going on?"

A murmur rippled through the gathered at Clinton's pained question. Jonah squeezed Ruby's hand, then stepped forward. Ruby crossed her arms, whether in defiance or defence, she couldn't quite tell.

Jonah took a few steps toward Clinton, stood to the side. "Clinton Pritchard, you've done unforgivable things..." He pointed back to the crowd like a defence lawyer would. "And you are going to hear these people out."

Clinton grunted and twisted back with great effort to the charred, smoking ruins behind him. With his bound hands he shielded his eyes from the bright morning sunlight and stared for a long while. He turned back to face Jonah. "I don't remember."

"Liar." Ruby uncrossed her arms, stepped out of the semicircle, and stood across from Jonah. Clinton looked up at her and frowned, his weary expression saying, "Not this again." She glared at him while pointing back at Jonah's grandma Polly. Whenever she'd met her in the past, the stoic baba always walked upright, gracefully, her long, grey-streaked hair and calm manner a picture of strength. But here, now, in the huddle of her daughter's arms she was suddenly defenceless and deflated, smaller in the way that only a woman who's just lost a child could be. Clinton followed Ruby's gaze, his eyes reluctantly taking in the old woman swiping tears from her cheeks. "Last night..." Ruby began, "you killed that woman's son." Ruby thought of Sasha and suddenly shared in Grandma Polly's anguish. Her tears came strong and without warning. "You monster," she said between heaving sobs. "How could you burn a man in his own home?" A collective din of horror and sorrow swept through the gathered. Jonah's mother and grandmother groaned in unison. Jonah's brother, Julian, standing next to them, dropped his head to his chest. Grandma Polly arched her head up, then dropped it into her palms.

In a voice that was pure sorrow she cried out, lamenting her poor son. "*Moy lubeshny syn.*" She nearly collapsed but Julian and Sharon clutched her, held her up. Ruby's mother stepped beside Grandma Polly and put her arms around her. Jonah was at Ruby's side now, hugging her.

"You okay?" he whispered.

She nodded, wiped her eyes and looked back at Clinton. His head was buried in his hands. He looked up. "I don't, I don't know what happened. I was drunk. It was an accident, okay? Fuck's goin' on here?"

Ruby watched as all of a sudden, the big Indigenous man, Jonah's Vietnam vet friend, Ben, lurched toward Clinton and grabbed him by the throat with his left hand. With his right hand he pointed to the gathered and spoke with unquestioned authority. "You watch your mouth around these elders, boy." Clinton coughed, looked at Ben sidelong.

fierceness in Ben's eyes together with the lines running down the sides of his face—claw marks that deepened with the conviction in his voice—restored Ruby's strength and resolve. From underneath her leather jacket she pulled out one of her hoodie's sleeves and wiped the tears that had wet her face.

Ben released his grip. "You swear one more time, boy, and I'm gonna knock your head clean off."

"There will be no more violence on this land." The booming baritone voice reverberated throughout the surrounding forest. It was unmistakably Ruby's father. She looked at him looking at Ben. "If you don't mind, sir."

Ben nodded respectfully, shot another warning glare at Clinton for good measure, then stepped back.

Emboldened, and with her heart knocking loudly in her chest, Ruby took a few steps toward Clinton. She stood next to him, but not too close. He tried to turn his head in her direction, winced and was forced to twist his torso in order to see her. He met Ruby's cold stare. His eyes were not those of the Clinton she had known even just a day before, when she'd confronted him. His eyes must've been blue at one time, but now they were dull, dark grey and bloodshot, the puffy bags beneath them black and red and threatening to burst. For a brief moment Clinton's eyes focused. He was present. He seemed to see Ruby for the first time, to really see her, not as an object of scorn or misogynistic pleasure, but as a human being. Was that possible? And then, just like that, he looked away.

Ruby turned to face the people. "Some of you here don't know but—" She pointed at Clinton. "—when I was nineteen this sad excuse for a man… raped me." Another murmur ran through the gathered.

Ruby's mother cried out, "No!" She grew faint and nearly collapsed but Big Nick hugged her into him. She buried her head into her husband's shoulder.

Clinton was silent and unmoving. Ruby's father stepped out from the crowd, holding Ruby's mother upright beside him. Ruby continued. "But last night I said what I needed to say to him." She looked at Clinton again. "What he needed to hear." Ruby knew that that confrontation could well have added to Clinton's rage, to whatever caused him to come to Yuri's place and do what he did. She suddenly felt weak. She shook the thought from her mind just as the sudden urge for escape coursed through her. When she turned back toward the crowd her mother and father were next to her, glaring down at Clinton with a rage in both their eyes that she'd never seen before.

If Virginia were alone in that moment, she'd raise her fist to the heavens and rail at God for letting this happen to her daughter. No prayers would be enough to vanquish an anger she had seldom felt in her life. An anger that now left her wishing death upon this cursed devil. "*Proklyatyy chort,*" she said under her breath. She'd never thought this way before. It was, of course, a mortal sin. But Virginia felt it now and thought she might just feel it forever. Of course, she'd had an inkling, hadn't she? A woman's sense? A mother's intuition? But she was always too afraid, too ashamed to find out the truth.

Throughout her people's history in Russia, Doukhobors had faced Tartar and Cossack raids on their villages; they'd felt the sting of whips and the slice of swords; they'd faced the wrath of the tsars, exile to the far reaches of the Russian Empire; they'd suffered Siberian imprisonment and torture. In Canada the Doukhobors were confronted with ridicule and discrimination by an unsympathetic public, endured smear campaigns by the biased press, were labelled as terrorists. But all of this the Doukhobors faced collectively. Nowhere in the prayer books, or prayer services, or through the stories passed down from grandmother to granddaughter was there any advice on how to deal with a daughter's rape.

The very word made Virginia shiver. She was loath to say it or think it. At least their dear Sasha wasn't a product of that terrible event.

Like a starving dog begging for food, Virginia bore holes into the man's skull with her desperate, razor-sharp look of hatred. Even though the Slocan Valley had its share of castaways and misfits—some of which Virginia referred to as no-goodniks—the pitiful excuse for a man sitting in the chair in front of her looked unlike any who had set foot there before. He was a villain straight out of a movie, the type of scowling, thick-faced, white man whose mug shot Virginia always saw on the news. She refused to name him, sure as the sky was blue that he was godless. And the more she sized up the *svoloch*, thought about what he had done to her Ruby, and to Sharon's poor brother, Yuri, and to God knows who else... the more unforgivable he was, too.

Virginia looked up at her husband, tense and puffed up and glowering down at the murderer with a look of disdain she'd only seen in Nick once before. She remembered it well. Ruby had been four. Virginia had held her little hand as they crossed Baker Street when a drunk driver ran a red light and nearly killed them. Unlucky for the driver, he immediately got stuck in traffic. Nick had yanked open his door, pulled him out of his car, punched him once square in the jaw, and with one arm, pinned him up against a wall by his neck until the police came. He might've choked him unconscious had Virginia not reminded Nick of what type of people they were, and if Ruby hadn't started crying and pleading with her father to stop hurting the man.

"Hey... look at us," Nick commanded to the bastard slumped in the chair.

Chattering swallows dashed and darted behind him. Until then Clinton didn't even seem to notice Virginia and Nick were standing in front of him. The bastard glanced vacantly at Virginia and then as he cast his eyes on Nick, scanning way up to see just how massive and angry her husband was; his eyebrows drew together and his cracked, swollen lips formed an *O* in a distinct look of worry. In the distance a dog barked. A chorus of caws made Virginia look up to see a murder of crows swooping and circling the curious scene on the ground. A gurgle and a murmur made Virginia follow the gaze of the crows to see Big Nick's big hand clenching the son of a bitch's throat. Both men's faces were turning red. None of the gathered made a move to stop Virginia's husband from choking the monster to death. Not Jonah, nor Ruby. Not Lewis or Ben. No one. The gurgling coughing gasps for breath were disturbing but Virginia was frozen. It was only when Swanny shouted for Big Nick to stop, that her husband released his grip.

As the man gasped for air, Virginia scrutinized him again and considered his rotten soul in relation to her people's history. Before

Tolstoy was regarded as one of the world's greatest novelists, before he was a pacifist and Christian anarchist, before he was an admirer of and patron to the Doukhobors, he'd gambled away small fortunes, slept with prostitutes and killed men in war. But in eventually embracing and living according to the simple teachings of Christ, as the Doukhobors had aspired to, Tolstoy allowed Christ to arise within himself. Virginia had always been taught that no one, absolutely no one, was beyond redemption. After all, what kind of God would deny the worst sinner a place in heaven? Yet, try as she might to draw from her faith as one draws water from a deep well, Virginia could not reconcile that this terrible man in front of her deserved anything but what awaited him in hell. If thinking this way eroded her faith, eroded her spirit, then so be it. He'd violently violated her daughter and threatened her family's safety.

The asshole was still eyeing Nick when Virginia cleared her throat and stepped in between them. "*Svin'ya,*" she said, looking him in the eyes and calling him a pig. Then she did something she'd never done before; she lifted her hand high above her head, clenched her jaw, and clawed a man across his face as hard as she could with bloodthirsty taloned fingers.

Standing with Ruby at the edge of the semicircle, Jonah watched Clinton take Virginia's talons without so much as a wince. As though he'd expected it, knew he deserved it. Blood instantly poured from the gouges across his face. Virginia pulled Big Nick away and they rejoined the crowd. With great effort and grunts, Clinton stood up for the first time. Together Ben and Lewis advanced toward him, but with his ankles bound he wasn't going anywhere.

"What do you want from me?!" he yelled, scanning the crowd. The effort this took depleted him. Right away he slumped back down into his chair. "Just ... just fuck ... just kill me already." A few snickers came from Jonah and Ruby's friends.

"That's not our way," Jonah's mother said, her arm still around Grandma Polly. This time, from the Doukhobor elders in the crowd, came mutterings of agreement.

Clinton raised his shackled arms onto the back of his head, closed his eyes and shook his head slowly in exasperation.

"That's too easy a way out for you," Jonah said.

Clinton opened his eyes and squinted at him. "Seeger. You ..." He pointed at Jonah. "*You* started all this." A weak, petty last act of defiance.

"No. He did not." Swanny had wheeled away from the safety of the group and had finally spoken up against his brother. Clinton peered at Swanny with loathing.

"Why did you kill my brother Yuri?" Jonah's mother asked, her voice quivering. A loud chorus of agreement swept the crowd.

Clinton dropped his head and stared at the ground, shaking his head almost imperceptibly. Obviously, he'd killed him because he'd discovered the relation, Jonah thought. Jonah took one step closer to Clinton and stooped over to his head level. "Yuri was an innocent old man, you piece of shit."

"A *good* man," Swanny echoed.

Clinton raised his head, shot his brother a wary look that suggested Swanny should know better. "I've taken out plenty of good men." He scoffed. "At least they were good at one point." He turned to Jonah, jabbed a finger at him. "Haven't you, soldier?"

"It was my job," Jonah shot back.

Clinton sneered, flashed his teeth, red from the blood that had poured down his cheeks and into his mouth. "It was *my* job too." He addressed the crowd. "How else was I supposed to make sure the nose candy and party treats you all gobble up on the weekends kept getting delivered without a hitch? Huh?" He looked up to the ravens still circling above. "You all think you're better than me."

Ruby laughed mockingly. "We *absolutely* are better than you."

Swanny spoke. "You deserve what's coming to you, Clinton."

Clinton levelled his gaze at his brother, grumbled, "Yeah, and what's that?"

Jonah watched his grandmother Polly and his mother step out from the group. Hand in hand they walked around Swanny and slowly approached Clinton.

"Closer," Sharon's mother said, lightly tugging her hand. They stood ten feet away from Clinton. Her mother always seemed to have this reserve of strength that so many women of Russian stock had. Sharon had it at times too, she supposed. But not quite like her mother. To remain resolute in the Freedomite ways even as the world around shamed you. To hide your tears even as the police dragged your children from your home. To raise your family with very little income when your husband was sent to prison. The strength it took to be the one to say that you and your daughter needed to address the man that killed their Yuri.

"Closer," her mother said again, this time tugging harder.

Sharon's heart had started beating faster the moment they stepped away from the security of the group. Now it was positively racing. *Och*, what good would it do to be closer to him, she thought. He was barbaric, stinking of alcohol and unwashed body.

Sharon and her mother approached until they were within five feet of him. This man called Clinton. Such a typical Anglik name, she thought. He rested his elbows on his knees, his head hung low in exhaustion. Lewis and Ben stepped closer now, too. Thank God they were there. Their proximity gave Sharon strength.

For many long uncomfortable moments, Sharon and her mother just stood there saying nothing. Finally, her mother adjusted her shawl, then spoke. "Hey mister. Do you have any children?" Her voice was calm but hoarse from crying.

Clinton shook his head without looking up.

She pressed on. "What does your mother think of the man you've become?"

"She's dead."

"If she were alive?" Sharon asked.

"She knew what she was getting into when she married my old man ... a biker."

Sharon's mother spoke again, her voice growing clearer. "What had my son... what had he done to you that made you so angry that you could do *this*?" She pointed at the smouldering ruins of Yuri's home to which Clinton had no response. "At least have the decency to look at me when I speak to you." Grumbles of agreement came from the crowd.

Clinton exhaled hoarsely but did not move. Lewis took one stride, grabbed Clinton by the neck and shoulder and yanked him upright in his chair. Clinton still kept his head down, avoided looking in the eyes of Sharon or her mother.

Sharon's mother wiped her freshly welling tears and took one step closer to Clinton. "I don't hate you," she said slowly and with strength.

Clinton raised his head and looked at her, his battered face contorted in bewilderment.

Sharon squeezed her mother's hand. "It's not our way," she added. She could feel Jonah's eyes on her and his grandma Polly. Ruby's eyes too.

Sharon's mother dabbed at her tears. "Hating you won't bring Yuri back... or fix all the suffering that I've been told you've inflicted on many people throughout your life."

Clinton closed his eyes and hung his head again. Sharon's mother turned around and waved the gathered to come closer. Everyone obliged and once the circle had formed around Clinton, Sharon's mother instructed in Russian that it was time to sing: "*Teper' mi poyom...* for Yuri."

It would not be easy, Sharon thought. It would not feel fully genuine. But would it be more painful than when she was a child locked in a school and shamed for her culture? Or when Virginia warned their high school friends that she was a Freedomite? Or when her marriage fell apart? When she gained a hundred pounds, and lost it, and gained it all back again? Would it be more painful than when she'd gotten the call that Jonah was injured in combat? Or when Jonah himself called last night and told her that Yuri was dead? Maybe it would. She would not say it for the benefit of this coward sitting in front of her; he was likely beyond redemption. She *would* say it for herself though, because there could not be, would not be any peace within her if she didn't. She would say it because she believed the Universe, life energy—God—was the embodiment of it. She would say it because by saying it she might just purify *herself* of all the darkness she had spilled onto people throughout her life. She would say it because it might just show Jonah and Ruby that by saying it, at least to themselves and to each other, and maybe to those that had done them wrong, they'd be manifesting a true and final act of love. She would say it because, if nothing else, her dear brother Yuri would've wanted her to.

"Clinton Pritchard," Sharon said.

He slowly looked up at her.

"I forgive you."

Ruby was shocked. Hell no. She could not forgive him. Not now. Not ever.

Jonah was shocked too, for he was only starting to understand how to forgive *himself*.

But as shocked as they must've looked when Jonah's mother said the words, Clinton's was an expression of total collapse, of oblivion, of an unenlightened mind misfiring.

And then the singing started.

Jonah's grandmother began solo, her now high, elfin voice immediately steeped in sorrow as she established pitch and tempo. The song of sparrows and chickadees suddenly ceased. The forest hushed. The May sun was now bright and warming overhead. Without needing to be told, Jonah understood that his grandmother had begun singing a funeral song in Russian, a send-off to her only son. The hairs on the back of his neck stood up. He could see Yuri now, stroking his Tolstoyan beard, a twinkle in his smiling eyes.

Foolishly, futilely, Clinton tried to look away from the penetrating chant. But Jonah's grandmother kept her eyes on him as though casting a spell, and kept singing the slow, mesmerizing elegy, her voice growing stronger with each tremulous word she drew out.

"*Idu V'mir Ya V'svoy Predvetchni*," Ruby whispered. She knew the psalm "I Walk into My Eternal Soul" from *molenya*; had been singing it since she was a child. The old Molokan funeral song that her ancestors adopted and made their own was told from the perspective of a person who had just died. As Grandma Polly sang it, it was Yuri that was speaking through her. "I'm going on a journey where the enlightened ones live," he conveyed, "a spirit realm from where I will not be returning..."

Ruby knew what came next. Grandma Polly finished singing the opening phrase of the first verse, its melody trailing off, reverberating eerily throughout the forest. A beat later, the congregation instinctually joined in for the next line and what would be the remainder of the song: Ruby singing in alto; her mother, soprano; her father, bass; Nadya, mezzo-soprano; and a handful of her father's Doukhobor co-workers and Yuri's old friends in the baritone and tenor range. Jonah's mother hummed along.

Every hair on Jonah's body instantly electrified. His stomach hitched, the ball of grief glowing hot and growing fast. His eyes stung and his throat clenched. He felt like he was going to be sick, as if his heart might spill out onto the ground along with the contents of his stomach. He didn't know what was happening to him.

The effect of the slow, harmonic, choral singing was like what Ruby always felt when she had been in the audience at a big music festival or a rave, standing in front of a powerful sound system, its subwoofers pulsing subsonic frequencies throughout the body. Her heartbeat had no choice but to align with the rhythm; her cells could offer no resistance to being shaken and flushed clean by the music. And so it was here too. It was unspoken but Ruby knew this much to be true; the gathered there in Yuri's yard were collectively singing a mighty, unstoppable and ancient harmonic sorrow. They sang for all the loved ones they too had lost. They sang for all those that had gone before them. They sang for Yuri.

And their singing, led by a powerful and grief-stricken elder woman, was shattering any emotional resistance that Clinton might have clung to. Ruby sang from the depths of her soul and watched as Clinton squirmed in his chair, cried out for them to stop. He raised his shackled arms above his head in a desperate, pathetic attempt to muffle the complex shapes of sorrow penetrating his ears. Remorse was an astonishing and terrible thing.

Ruby felt Jonah squeeze her hand tight. He was nearly doubled over, rocking back and forth. She thought he might be sick. Tears poured from his face.

Not since being separated from Ruby seven years earlier, and the phone call where she'd told him that it was over between them, had Jonah fully cried. Not even through all the horrors of war, and the losses he'd suffered, was he able to conjure freely flowing tears. They'd been resolutely locked away. But now by some miracle of sonic magic it was as if every door and window to every dark room that he'd ever sealed shut inside himself was suddenly blown open, curtains fluttering and whipping from a strong, soothing breeze. Jonah was so goddamned heartbroken about Yuri, about the horrors of war, and at the same time so relieved it was over with Clinton, and so ecstatic to have Sasha and Ruby in his life, that there was no stopping the tears that flowed effortlessly now as his people sang the saddest song he had ever heard.

By now Clinton had fallen to the ground. He writhed and begged for the singing to stop. He cried that he was sorry, but his voice was drowned out by the funeral song that would not stop until it was ready to.

When it was finished, it seemed as though the world had been hushed. And then a light breeze ruffled leaves in the surrounding forest. After a few moments the crowd stepped back and enlarged the circle. Ignoring the pathetic and pained mutterings of Clinton, who was still fetal on the ground, Grandma Polly turned to face the gathering. Her voice was strong. "In our tradition," she began, "we ask that if for any reason my son... Yuri Kazakoff, has offended you..." She choked back tears. "We ask that you please forgive him."

And the Doukhobors in attendance replied, "May we all be forgiven."

* * *

For the past fifteen minutes Jonah knew they had been there, waiting respectfully at the end of Yuri's driveway, just as Jonah had requested. The night before, his friends Cedar and Trevor had talked to their old high school friend who had become a cop. And now that friend led six of his fellow officers past the crowd to where Clinton lay. They handcuffed him, picked him up from the ground, arrested him for the murder of Yuri Kazakoff and took him away.

As Jonah walked hand in hand with Ruby, his mother and Grandma Polly, he glanced back at what was once Yuri's home. And that's when he saw it. He stopped walking and gestured for all to see what he was seeing. Above the smouldering ruins, a lone white feather suspended in the breeze, gently and playfully twirled in a beam of sunlight, as though waving goodbye.

As of October 2022, the bad blood generated over many decades between the various Doukhobor factions has been laid to rest.

The Sons of Freedom survivors who had been incarcerated in the New Denver prison school as children still await a formal apology and reparations from a British Columbia government that refuses to offer any.

Today there are an estimated 120,000 Doukhobors and their descendants living primarily in Canada, the United States, Russia and the Caucasus region. Many have forgotten their roots and their culture. Yet many more are rediscovering their Doukhobor identity each and every day.

EPILOGUE

Slocan Valley, British Columbia, July 2005

As soon as Jonah heard the unmistakable growl of the diesel engine, he spun around, and, as if reaching for a M18 Sig Sauer handgun, he gripped the head of the hammer hanging in the tool belt around his waist. Yanking it out he called to Lewis who'd been sitting on the grass eating sandwiches with Nadya under the welcome shade of an evergreen. But Lewis had already hopped to standing, having himself heard the black Hummer slowly rolling along the gravel driveway that wound around the side of the Samarodin house to the back forty.

"Shorty..." Lewis said to Nadya as he handed her his keys. Without taking his eyes off the tinted windshield of the Hummer, Lewis gestured to his Ford F-150 parked fifteen metres to his left at the edge of the property. "My duffle, please. Behind the seat. On the double, Momma."

Sasha had been passing nails to his dad, happy to be helping build the new house they'd be living in soon. He held out a palm full of nails and looked up at his father. "Is this enough, Daddy?"

Jonah kneeled before Sasha, received his palmful of nails, poured them into the nail pouch of his toolbelt and said, "Plenty, Sash. But hey, now we're going to do something else. Kind of like hide-and-seek, with your momma, okay?" Sasha grinned and nodded.

Covered in sawdust and blowing her bangs away with a puff, Ruby stepped through what would eventually be the front door of the two-storey structure they'd been building for the past two months. A few seconds later Big Nick appeared behind her in his grease-stained overalls and t-shirt soaked from working in the summer heat. Ruby's heart hammered in her chest as she ripped the safety goggles off her head, crinkled her eyes and peered at the incoming SUV. "Fuck, is that...?" How would he have gotten out of prison already? Ruby wondered, as panic gripped her. She looked down at Sasha. She'd grab him and flee into the woods. She patted her back pocket and felt her cellphone. She'd call 9-1-1 as they fled.

Jonah placed his hand on the back of his boy's head of curls. "Take Sasha and go," he said to Ruby, pointing toward her parents' house. Jonah's mother had been making borsch and *pyrahi* with Virginia in the Samarodins' kitchen. Neither woman needed this shit anymore. None of them did, Jonah thought. "Take the moms and go into the root cellar, baby," he said to Ruby.

Ruby was frozen with indecision until Big Nick placed his meaty hand on her shoulder. "*Idti*," her father commanded her to go. She jumped off onto the grass next to her son.

Peering up at his mother, Sasha spoke. "Daddy said it's time for hide-and-seek now."

"Uh, yeah, that's exactly what we're going to do, baby." Ruby effortlessly scooped Sasha into her arms and took off across the lawn toward the stone path that cleaved the garden and led to Ruby's parents' house. Nadya was hot on her heels. Big Nick turned and stomped back into the depths of the unfinished house. Lewis stepped to Jonah's left flank, crouched and unzipped his duffle bag.

"Shit," Jonah said. Two weeks earlier he'd somewhat ceremoniously discarded Tupac. Along with Ruby, Lewis and Nadya, Jonah had stood on the timber deck of the old Doukhobor Suspension Bridge that spanned the Kootenay River just below Verigin's Tomb in Brilliant. He'd pulled the handgun from a backpack, stepped onto the iron railing, and peered down at the churning emerald waters fifty feet below. The others stepped onto the railing and joined him. They all looked around to make sure no one was watching. Then, without any fanfare, Jonah reached over the side of the railing and let the gun fall from his hands. Three seconds later it made a small splash and quickly disappeared into the depths.

"Bye-bye Tupac," Lewis had said, waving his hand at it.

Ruby had turned to Jonah, grabbed his face, squished his cheeks together and kissed him on the lips. "Your very own Burning of Arms."

Jonah looked back over the railing just to make sure the gun was really gone. "Yup," he'd said and nodded.

Lewis chuckled. "More like the drowning of the arms, yo." He'd slapped Jonah on the shoulder. "Now you owe me whatever five hundred bones is in your Canadian play money, bro."

With the Hummer slowly approaching, Lewis looked at Jonah gripping his hammer tight. "Betcha miss Tupac right about now, huh?"

"Shit, shit, shit," Jonah said as he ripped off his Skull Skates t-shirt and chucked it at his feet, ready for combat. He groped his chest and felt for his silver Cossack pendent dangling from his neck, rubbing it between his forefinger and thumb.

"Ah, it's gonna be that kind of party, is it?" Lewis slid his own t-shirt over his head, flexed his intimidating, muscled upper body and emitted a low growl in anticipation of what may come.

Exasperated, Jonah said, "Two months only? What the fuck, did he bust out?"

Lewis responded by pulling his handgun from the duffle. He released the magazine to check that it was fully loaded. Satisfied, he palmed it back up into the grip and secured it with a click. He'd keep the gun hidden behind the bag. At least for the time being.

The Hummer rolled to a stop ten metres away at the end of the driveway and sat idling.

Ruby was halfway through the garden, Sasha bouncing in her arms as she ran, with Nadya in tow, when the Hummer sounded three short honks. The passenger door opened just as Big Nick stepped out of the partially built house and onto the deck gripping a Husqvarna chainsaw, his expression that of a pissed-off gorilla. He lifted the chainsaw to chest height, yanked on the starter cable and revved the saw to life. Its buzz echoed through the surrounding forest. Jonah glanced back up at Ruby's dad and wondered what exactly Nick had planned, considering he was a staunchly pacifist Doukhobor.

A woman with long brown hair, wearing large designer sunglasses and a pink track suit hopped out of the Hummer's passenger door wildly waving her arms as if in surrender. "Don't everyone lose their shit all at once!" Quickly she opened the back passenger door.

Having stopped in their tracks at the sound of the horn and chainsaw, Ruby and Nadya circled back and now crouched at the edge of the garden, cautiously poking their heads from in between rows of young corn. Sasha hid behind them. Lewis, Jonah and Big Nick—who continued to menacingly rev his saw—strode defiantly toward the SUV just as the woman grunted, yelped in pain and yanked out a collapsed wheelchair.

* * *

"Swan," Ruby said, waving her cellphone mockingly in front of her, "you got one of these now. Use it." Jonah and Ruby sat on the deck of their unfinished home, both visibly relieved it was Swanny and not Clinton that had paid them a visit. Sasha was tucked in between them alternately gawking at the unsmiling man in his wheelchair, then at the pretty woman Swanny had introduced as Brandi, his girlfriend.

Brandi splayed her fingers in front of her to assess her hot-pink nail extensions. "Exactly what *I* told him."

Swanny fidgeted in his chair, lightly hit his thigh with a clenched fist and attempted a smile. "Sorry, didn't mean to send everyone's cortisol levels spiking through the roof. I just, I completely forgot that ..." Swanny threw a thumb back toward the Hummer. "That I claimed it as my new ride. And yeah, I guess the illegally tinted windshield didn't help matters. So... got to rectify that soon."

Lewis and Nadya had continued eating their lunch on the lawn a few metres away. Big Nick and his chainsaw were back in the house where he resumed hammering nails into plywood. Across from the garden and the orchard, past the old weeping willow and its tree house, Virginia and Sharon stood on the deck of the Samarodin home, sipping lemonade, craning their necks to see what all the commotion was about.

"You look good, Swan," Ruby said, pointing at his new short haircut and clean new clothes.

"You can thank me for that," Brandi said cheerily. Swanny reached for her hand and gave it a squeeze. Then he sighed the sigh of someone shouldering bad news.

"What's up, man?" Jonah said.

Ruby raised her eyebrows and asked, "Everything okay?"

Swanny nodded, glanced at Brandi. She averted his gaze and resumed examining her nails. Swanny looked back at Ruby. "Hey, saw a commercial for the next *Conan* episode. You back with your band?"

Ruby knew he was deflecting. So be it. "Sort of. Taking this li'l man," she said as she tousled Sasha's hair, "and Jonah to New York for my final performance with Caravana. We're going to stay for a week afterward and be cheesy tourists—Empire State Building, MOMA, Central Park, shopping, that sort of thing.

"And then when we get back, we're hella busy," Jonah chimed in.

Ruby smiled widely and said, "Yup, he got a bank loan and is taking over the skate shop in Nelson. And I'm going to start working on a solo album."

"Congrats you guys," Swanny responded with as much enthusiasm as he could muster. His hands gripped the wheelchair's push rims and he propelled himself closer to Jonah and Ruby. He gave them each high-fives, fist-bumped with Sasha, then wheeled back to Brandi. "Well, we should be going."

"You just got here," Ruby said. "Stay for a bit, I'll grab some beers from the house."

"Thanks, but I really just came to say a quick hi, and pass along some..." Swanny took a big breath. "Some news." Swanny flicked his head back toward the Hummer. "Come with me to the truck. Just the two of you?"

"Everything okay?" Jonah asked as they made their way out of Sasha's earshot.

Swanny spun on the gravel driveway to face Jonah and Ruby. They tightly held each other's hands. Swanny looked past them to see Brandi chatting with a blushing Sasha.

The serious look on Swanny's face sent Ruby's heart plunging into her stomach. She'd been completely sober for the past two months. No, no, no, she thought. Please no. God, how she didn't need to be tested like that right now. "He's... Is he getting out?" she asked with a withering look.

Swanny closed his eyes and shook his head.

"He's already out?" Jonah fixed Swanny with a look of outrage. "How? He was sentenced to—"

"No, no, no, it's none of that," Swanny said, waving his hand at Jonah. Even with Brandi's help to spruce up Swanny's home those past few weeks, it had still felt stuffy and claustrophobic with the memory of his brother. The truth was Swanny *had* thought of calling Ruby before paying a visit, but what he needed to share with them deserved open air. Again he breathed deeply, forced his chest to unclench a little. "You guys need to know; I just learned yesterday that Clinton is... gone."

Ruby snapped her head back. "What do you mean *gone*? Like, missing?"

"Like, dead," Swanny said. "Rival gang jumped him in the prison yard and stabbed him to death."

Ruby and Jonah stood frozen, looked sidelong at each other, both unsure what to do. Ruby's shoulders visibly relaxed. They both simultaneously expelled great relief.

At one time, on the battlefield, Jonah might've pumped his fist in celebration of his enemy's death. But he felt Yuri's eyes on him now, could see their crisp, blue clarity. Jonah thought of his uncle's gentle wisdom and understood that he was not that crude young Marine anymore. Besides, if karma actually was a thing, Jonah might well feel its force one day, too.

Ruby thought she might experience closure through Clinton's execution, but... she wasn't sure what she felt. Did a part of her hold out hope that he might've one day straightened out his heart and sought her forgiveness? Jonah's family's forgiveness? Swanny's? That would've been a longshot to say the least. And now, well, she supposed he got what he deserved. "Don't know what to say," Ruby responded flatly.

Swanny frowned lightly, shrugged. "Don't have to say anything. It's over. Fully, completely over. I'll mourn in my own way."

No more bloodshed. Jonah reassuringly squeezed the hand of Ruby Samarodin, the mother of his child and the love of his life.

"Oh, one more thing," Swanny said, eyeing Jonah. "When I played you Yuri's last message to me, the night… he died, I didn't play the whole thing."

"Okay…" Jonah said.

"Based on the conversation Yuri and I had a few months ago, he'd done some internet research for me at the college about my mom's side of the family. Turns out in 1909, along with a few other families, they moved from Blaine Lake, Saskatchewan, to Shafter, California, near Bakersfield, 125 miles north of LA, to escape the winters that reminded them too much of… Siberia."

"Siberia?" Ruby said with a perplexed look. "So… you got some Russian blood?"

"Even better. The family moved to Cali to start a colony…" Swanny smiled. "Their last name was Popoff…"

Ruby's mouth fell open as it dawned on her. "Doukhobors? Y-you have Doukhobor roots?!"

Swanny's grin spread across his face as he nodded. "Bingo!"

Ruby squealed as she stepped toward Swanny, bent over and hugged him. Afterward, he glanced at Jonah. "It didn't feel right to mention the rest of Yuri's message at my place that night… but I thought you guys would like to know."

"I don't get it," Jonah said. "How did you not know all these years? Like, was your mom ashamed or something?"

"No, I don't think so. It just never came up."

"Yeah." Ruby nodded. "Living in the US for so long, I've heard that branch of Doukhobors assimilated a lot quicker than we did up here. Your grandmother, your mom—they maybe never knew much or cared much about their roots. They fully embraced being American."

"Well, whatever the reason," Swanny said with a smile, "I'm happy, and honoured to be a part of the club."

Jonah stepped toward Swanny and high-fived him. "To being black sheep."

"Black sheep," Swanny echoed.

"Might explain why you chose a more peaceful path than Clinton," Ruby said.

Swanny nodded. "Maybe... Maybe it's in my DNA."

ACKNOWLEDGEMENTS

Many thanks and much love to my parents Ann and Fred and their respective Makayev and Chursinoff families for raising me in the Doukhobor tradition amongst the wild beauty of the Kootenay region. I owe a debt of gratitude too to my brothers Tom (RIP) and Nick for introducing me to the magic of music.

Thank you to Silas White and Emma Skagen at Nightwood Editions. I can't thank Emma enough for her insightful edits and for graciously enduring a debut author's nerves and fussiness.

My deep gratitude to Nick Kootnikoff Sr. (RIP) and his son Nick Jr. for sharing stories of a Sons of Freedom upbringing, some of which were not easy to share. Gratitude goes out too to those who shared difficult stories with me about being incarcerated as Sons of Freedom children at the New Denver residential school.

I'm indebted to Sgt. Peter M. O'Connor USMC Infantry for the candid conversation we had about his combat in Fallujah, Iraq and who served as the initial inspiration for Jonah Seeger's character. Many thanks as well for Peter's feedback on the chapters where Jonah is in the United States Marine Corps.

A big thank you to Jesse Gould, former United States Army Ranger and founder of the Heroic Hearts Project for feedback regarding combat veterans suffering from PTSD.

Much gratitude to Helen Walsh and Zalika Reid-Benta at Diaspora Dialogues and its Long Form Mentorship program in which I received invaluable guidance and feedback from authors Megan Gail Coles and David Layton. Additional thanks to David for pushing me to dig deep and for his continued friendship and inspiration.

A big thank you also to Vancouver Manuscript Intensive who paired me with author Aren X. Tulchinsky whose guidance and rounds of feedback helped shape *The Descendants,* and whose boosts of morale kept me afloat during the darkest days of the pandemic.

I'm grateful to J.J. Verigin Jr., executive director of the Union of Spiritual Communities of Christ and spiritual leader of the USCC Doukhobors for his candid discussions about Doukhoborism with me over the years and for allowing me to use his real name for his character in the novel.

I'm grateful to the following sources that I used to research for the non-fiction chapters: *The Doukhobors* by Woodcock and Avakumovic; doukhobor.org; *Maclean's*; *The Globe and Mail*; *Nelson Daily News*; *Castlegar News*; *Vancouver Sun*; *Doukhobor Incantations Through the Centuries* by Svetlana A. Inikova, translated by Koozma J. Tarasoff.

A big thank you goes out to Stephanie Harvard, Wes Regan, Mimi Asabea, Val Litwin, Tamara Terry, Tim Wenger, Sara Quin, Kinnie Starr and Jonathan Kalmakoff for providing invaluable feedback on *The Descendants*. An additional thank you to Jonathan for his expertise regarding the non-fiction, historical vignettes that appear in between chapters. Thank you to Juliana Moore for sharing what it's like to be a teenage girl and to Marta Jaciubek-McKeever for sharing what Romeo was like as a young boy.

Thank you to Natasha Jmieff for allowing me to use her poetic adaptation of the Doukhobor prayer "Our Blessed Home" originally published in *Singing Our Prayers: 90 Doukhobor Psalms,* available from the USCC.

Many thanks to Tegan Quin and Sara Quin for permission to use an excerpt from their song "Where Does the Good Go." I'm indebted to them and all the bands and singer-songwriters I've played with over the years for allowing me to part of their music.

And lastly, thank you and boundless love to my partner Dele Oyinloye for her patience and support during the final drafts of a novel that was fourteen years in the making. My heart overflows for the new family we are starting and my pen eagerly awaits the many new adventures and stories to come.

PHOTO CREDIT: Brendan Meadows

ABOUT THE AUTHOR

Robert Chursinoff was born and raised in the Doukhobor community of British Columbia's West Kootenay region. He draws inspiration for *The Descendants* from his upbringing and his years spent drumming for Grammy-nominated duo Tegan and Sara, Australian pop star Ben Lee, the Be Good Tanyas, Juno-nominated performer Kinnie Starr, the Belle Game and many others. His writing has been published in the literary journal *Blank Spaces,* the anthology *Just Words Volume 4,* and online in *Vice, Nowhere Magazine, Upworthy* and *Matador Network.* As a scriptwriter, he has worked on dozens of Red Bull Media House documentaries and series. He lives in Vancouver, BC, on the traditional, unceded territories of the Musqueam, Squamish and Tsleil-Waututh Coast Salish peoples with his partner, their child, and their dog.